D1526908

## Praise for William Jack Sibley's *He*

*Independent Publisher Book Awards (∠
Gold Medal Winner - Humorous Book of the Year, 2022
*Selected, <u>10 Best Books by San Antonio Authors, 2021</u>

"Opens with a killer scene in which a woman driving home in the wee hours nearly runs over her elderly father, lying in the road. The rest of the book lives up to the promise of the opening pages!"
- *San Antonio Express News*

"Sibley crams this quirky Texas epic with humor, contemporary issues, and oddball characters. Sibley manages to keep all the plates spinning while offering a strong sense of small-town Southern life. This eccentric, multifaceted story has a great deal of heart."
 - *Publishers Weekly*

"5 of 5 rating. Aside from being a comic tour de force, (it) also offers contemplative moments focusing on real human emotions like life, death, love and loss. That Sibley can tug at the heart at the same time as making the reader laugh is testament to his skills. Sibley is a serious talent." - *Indie Reader*

"What the story is really about is finding happiness and what a fun way to read about it. Filled with wonderful humor and satire, I was unable to put this down and finished it in one sitting."
- *Reviews, Amos Lassen*

"Sibley's sense of comedic timing is impeccable, and his ability to squeeze humor out of almost every line in the book is incredible. An intelligent and witty must-read piece." – *Readers' Favorite*

"...should be on everyone's shelf. At the core is a woman who loves a man who's in love with another man, but the colorful prose and wildly memorable dialogue introduce us to a load of small-town characters. We'd love to see this turned into a movie."
 - *He Said Magazine, Dallas*

"Every book has characters and a setting, but it's a rare occurrence when you stumble upon a book in which the setting itself is a character. In the end, it's a story about pursuing happiness even when it doesn't look the way people are used to." - *Booktrib*

"This book is no doubt a different kind of love story with hilarious characters. The emotional interaction is perfect. This is such an entertaining and beautifully written book. I had to save the best for last. The biggest positive of the book are the rich dialogues."
- *Online Book Club*

"A delightful, rollicking romp. There are hilarious riffs and set pieces, a bon mot about every other paragraph, and scads of wonderfully authentic details. It's a really bold book. A remarkably successful pastiche of important cultural themes. It's a distinctly individual work with very unexpected twists."
- *Charlie Smith, Author*

"A story with humor, action, and a lot of passion. This novel felt like watching a movie. Sibley held nothing back and gave readers everything to make this story as interesting as possible. The dialogues are as entertaining as they are revealing. The characters are chasing different forms of happiness without realizing that their happiness is just a step behind them." – *Readers' Choice*

"A rich, funny, entertaining read. *Here We Go Loop De Loop* is a cracker. It had me laughing out loud and I admit to a few tears too. If you're looking for something that will have you immersed for hours, then grab this with both hands." - *Smashbomb*

"An ode to Texas, and a hilarious one at that. The characterization is what really stands out here. Sibley does a marvelous job with it, creating characters vibrant and unique. The recipe for a brilliant book." - *Bookshelves And Teacups*

"An entertaining and very funny novel. Sibley breathes joyous life into a world that is sometimes strange and sometimes off-kilter but always recognizably real." - *Lit-Nuts*

## Praise for William Jack Sibley's *Any Kind of Luck*

*Lambda Literary Award, Finalist
*Foreword Review, Book of the Year, Finalist
*Texas Institute of Letters John Bloom Humor Award, Finalist

"*Any Kind Of Luck* is lively, funny and moving. Sibley is off to a good start." — **Larry McMurtry, author of *Lonesome Dove* and *Terms of Endearment***

"One of the best from 2001!"
— **Jesse Monteagudo, *The Book Nook, Gay Today***

"Sibley's tale is humorous and full of memorable characters and laughs. His vivid writing style is fresh and unique; his use of unusual metaphors and descriptive text sets him apart from the ordinary. The story is thoroughly entertaining, and readers will easily identify."
— **Amy Brozio-Andrews, *Inside The Cover Book Reviews***

"Hilarious characters and breezy but comically entertaining plots that don't strain the brain. Enticing and nutty...an energetic, frenzied take...wildly funny...charming material...spicy, endearing characters. It will certainly make you giddy, an emotion we could use more of these days."
— **James Piechota, *The Bay Area Reporter***

"Sibley has written a valentine to his home state (Texas)."
— **John Griffin, *San Antonio Express-News***

"If you've forgotten what it's like to read just for fun, pick up *Any Kind of Luck*...a very affectionate look at life in a small Texas town ...Sibley captures it so well, you might feel as though you've been home again."
— **Ella Tyler, *The Houston Voice***

"What a first novel it is! The author has a grasp of the metaphor that rivals Tom Robbins. Sibley creates a story so fresh and new that it blows past the reader's expectations."
— **Graham Averill, *The Fort Worth Weekly***

"To mix serious fiction with laugh-out-loud humor is a difficult task, but William Jack Sibley has succeeded in doing just that...strong characters and inspired dialogue...marvelous ability to create believable characters facing trying situations with dignity and humor."— **Juliet Sarkessian, *Lambda Book Report***

"Funny, engaging and all-around delightful...Sibley's writing is honest, refreshing, reflective." —**Kim McNabb, *Chicago Free Press***

"Engrossing...the storyline is detailed, the characters treated with love and dimensionality...the message is that of healing and love without being preachy." — **Jess Littleman, *Quest***

"An incredibly colorful cast of characters...will certainly provide a hoot!" — **D.L. Trout, *Gaywired***

"*Any Kind of Luck* proves that it's no disgrace to come from Texas. It's just a disgrace to have to go back there. If you don't think this book is funny, you deserve the death penalty!" — **Kinky Friedman; novelist, musician, nominee Governor of Texas**

"Witty, charming and spiritually touching. If Noel Coward had been a novelist, his book might have read something like this."
— **Arthur Hiller, director of *Love Story***

## Praise for William Jack Sibley's *Sighs Too Deep for Words*

*National Indie Excellence Book Award, Winner
*USA Best Book Award, Winner
*Lambda Literary Award, Finalist
*Foreword Review, Book of the Year, Finalist
*Balcones Fiction Prize, Finalist

"Novelist and playwright Sibley (*Any Kind of Luck*) returns with a melodramatic, spunky tale of good intentions, mistaken identity, and mixed signals...Sibley demonstrates dexterity in prose, deft characterization, and command of a fresh, contemporary plot line about redemption and starting over that entertains with feel-good appeal." — *Publishers Weekly*

"Sibley blends skillful storytelling with a sharp insight into human nature in this darkly humorous, intricately plotted tale..."
— *Kirkus Reviews*

"A multiple character study of what happens when 'providence' brings together an entire cluster of people who impact each other. If you like books delving into internal existential questioning and interpersonal development – then by all means go for it. "
— *Goodreads*

"The last page made everything fit perfectly. This is a love story, not the typical one our society has written. It takes all these strange life events to realize that the person he loved most was there all along."
— *Wordpress*

"If you are looking for a different kind of love story, you should check this out ... I'd recommend it." — *TeenainToronto*

"The characters are wonderful and the plots of mistaken identity, sexual confusion and coincidence are great fun. Sibley excels at dialogue and the idea of mistaken identity works beautifully and it remains funny throughout. The characters are great and following his journey is just fun. What happens you will have to find out for yourself as you read. One of the most human stories I have read in a long time." — *Amos Lassen Reviews*

"I absolutely fell in love with this book. The story is so multifaceted; there are a lot of characters, and each character is embroiled in their own love-related turmoil. I found a lot of the emotional interactions in the book to be really beautiful. I thought the writing showed a tremendous amount of depth and heart, and the story was truly original. The book really makes your rethink what it means to "love thy neighbor." — *Tiffany's Bookshelf*

"This is going on my favorites list of 2013. Goodness gracious what a great read. The characters, the dialogue, and the story came together so beautifully. This book will make you go through every emotion possible. It was such a roller coaster ride. Full of laughs, deceit, misunderstandings, and downright craziness. I absolutely loved the characters. The story kept me enthralled. It was just very human. You don't really see gay, straight or in between. You don't see religion, society, lies, mistakes, or secrets. You see all that makes them human. This is such a beautifully written book. It is heartfelt, thought-provoking, and emotional. This will leave you smiling."
— *Librarything*

"Uses farce to critique mainstream society's expectations with gambits as improbably successful as the novel's own trajectory."
— *San Antonio Current*

"For all of their bitchiness, surface superficiality and forgivable flaws, some of the characters in *Sighs Too Deep for Words* are also funny and humane people at heart, despite their politics and 1 percent ways. That's not to say Sibley doesn't take a lot of things to task in this heartwarming tale, including America's health care system, Hollywood, Tea Party members and oil companies. There are outlandish zingers, some hilarious one-liners, very original similes and plenty of surprises as a group of residents in the small coastal fishing village of Rockport, Texas, come to know one another through chance and coincidence." — *Oscartude.wordpress*

# HERE WE GO
## LOOP DE LOOP

### A TEXAS MYTH UNPACKED

WILLIAM JACK SIBLEY

© 2021 William Jack Sibley

Published by Atmosphere Press

Cover design by Kevin Stone

**Loop De Loop**
Words and Music by Teddy Vann
Copyright (c) 1962 by Morris Music, Inc.
Copyright Renewed
International Copyright Secured - All Rights Reserved
*Reprinted by Permission of Hal Leonard, LLC*

Thanks to Nancy Cook Monroe for copyediting, and Azza Kamal and Hala Spiers for their Arabic translation.

atmospherepress.com

*Dedicated to Mrs. Judith Spitz, my Senior High English/ Creative Writing teacher at Edgemont High School, Scarsdale, NY. She once told me I was the only student she'd ever taught who wrote in the first person and killed himself at the end of every story.*

"Here we go loop de loop

Here we go loop de li

Here we go loop de loop

All on a Saturday night"

"Never trust the teller, trust the tale."
D.H. Lawrence

# CHAPTER ONE

The drunk she nearly ran over, now lying in the middle of the road at one-thirty in the morning, was none other than her father, Pete Pennebaker. She'd missed flattening his head by a hair. Stopping the car quickly beneath a lone mesquite tree, she flung open the door of the battered Mercury Montego and immediately threw up on the moon-lit-ravishing, *caliche* road. Marty Pennebaker had thought of killing her father many, many times in her forty-two years, but never quite so spontaneously.

"Daddy, Daddy...are you dead?" Marty wiped her chin and tried grabbing the can of Old Milwaukee before it rolled from her lap and spilled onto the road. "Shit."

"Mar...Marty, that you?" Pete Pennebaker wheezed as he rolled over on his side. "Where in Jesus' name am I?"

Marty yanked the hair from her eyes and unbuckled the single strap seat belt. "Out on Peeler Ranch Road. How in hell did you get out here?"

"I don't...recall. I think...think I was checking the fence line."

"In the middle of the night? I nearly ran you over! How much you been drinking?"

"How much *you* been drinkin'? Hadn't I told you before don't ask a drunk for particulars."

Marty held her stomach, hoping to suppress another heaving. Stepping outside the car, she knelt slowly beside Pete. "Daddy, you gotta stop wandering off like this. I don't mind you getting killed but I don't want to be the one to do it."

Pete lifted his head, the car headlights causing him to squint. "I don't mind dying neither but there's gotta be a better way to go than being eaten alive by fire ants." Pete slapped at his head. "Get me outta here!"

Marty glanced around at the Montego – car door open, Kay Starr on the CD belting "Wheel of Fortune," crazy ass turn signal blinking a mile a minute. Last time she tried hauling Pete into the back seat, it took her, Jacinta the maid, and Nestor the ranch foreman twenty minutes to pick him up and transport him. He'd broken his foot sailing off the front porch of the Big House while demonstrating how to cut the nuts off a boar hog. He'd had enough Canadian Club and Sevens at the time to float a sack of corn cobs. He fought, kicked, and hollered all the way to the car, shouting that we "Goddam backsliders" weren't taking him nowhere. A week in the county hospital just made things worse. Pete's daily, incessant, unvaried rants were as predictable as a Baptist preacher's tears on Sunday: "Godammit! Everything's wrong with Texas nowadays! The 'foreigners,' liberals, atheists, gay love, free love, shackin'-up love, way-too-much-love-in-general-love, RINOs, libbers, hippies (*hippies?*), yuppies/buppies/puppies, Austin, Hollywood, Washington, New York City...hell, Fort Bend, Indiana!" They were all the fountainhead and ongoing disembowelment of society, decency, and moral rectitude of Texas and the nation. Everything today in the Lone Star State, by his yardstick, was a shithole of whining miscreants.

Naturally, it served no purpose to remind him that Texas was ruled by a conservative Republican Governor, conservative Republican Senate and Congress, conservative

Republican gerrymandered voting districts, conservative Republican mega churches; conservative media, conservative businesses, conservative voucher schools, etc., etc., etc. Apparently, as Marty frequently pondered, the only thing truly not conservative in Texas anymore was Pete Pennebaker's prodigious drinking.

"Hon, you're gonna have to pay a plastic surgeon to put a new nose on me if you keep dragging my head thataway."

Marty sat down on the road, exhausted. "Daddy, I'm trying. I really am. You're not that easy to move. Can you just help me a little bit?"

"Call Nestor or Fidencio on your mobile."

"There's no service out here! My God, you're already a couple of miles from the house. What were you doing?"

Pete semi-lifted up on his elbow and squinted at Marty, "I went out to take a pee on the back patio and I heard somebody calling off yonder." Pete listlessly tossed an arm in Marty's direction. "It sounded like your brother, Tom."

Marty leaned her head against the side of the car and exhaled deeply. "You couldn't have heard Tom. Tom's been dead for over a year now."

Pete bellowed, "I did! You hear me - your brother has not left us yet. He's here, on this ranch, on this land, just as sure as the devil's got horns. Something's preventing his earthly departure and I'm gonna help that boy get to wherever he's goin'. I got to–that's my only boy."

Marty closed her eyes and shook her head. What did it matter reminding him that she was his only girl. She was the one who left a Manhattan career, friends, culture, intellect, art, stimulation, and a for-real *inamorato* to return home to Rita Blanca, Texas...for *this?* Life with an angry, alcoholic, fallen apart old megalomaniac? And 50,000 acres of prime brush country immoderately blessed with oil, gas, uranium, lignite coal, fat Brangus cattle, show quarter horses, 250 angora goats, 18 species of exotic wildlife, hunting camps, whitetail deer, javelinas, cougars, bobcats, quail, turkey, an olive grove with 400 producing trees, four large homes, bunk houses, barns, offices, trucks, jeeps, ATVs, dozers, tractors, a landing strip, and one small helicopter. As she would dryly inform her sophisticated New York coterie of swells, "It's not exactly the heat that's bringing me back to Texas. There's some *business* to attend to."

*Los Abuelos'* ("The Grandparents'") ranch had been bought originally by her great-grandparents, Hiram and Violet Pennebaker, back in 1896, when land went for between fifty and seventy cents an acre and mineral rights were mostly theoretical. That they held on to the theoretical through the years said a lot about their faith in the unknown. Pete Pennebaker had already lived through four oil booms and busts and saw no reason for them not to continue forever. "God only knows what all's down there. Don't you ever go poor-mouthing this godforsaken old country. It'll save your butt every time!"

Marty sat on her heels and leaned toward Pete. "Daddy, put your arm around my neck, and let's see if I can scooch you a little closer to the car door."

"Cain't"

"What do you mean you can't?"

"It's broken."

"What?"

"My arm. Feels awful bad."

Marty let out another sharp puff of air and took off the light sweater she was wearing, folding it. "Here, put your head in my lap. Somebody'll be along soon enough. Some old cowboy, some oil field worker–they'll stop and help us."

Marty lifted Pete's head slowly and stretched her legs out before her. He grimaced slightly. "Son of a bitch, they may have to cut this arm off."

"I doubt it. You said the same thing when you broke your foot."

"I ain't going back to that hospital!"

Marty sighed, "Betty Ford's where you need to be. That or the 'Crazy House.'"

Pete frowned, "Always had a mouth on you. Just idn't becoming on a young lady."

"I'm not young and I'm no lady and I wonder where the hell I got that mouth from?"

Pete sighed, "Your mama tried, that's all I know. Never heard a cuss word or a bad notion out of your brother's mouth his whole life."

Saint Tom, the "brother from heaven." There were two inerrant constants in Marty's life, the crow's feet that were advancing daily on her face from character-defining to Georgia O'Keeffe death mask, and the sheer infallibility of her late, gay brother Tom's irreproachable rectitude. If it wasn't for that pesky gay part (or perhaps in spite of), he'd surely have given the Pope a run for his money.

"Well, I did. He cussed plenty down at the Medical Center in Houston when he got...sick."

The "A" word was still never mentioned in the Pennebaker household. AIDS was something that happened to trashy, loathsome reprobates unworthy of the Pennebaker sobriquet, "a Christian *and* a Cowman"–equal virtues. Of course, in Texas nearly everyone claimed to be Christian, from bank robbers to topless dancers. And for sure, many Texans did indeed become excessively Christian the closer they got to actual sin. (As a rule, the louder the Christian condemnation, the more one needs to start clutching his or her wallet and/or genitals– you're about to get screwed.) But a "Cowman"–that was the highest accolade of all. For a man of such fine and noble caliber, it was an honor for a shit-on-his-boots dusty cavalier to navigate your fine Persian rugs any hour of any day.

"He had a right to cuss. They couldn't find a cure for his ailment. Hell, anybody would. A terrible shame losing such a fine boy in the prime of his life. Terrible. You've no idea what that did to your mother'n me."

If Marty knew anything at all it was that negation and recalcitrance counted for high virtue in the Pennebaker clan. It could get you through near anything. Almost anything. She pulled Pete's collar up around his neck and glanced at the sky. It was actually kind of beautiful out. A half-moon at forty-five degrees light breeze from the southeast made for a quite tolerable mid-70s temperature for a June night. She listened as a distant owl called its mate. Her slight beer buzz had departed with only a faint headache ensuing. Perhaps throwing up had been the best thing after consuming the four beers at her high school chum Wendy Barrera's house. Wendy was recently divorced with three kids and worked as a gate guard for an oil company near Cotulla. They really had nothing in common anymore except drinking beer and talking about high school inanities, but it was someplace to go in the long, long evenings that stretched before her each night like an endless stream of digression.

Marty thought to herself as she flicked at gnats buzzing Pete's forehead. 'What's to become of me when he finally goes? Should I sell out? Four generations of unyielding Anglo gourd-headedness vanquished to Houston and Dallas banks with the flourish of one shaking hand. For what? What did it all mean? These hard-assed Christian cowmen and women who worked the South Texas land like it was God's own personal munificence for their actually agreeing to stay put there. It was not now, nor had it ever been, a "love at first sight" environment. There were no Rocky Mountains, majestic seashores, European quaintness or cultural touchstones to immediately charm one. It was just hard, flat, hot and cruel. And it had a way of eventually seizing one's imagination and forcing a body to constantly fill in the blanks for what may or may not be missing. It was a game she played nearly every day. Is this something to be improved upon or is it exactly perfect in its own imperfection?'

"Marty."

"Yes?"

"There's something crawling up my trousers."

In an instant Marty was on her feet, frantically brushing her legs, hair and arms. She quickly kneeled back down to roll up Pete's cuffs.

"Which leg?"

"Right."

"What is it?"

"Dunno. Feels like a goddam scorpion!"

"Undo your belt buckle. I can't get the pants leg over your boot."

Pete began fumbling with his one good arm. "Aw, shit!"

"Did it bite you?"

"I gotta pee."

Marty had a look of consummate terror. "Daddy, let's concentrate on one issue at a time."

"Cain't! Gotta go."

Anxiously, Marty began unfastening Pete's Mexican belt buckle. She reached around behind his head to lift him and slowly they both rose precariously as if two small lava islands were erupting somewhere in the Pacific.

And then Mount Pinatubo blew.

"Aw, Jesus!"

Somehow, by the grace of an understanding savior, Pete had managed to free his willy from his cotton shorts in the precise millisecond before impending deluge. Marty balanced him steadily against the car hood while looking elsewhere and silently itemizing the precise ingredients in a good gazpacho. Just another commonplace day in the life of a ranch heir's uneventful existence.

"What happened to the scorpion?"

"I think I drowned him."

Marty exhaled, smiled and recited aloud, "*How far that little candle throws his beams! So shines a good deed in a weary world,* Mr. William Shakespeare."

Pete zipped up his fly and spit. "I told your mama we weren't wasting our money sending you to that Ivy League school back east. Don't hardly know which end of a cow to feed but you can for damn sure come up with the dangdest little ditties for purt' near every occasion."

"Every family needs a bona fide wag, right, Daddy?"

"Wag? What I need's a drink. You got any beer left?"

Marty shook her head. "All gone."

"Got a flask? A 'traveling bottle'?"

"Nope."

"Damn. Well, like the old preacher used to say, 'You cain't always get what you want but if you pray hard enough you can start wanting something else.' Help get me into the back seat, shug."

Marty slowly turned Pete toward the rear door. Gently, steadily she lowered him into the car's sofa-sized hind pew. The Montego had been in the family since 1972. Pete had refused to part with a vehicle the size of a gunboat that could carry bales of hay and saddles in the trunk plus five *vaqueros* and several sacks of feeder cubes on the hood. Marty inherited the tank, which she nicknamed "Stubby Kaye," upon returning home. Short of her three-legged stray bitch, "Gloria Mundi," she found wandering down a highway and brought home to raise, Marty revered the Montego above all her possessions. It had unmistakable *brio.*

"I don't know how we did it, but you're in the car, Daddy. Let's get you to the hospital." Marty started the ignition.

Pete lifted his head. "Wait. I need to talk."

"Talk? What about your arm?"

"It's not hurting so bad. Now's a good time to...talk."

Marty stared at Pete in the rearview mirror. She recognized that determined look of his which meant time must stop, planes must land, legislatures recess–Pete was about to elucidate. She rolled down the electric windows and turned off the motor. For a good minute and a half, they sat in silence. Marty could feel that familiar tightness in her stomach that emanated from these consequential "talks."

"I got cancer."

"I know."

"Who told you?"

"You did, Daddy. About a month ago. You were drunk, so you wouldn't remember."

"Well, I'm gonna die." Marty bit her lip and stared at nothing. "Everything goes to you, ya know." Marty continued staring. "Just answer me this, have I been a terrible father?"

Marty took a deep breath and exhaled. "Daddy, why are we doing this?"

"Have I?"

"No, you were not terrible. You were just...unpleasant to be around a lot of times."

"Well...shit. Life is an unpleasant thing, mostly. You get a few bits of happiness here and there–but by and large, it's the shits."

"And thank you for sharing so abundantly through the years."

"Have you had an awful life? Did your mother and I deny you anything we thought would make your life better? You know I'm a poet too. *'How sharper than a serpent's tooth it is to have a thankless child.'* My mama drilled that into me from the Bible when I wadn't even weaned off a titty rag."

Marty shrugged, "It's Shakespeare too, but why split hairs."

"You listen up...you got some powerful decisions to make. You gonna inherit one of the finest ranches in South Texas. My Lord, girl, any man alive would give his heart and soul to be handed an opportunity like this. And ever' time we try to have this same talk you act like I'm throwing burning coals at ya. What is it? What is it you wanna say, can't say...talk to me! Speak, girl!"

Marty gripped the steering wheel like it was a wild animal about to swallow her whole. She glanced again at her father's pleading face, a face she'd of late come to recognize instantly in her own morning mirror or whenever she entered a room and caught her distant reflection. She was and always had been Pete Pennebaker's girl child, in umpteen ways.

"I can't give you the answer you want to hear."

Pete bellowed, "Why?"

Marty turned instantly around in the front seat and glared back at him, "Because I don't know! I don't know what I'll do. What I *have* known my whole life is how this place, this isolation out here, this wildness, can turn a person into a half crazy, half uncontrollable misfit, and I am already well on my way to the bughouse as it is. It consumed Mother, it consumed Tom and it for God sure has devoured you. I am not willing to spend the rest of my days alone out here, mad as a hatter, drinking myself into a coma just so other crazy-ass people can say, 'Look, there goes Pete Pennebaker's fine, upstanding, alcoholic, spinster daughter. I hear she turned out crazier than all of 'em put together.'"

Pete squinted, staring back. "Why'd you never marry, Marty?"

Marty whirled back around in the front seat and started the car.

"You're going to the hospital right now."

"Stop the car." Pete placed a rough and swollen hand on Marty's shoulder. The touch of her father was such a rare and unanticipated occurrence it sent shivers through her. "Just stop for a minute...please."

The car rolled a few extra feet, then Marty braked and shut off the ignition. Sticking her elbow out the window, she rested her head in her hand.

"I waited too long."

"Too long?"

"Yep. I kept waiting for the right one to show up. The one

who was already 'up and running.' All I seemed to attract were the ones sitting on the sidelines. Oh, there were offers, a number. Cute guys, sweet guys, interesting guys–but I kept thinking, 'Hold on, the right one's coming. Don't be rash, you're in no hurry. You've got work, friends, travel, diversions...'" Marty made quotation marks in the air. "'Trust the Universe!' Well, the Universe fucked up. I waited too long, Daddy. But there are worse things than going through life mateless."

"Hell, you're still good-looking, smart, got a sense of humor–half of which I don't get–and you're gonna be rich!"

Marty smiled ruefully, "That's helpful."

"I'm serious, it's no good living alone. Everyone needs a partner."

"Not everyone, Daddy."

"Everyone! What are you, some kind of freak? A robot? I know you think it's 'cause your mama and I fought too much you can't be happy with someone. We fought every goddam day of a forty-two-year marriage, so what? We loved each other, didn't we? People fight, they make up, they fight again– big fuckin' deal." Pete leaned forward. "Don't wait for perfection. You wouldn't be happy with that neither. Settle for something decent, honest and loyal–and put up with their annoying shit cause they're the ones gonna be cleaning your drawers one day."

Marty stared at her father not knowing, as usual, whether to laugh or fall to the ground gnashing her teeth. If he knew or even suspected that she was seeing–hell, sleeping with–that shiftless, no count, worthless, trifling neighbor down the road, Pettus Lyndecker, his head would explode. The Lyndeckers were white trash. No two ways about it. How they'd managed to hang on through the generations to three thousand acres of the roughest, hardest, ugliest brush country in south Texas was an aberration to everyone. Old man Lyndecker had spent time in the federal pen, the mother ran off with a trucker years ago, the seven kids grew up fractious, mendacious and indolent–and they were all the best-looking things in the county. Every one of them, big, cocky, healthy-looking criminals. Pettus, the oldest, could've had a career in the movies playing brooding studs. Even after two failed marriages, four kids, one bankruptcy and a half-assed attempt to run for sheriff, he was about the sexiest thing Marty had ever laid eyes on. And the entire situation between them was as utterly farcical as a wig on a rooster. Just sex, period. Pure D SEX! And frankly, about the best she'd ever had. And yes, there're Astrodomes full of literature pertaining to the glories and *sine qua non* of a healthy sex life. But what do you do with a man that cuts his toenails with a pocketknife after coitus and not only has never heard of "Hedwig and the Angry Inch" but seriously asked if the "head wig" was to hide baldness or something? It's cute just once. A series of these rustic, indifferent utterances began to wear on Marty like an attack of dishpan hands. Sex good, the rest–not so *bueno*.

Pettus started showing up weeks after Marty's sudden return from New York to care for her dying mother, Lila B. By the time Lila B. passed, Marty had already lost her rent-controlled two-bedroom on the Upper West Side. The prying super in her building grilled her subletters mercilessly till finally, the jig was up. What was she returning to New York for anyway? She'd managed a gallery, was a Girl Friday for a well-known artist, dabbled in real estate, tried consulting work with several museums–it was all dog-paddling till someone or something, *somehow* put a focus on those daily, methodical exertions that were supposed to be leading to the inevitable. What? What was it exactly that didn't happen?

"Did I raise a stink when your brother turned out queer?"

Marty shook her head, sighing. "We don't say 'queer,' remember?" Marty glanced at her father in the rearview mirror. "We don't say nigger, wop, kike, chink or greaser either! Remember this conversation?"

Pete snorted and spat out the window, "You lived in New York too long. I ain't putting nobody down. Hell, I'm an old ignorant, reprobate–call me whatever you want, don't make me no matter."

"That's cause you're in *charge,* Daddy. You and a handful of others run the county–the banks, the schools, the churches, the businesses–it's all a white man's heaven. It only matters what they call you when you're powerless."

Pete looked out the window, frowning. "I never said a word about your brother becoming a fruit."

Marty exhaled loudly, rubbing her forehead. "He didn't 'become' a 'fruit'! You don't *become* what you already are! Jesus Christ, Daddy, let that one go, will ya?"

Pete seemed transfixed on a distant object. "I seen it my whole life. Nothing unusual. Bulls humping bulls, stud horse humping a gelding–hell, an old dog will fuck a fire hydrant. Nothing strange about it. But one day you grow up and you assume some responsibility in your life, and you do the right thing."

Marty stared out the driver's side, shaking her head.

Pete spoke louder. "Men liking men, women liking women–I seen it all! Nothing new under the sun, believe me! But one day you gotta buckle down and just do the right thing! What I'm trying to tell you is, just like your brother, take some responsibility in your life. It ain't a damn cruise to paradise out there."

Marty turned around again. "I...truly...have no idea what you're talking about."

"I didn't give a damn if your brother liked boys! That was his own hang-up–but dammit, a man has to pull in his cinch and make his way in the world. We don't always get to be who we think we ought to be."

"And he did exactly that! He stayed here, played it YOUR way, did YOUR bidding, lived YOUR vision of reality–ALONE! He lived and died alone, Daddy. You'd have no more gone along with him bringing a boyfriend out here–provided he'd even found someone crazy enough to do such a thing–than the man in the moon. Admit it!"

"I'm not saying that. That...aspect, never came up. Your brother was a fine man. He did the right thing."

"And the right thing for me, Daddy, is to do what? Marry some old boy, any boy, and just suck it up? So I won't be 'lonely?'" making quotation marks with her fingers again. "My God, you're absolutely terrified I'll sell this place the afternoon you're buried, isn't that right? So it's better for me to have some 'man,' any 'man' in my life, who can run herd on me and my wild, impetuous, crazy-ass female ways. Is that the story we're telling here?"

"Lord God a-mighty, talking to you is like spitting in a fan."

"And talking to you is like standing under Niagara Falls with an umbrella." Marty glanced in the rearview mirror. "Thank God, here comes somebody."

Pete turned around to look. "What kinda crazy sumabitch is out driving this back road at two in the morning?"

"Some sumabitch like us, I imagine." Marty turned to Pete. "And listen to me, you can just get that notion out of your head that I need someone to 'complete' who I am or whatever fiction it is you've conjured up for yourself. What I do with my life is my business. I do not need a man to fulfill me, ennoble me or shield me in any way, shape or form, *comprende?*"

The pickup rolled up alongside them and stopped. George Strait was singing softly on the radio as a man got out of the driver's side and strolled casually over to Marty's window.

"Evening. Y'all having a tea party out here?"

Marty stared at the man briefly, then smiled.  "Hello, Pettus. How's your night been going?"

# CHAPTER TWO

The Dusty Rose Flower Shoppe had not made a sale in over three days. Twin sisters Darcy and Delilah Lyndecker stared out the front window of their tiny "Shoppe" on Main Street and grimaced.

"I don't know what we're gonna do. We're losing all our business to that bitch." Darcy grumbled, crossing her arms.

"Don't say bitch, say 'mean girl.'" Delilah corrected her sister as she snipped dead buds off a kalanchoe.

"Mean girl's a real bitch." Darcy shook her head and crossed to the coffeemaker. "Sorry, Lilah, but since you got out of Christian rehab I can't hardly understand you anymore."

"My counselors told me it's lazy and un...unbefitting to always use swear words instead of a proper noun. They said you're not utilizing your God-given potentiality."

Darcy stared at her sister. "I don't even know what the fuck that means. How many times did I tell you to lay off the meth, lay off the meth–that shit is *caca*. And what happens? Bam! Court gives you six months in the Jesus Nuthouse and you come outta there singing 'The Sound of Music.' Nobody can understand you anymore, Li!"

"Well, I'm sorry for trying to better myself. I did learn stuff while I was there."

"And now you're here!" Darcy pointed out the window. "And this mean girl bitch is eating our lunch! Who does she think she is? Carol Ann Jansky's old man throws a boatload of money at her to keep her big butt occupied and what does she go and do? Opens a Flower Emporium right across the fricking courthouse square from us. I mean, it's fucking un-American."

"Why is it un-American, Darc?"

"It's un-American cause we're getting screwed, that's why! All that shit in the Constitution about pursuit of life, liberty and...and...making money.  She has deliberately screwed us, royally."

"Well, Carol Ann Jansky's got issues, everyone knows that."

"You got that right. Her 'issues' mean we're gonna lose this store. Then what's gonna happen to us? You going back to teaching day school for a buncha drippy-nose toddlers? What am I supposed to do?"

"You could open your modeling academy again."

Darcy snorted. "Yeah right. That lasted about half a year. These heifers around here don't know modeling from goat roping. When you've had your hair done at Walmart your whole life, your fashion sense gets a little warped–know what I'm saying?"

Delilah stopped arranging the strawflowers before her. "Well, I learned a lot."

"Like what?"

"Like how to walk and how to sit and how to stick your boobies out for a more 'accentuated line.'"

Darcy smiled and shook her head, "Oh, Li, you were listening! I swear I'd look at you in those classes sometimes and all I'd see was that hideous meth grin of yours and I'd think, 'Girl doesn't have a clue, not a clue, unh-unh.'"

"Of course I was listening! You know all drugs aren't bad. I mean, everybody takes aspirin."

Darcy stared at Delilah, expressionless. "Yeah." She began rummaging through the pile of mail sitting in a basket by the front door. "Did we get a paper yet? Who died? Who got engaged? Who's in the hospital? We gotta work it, sister. I mean, if this bitch is gonna steal all our trade we gotta fight fire with 'ire'!"

"Huh?"

"'Fire with ire.' It's a play on words. You know, like, 'What's good for the goose is good for the granny.'"

Delilah nodded, smiling, "Oh...right. Like, 'It takes two to tangle!'"

"That's it."

"Or 'Look before you creep.'"

"Um-hmm."

"'Still waters run cheap.'"

"Stop!" Darcy held up the newspaper. "Oh my God, old lady Pettigrew died. Isn't that a shame."

"Who's that?"

"I have no idea, but her loved ones need to buy a shitload of carnations from us, today! Now think–how do we let them know we have the best flowers, best deals and best customer service in town?"

Delilah stopped her arranging and glanced up. "Well...we could send them a coupon."

"Oh sweet Jesus, that's brilliant! A coupon. Now how do we get a coupon to the family?"

"Well, I would probably just mail it or you could hand deliver it if, like, you know, time were not a big issue kind of thing."

"Darc, honey, we're in the flower business. Time is kind of a real big issue, ya know? Nobody wants dead flowers for their dead kinfolk. Now I need you to pull in both sides of your bipolar brain and help me with this coupon conundrum."

"What's a...conundrum?"

"It's like parsley–that thing on your plate you don't want."

"Oh. I thought it might have something to do with the Post Office."

Darcy stared at Delilah blankly then shook her head and instantly began pacing. "Fuck it." She walked around the shop with her hands on her head. "So...coupons. The funeral is in two days, we don't know who the family is or where they live. They're probably going to call the mean girl bitch because her daddy paid for that big, honking half-page ad in the paper. Think, Lilah, think!"

"I'm thinking. Oh I know–don't we have a website? Couldn't we just put the coupon on the website?"

Darcy instantly high-fived Delilah. "That's it, girl! You are on fire today. Why didn't I think of that?"

Delilah shrugged, "It's a conundrum?"

"Wait a minute. Don't we owe that computer guy some money? Like we haven't paid him in a couple of months?"

"It's been a year. You said we should stick it to him 'cause you didn't like the song he put in the background on our webpage."

Darcy nodded vigorously, "Guns N' Roses? Really? Our name is The Dusty Rose and all he can come up with is Axl Rose singing, 'Welcome to the Jungle'?"

Delilah frowned. "It did seem a little strange, didn't it?"

Darcy mimed typing on a keyboard. "'Hmm, my wife's having a hysterectomy today–I'd like to order some flowers. Oh, 'Welcome to the Jungle,' cool. I wonder if they'll throw in a couple of Uzis and an AK47? She'd go for that.'"

The front door suddenly opened and a heavyset woman roughly the twins' age walked in holding the hand of a four-year-old child. "Haaaay!"

The twins both replied simultaneously, "Haaaay, Vonnie."

Vonnie Pawlik fanned herself with a handful of mail and glanced around the store, blinking, "Well God, I figured y'all would be up to your butts in pink, pink, pink by now." Vonnie turned to address the child sternly. "Tanya, don't touch anything!"

"What do you mean?" Darcy asked.

"Well, God, everybody's talking about it. Junior Bosquez is throwing a *quinceañera* for his daughter, Tiffany, and he's supposed to be going all hog on the decor. They've got the hall down at St. Andrews booked and Little Joe Y La Familia are playing. Damn, it's gonna be big. Tanya, don't touch anything!"

Delilah spoke slowly, "Didn't we do the casket cover of *'pink hydrangea, larkspur, stock and waxflowers, accented by ivy, eucalyptus and leatherleaf fern'* for his mother's funeral?"

Darcy stared out the window, toward the courthouse. "You forgot the irises. LOTS of lavender irises. We gave him just what he wanted, and he paid good money too. You don't own three auto repair shops in this county and stay a poor man long." Darcy eyed Vonnie with a tight smile. "No, Vonnie, we haven't heard a word about the big *quinceañera*. I don't imagine we will since mean girl..." Darcy glanced at little Tanya and corrected herself, "*witch*...across the square is determined to drive us out of business. Tanya, don't touch anything!"

Vonnie clasped her envelopes to her chest. "I know! It's terrible, terrible! Really, all I've heard the past couple of weeks is, 'Carol Ann Jansky's running those two Lyndecker twins right into the Poor House.' It's not right, it's just not right, y'all! Tanya, put down that sequined cross!"

Darcy folded her arms. "I oughta go over there right now and give her a piece of my mind."

Delilah finished her second strawflower arrangement and sighed, "Won't do any good. She's bigger than you."

"And meaner. Way meaner. I saw her beat up Cindy Kendall back in high school–it was uhg-lee." Vonnie grabbed the figurine of the Virgin Mary from Tanya and smacked her hand. "What did I tell you? Now don't make mama angry or we're not going to Dairy Queen for lunch." Tanya immediately started wailing and Delilah brought her a sunflower.

"Here, honey, you want to play with the pretty flower?"

Tanya took the blossom and threw it on the floor. "No!"

"Tanya Marie Pawlik! Shame on you!" Vonnie leaned down and scooped up the flower. "She's just like her Daddy. Muleheaded as can be. Her brother Bruce can play with flowers and little figurines all day long and you never hear a peep out of him. What makes kids so different, I wonder?"

Delilah smiled at Vonnie. "It's like parsley on a plate. Just there to confuse you."

Vonnie nodded, mystified.

"Well, I don't care, y'all. I'm going over there right now." Darcy pulled her hair back into a tight ponytail and used the scrunchie on her wrist to cinch it.

"Darc, now wait a minute..." Delilah walked toward her.

"Oh Darcy, you think you should?" There was just the slightest quiver of excitement in Vonnie's voice. "What are people gonna say if y'all have a big scene?"

"They're gonna say, 'Thank God somebody in this horseshit town has the *cojones* to stand up to Missy Jansky and her royal high-and-mightiness.'"

"Darc, I don't think you should. Really now..." Before Delilah could finish her sentence, Darcy was out the door aiming for the Flower Emporium like a heat-seeking missile. She and Vonnie stood watching out the front window.

"I knew I should've never let my day school teaching certificate expire. How much you think a courthouse secretary earns?"

Vonnie looked at Delilah. "Can you type?"

Delilah shook her head. "Nope. But I'm really good on the phone. I've been told that my whole life. People just love the sound of my voice. It's uncanny."

Vonnie, unsure where to go with that revelation, nodded slowly and turned back to stare out the window.

\*\*\*

As Darcy entered The Flower Emporium, the overpowering smell of potpourri stewing on a burner caused her eyes to burn. Blinking nonstop, she glanced around the store, which was busy with customers. Everything was new and fresh and sparkly and over-the-top *girly-girl*. Taylor Swift was crooning softly in the background. 'Strong men would need testosterone shots after five minutes of this froufrou,' Darcy thought to herself. There was Old Lady Delmer looking at vases, hairdresser Billy Mapstone studying silk flowers, Brittany Hinojosa buying roses...what the hell was going on? These were *her* customers. Or at least they used to be.

"Oh, hi, honey. How're you doing today, sweetheart?" Miss Delmer smiled agreeably at Darcy like it was just another day at Walmart.

"Fine, Miss Delmer. How 'bout yourself?"

"No complaints, no complaints. They're still working on that colon cancer thing of mine, but it's all just fine, just fine."

Darcy smiled, "I'm glad to hear it, Miss Delmer. You come by and see us now." Darcy continued walking slowly. She passed Billy, who was holding up several large silk calla lilies.

"Oh hey." Billy whispered softly, "Girlfriend's way overcharging for these. I can get them at Michael's in San Antonio for like half this."

"Really?"

"Darn tootin'! What are you doing over here, checking out the new rival?"

"I could ask you the same question?"

"Pumpkin, I gotta be nice to everybody. Being a hair burner's like being Jesus, ya know? You gotta spread the love or they'll be at your door with pitchforks faster than you can say *Garnier Nutrisse!*"

"Thank you, Billy. If I'm still alive next week, put me down for a blowout on Wednesday."

23

Billy looked quizzical while Darcy drifted away as if pulled by some invisible cord. He shook his head and mumbled to himself, "Girlfriend's gonna get spa-a-a-a-nked."

Darcy emerged from around a display of wicker baskets to finally see Carol Ann standing behind the register making change for Brittany. Carol Ann caught Darcy's eye and instantly beamed back a blinding smile that could melt steel.

"Haaaay! I've been meaning to get over and see y'all!" Carol Ann finished counting coins and slapped the register shut. She moved around the counter and tottered toward Darcy, hands in the air, all squeals and giggles. With her long, perfectly coiffed blonde 'do, pink sequined headband, pink pinafore mini and pink sequined sandals, Carol Ann Jansky may not have been the *ultimate* small-town Barbie but she was doing her damnedest to fill the void. "How've you been? I love that blouse. How's Lilah? What's that good-looking brother of yours been up to? He is so baaad!"

Darcy muttered under her breath, "Cut the shit, Carol Ann. I'm about nine seconds away from slapping the dizzy right off your face."

Carol Ann stepped back as if suddenly smelling a gas leak. "Wh...what?"

"You heard me. How dare you do this to me and my sister!"

"What are you talking about?"

"This...this 'Emporium' from hell! That's what I'm talking about! My sister and I opened our store four years ago and we have busted butt to make a go of it and now you come in and open the SAME G.D. STORE right across the parking lot from the courthouse? Are you completely brainless? Do you think for one second this tight-ass town can support TWO flower shops? What on earth were you thinking, Carol Ann? WERE you thinking!?"

"I...I can't believe you're saying this to me. I thought we were friends."

Darcy raised her voice, "Friends don't fuck each other out of making a living!"

By now Miss Delmer, Billy and Brittany Hinojosa were staring as if watching a living Biblical parable. And not the one about the meek inheriting the earth either.

"I haven't had a customer for three days now! Can you guess why?"

"Maybe they're looking for something new and different?"

"New and different, my rusty butt! They're all over at your place cause you're stealing my customers. I don't have a daddy that can throw thousands of dollars at my skanky butt just to get me out of the house."

"I don't have to listen to this. I'm calling Daddy."

"Yeah, you do that Carol Ann–you call Big Daddy. And while you've got him on the phone, you be sure and tell him about the time you gave half the basketball team head that night at Brandon Schuler's pool party."

Carol Ann gasped, "Well, at least I never had a three-way with the preacher's kid and his pimple-faced cousin from San Angelo!"

"That's different! *Everyone knows I'm a slut!*"

Billy held up a handful of glass beads, clearing his throat. "Um, are these on sale?"

Darcy glanced over her shoulder. "They're cheaper at my place."

"And cheap's the word! People stopped going to The Dusty Rose 'cause everything in there is old, tired and DUSTY. Why don't y'all buy a vacuum cleaner and just suck all that trash out of there?"

"Why don't you buy a can of Raid and suck on that?"

"Girls, girls, please–I hate to hear all this bad talk between two old friends. Now why can't y'all just be Christian and give each other a hug and stop this bullshit?" Miss Delmer dabbed at her temples with a tiny white handkerchief.

"It's kinda hard, Miss Delmer, when someone you used to

think was your friend deliberately sticks a knife in your back. What am I gonna do when she runs me and my sister out of business? It's not like General Motors is recruiting round here, ya know?"

"Well, I 'spect I'd call that preacher's kid and see if his daddy's hiring anyone down at the church." Miss Delmer smiled at Billy. "It's always the personal touch that makes the difference."

"That was ten years ago, Miss Delmer! And I don't want to work at the church, or the school, or the bank, or the motel–I want to stay right where I am and do what I've been doing."

Billy Mapstone chimed in, "Suit yourself, sweetness, but Carol Ann's got a point. Y'all need to get in there with some Ajax and a mop bucket and scour that place down. Looks like it hasn't had a real good scrubbing since Rosalynn Carter ran the White House."

Brittany Hinojosa finally spoke after staring wide-eyed during the entire skirmish. "I really, really like your place and I think your prices are good and your sister Delilah is so nice and everything, but sometimes, sometimes y'all just don't have, like, the newest, coolest stuff. Like Carol Ann's got this really neat room freshener called 'Attitude Heaven' that's just so, like, *fresh*. I mean, you know, people just want to stay...current."

"Trendy." Miss Delmer interrupted. "You don't want to feel like you're that last one to know what's hot."

Billy placed an arm around Darcy's shoulder. "Babe, I will never NOT be your customer. But y'all need to give some serious thought to gussying up the place. It's just gotten way too 'Mayberry' over there. I feel like Aunt Bee's gonna come waddling in carrying a dead cat and *The Saturday Evening Post* rolled up under her arm half the time. Seriously."

Darcy eyed them all with a look meant to annihilate. Finally, Carol Ann spoke. "She won't listen. She'd rather attack me than face up to her own shortcomings. It's okay. We'll see who wins in the end. We'll see."

Darcy glared at Carol Ann momentarily then turned and walked out of the store, snatching several packets of bluebonnet seeds off a display rack and tossing them high in the air.

***

Delilah stared a long time out the front window of their shop. She half expected to see a cop car and ambulance pull up in front of the Emporium, sirens blaring and a big city news team following close behind. Lord only knew what kind of mess Darcy had gotten herself into. She loved her sister more than life, but she could be a ginormous canker sore. Delilah turned anxiously and walked to the refrigerator case. Inside sat one sad little baby bouquet for Mrs. Pendergast's third girl, from her husband, the junior high band instructor. Was he ever coming in to pick it up, she wondered? Those daisies are absolutely on their last legs. Delilah closed her eyes and held her hands high in the air. "Lord, this is getting depressing. Send us some business, Lord. I don't care who it is, just find 'em, bring 'em in and get 'em to spend at least fifty dollars on a 'Summery Spray of Joy and Laughter' arrangement. Amen."

The door's electronic signal buzzed and Delilah smiled, eyes heavenward. "You rascal, you!" Turning around she saw the most handsome man walking into the Shoppe. She muttered to herself as she approached the stranger, "Lord, you're really on a roll today."

"Excuse me?"

"Just talking to God. How are you this fine June day? What can I do you for sir?"

Chito Sosa at forty years old was at his peak of male beauty. An old Hollywood playboy veering toward a mélange of George Clooney, Tyrone Power and that Cuban heartthrob from *Dancing With The Stars*, whoever he was. Delilah's head was spinning.

"Well, I came in to buy flowers, oddly enough."

"You came to the right place, yessir. We got everything from roses to gladiolas, birds of paradise, asters, delphiniums, dahlias, freesia..."

Chito smiled, "Alright! Okay. Looks like I did come to the right place. I actually need two different orders."

"Yes sir! Even better."

"One's for...a gravesite."

"Oh, how nice. You know people don't put fresh flowers on graves much anymore and I can't really understand why. It's so much nicer than the plastic flowers that wither in this heat and end up looking like something that's been through a nuclear blast. Depressing, really. How much you want to spend?"

"Oh, I guess around $100 for each order."

"Wonderful!" Delilah began writing on a receipt pad. "May I have your name please?"

"Chito Sosa. C-H-I-T-O, Sosa."

"Excellent. You know when you came in here I said, 'Gosh, he looks just like a movie star,' but I couldn't quite place it. Who do people tell you you look like?"

Chito smiled. "My father."

"Wow! Y'all have been really blessed in the looks department, I'll say that. You're not from around here?"

"No, no–I live in London."

"England?"

"Most of the time. I travel a lot."

"Golly, how exciting. I've never been to England. Well, I've never been anywhere. But I looove the Travel Channel. Did you want to put this on a card or pay cash?"

Chito reached for his wallet, "No, no, I'll put it on my card."

"How would you like a spray of roses? We'll put it in a pretty vase with water and if it's in the shade they'll last at least a couple of days anyway."

"Fine."

"Did you want to put a note with that?"

"A note?" Chito thought momentarily, then replied, "Yes, just say 'For Tom, forever...in my thoughts.'"

Delilah continued scribbling, "...in...my...thoughts. There. And the other one?"

"Oh, I don't know. Something colorful, cheerful."

"I know just the thing! It's called 'Easy Breezy' and it's one of our best sellers. It's like a big box of Crayolas. Sensational! Did you want a note card for that one too?"

Chito stared at Delilah. "Um..."

Delilah smiled back. "Maybe?"

"Actually, you might be able to help me. I'm trying to locate an address so I can personally deliver the flowers."

"Oh yeah? Sure, I'll try."

"They live on a ranch outside town."

"Me, too! Maybe I know them."

"Her name is...Marty Pennebaker."

Delilah stared stone-faced for a second then half smiled, "Oh sure. I know Marty...well. If you're headed out that way I can draw you a map, if you like."

"Thank you, that would be very helpful."

Delilah tore a back page from the receipt book and began to draw. She suddenly stopped and looked up at Chito. "Are they expecting you?"

He shook his head. "It's kind of a surprise."

Delilah nodded slowly. "Uh-huh. Well...surprises are fun!"

# CHAPTER THREE

Marty idly ran her fingers thru Pettus's hair. It was longish and brown-gold and it was wavy in just the right, interesting places. Pettus's scent was pleasantly musky, with notes of Right Guard and Tide. The overall sensation, however, was primarily of horse, hay and clean sweat. "Why can't they bottle this and call it MAN? I could make a killing in New York–hell, in Beijing," Marty pondered as she continued stroking his hair.

Pettus rolled over on his side and exhaled. Their lovemaking had been its usual vigorous, eager exchange. In the bed department, Marty had zero to grouse about. Pettus worked hard at pleasing a woman. Out of bed was a different headline.

"Damn, I'm getting gas," Pettus remarked nonchalantly.

"Would you mind stepping over to the window, please. It's already a little stuffy in here."

"Nah...maybe it's gone...can't tell. Probably that Mexican dinner I had over at Reyes Cafe."

"I don't know how you stay so slim. You eat everything under the sun."

Pettus curled his lip. "Beats me. I think it's why my first

wife left. She gained forty pounds while we were married, and I probably lost. Just barnyard genetics." Pettus rolled back over and ran his tongue slowly around Marty's nipple. "You taste like Dentyne."

"Dentyne?"

"Yeah. Somebody else been licking on my friend here?"

"No. Your 'friend' remains thoroughly unsullied. Dentyne?" Marty frowned and sniffed under her arms. "Where do you come up with this doggerel?" She rose from the daybed and pulled her T-shirt over her head.

"I like the way you talk," Pettus grinned at her mischievously.

"Thanks. I like the way you smell. I gotta get back to the house and see how Daddy's doing."

Pettus reached out an arm, taking Marty's hand. "Let's do it again."

Marty smiled. "Can't. It's almost seven. Daddy's already up, had coffee and raising hell."

"When am I gonna see you again?"

"Soon."

"You're always in such a big hurry every time we're done having a little fun. You don't like seeing a smile on my face?"

Marty grinned back, pulling on her boots. "I like your smile just fine, Pettus, but you know what this is. It's two adults who've been around the track one too many times and they're both afraid they might know too much to start believing in make-believe again."

Pettus stared at her. "You call what we just did over here 'make-believe'? Damn, and people say I'm an old scoffer."

Marty walked over and rubbed his head. "No, it wasn't make-believe. It sure wasn't. I gotta go."

Pettus grabbed her arm, "What is it you don't like about me, exactly? I know you like the sex; we both know that. But there's something in me you just can't wrap your head around. What is it? I'm too country, too poor, too redneck, too...what?"

"I'm fine with the way things are. I'm not unhappy, really."

"But you don't want your daddy to know about us."

"Pettus–he's not going to change. I don't know what all the bad blood's about, I don't care. But I respect him as a daughter, on most levels, and I know it would only upset him if I started bringing you around."

"So I'm just the mangy old dog you throw a blanket over whenever company comes." Pettus flung back the sheet covering him and began to dress. He had the body of a man half his forty-five years. It was ridiculous, really. Marty knew her girlfriends in New York would have killed her if they knew she was playing hard-ass with such a hunk.

"Don't be mad. Give it some time. Let's just see how it goes."

Pettus whirled around, yanking up his tighty-whites. "You know, I could be sleeping with any number of women right now? You know that?" Marty gave him a "And your point is?" look. "But I don't, and that's the part that confuses me. You don't even like me that much and I'm still hanging around." Pettus thumped his chest. "That ain't me!"

Marty took a deep breath. "See you tonight?"

Pettus pursed his lips and sat on the bed pulling on his socks. Marty opened the door to the double-wide and stepped down the concrete stairs. The *Los Abuelos* hunting camp was deserted and silent but for the distant cooing of mourning doves. Her father had built the compound for a hunting club from Dallas years ago, on a far corner of the ranch. During off-season it was as quiet and undisturbed as an Orthodox monastery. With its massive fire pit, shady mesquite/ mountain laurel/ coma trees and high hilltop perspective, it was one of Marty's favorite parts of the ranch. Starting the ignition of the ancient ranch Jeep, she looked up to see Pettus now standing at the trailer house door. He called out.

"What time tonight?"

Marty waved back, "The usual. See ya later." Marty shifted

into first and drove off. Pettus sat on the steps and pulled on his boots. He paused momentarily, stared at the disappearing Jeep and absentmindedly reached in his shirt pocket for a stick of Dentyne.

\*\*\*

Marty loved early morning at the ranch. The air was fresh and cool before the summer sun had a chance to beat hell out of one's senses. The smells of dirt, manure, sage, lantana and horsemint mixed in with the heavy dew made a heady fragrance she'd loved since childhood. Racing in the Jeep, the moist air whipped around her head, tangling her hair. That was the great, freeing thing about being on the ranch. You could just "be." There was nothing to live up to, affect, imitate, aspire or begrudge. Which of course contained its own peril. Marty had always known that if she *didn't* try, *didn't* make the effort, her life would eventually devolve into some facsimile of a flat-screen appliance conveying only the vaguest of sentient thought and emotions. There was more to it all, she always knew that!

The ranch was big, legendary and "home," but it had never been "*the* home." She left after high school and had only intermittently returned. Sometimes eagerly, sometimes not. It was the ponderous responsibility of now being "the sole heir" that made her life an ongoing series of "fugitive from providence" interludes. With a dying father and a pleasurable but inappropriate bedmate to allocate the hours with, she once again felt herself drifting heedlessly into the all too familiar inertia of going with the tide.

Suddenly, fast as a jackrabbit, a whitetail buck jumped from behind a stand of *guajillo* brush and ran across the road, mere feet from the front of the Jeep. Marty slammed on the brakes and watched in awe as the big devil disappeared into the undergrowth. He must've had a fourteen-point rack, she marveled. Although not a hunter due to Pete Pennebaker's admonition, "They pay us too much money to shoot those varmints. Leave 'em alone!" the sheer thrill of coming face-to-face with such a resplendent beast stirred her steadfast, adventurous soul. Growing up on a ranch had indeed taught her two very important life traits: grit and no sniveling. That, and when you fall on a patch of prickly pear, swear as loudly as possible; it effectively dulls the pain.

She'd even had a chance to demonstrate that bit of country-fried wisdom once at a party in Malibu. She'd been dating a screenwriter and there was a big whoop-de-doo at some sitcom star's home. She twisted her ankle coming down a flight of stairs while wearing a pair of ridiculous nine-inch Louboutin heels she imagined made her look ultra *comme il faut*. Lunging across the room, she stepped into one of those flush floor "flame and glass" rock/fire things that were designed to impress everyone with your ability to read *Architectural Digest*. Marty scorched her ankle but it was the smell of a half-burnt pair of $900 shoes that caused her to roar out a string of profanities her daddy would've paid good money to hear. It ended up being her last date with the screenwriter, but she did get to meet Lionel Richie, so it wasn't a complete washout.

Marty pondered as she drove. What a weird, serpentine life she'd constructed for herself. Born and raised in Texas, college in New England, first job in New York, then L.A., then Santa Fe, a stopover season in Paris, soul-searching in Asia, full-on hedonism in Rio for a few months. Each destination was meant to be the semi-permanent solution, with or without the semi-permanent partner, in the semi-perfect environ. Could anyone blame her for being a gun-shy, perennially twelve-year-old mess? It was never right, or it was never right for long enough–or quite possibly it was usually *too* right to not come crashing down as every dream always seemed to insist upon. Was it mostly her, the men, the situation or the circumstances? Why did things always seem to sour despite the billions of brain cells and massive heart vibrations focused laser-like on those objects of desire? Her therapist told her once she was too "expectant." "Expectant of what?" she'd asked.

"You're always hanging on tenterhooks! Always expecting the inevitable instead of accepting the possible."

This statement puzzled Marty for a very long time. Was she saying, "Live for the moment and to hell with the outcome?" Or more of a, "Just flow! If you really got what you thought you wanted, you'd just end up throwing it all away anyway"?

A large covey of quail, unusual for this time of year, was browsing in a salt flat just off to the side of the road. The chicks, tiny as gherkin pickles and each frenetically vigilant, raced off behind their mamas into the thicket. In South Texas the saying went, "Everything eats a quail." And it was true–humans, dogs, cats, snakes, coyotes, roadrunners, hawks, even fire ants. And yet, they returned, season after season, regardless of drought, disease, inclement weather, scarcity of food, manmade disasters–they always returned. They were the true "phoenixes of the chaparral." How one survived in a place that wanted to destroy your existence every single day was a riddle, indeed. Marty had no glib answer, just saw it as proof that anomalies are as critical to life as life itself.

Putting the Jeep into third, she climbed the last rock hill before reaching the big house. Turning the bend in the road was a sight she never tired of. Her mother, Lila B., had designed the white Spanish Colonial *hacienda* with the massive rusty red tile roof herself. It had always looked to Marty, from this perspective anyway, like a way station on the old Spanish *Camino Real*. So many of the Spanish-influenced homes in the Southwest today were like assembly line Taco Bells. Slapdash, cheap-looking and monotonous–they had all the charm of a can of refried beans. Lila B. had spent years working out the details: planning, designing, siting, tracking down a gifted tile man, bringing stone masons up from Mexico. It was, as she proudly said, her masterpiece.

Lila B. Hoover Pennebaker was descended from a long line of faded Alabama gentleman farmers. As she used to tell visitors after a few Manhattans while relaxing on the back patio, "The plantations are all gone, but we did manage to hold on to all the silverware and pretensions." Meeting Pete Pennebaker at a college football game in Austin during the Korean War sealed her destiny. It's true, they fought every day of their married lives but they were an impressive team. Each finishing the other's sentences, same views on how to run the ranch, same politics, same sense of humor, same lapsed Episcopalian proclivities. And the arguments? They fought about the weather, the future, the past, who left the door open, who fed the cat, why'd you buy that hat?, Aunt Vi was not a Baptist!, why are we watching this show? I smell your boots!, why is this magazine on my chair?, who was that actress in *Written On The Wind*?...and on and on it went.

And then there was Marty, the wellspring and occasion for daily dissection. Pete wanted Marty and Tom nearby, all the time, on the ranch, learning ranch ways, doing ranch things. Lila B. wanted them to "fly."

"You see the world, honey," Lila B. told them each. "You live and you learn, and decide what's best for you. This old ranch will always be here. One day you'll fly back home again—maybe, maybe not. But you'll never know what you never missed if you don't at least jump off that branch and fly!" Marty took the advice and winged headlong into the fray. Tom either ignored or sidestepped it altogether.

As Marty pulled into the hacienda's walled courtyard, a passel of stray mutts surrounded the Jeep, wagging, licking, sniffing and slobbering in unison. Gloria Mundi, Clara, Dingbat, Scoot, Festus, *Pobrecita* and Whiz—all of somewhat dizzy parentage and only marginally interested in earning their keep as the ranch's security detail. The house rules were simple: "If somehow you find us out on this isolated spread, you are free to stay; food and doctoring provided *gratis*. However, if the grub's not to your liking or you're sentimental about your reproductive organs, the front gate is thataway!"

Walking down the arcaded portico and followed by the unyielding hounds, Marty could hear Pete already rumbling in the distance. Entering the kitchen, she smiled at Jacinta, the housekeeper, who stood in front of the stove frying an egg.

"Good morning, everybody! How's everyone this fine, beautiful morning?"

Pete folded his paper and dropped it on the kitchen table. "Every night, out again. Where you go every night?" Even for an eighty-six-year-old, tough as a boot *hombre* whose vanity was as distant as Mars, Pete looked like hell. Arm in a sling, cut on his brow and cheek, puffed-up bruised lip, hair askew like a buzzard's tangled nest, he wasn't exactly ready for the Kiwanis Club annual photo.

"I told you, Daddy; I've been staying at the hunting camp. It's quieter up there and I can read and do my business in peace. Jacinta, have we got any more soymilk?" Marty poured herself a mug of coffee while Jacinta searched in the pantry.

"I don't like you staying up there all by yourself. Old man Jessup got broke into a while back. Buncha outlaws stole saddles, tools, even tried to drive off with his propane tank."

Marty sipped her coffee. "I've got a gun. I know how to use it."

"You shouldn't be up there all alone. It ain't right."

Marty took the container of soymilk from Jacinta and poured herself a bowl of cereal. Taking a spoonful, she grimaced. "Yum. Warm bran flakes."

"Why don't you sit down and have an egg, some toast, *frijoles* and bacon? Hell, you can't go all morning eating just straw."

"This is all I want." Marty looked at Pete. "Daddy, would

you like me to comb your hair? It looks like one of the dogs has been slobbering on you."

Pete frowned. "Now that this right arm's banged up, I can't comb with my left hand for nothing."

Marty sat her bowl on the table. "Where's your comb?"

"Back pocket."

"Let me get a glass of water so I can style it a little." Walking to the sink, she filled a goblet and headed back toward him. Jacinta followed her with his breakfast. Same breakfast he'd eaten nearly every day of his life: white toast, no butter, teaspoon grape jelly; one egg, sunny-side up; scoop of pinto beans; slice of bacon; one jalapeño. Breakfast.

"Which pocket's the comb in?"

Pete leaned forward, "Right...no left...hell, I don't remember."

Marty reached around and felt the rear of his khaki britches. "Here it is." She dipped the comb in the water glass and began to detangle his fine, white hair into semi-respectability.

Pete ate his breakfast in silence, enjoying the attention. Marty used to comb his hair as a child, entertaining them both. Back then his hair was thick and black, and he'd let her put curls and spikes and waves in it, enjoying a good laugh at the results. But it had been a long time since those amusements. A lot of tears, silences and grudges had welled up on both sides so that now, only occasionally, did the old father/daughter routine manage to surface.

"There. Looks pretty sharp to me. What do you think, Jacinta?"

Jacinta turned, smiling. "Oh yes, very handsome. But soon you're gonna need another haircut, yes sir." Jacinta was the official ranch barber, even trimming Marty's hair a few times.

"Don't let it get too shaggy, 'Cinta. We don't want anybody thinking he's some thief come to steal our saddles."

Marty picked up the glass and started to move when Pete

grabbed her hand. Not looking at her directly, he mumbled softly, "Thank you, darlin', appreciate it."

Startled, Marty started to speak but couldn't. Was this the new Pete, the dying-of-prostate-cancer Pete with the subdued touch and more appreciative *mien*? Hard to say. Whatever it was, it threw her momentarily. She exhaled and smiled. "No charge today! It does look good, if I do say so." Jacinta nodded in agreement.

Pete wiped his mouth with a napkin. "Somebody called this morning. Wants to come out and visit with us."

"Who?"

"I can't remember. I was trying to shave when he called. I didn't get all the particulars."

"Wonder what he wants?"

Pete shook his head. "Lord only knows. If it's one of those Jehovah's, I'm running his butt off 'fore he gets comfortable."

"Well, I've got to wash up. I need to run into town later. Do y'all need me to pick up anything?"

Pete glanced at her, smiling ruefully. "You can get me some Fountain of Youth pills. I've had it with old age."

Marty smiled back as she headed out the kitchen door. "I hear ya, Daddy, I hear ya."

\*\*\*

The dogs were barking so loudly that the sole house cat, Granny Clampett, had run up the waterspout and was watching from the roof like a terrified gargoyle.

"Quit it! Hush! *Pobrecita,* Scoot–be quiet!" Marty, fresh from the shower, had changed into a comfortable cotton shift and sandals. Reaching for the buzzing front door, she stepped around the yapping dogs and opened it quickly. "I'm sorry, these dogs don't get enough visitors, they get a little..." Marty stopped talking and stared at the handsome man before her.

"You must be Marty."

She spoke hesitantly. "Yes."

"My name is Chito Sosa. These are for you." Chito handed Marty the bouquet of flowers he was holding in his hands.

"M...my goodness. What is this...I don't. I'm sorry, would you like to come in?" Chito stepped into the hallway and gingerly made his way around the now quiet, intensely sniffing dogs.

"You have a beautiful home."

"Thank you. I'm sorry, it was Chee...?"

"Chito." He offered his hand to Marty. "I was a...friend of your brother's."

Immediately it started coming into focus. Was this Tom's "friend?" The one she'd never met but had heard constant rumor of?

"So nice to meet you. Um–let me put these in some water. Can I get you something to drink, coffee, tea–anything?"

"No. I'm fine, thanks."

"Please take a seat in the living room. I'll be right back."

Chito stared around the large baronial room. The dogs followed his every step, intent on imprinting his scent. He stopped to pick up a family portrait on the mantelpiece and rubbed his hand lightly across the surface.

"Did anybody offer you a drink?" Chito turned to see Pete leaning on his cane, standing by the entry.

"Yes, thank you. You must be Mr. Pennebaker?"

"I am."

Chito moved to grasp his good hand holding the cane. "Chito Sosa."

"Had a fall here recently. Messed up my arm. Sosa? I knew some Sosas from down in the Valley once upon a time. Big ranching outfit. You any kin?"

"It's possible. My family's from Monterrey. We seem to have family everywhere."

"Oh yeah, if you've got any money you'll have family all over the planet." Pete waved his cane in the air. "Sit down, sit down!" Chito sat in a nearby leather club chair while Pete lowered himself onto the sofa. "What brings ya out this way, Chito?"

Marty re-entered the room and stood silently near the doorway.

"Well, as I was telling your daughter, I was a...good friend of your son, Tom." Pete's expression was a blank stare. "And I've been wanting to come for some time now to express...my condolences. You see, Tom and I...we both..."

Pete's eyes narrowed indiscernibly.

"We both were very fond of...music. Classical...music. In fact, I'm a bit of an amateur singer myself. Anyway...I wanted to return something."

Marty spoke softly. "What is it?" Chito reached into his coat pocket and produced an envelope.

"A check...from Tom to me...for two hundred fifty thousand dollars. He mailed this to me before he died." Chito handed the envelope to Pete, who opened it, staring blankly.

"But...why?"

Chito looked at Pete, then at Marty. "We were married three years ago...in Boston. He wanted me to have some...security, I guess. The main thing is, I don't need the money. I'm doing fine. I just have a favor to ask."

Jacinta entered the room carrying his vase of flowers and said, "Que bonita! Fresh flowers always bring good luck to a home."

She sat the arrangement on a buffet and turned to them. "Will there be one more for lunch?"

# CHAPTER FOUR

Darcy stared at her plate glumly, whirling the Kraft macaroni and corn nuggets into a sculpture of viscous gluten.

"Why do we eat such horseshit around here?" The seven members of the extended Lyndecker clan, sitting at the table with her, looked up with their mouths full and chewing.

"Whassa matter?" Uncle T.T. belched and reached for another boiled hot dog. "Ain't you get enough to eat?"

Darcy shoved her plate away and rose from the table. "This stuff is killing us. We should be eating organic and GMO-free and non-processed and probably vegetarian."

Pettus drained his mayonnaise jar of iced tea and slapped it back on the table. "Great, you get your ass home early enough to make dinner some night and we'll try all that shit you're talking about."

"I ain't no vegetarian." The baby of the family, eighteen-year-old Thaine, glared at Darcy as she dropped her paper plate in the trash can. "People who raise beef for a living aren't like those fruit and nut jobs out in California." Cracking up, twenty-one-year-old brother Cody blew bubbles in his iced tea.

Oldest sister Darlene gazed stoically out the window. "The

Chinese have invented a drug that erases all memories. You can live every day free from your past. No sadness, no regrets, no desperation."

They all stared at Darlene as if Captain Kirk had just beamed himself into the room.

"Can someone pass the hominy, please?"

Uncle T.T. lifted the bowl of canned hominy and handed it to Darlene. "Well, now Darlene, hon, does this memory pill come with a little map case you forget where you left it at?"

Cody and Thaine immediately began snickering. Darlene stared at her lap, "It only erases memories, not common sense."

Pettus cleared his throat. "Well, that's a good thing cause you'd hate to go around all day trying to remember if you'd wiped your butt or not." Pettus doubled over in laughter as Cody, Thaine and T.T. joined in. Darlene bit her lip, trying not to laugh.

Darcy scooped a bowl of ice cream and placed the container back in the freezer. Standing behind Darlene, she glowered as she shoveled spoonfuls of cherry chocolate pretzel in her mouth. "You just say these ridiculous things to get a reaction, don't you?"

Darlene turned to her sister, mystified. "What?"

"It's how you get anyone to pay attention to you. Say something completely outrageous, play the fool, you'll get a response. Don't you ever get tired of being everyone's idiot?"

Pettus turned quickly to Darcy. "Hey, hey, hey!"

"It's true! Everyone knows Darlene can't carry on a normal conversation so she just says anything stupid so she won't feel left out. Isn't that right?"

Darlene turned to her. "That's right, Darcy. Some of us actually know our shortcomings. You, on the other hand, wouldn't know a personal flaw from a virtue if it rose up and bit your nose off."

Darcy pulled the spoon slowly from her mouth and made

a perfect small "o" with her lips. "Oh, but you're wrong. I find pointing out people's flaws a necessary virtue. Keeps the asshole quotient to a reasonable number." Darcy turned and walked out to the back porch. They all stared at each other with confused looks.

Pettus finally spoke. "What's eating her?"

Delilah, who'd been silently reading her latest issue of the *Baptist Standard*, quietly sat the magazine down and cleared her throat. "We're going to have to kill Carol Ann Jansky, that's what. She's taken all our business from us. My God, she's even put in a 'Wine-a-rita' machine down at the Flower Emporium. Don't you think there's something truly evil about a person that carries spruce sachet in their pockets, so they'll smell like Christmas all year long?"

Uncle T.T. smiled. "Well, hon, that's the good old American way. It's called competition. Maybe y'all just need to try a new tack. Outsmart the little strumpet!"

Delilah shook her head and sighed. "Oh, Uncle T.T., music ability doesn't really count for much in the business world."

Uncle T.T. stared at Delilah, lost.

"I brought my zither and played in front of the store awhile back and all it did was run people off."

"Honey, a strumpet is not a musical..."

Pettus interrupted. "Y'all gotta figure something out cause you still owe me eight thousand dollars of the ten I loaned you, and I, by God, can't afford to shrug that off."

"You'll get paid."

Thaine rolled up a piece of white sandwich bread into a hard ball and bounced it off Cody's head. "What's a strumpet?"

"Cut it out, dickhead! You're so stupid you don't even know the instruments in an orchestra."

"A strumpet is not a musical..."

Darlene picked up her plate and stood. "Prostitute! That's what it is. A strumpet is a prostitute."

Thaine looked at her wide-eyed. "Is Carol Ann Jansky a

prostitute?"

Cody snorted, "You dumb shit. You couldn't afford her even if she was."

"Is Carol Jansky a ho?"

Delilah shrugged. "Don't be so immature, Thaine. Nobody cares what her ethnic background is."

Pettus wiped his mouth with a paper towel and sat back in his chair. "Y'all need to figure out a plan to keep that store open but you can forget about trying to one-up the Janskys. People like us don't count to the Janskys of the world. They gonna do whatever they damn well please and you trying to impress or outshine 'em ain't gonna amount to a sack of grass burrs to those folks."

Darlene dropped her paper plate in the trash bin and smiled. "Sort of like you and Marty Pennebaker, huh?"

They all turned to Darlene. Pettus effortlessly tossed his paper plate across the room into the garbage can. "Girl, I don't believe I'd go there if I were you."

"Go where? Is it supposed to be some secret you're seeing Marty? Just 'cause they have the biggest ranch in the county doesn't mean we don't count in their world, does it?"

Uncle T.T. shook his head, "Umm-mmm. Darlene, you have an uncanny ability to always say the wrong thing at the wrong time to the wrong person in the wrong place. Truly a gift!"

"Well, if we're not supposed to know anything..."

Pettus leapt from the table and glared at Darlene. "Look, it's no secret. You can tell everybody you know. What if I AM seeing her? Maybe she likes me, how 'bout that? A lot!" Pettus pointed toward Delilah. "I, however, am not competing in the same business with someone who's far richer, far more powerful and far more devious."

"You sure about that?" Darlene turned to exit the room, murmuring softly to herself. "They gonna do whatever they damn well please...grass burrs and all."

Stepping onto the back porch, Darlene saw Darcy huddled on the porch swing resembling a just-hurled Raggedy Ann.

"I'm sorry about Carol Ann being such an inconsiderate sow. What are you going to do?"

"Oh, don't act like you give a shit, Darlene. You've hated the Shoppe ever since we opened it. Now that you're finally a big nurse's aide–God knows how many years you've been trying–you think you're on *Grey's Anatomy*. Just..." Darcy waved her hand. "Go away."

Darlene crossed her arms and smirked. "Poor little Darcy. I'd expect Lilah to cut and run, but you? I thought you were the Rambo of the family." She shrugged. "Guess not."

Darlene turned back to the kitchen. "I had a killer idea for you, but since you'd rather pout, I guess I'll just keep it to myself." She paused at the door, waiting.

Finally, Darcy spoke in a low monotone. "What?"

Darlene turned and rushed to shove Darcy's feet off the swing. "Move. I can't stand that little fish-mouthed cow any more than you, but you've got to be smart about these things."

Darcy looked unconvinced.

"Sell her the Shoppe!"

"Oh, Darlene–is that all you've got? That is so freakin' lame. We owe Pettus eight thousand dollars, near twenty thousand back mortgage on the building, all our suppliers, creditors, utilities, phone, taxes–easily another twelve to sixteen thou. Forget ever showing a dime profit for either of us, you think Miss Pink Pussy's gonna write us a check for over fifty thousand and just bury the hatchet? Dream on, girlfriend."

Darlene idly pushed the swing with one leg and answered thoughtfully, "Well then, you're just going to have to kill her."

"Exactly."

"I mean it's no big loss. She's between husbands, no kids–I don't even think she goes to church anymore."

"She doesn't"

"No big loss."

"Nope."

"Wouldn't it be great if we had a volcano nearby she could accidentally fall into?"

They both nodded, then sat in silence. Delilah walked onto the back porch eating an Eskimo Pie.

"I know what y'all are thinking." They looked up at her, expressionless. "How can I still be hungry after all that supper? I'm not, really. Just nerves. This has been a day of Biblical proportions!"

Darlene shook her head slowly. "What does that mean?"

"Well, think about it! The Lord was testing all my pillars of faith today. There was so much tension over at that shop I thought any minute I might just run into the street, render my garments and gash my brains with a sharp rock."

Darcy pursed her lips. "That would've been different."

Darlene shook her head. "Just another day at the Lyndecker Home of Biblical Contortions."

"Y'all can make fun if you want, but I don't know what I would've done if that beautiful man from London...or Mexico...hadn't come into the Shoppe."

"What man?"

"Chico or Cheeto, something like that. He ordered two great big sprays of flowers–the 'Easy Breezy' and the 'Scarlett O'Tara'! We cleared over two hundred dollars on those alone!"

Darcy leapt up from the swing. "Lilah, you didn't tell me about that!"

"I didn't? Well, I meant to but I was just so shaken by the revelation that was occurring before me. He was like this beautiful angel come to Rita Blanca. Like a mini rapture, only without people flying in the air."

"Who did he buy the flowers for? Do we know them? Where's he from again? Why's he in Rita Blanca?"

Darlene chimed in eagerly. "Good looking? Like crazy handsome or just cleans-up-well? Wedding band? Did he have a 'money vibe'? Did he use a credit or a debit card?"

Delilah stepped back, alarmed. "Gol-ly, I'm not the F.B.I. Y'all want me to be Herbert Hoover and I'm just not!"

"Edgar."

"I told you his name was Cheeto!"

Darcy exhaled loudly and crossed her arms. "What difference does it make? Two hundred bucks isn't going to save our asses from the beating Pink Poodle Butt is handing us. Next time, Lilah, if there ever is a next time, tell me when we have a sale! I'd like to experience more fully that feeling of fleeting wealth, you know?"

"Well, if you want to know more about him, why don't you call Marty Pennebaker? He bought one assortment for her and one for her brother, Tom, out at the cemetery."

Darcy and Darlene stared at Delilah.

"You mean...Pettus's Marty?" Darlene asked warily.

Delilah nodded.

Darcy looked incredulous. "He bought flowers for Marty...and Tom Pennebaker?"

"That's what I said. And he used a credit card, platinum. And he was very good-looking, and he smelled a little bit like a brand-new leather billfold."

Darcy and Darlene glanced at each other; shivers of vague potential seemed to lurk in the ethers.

"So...good looking Englishman, Mexican–whatever–unbeknownst to anybody, walks into the Shoppe and buys two pricey assortments for...Marty..."

"And her late brother," Darlene interrupted.

"Why?"

"Relative, friend–ex-boyfriend?"

"Whose?" Darlene nodded slowly. "Ohhh, I getcha. Marty...or gay brother?"

Delilah jumped in. "Y'all don't know he was gay. That was just a rumor."

"Honey bunch, if it eats carrots and has a fuzzy white tail

it ain't an alligator, okay?"

"I don't know what y'all are getting at, but I don't want any part of it."

Darcy spoke softly. "I wouldn't say we're getting at anything, Lilah. I wouldn't say the opposite either. I'd just say it might be an opportune moment to investigate any hint of likelihood when it lands in your lap."

"What likelihood?"

Darlene snapped, "Oh, Delilah! Don't you ever wrestle with the windmills of your mind, or is it all just the Carpenters playing in there?"

Delilah looked bewildered. "The windmills of your mind? No, I don't think the Carpenters ever recorded that one, but have you ever heard Karen sing 'Ave Maria'? You'll burst into tears."

Darlene smiled stoically. "I can guarantee it."

"Listen up! I don't have a clue where any of this is going," Darcy huffed, "but we have to do something or we're going to be out on the street selling Chiclets from a cigar box. Now we've got to put our heads together and figure out a plan. I'll be damned if I'm going to let fish-mouth run me out of my own hometown in her pink Barbie Jeep."

Darlene put a hand on Darcy and Delilah's shoulders. "Sisterhood is powerful. I'm here for you both in your hour of need. Either we break the bitch's back or...or..."

Darcy spoke in a low growl. "We kill her."

\*\*\*

The Jansky home, located five miles outside the "Rita Blanca Pop. 6,732 City Limits" sign, was referred to locally as "Fort Tuscany." Barbara and Clayton Jansky, Carol Ann's parents, had vacationed in Italy a decade or so earlier on a Farm Bureau tour and Barbara came back obsessed with all things Tuscan. As a result of the last South Texas fracking boom, the Janskys were able to hire a San Antonio architect and construct a somewhat unique facsimile of what a Texan's-first-trip-to-Europe version of authentic Italian was. Not an uncommon phenomenon at all; similar housing variants of "Instant Italy" were popping up all over South Texas (or as they were referred to by local arbitrators of taste, "Big Ass Texas Tuscan").

Basically, it was a typical Texas ranch house on spaghetti steroids. Everything was BIG, in a Disneyworld/Italian sort of way. From the oversized leather club chairs that could easily fit two adults, to the Hill Country limestone fireplace large enough to roast an Angus bull, to the granite-countertop-by-death kitchen–it all screamed Olive Garden *simpatia*. Overwhelming, overproduced and essentially, overdone. But noticed, it got!

Carol Ann Jansky sat at the "Country Italian Farmhouse" kitchen table and flipped her long blonde hair off her shoulders, sighing the sigh of a fishmonger stuck with an unrefrigerated three-day-old tuna. It all stunk. Between marriages (one down, how many more on the way?), Carol Ann had moved back to Fort Tuscany to "gather stock," as her mother, quite unperturbed, put it. It wasn't the ideal state of affairs, but it would have to do until that, it, or him showed up to alter her current situation. Meanwhile, she stewed. Glancing up at her mother, who was slicing tomatoes at the kitchen counter, she moaned, "I mean...ewww...it was just so...common!"

Barbara continued slicing, "They're all common as dirt. I'd as soon buy a used car from Charles Manson before I'd let a Lyndecker try to sell me anything."

"Darcy just stood there in MY store and attacked me in front of MY customers like I was some ninny that was going to go crying out into the street."

Barbara began flicking tomato wedges into the salad bowl as if she were attempting to harm the lettuce. "What burns me up is that they somehow have come to the very wrongheaded conclusion they're the only game in town. Ludicrous!"

"My God, what about free enterprise and competition and open markets? This isn't Communist Russia."

"I don't think they're Communist anymore, shug–but point taken." Barbara energetically tore off a swath of Saran Wrap and tightly covered the salad bowl, placing it in the refrigerator. "Thank goodness your father wasn't there. He'd of bitten her head off, or worse."

Carol Ann slapped a bejeweled, manicured hand on the table and rose. "Well, I'm certainly not going to take it lying down."

"No ma'am."

"I'm going to march into their store tomorrow morning and give them a piece of my mind."

Barbara looked up from wiping the countertop, alarmed. "Now honey, there's two of them. Let's not be rash. I'll call some of the girls and we'll all go in as a group."

"Oh, Mother, would you?"

"Of course! I've had it up to here with those Lyndeckers. That horrible old daddy that went to the pen–he had the nerve to inform me once that I shouldn't be on City Council because I didn't represent the working man. *The working man!* As if a Lyndecker had ever done an honest day's work in their entire lives! I told him he could just remove himself from my presence and go crawl back under the rock from which he sprung because this WORKING WOMAN had a job to do!"

"Oh, Mother, you always know just the right thing to say. I wish I had your gift."

Barbara moved around the gleaming granite counter and placed a hand on Carol Ann's shoulder. "You're beautiful, honey, inside and out. That's the main thing–always let your outside be a reflection of what's truly deep inside yourself."

Carol Ann anxiously twisted a platinum and turquoise bracelet with pave diamond inlay that her father had given her on her twenty-first birthday.

"Yes, Mother, I try so hard to be beautiful, but sometimes...sometimes I feel like I'm the only person in the world that even cares anymore. It can be...a huge burden sometimes!"

A small tear slid down Carol Ann's flawless pink cheek and Barbara wiped it away.

"Everyone loves you, precious. They want to be you! You show people what they're capable of–joy, happiness, beauty and high principles."

Carol Ann smiled and hugged her mom.

Barbara continued, "Your daddy and his daddy didn't inherit all this money we have for nothing. It takes talent and brains and big-city lawyers to hang on to what God has blessed us with! Don't forget, Carol Ann–you're where you are today because someone made a lot of money once upon a time and your Christian duty is to hang on to it with everything you've got and not squander what the good Lord has so abundantly endowed."

Carol Ann again hugged her mom and then looked innocently into her eyes. "But I really hate her, Mother. I hate Darcy Lyndecker like I hate *faux* Prada. Sometimes I just want to take her smug, white trash face and squeeze it into a tight little ball of bloody ooze. Is that so wrong?"

Barbara smiled and brushed Carol Ann's hair. "Darling, we all have to learn to channel our impulses into more appropriate aspirations."

"Like what?"

Barbara grinned. "Well, for starters, maybe their store will burn down!"

"Mother!"

"Oh, it's just an idea. Goodness, I'm certainly not suggesting you go over there and light a match. But, who knows, maybe somebody else might have a similar idea. You never know."

Carol Ann's eyes glistened. "Of course, you never know. I mean a person can't be responsible for another person's actions, can they?"

Barbara shook her head.

"And if someone were to act on a person just thinking out loud, well, what's to be done about it?"

"Exactly."

Suddenly a dark cloud crossed Carol Ann's features and she frowned a tiny Botox-tightened grimace. "But who would be that stupid? I don't know anyone that stupid."

Barbara appeared stumped as well. "It would definitely require someone with just minimum intelligence. I mean, if you thought too much about it all, you'd probably want to pass on it.

"Who do we know that's as unintelligent, mean and low-life as the Lyndeckers?"

Barbara placed a hand on her hip. "Well, those two younger brothers of theirs certainly wouldn't win any Citizen of the Year awards."

"Who? Cody and Thaine? Mother, there's not enough brain cells between the two of them to spread on a cracker. And why would they want to burn down their sister's store anyway?"

Barbara clucked and shook her head. "I can't imagine, unless there was money to be made."

Carol Ann let this thought settle in her head. "Oh, I don't know. They're both just too simple-minded for words. They'd probably burn down the wrong store."

Barbara turned and walked swiftly back toward the butler's pantry, a room only slightly smaller than your average one-bedroom New York City apartment. Reaching for a spray bottle of granite polish, she began burnishing the Sienna *Cinque Terre* slabs her decorator had found wholesale from a going-out-of-business Houston dealer. Speaking calmly, she buffed the stones with the focused conviction of a transgressor seeking penance. "All I know is–sometimes you have to be the spark of an idea. You don't go lighting the bonfire, yourself. No ma'am. You stand back and direct the wind to blow in the direction you're aiming. Let someone else carry the torch of restitution."

Carol Ann moaned, "Oh, Mama, this is all getting too confusing. Couldn't I just accidentally drive my car through their front window? Maybe the whole thing would collapse."

Barbara stopped rubbing and looked at her. "Your daddy is not buying you another new car this year! You can forget that." Barbara returned to the task at hand, thinking aloud, "Was it Darcy or Darlene who got that oldest boy sent up to reform school for half a year for breaking into Old Lady Wheeler's home and stealing all her guns?"

Carol Ann nodded. "Yep. And her sewing machine."

"And the younger one, Thaine, wasn't he on juvenile probation for selling pot to that Methodist preacher's kid? I think it was Delilah who turned him in when she got out of rehab."

"Yes."

Barbara looked up from her cleaning and brushed her forehead with her arm. "I'm just saying. I doubt there's a lot of love lost between those brothers and sisters. Right price, right offer–done in the right, indirect kind of way–well, who knows, the Flower Emporium could come out smelling like a rose."

Carol Ann looked at her mother and slyly grinned. "And farewell, Dusty Rose–the late, great!"

# CHAPTER FIVE

Pete, expressionless, slowly handed the check to Marty. She stared at it as if it were some missive from another world. It was clearly Tom's handwriting, written on a checking account from the local Rita Blanca First National, an account Marty assumed had been closed soon after his death.

"Married? You...you were married to Tom?"

"Almost three years ago." Chito glanced at Pete apprehensively. "He didn't want you all to know. He didn't want to cause you any embarrassment."

"Embarrassment?" Marty spat out the word as if it were something disagreeable in her mouth. "I'm his sister! Why would he not tell me? What would I be embarrassed about?"

Again, Chito looked at Pete, who continued to stare in vacant silence. "I think, maybe, he thought it would cause too much...disruption."

Marty sat slowly on the edge of the sofa and exhaled. "All those trips to the doctor. Distance. The weeks of seeing specialists, surgeons, healers, practitioners–God knows what..." she looked up at Chito, "he was with you?"

Chito nodded. "We got an apartment together in Boston."

Marty smiled ruefully. "Boston. About as far as you can get

from Rita Blanca and still be just one time zone away." She looked at the check again, then back at Chito. "How did you meet?"

"I'm an investment banker. I travel a lot. Right now I'm based in London, but several years ago I was working out of Houston. My family, we're originally from Monterrey, Mexico, and when my father got sick, he came up to Houston for treatment and stayed with me. We both met Tom one day in the cafeteria at MD Anderson. It was...as they say...meeting the right person at the right time."

Marty shook her head and spoke in a trance-like voice. "Married. We didn't know. He didn't want us...to know." She put her hand to her mouth, stifling a lump in her throat. "Why would you not be with him in his final days, Chito, and attend his funeral?"

Chito stared at the floor. "More than anything, *anything,* I wanted to be with him. You have no idea how we fought over this. He was very clear, angry even. He did not want his family brought into his new life."

A silence fell on the room like a sinking veil of contrition. Finally, Pete, who'd been mute the entire time, cleared his throat and spoke slowly in a hollow, distant voice. "Well...this has been...quite a riveting preamble, Mr. Sosa. I thank you for returning my boy's money. But it seems apparent that it was intended for you. Why, I don't know exactly, but if that was Tom's intention, then he surely had his reasons." Pete took out a handkerchief from his back pocket, blew his nose and wiped his mouth. "This...marriage business. I don't know much about it, 'cept what I read in the paper. I fathom it's legal now just about everywhere. World ain't gonna stop turning if it is. So be it. I think I understand Tom's reasoning for keeping you...at bay. Folks round here, they ain't entirely ignorant, just slower to take things in, that's all. You got the Bible telling you it's okay to kill this one but not that one, hate this one but not that one, listen to this one but not that one, love this one but not that one–is it any wonder the whole world's a goddam mess? No, Tom didn't want you here 'cause I think he knew you wouldn't be accepted. That's the part that hurts." Pete tapped at his chest, "It hurts my heart that we couldn't, father and son, get through this thing that separated us his whole life. And I don't know why that had to be–'cause I loved that boy! But I guess I always wanted him to be something he wasn't. I wanted to protect him from the world. And I'm ashamed I couldn't rise above my own pitiful shortcomings. A terrible, senseless shame."

Pete wiped his eyes and blew his nose. Marty rose, wiping her own eyes and walked to stand behind him. She placed a hand on his shoulder and he shakily reached up to pat it. Marty cleared her throat and spoke, "Mr. Sosa..."

"Chito."

"Chito. You can see this has all been something of a...shock for us. Not sure what you'd like for us to do at this point. I think my father wants you to keep the money. If there's something of Tom's you'd like for yourself–photographs, books, clothes..."

Chito shook his head. "No. I have the memories in here"– he pointed to his heart–"and here. What Tom wanted, what he spoke about over and over. He wanted to *change* Rita Blanca. To make it a..." Chito struggled, trying to find the right words. "A better place."

Pete and Marty were dumbfounded. Marty shook her head. "Better?"

"Yes!"

"You mean like...a park, or something?"

"I'm not sure! That's why I'm here. I want you to help me find a way to fulfill Tom's bequest. How do we make here...a better place?"

Jacinta suddenly entered the room and announced, "Lunch is served."

Nobody budged. Finally, Pete raised his cane in the air and

shouted, "Burn it down! Only damn way. Start all over again and rebuild from the ashes."

Chito half-smiled. "Yes, well maybe there's a less...dramatic way to help."

Pete stood slowly with Marty's assistance and stared back at Chito. "Son, I don't know who you are or what you are or what you think you are–it don't matter. If Tom Pennebaker thought enough of you to partner up with, that's good enough for me. You're welcome to stay here long as you want. Hell if I know what can be done for piss-poor little Rita Blanca, but we'll for damn sure figure it out. Now come on in here and dinner with us. We're simple country folk, we eat our big meal of the day at noontime."

Pete put his good arm around Chito as they walked slowly toward the dining room. Marty followed behind and pondered two thoughts simultaneously: What in the name of God just happened here in this living room to change their lives so immutably, perhaps forever? And damn, did Tom Pennebaker ever know a good-looking man when he saw one!

\*\*\*

The three Lyndecker boys sat in the front seat of the family's 1981 Dodge pickup and stared glumly ahead. It was hotter than Cinco de Mayo in Nuevo Laredo. The sweat stinging Pettus's eyes was incessant. He wiped and cursed, wiped and cursed as the pickup jerked and careened along the rutted ranch road. Cody and Thaine, dazed, shared expressions of apathy and disgust.

"She's probably dead by now," Cody mumbled.

Pettus, hands gripping the wheel, glanced over at Cody by the door. "When'd you see her last?"

"Yesterday morning. She was already up to her titties bogged down."

"But you didn't bother to say anything 'til today?"

Cody jerked his head to the left. "Pettus, I told ya, I went back to the house for a rope. Uncle T.T. wanted me to give him a ride into town, by the time we got back the pump at the well house went out and we worked on that sumabitch 'til near sundown. Thaine was off steer roping at the arena–wadn't nothing we could do about it."

"Third damn bitch we've lost this summer. You better hope she's still alive."

Cattle wading into the middle of South Texas stock ponds during the scalding heat of summer was nothing new. The possibility of their getting bogged down in the mud was a ranching fact of life. A cowman's part-time job in the summer was riding the *senderos* and back trails of a place and keeping an eye out for poor, worn-out, potential drown victims.

Thaine leaned across Cody and spit a wad of snuff out the window. "I ain't going in to pull her out. I ain't wearing any underwear."

Pettus snorted, "You'll go in if I say you will. We've all seen your tallywacker before. It ain't nothing to write home about."

Cody hooted and slapped Thaine's thigh. "You 'fraid Cindy Keelahar's gonna drive up and see your goober way out here?"

"Shut up, dickwad!"

Pettus eyed Cody. "Don't go getting all full of happy cake– you're going in there with him."

Thaine reached over and dug his nails into Cody's knee, mimicking his previous taunt. "You afraid Debbie Wylie's gonna see your goober?"

Cody jerked abruptly and threw off Thaine's hand. "Bitch! She's seen my dick more times than you've ever pounded your pillow at night. Who gives a shit? I ain't wearing underwear neither and I don't give a good damn!"

Pettus shook his head. He thought briefly about asking what this ban on underwear thing was all about but decided he really didn't want to know anyway.

Turning the corner of the old back ranch corral, Pettus

pulled the Dodge up to the rim of the stock tank and shut off the ignition. He squinted. "Well...she's still alive."

There, in the middle of the tank sat a very large, very tired and very irritable Santa Gertrudis cow. Her horns extended, easily, a foot and half on both sides of her head.

Pettus emitted a small whistle. "Now begins the rodeo." He cracked open the squeaking truck door and grunted, "Okay, men–let's get to gettin'."

Slowly, they all stepped out of the pickup and Pettus reached behind the back seat to retrieve a lariat. He tied one end of it to the winch in front of the truck. Thaine and Cody eyed each other warily and began stripping behind the tailgate. They removed their articles of clothing as delicately as if they were made of gossamer silk, carefully folding each ratty T-shirt and pair of holey jeans with the solemnity of a papal sacrament.

"Quit looking!"

"I'm not looking at your tiny meat, asswipe."

"Shut up!"

Pettus laughed and spit, "Okay, children, quit acting like you never seen a grown man's pee-pee before. I don't want this to take all day. Come on."

Last to be discarded were the threadbare socks. Standing there before God and nature with their red sunburnt backs and snowy white butt cheeks–looking for all the world like two Hostess Sno-Ball mounds–Pettus chuckled again. "Come on strawberry and vanilla, let's get Granny pulled out of here."

Cautiously the boys tiptoed toward the pond's edge, carefully avoiding sticker burrs and cow shit. They cupped their manhoods with both hands, somehow managing to retain a distant semblance of their masculine dignity.

Pettus threw the rope after them, splashing cool water on their ivory legs. They both flinched.

"Sure wish I had a camera. *Playgirl Magazine*'d pay good money to see those fine white heinies."

Thaine suddenly flinched. "Shit, I think I stepped on a turtle."

"You better hope you don't step on a snake," Cody said.

Pettus took off his cowboy hat and wiped his brow. "Ain't no bad snakes in there, just the good ones. Let's go, *compadres!*"

Both boys slowly approached opposite sides of the confused cow. She stared at each as if they were little green men and little green men were definitely not on her dance card at present. Cody tried gingerly placing the rope over her head. She'd have none of it. She snorted and huffed and flung those sharp horns of hers around like a circus knife act. Cody handed the rope to Thaine.

"Here, try it on your side."

Thaine repeated the procedure several times with the same results. Granny was pissed as hell for being stuck in the mud this long and she for sure wasn't going to put up with any Martians trying to mess with her.

Pettus called out, "Put the damn rope on her horns! What's wrong with you two? You're both acting like city boy Yankees."

Thaine hollered back over his shoulder as Granny splashed him good with her thrashing head. "She's acting crazy. If it goes around her neck she'll choke to death when we pull her out, and she won't let me get it around her dadgum horns!"

Pettus shook his head in disgust. Exhaling sharply, he began muttering to himself as he started pulling off his boots. "Buncha little girls. Never shoulda brought 'em out here. I knew I'd end up doing it myself."

Pettus paused at the front of the truck in his old boxer shorts and stared stony-faced out at the pond.

"No sense riding home in wet drawers. Outta the way, babies." He slipped out of his boxers and tossed them on the pickup's hood. As he stepped briskly into the water, Cody and Thaine began hooting.

"Don't let a big ole snake bite your ding-dong!"

"Ooh daddy, I've got a gay friend down in Corpus that'd sure like your number." They continued snickering.

Pettus dove in and paddled toward them. "Shut the fuck up. You two about as worthless as pussy on a billy goat. Give me that rope."

Thaine tossed the knotted end to Pettus. Standing directly in front of the cow, Pettus eyed her with steely determination.

"Now you listen to me, you fractious old bitch. I'd just as soon leave you here to die, but that'd cost me some hard-earned money and I for damn sure ain't throwing any of that around, so you just lower your head, sister, and we'll all get out of this piss hole *muy pronto. Comprende?*"

As if by some unseen remote, Granny slowly dropped her horns just enough for Pettus to gently slip the rope over them. Letting the lasso touch the top of her forehead, Pettus quickly jerked it tight.

"That's how it's done in the movies, boys!" Pettus grinned.

Thaine and Cody both whistled and shouted and even Granny seemed resigned to her new state of affairs. Wading back toward the truck, the three of them ascended from the watery mire, their bodies covered in black mud and slimy weeds.

Cody groused, "Shit, how we gonna get this crap off our..."

Pettus interrupted, "We ain't. Might as well just let it dry 'til we can get home and shower."

"Aw, fuck. This shit is nasty." Thaine futilely wiped at his legs.

"Fifty years of cow shit, piss, bird crap, hog pooty, deer urine and coyote scat–nectar of the South Texas gods! Come on–let's pull this ole *puta* out and git."

Pettus grabbed his underwear from the truck hood and tossed it on the dash. Hopping into the front seat, he started the ignition and engaged the winch. Nothing. Trying again, he flipped the toggle switch a few more times. Nothing.

"Shit."

"What up, my man?" Cody, standing outside the truck window, grinned at Pettus idiotically.

"Shut the fuck up, Cody. The damn winch is broke."

"Figures. Nothing ever works around here when you want it to. It's the Murphy's Law of the Lyndecker Clan."

Pettus looked wearily over at Thaine. "Thank you, Socrates. Y'all go stand out of the way–I'm gonna back her out with the truck."

Thaine and Cody hobbled off to the side, avoiding cactus and thorns. Pettus shoved the old Dodge into reverse and then...nothing. He'd parked too close to the lip of the pond and now the front wheels were stuck in the mud. The old retreads in the rear, smooth as a tabletop, couldn't get any traction on the baked soil. They spun and smoked and squealed just like a thrilling day at NASCAR.

"Son of a bitch!" Pettus slapped the steering wheel, then lowered his head against it. The boys by now were standing under a nearby *huisache* tree, scratching their naked butts and looking slightly anxious. The cow in the water appeared to be wondering how in hell she'd ended up with these harebrained aliens in the first place.

"What are we going to do now, Pettus?" Thaine inquired hesitantly.

Pettus peered over at them both with a mad gleam in his eye. "We're going to hold hands and dance around the fucking Maypole! What do you think we're going to do? Get your asses in front of the truck and start pushing!"

Thaine and Cody looked at each other with expressions of pained forbearance.

"I don't get paid enough for this shit," Thaine muttered.

"You don't get paid anything, asshole."

Positioning themselves on each side of the front headlights, Pettus called out to them, "When I say 'push,' you start rocking her and push like hell. PUSH!"

Pettus floored the gas and the rear wheels smoked and screeched like a foundry in hell. Nothing. Taking his foot off the gas, Pettus leaned out the window. "Let's try it one more time. When I say...PUSH!"

The boys leaned into the hot metal of the hood and gave it all they had. They bounced the worn-out old shocks up and down as if they were rubber yo-yos, straining and grimacing like mighty Gladiators of the Chaparral. The only things they'd both excelled at in high school–football and weight training–seemed to have paid off. The Dodge suddenly flew out of the mudhole so fast both boys ended up face down in the muck. And right behind them came ole Granny cow sailing across the pond like a bovine yacht! If Pettus hadn't slammed on the brakes quick as he did, she'd have ended up in the surf on Padre Island.

Pettus whooped and jumped out of the cab. Seeing both boys face down in the mud, he hollered again and threw his hat in the air. "Y'all take your time. Those mud baths are supposed to keep ya looking young and pretty." Pettus chuckled and went back to put on his boots. Thaine and Cody rose slowly from the mire and stared at each other.

"You look like shit."

Cody cuffed a handful of mud at Thaine. "Give that boy an A! You think that might be cause I'm sitting in shit just like you, Soccer-teese?"

Thaine jumped on Cody and they began wrestling in the mud–laughing, spitting and flinging ooze like a pair of Amazonian river otters. Pettus ignored them as he walked over to Granny cow, now lying on her side and staring straight ahead, thunderstruck.

"Gramma, you okay?" Pettus walked around the cow and examined her. She didn't seem to be wounded at all, just a little stunned. He reached over to gently remove the rope from her horns.

"Now you be a good girl and don't give me any trouble.

That's it. Thank you, sweetheart. Let me see you get up on your old haunches."

Pettus removed the rope without provocation and gave Granny a small nudge with his boot. She continued to lie still, breathing quietly. He nudged her again.

"Come on, gal. After all we done for you, don't just lie there like a rock, git up!"

Pettus poked her a little harder this time, and like a NASA projectile, she leapt to her feet, snorted and whipped around, aiming for Pettus, who by now was racing toward Cody and Thaine at the speed of batshit loco. The cow chased the three of them in and out of the pond for a good minute or more.

Unseen and unheard, Marty Pennebaker and her passenger, Chito Sosa, drove up on the berm of the tank pond in her Jeep. Turning off the ignition, they stared in wordless wonder at the scene transpiring below.

By now, Granny had the three of them hip-deep in the water. They were waving and shouting and cuffing spray at her, but she held her ground, occasionally lunging forward and shaking her horns. With each lunge, the trio jumped further back into the pond. It was like watching a game of Chicken performed by primitive mud people from a *National Geographic* documentary.

After a moment, Chito spoke to Marty in bewilderment. "Is it...some kind of game?"

Marty squinted, shaking her head. "Hard to say. Might just be bath day at the Lyndecker ranch."

At that moment, Granny took one final dive toward the cluster of slightly wounded machismo huddled before her, then whirled and skedaddled, tail held high, making a beeline out of the pond trap and into the open pasture. Instantaneously, as if they'd just learned they'd won the Powerball, all three Lyndeckers began laughing uproariously. Cody and Thaine picked Pettus up and tossed him into the air. Pettus grabbed Thaine sideways between the legs and shoulder and flung him across the water. There was so much howling and hollerin' going on, Marty thought it sounded pretty much like a pack of coyotes finding a dead javelina in the brush.

Slowly the men emerged from the South Texas Nectar of the Gods and Marty noted to herself that they were indeed unusually healthy-looking specimens. Not an ounce of fat on any of them and all the appropriate musculature in just the right places. It was also apparent to her that being less than amply endowed was not a Lyndecker issue, nor one any of them would ever have to face. Marty suddenly turned to Chito to speak, then stopped abruptly. He had a look in his eyes that could aptly be described as riveted.

"I guess this is something you don't see too often in London."

Chito shook his head. "You don't even see it on the nude beaches in Ibiza!"

Marty laughed and turned to call out, "Hey! Is the show over already?"

The three of them whirled around and looked up at the embankment where they were parked.

"Son of a bitch!" Thaine and Cody cupped their genitals, and Pettus just stood there, grinning broadly.

"How long you been there?"

"Long enough to have seen the best live-action drama in Texas. You oughta take that show on the road."

"Might just do it." Pettus nodded toward the boys. "Don't know if my backup team's quite as eager to let it all hang out, though."

"Shit." Cody hung his head and waddled back toward the truck. He called out to Thaine, who still appeared shell-shocked, "Come on, dickwad, put your *chones* on." Thaine turned and shuffled obediently behind Cody.

Marty called out, "I'd like you to meet somebody, but you might want to put on your own *chones* first. You know, just to be polite."

"Not a problem. Sure feels good though, taking a cool dip. Sure you don't want to join me?"

Marty smiled. "Tempting, but I didn't bring a swimsuit."

Pettus smiled a roguish grin. "Aw, shucks."

Cody, tugging on his boots, called out to Pettus, "Quit showing off, and put your damn clothes on!"

Pettus grinned again. "Yes, Daddy." He turned and walked back toward the truck. Marty had to admit, the backside view of Pettus was just as satisfying as the forward assessment.

Chito cleared his throat., "What...gym does he go to?"

Marty laughed. "I doubt he's seen the inside of a gym since high school graduation. That is what we ranchers call 'natural selection.' It's in the genes, g-e-n-e-s. Generation after generation of selective breeding, or in the Lyndecker instance, random procreation with maximum results."

"They're all very...striking."

Marty nodded. "In some ways..."

Thaine was suddenly heard protesting loudly in the distance. "Aw man, I think I got chiggers on my nuts!"

Marty continued coolly. "...In other ways there's occasionally a sense of...shortfall."

Pettus–caked in mud under his pants, shirt, boots and hat, now properly adhered–came walking up the side of the slope and held out a grimy hand.

"Pettus Lyndecker. Welcome to Rancho Lower Class."

Chito jumped from the Jeep and shook Pettus's hand eagerly. "Chito Sosa, pleasure to meet you."

Pettus slowly pulled his hand back and shook it in the air. "Sorry 'bout the mess..."

Chito grinned brightly. "Not a problem. Not a problem at all."

Pettus smiled, then wiped his brow with his forearm. "So what brings y'all out here on this fine summer day?"

"Chito and Tom were," Marty glanced at Chito, "very close.

He's come here to, well, make us an offer. It seems Tom set aside some money to make improvements in Rita Blanca."

"Improvements?" Pettus looked amused. "Like put in another liquor store?"

Marty pursed her lips. "Or maybe something the kids could use. Chito, why don't you explain?"

Chito cleared his throat and spoke softly. "Well, I asked Marty to introduce me to another area rancher. Someone from here, like Tom was. I never quite understood what his...connection to this place was. Why–when it's sometimes so hard just to survive here–why stay? He couldn't explain it to me exactly, but it was a genuine and very deep commitment. When he died, there was a sum of money he set aside to, somehow, make life a little better in Rita Blanca. And I guess I'd like your input."

Pettus stared at Chito for a moment then peered over at Marty. He laughed and shook his head. "That's what I like about rich people. Always thinking about how they can help the poor bastards they screwed over on the way up."

Marty started to interrupt, as Pettus held his hands to his ears. "Now...don't go getting all huff n' puff. I'm not talking 'bout the Saint Pennebakers. Lord amighty, I'm just saying– must be nice having enough *dinero,* no matter how you got it, to spread it around and help all the little people."

Marty got back into the driver's seat and started the ignition. "I knew this was futile. Sorry to ruin your afternoon swim, Pettus."

Pettus reached over and switched off the ignition. "Did I say I wouldn't be of any help? Did I say that? Sure, I'll give ya ideas, Chito, my friend, lots of 'em. I'll fill your head with more suggestions than a dog's got ticks. You let me sit on it a bit. Come around and see me tomorrow–we'll have a nice, long visit."

Marty started the ignition again. As she backed the Jeep down the incline, she called out to Pettus, "Try to remember your manners, okay?  We have a guest here."

Pettus grinned and bowed deeply, sweeping his hat cavalierly before him.

# CHAPTER SIX

Chito hung up the phone after speaking to his father for over thirty minutes.

"What are you doing there? What about your work in London? You can't afford to take the time off. Get on with your life–you have many things to accomplish still!"

His father's stern words skipped around his brain like ghosts and goblins in a distant *PacMan* game. Staring around his cheerless room at the Best Western, he rolled over on his side in bed. What *was* he doing here? What was it about Tom's passing that kept him so uneasy? It was true, he couldn't let go. Not yet. And yet–he didn't have a clue, not a whit, about why he was truly here. Tom had always kept him so effectively removed from his ranching existence, it had always seemed more make-believe than anything of real plausibility. And these people! They were tough, hard-bitten pragmatists of an entirely new strain to him. Even Marty. Respectful and genial as she was, there was a form of nondisclosure about her. Ask, but don't ask too much. Seek, but don't expect easy answers. What was she hiding? What did she aspire to? What was she avoiding out here in all this desolation?

Chito rose from the bed, stared in the mirror and ran his

fingers through his thick, black hair. A vision of a nude, mud-covered Pettus suddenly entered his thoughts. If there were ever such a thing as Old West porn, he'd witnessed something akin to it this afternoon! He for sure had never experienced *anything* remotely orbiting that kind of unrestrained male exhibition in his life. It still made him a little weak-kneed just thinking about it. Of course, *all* men love to *strut* and preen and show off from time to time–but this? This was something out of *Satyricon Meets Hot Daddy on the Range*.

Chito poured himself a small glass of scotch and sat back on the edge of the bed. Gazing at the nailed-to-the-wall print of a cowboy roping a longhorn steer, it suddenly occurred to him: These people venerate a past that no longer exists. Mr. Pennebaker, with his gruff and irritable nature–he's mad because he lives in a world he doesn't understand or identify with. Marty's troubled because she's trying to fulfill some role as *doyenne* of an imaginary empire. And Pettus–well, what's wrong with Pettus is what makes him right–all cocky arrogance and droll bluster, and as spurious as a teenage Homecoming King.

There was a sudden knock at the door that shook Chito with back-to-reality urgency. Standing quickly, he threw on his shirt and opened the door.

"Mr. Sosa? You may not remember me. I'm Delilah Lyndecker from The Dusty Rose Flower Shoppe."

Chito blinked and squinted as the bright afternoon light temporarily blinded him. "Y...yes?"

"I'm sorry, I didn't mean to bother you. My friend Jamie Dinkins runs the front desk here and said you were staying in back. I hope I'm not interrupting?"

"No, no. I remember you. The flowers were beautiful. Please, would you...come in?"

"Oh, that's so sweet. I can only stay just a minute." Delilah looked around the dark, generic-blah motel room and gushed, "Oh, this room is darling."

Somewhat dubious, Chito followed her eyes.

"Please, have a seat." Delilah sat in the one chair by the Formica tabletop near the front window. She looked at Chito seated on the edge of the bed and smiled.

"Well, how do you like our little village so far?"

He nodded. "Noteworthy."

Delilah laughed, "Oh yes! No place like Rita Blanca, that's for sure."

Again, they both nodded and smiled agreeably. Finally, Delilah leaned forward, purposefully.

"Well, I'll just get right to the point, Mr. Sosa. Would you be interested in buying our flower shop?"

Chito's deadpan expression quickly turned to one of befuddlement.

"I'm sorry?"

"Our flower shop, The Dusty Rose, the one you were in- would you be interested in making us an offer on the store?"

Still befuddled, Chito asked, "Why would I want to buy your store?"

Delilah wrinkled her nose and looked thoughtfully at Chito. "Now, I can't tell you precisely why you need to do this, but I will say I have prayed and prayed over the matter and the answer that came to me in a blinding flash was, 'Go see Mr. Sosa and make him a deal.'" Delilah beamed ecstatically. "Can't you just feel the angelic vibrations surrounding this?"

Chito turned his head slowly from side to side. "No."

Delilah looked awed. "No? But that little bitty voice inside me said you'd be very open to the matter."

Chito stood and poured himself another scotch. "I don't know whose voice you've been hearing, but my inner voice says, 'No...and NO!'" Chico pointed his glass toward Delilah. "Scotch?"

Delilah looked bewildered. "I'm not supposed to drink in public. I promised my Christian rehab counselor."

"Rehab?"

"I became a little too dependent on Meth, X and Snow."
Thrusting her hands high in the air, she cried, "Praise the
Lord! That's all in the past." She leapt to her feet. "Mr. Sosa…"

"Please call me Chito."

"Cheeto, I'm just afraid something bad's gonna happen if
you don't help us out."

"Bad? Like what?"

"I can't say. I don't want to get my sisters in trouble."

"What kind of trouble?"

"Don't know, but they may do something they'll regret,
we'll all regret, and you can help us out right now by buying
the Dusty Rose and freeing us from eternal damnation!"

Chito calmly took a sip from his drink. Was *this* what Tom
had in mind when he'd said, "Help the town?"

"What did you say your last name was?"

"Lyndecker."

"Are you related to Pettus Lyndecker?"

Delilah looked startled. "He's my oldest brother. How do
you know Pettus?"

"I was taken out to meet him yesterday–and your two
other brothers."

Delilah gulped, "Oh gosh, I hope they weren't vulgar or
anything. They're all good boys basically but sometimes the
devil gets ahold, and he just won't quit 'em."

Chito sipped his scotch and ruminated. Pettus, Delilah, the
ranch, the Dusty Rose…some kind of vague association was
emerging from the fog, but he hadn't a clue as to what any of
it meant.

"Do you know Marty Pennebaker?"

Delilah nodded. "My whole life."

"I don't mean to be personal, but is she seeing your brother
Pettus?"

Delilah stammered, "Well, I shouldn't talk out of school
and Pettus has never breathed a word, not one word to any of
us, but yes, I 'spect everyone in town knows they're…having a

dalliance."

Chito smiled. "I'm supposed to meet your brother later this afternoon. Why don't we drive out to your place together?"

Delilah panicked. "Oh, no! That's not such a good idea. All the Lyndeckers at once? That's like asking a lion tamer to drop the whip and chair and just use his smile."

Chito laughed, "Bad as all that?"

"Worse, I'm afraid. So...Cheeto...I wouldn't be here if I didn't think there was some small nugget of possibility in this whole predicament. Now, I know you have money..."

"I do? How is that?"

"I'm sorry, but these are desperate times. I looked your name up on the internet from your credit card. Francisco 'Chito' Treviño Sosa; age forty, Investment Banker/ Stockbroker, son of Felipe Trevino, beer baron of Monterrey, Mexico...more?"

Chito shook his head. "Marvelous thing, the internet. Still, doesn't mean I'm going to buy your store."

Delilah stepped forward and took Chito's hand. "My family thinks I'm crazy. Well, isn't everybody, just a little? But I do know people"–she touched her heart–"in here. From the minute I saw you, I knew you were a good man. A man with a conscience. Someone who longs to help others–don't ask me why, I just know it."

Chito looked at Delilah, then drained the last of his scotch. "I have to go meet your brother. Shall we pick this up at a later date?"

***

Marty held her glass of scotch at arm's length and squinted through it, aiming toward the waning sunset. The amber reflection augmented in the cut crystal was as striking and incendiary as a Jackson Pollock outburst. God, she missed New York at certain melancholy intervals in her long Texas retreat.

She missed the unscripted life that rose up every second of every day to either knock you sideways or propel you forward into the very best version of yourself, no matter how brief or implausible. Here, in Texas, it was more a question of persistence. The challenges, the stimulation, the joy and anguish of day-to-day Manhattan were vanquished. It was all now fairly inevitable. Breakfast, diversion, lunch, distraction, dinner, limbo–then–quietus. Repeat.

Sitting on the patio late in the afternoon, with the dogs at her feet and her single malt Macallan in hand, had become her daily consolation. For a brief interval she wasn't anywhere–not New York, not Texas. She was infinite. A spirit, holding spirits, orbiting spiritual oblivion. Rapture.

She took another sip then touched the cold, wet glass to her forehead. Why were the men in her life always such paradoxes? Never once in her forty-two years of existence had she ever met a man and immediately thought to herself, "You, I get!" It was always, *always,* "maybe, kinda, sorta" do I truly comprehend you and this masculine guise you're offering up here. With women it was different. There was either immediate insight and affinity or sudden wariness. Nearly always. Was it not just easier to interpret members of your own sex, period? True, the S-E-X portent that sometimes arose with members of the opposing team was vanquished with the sisters. Men were the pinnacle posturers–even the average, "normal," run-of-the-mill ones. Fact: they all thought of themselves as Captain America on most days of the week.

And then there was Chito! Marty took another long sip, letting the image of Chito materialize before her. He was definitely the standout racehorse in a pen full of mules. Yes, Marty was as capable of objectifying as much as the next female chauvinist. She hadn't been with Pettus for his intellect, exactly. But there was a calmness and intelligence about Chito that captivated her from the very first moment. Of course, they hadn't communicated much beyond niceties and the weather, but still, what was it about her brother-in-law (brother-in-law!) that so thoroughly drew her in? Did she and brother Tom share more than just freckled cheeks and double-jointed left wrists? Could their familial inheritances have provided each with shared affinities for the same men? It was an interesting notion but nothing substantive to hang your hat on. Good is good wherever you find it. Every blind man follows his nose at mealtime and it can be safely assumed the average cat would rather purr in Cary Grant's lap than in King Kong's.

And Pettus. Oh God, Pettus! Is there no end to the man's audacity? Yes, it was funny and brash and perhaps the perfect introduction for a foreigner like Chito to South Texas mores, but Lord have mercy! The sight of the three Lyndecker "Graces" wrestling in the mud was a vision that Marty was certain she'd carry well into the next world.

The cell phone buzzed. Startled, Marty returned from her distant reverie. She picked up her iPhone. "Hello?"

"Marty, is this you?"

"Yes, who's calling?"

"It's Carol Ann Jansky, how are yewwww?" Marty's ear filled with the sugar-sweet timbre of Texan "sincerity" to the power of ten.

"Oh, hi Carol Ann."

"It's been so long; I just haven't seen yewwww in ages!"

"Yes, it has been awhile."

"How've you been?"

"Oh, good, real good–and you?"

"Oh, I'm just fine as wine, ah-ha-ha-ha!"

Marty held the dripping glass again to her now slightly aching temple. "That's good, good. Any news out your way?"

There was a brief silence on the other end, followed by a long exhalation.

"Well, to tell you the truth, Marty, I'm having just a tad bit of a dilemma here."

"Oh? That doesn't sound good."

"No, it doesn't."

"Anything I can do to help?" Marty immediately regretted saying it the second it left her mouth.

"That is sooo sweet! You have just always been the sweetest person to everyone in town."

Marty laughed, "I wouldn't go that far, not hardly. What's up?"

"Well..." Carol Ann cleared her throat in a squeaky, three-octave emanation. "Excuse me! I must've swallowed a bug or something. Let me get a smidge of water."

Marty stared listlessly at the vanishing sunset, suppressing the urge to hop on a passing rocket ship and chase after it.

"There, I'm back. You there?"

"Here."

"So sorry about that. Isn't it just awful when you get something in your throat and you can't talk?"

Marty didn't imagine this was ever a remotely significant concern to Carol Ann...ever.

"Well, it's like this–you know whose happy birthday is coming up next week?"

"Who?"

"Daddy Pennebaker, that's who! Don't tell me you forgot now, Miss Marty?"

"I didn't forget," Marty said forgetfully.

"Of course not, and of course I know you're in the habit of buying flowers for your dear daddy down at the Dusty Rose, but Marty, I just want to take this opportunity to offer you the chance to try something completely different this year. I'm offering all my new customers a twenty-five percent discount on any purchase at the Flower Emporium! We have some of the most breathtaking collections to choose from, and I just have to tell you, our 'Masculine Flower' series is out of this world..."

"Carol Ann."

"...I don't know where you can find flowers this fresh, this gorgeous, outside of Dallas..."

"Carol Ann!"

"Um-hmmm?"

Marty took a deep breath. "I really appreciate the offer–it's very thoughtful of you, but I really wasn't even planning on buying any flowers this year. I was thinking I'd just get him a new coffee mug or something."

Carol Ann spoke as if she'd suddenly been dropped inside a deep well. "A mug?"

"Or pocket comb. He doesn't need or want a thing."

Again, the voice from *Twenty Thousand Leagues Under the Sea* croaked, "I just, I just...I don't know what to think. Your daddy's such a huge, prominent person in our town. A comb?"

Marty was starting to feel the non-editing effects of her scotch, "Yep. He doesn't need any flowers, Carol Ann. It's sweet of you to ask though. Anyway, I usually end up getting flowers at the Dusty Rose, out of habit, I guess. I do hear you've got some really cute things. I want to come in this week and take a look around."

Silence. Marty started to speak again when she heard what sounded like a puppy choking on a sock. "Carol Ann–are you there?"

A deluge of muffled whimpering issued forth. "Everyone hates me. They do. Those hateful Lyndecker girls say awful things about me. All I'm trying to do is make a living and make my mama and daddy proud. Is that so wrong?"

"Carol Ann, I..."

"You have no idea how mean those two have been to me, particularly that Darcy. Oh, she's evil, EVIL! Whatever happened to free enterprise? Isn't competition supposed to be good for the country?"

"Well..."

"Do you know Darcy came into my store and caused a

scene, a hissy fit right out of some first-grade shoving match. I was mortified! I don't know what to do anymore. I'm just reaching out to every friend I have–please, please, let's stop the pettiness. The Dusty Rose has got to go!"

Marty leaned forward in the wrought iron patio chair. "But Carol Ann, what about 'free enterprise' for the Lyndecker girls?"

Carol Ann trilled, "That's what I'm talking about! Free enterprise means you stand or fall on your own merits. If everyone stops buying at The Dusty, then it proves the true worth of our capitalist system. Survival of not only the fittest, but the best! The American way!"

Marty shook her head and drained her drink. "Ayn Rand, a nation turns its lonely eyes to you."

"Ann who? Should I give her a call too?"

Marty stood, reaching down to scratch the head of Gloria Mundi, who'd been sleeping nearby. "Carol Ann, I've known the Lyndeckers as long as your family. I'm really not going to start choosing sides at this point in my life. Rita Blanca's a small town–we already know too much about everybody as it is. What good does it do stirring up a provocation when absolutely no good will come of it?"

Carol Ann's tone changed from whimper to stony. "It's Pettus, isn't it? He's got you wrapped around his little finger– I know, I know–I've been there. He's good, real good. The problem is, Marty, face it, you're just another notch on that old cowboy's belt. Aren't I right?"

Marty, mouth open, wasn't sure she'd heard what she was hearing. "Excuse me?"

"Come on. You know as well as I do how many women he's been through in this town. When you gonna stop kidding yourself? The minute you show him the slightest interest, the slightest hint you just might be thinking about a future together–he's gone! Goner than a rat on fire straight outta hell!"

Marty stammered, "I have to go..."

Carol Ann hissed, "Nobody's getting any younger around here, Marty, know what I'm saying? You're not going to keep him interested forever. Turn the page, move on–the Lyndeckers are trash, face it."

Marty tapped the phone screen with force, hanging up on the hussy. Momentarily dazed, she swept a hand through her hair as if trying to brush out imaginary debris. "Nobody's getting any younger around here." The little witch! "And to think I even taught her in Vacation Bible School."

Marty picked up her empty glass and started back for the kitchen when she noticed a car coming up the road. The dust tail flying up behind was as high as the house. Someone was moving at a good clip. "Lord, now what? Save me from killing the next son of a bitch that wants *anything* from me." Marty shook her head and, followed by a pack of hungry canines, disappeared into the cool confines of the Pennebaker hacienda, shutting the world behind her.

***

Pete Pennebaker finished peeing onto the clump of prickly pear beside the road, and with one good hand managed to zip up the fly on his khaki trousers. He turned toward Nestor, his number one *vaquero,* and coughed and spit.

"No, I tell ya, back in the day, hell, I wadn't no bigger'n five or six, me and Daddy was driving along out here in his old Ford and I swear, sure as shit, we stopped to pull a log out the road and damned if an old mountain lion didn't jump outta that creek over yonder and start for us like some kinda mortal trepidation."

Nestor smiled. "Did you shoot him?"

Pete shook his head, gazing into the distance. "We got in the car and locked the doors! Daddy said there wouldn't be any of 'em left one of these days. Let 'em be. He was right. Old country has changed a lot."

Pete stared off at the gas flares surrounding them from the frack wells on his property. At night the entire sky was lit up with the glare of an orange inferno. There were thirty-one producing wells on his place, for shale oil and natural gas. It made him a very wealthy man but did nothing for his peace of mind. From the hundreds of oilfield workers that swarmed the ranch during fracking procedure, the constant noise, the stink, the tremors, the pipeline disruptions, the threat to the water, the air, the land, then the lease hounds, oil company brass, the lawyers, estate planners, tax accountants, financial advisors–no, it hadn't made him one bit happier. Just richer.

Pete, with some difficulty, hoisted himself up into the passenger seat of the pickup, and Nestor started the ignition. No bout of inclement weather, no scorching sun provocations, no run-of-the-mill health maladies–virtually nothing prevented Pete and Nestor from making their daily rounds out on *Los Abuelos*. Day in, day out, they made the same three-hour *vuelta* circling the ranch, allowing for minor modifications dependent upon Pete's mood and/or sudden notion.

"Let's turn up here and head over to the *Catarina* pasture. How'd we do on that downed fence?"

Nestor replied, "It's up, but I don't know for how long. The deer and hogs run through that low place and keep popping the wire."

Pete didn't answer but gazed out at his land. He pointed to a pair of heifers standing under a cluster of *coma* trees.

"Those two bald-faced heifers over yonder. Let's get 'em in the pen next working. Sure want to wean 'em from their mamas. Gonna make some fine brood cows."

They continued on in silence. Pete's eyesight would be called compromised at best, but he could usually spot a sick goat or lame colt off in the pasture long before Nestor. He suddenly kicked at the floorboard.

"Stop!"

Nestor quickly brought the truck to a halt.

"Now, back up."

Nestor slid the gears into reverse and slowly began working his way back up the caliche road.

"Stop now!" Pete pointed off into the brush. A blue object was sitting on the ground about fifty yards away. "What's that lying out there? A shoe?"

Nestor shook his head, "*Quien sabe, Señor* Pete*?*"

Pete opened the passenger door with his good hand and unsteadily stepped out. Nestor followed quickly to the other side.

"Goddam oil field trash always throwing shit out the window. You ever catch any of 'em doing it, give 'em hell. You tell 'em Mr. Pennebaker's gonna throw their butts off the place if we catch 'em!"

Nestor nodded. He trailed closely behind Pete, watching his every rickety step with caution. Finally, they came on what looked like a man's sneaker, lying on its side. Nestor bent down to retrieve it and hand it to Pete. Pete examined it, then looked around to see if there were other signs of litter, lifting his sweat-stained Stetson and wiping his brow.

"Don't look all that old, does it? You reckon somebody was out here walking around?"

"Possible," Nestor replied.

Pete dropped the shoe and shook his head. "Damn crazy people. Probably decided to go arrowhead hunting or some such shit. Let's *vamos*–too damn hot." Pete started to turn back for the truck when Nestor grabbed his sleeve. Pete turned around then followed Nestor's eyes toward a cluster of tall *sacahuista* grass. A child, virtually concealed in the weeds, was glaring at them with the dead-eyed stare of a zombie.

Pete blurted out, "Son of a bitch! Nestor, get that kid." Nestor walked quickly toward the child, who suddenly unfroze and began to flee. Nestor lunged for the youngster and hollered back to Pete.

"It's a little girl."

"Bring her here. Get her back to the truck where there's shade and water."

The girl struggled in Nestor's arms, whimpering and trying to speak. Nestor hurried past Pete, who hobbled behind them as fast as he could. Reaching the truck, Nestor laid the girl down on the front seat. Retrieving a warm, unopened bottle of water, he held it gently to her mouth. The water ran in rivulets down her lips and cheeks. She finally opened her mouth and swallowed, coughing and sputtering.

"*Pobrecita. Despacio nina, despacio.*" Nestor cradled her head with his forearm. By now, Pete had reached the truck, calling out.

"Did she take some water? Poor little thing. Here, wet this hanky." Nestor turned to pour water on Pete's clean, white handkerchief. Stepping forward, Pete leaned in over the child's face and patted her flushed skin as tenderly as a newborn infant.

"*Mi niña, a donde vas?*" To Nestor he said, "No telling how long she's been out here. We're a helluva long way off the usual illegal routes. How you reckon she got out here?"

Nestor shook his head. "*Quien sabe*...we better look and see if there's any more out there." Nestor drew another bottle of water from behind the seat and handed it to Pete. By now the child opened her eyes and looked at Pete as he continued to dab her face with the wet coolness.

"It's all right, honey. Drink a little more water...slowly, slowly...that's it. Good girl. *Como se llama?*"

The girl continued to stare at Pete in wide-eyed shock.

"We better get her into town to the hospital. Nestor, make a quick run down through there and see if you can spot anybody else. Surely she wadn't out here by herself."

Nestor turned to scramble into the brush when suddenly the little girl jumped in the front seat and screamed, "*Alab!*"

She bolted from Pete's grasp and ran past Nestor, racing back toward where she'd been hiding.

Pete called out, "Don't let her get away! Grab her 'fore she gets hurt."

Nestor ran after her, but she darted before him like a deer, calling loudly in some babble that Nestor didn't understand. Racing toward a small ravine lined with black brush and stunted mesquites, the girl disappeared into the undergrowth. Nestor called out to her.

"*No tienes miedo. Queremos ayuda!*" Silence. He called again.

"*Escuche niña, vuelve!*" Stumbling down the side of a small gully, Nestor saw ahead what the girl had been pursuing. A man's body lay partially hidden in the scrubby ravine. He was missing one blue sneaker. As Nestor approached, the girl looked up and repeated to him, "*Alab.*"

# CHAPTER SEVEN

Darcy lay in bed staring at the ceiling with an expression that could be described as a keen likeness to Biblical illustrations of Job's forbearance. Dr. Finley pulled the sheet over her chest and turned to face the rest of the Lyndecker clan huddled in the back bedroom she shared with Delilah.

"She'll be fine. Mostly superficial. Tetanus shot will take care of any infection. There's a deeper laceration on her thigh, but I sewed her up good. I don't even 'spect it'll leave much of a scar." He grabbed his old satchel and stood.

"You're lucky I live out this way. Saved y'all a trip to the hospital."

Uncle T.T. ran his fist through his hair and held out his hand. "Doc, we appreciate it. I tell ya, we got a real scare when Darce come running out of the barn screaming and hollering like she was on fire."

Dr. Finley shook his hand and started for the bedroom door. "Well, it's in the hands of the sheriff now. Whoever attacked her–seems like they were trying to scare her more'n anything else. Good night, y'all."

Darcy rose feebly in her bed and spoke hoarsely. "Th...thanks, Doc Finley. You're a good man."

"You rest up, Darcy. Come see me in the office in a couple of days. You'll be fine."

Pettus walked out of the room with Dr. Finley, shutting the door behind him. As they headed down the hallway, Pettus grabbed his shoulder. "Say, Doc, you know how much we appreciate you coming out this way. You've come to our rescue more times than any of us can remember."

Dr. Finley walked on slowly. "We all got a job to do."

"Listen, about paying ya for tonight..."

The doctor stopped and turned. "Your mama and I went to school together, Pettus. Your granddaddy took me hunting a hundred times when I was a kid. You drove my wife to the airport in San Antonio when her sister fell ill. It ain't about money. I got bills like everybody else, but I got friends I value more."

Pettus stared at Dr. Finley, mute.

"How 'bout you give me thirty bucks for gas and we'll call it even?"

Pettus cleared his throat anxiously. "That's fine, that's fine Doc." He slushed, "Let me go find thirty dollars."

Dr. Finley turned on his heels and headed for the front door. "You'll pay me when I see you. Make sure Darcy takes all those antibiotics I left her."

"I'll do that. Thank you." Pettus stood at the front door and shook his head. Where in God's name did he think he was going to magically find thirty dollars, just like that? He never carried any cash on him. There was never anything he needed to buy worth over ten dollars cash anyway.

*** 

The remaining Lyndecker clan stood frozen, clustered around Darcy's bed, half expecting her to levitate.

"What are y'all looking at? You want me to spit pea soup or something?"

Darlene cleared her throat. "We just want to know if you need anything. We're right here if you need us."

Cody stcppcd forward from the back wall. "Dadgummit, Darce, you didn't get any kind of look at who done it?"

Darcy turned her head slightly. "I told you, it was dark in the barn. Sun was setting. I'd just gone in to get an extra garden hose to water my zinnias and somebody jumped me from behind."

Thaine nervously ran his hands up and down the thighs of his jeans. "Which way did they run off? Toward the creek, up to the horse stalls?"

Darcy grimaced. "Look–he, she, it–knocked me to the ground after they'd finished their little sword dance and I had so much dirt and hay in my eyes, I couldn't see a thing."

Darlene asked eagerly, "You think it might've been a *she*?"

Darcy looked at Darlene knowingly. "I couldn't tell."

Uncle T.T. began herding the cluster out of the room. "Well, sister, you just lie here and try to get some rest. Delilah can stay in Darlene's room whenever she gets back from town. Where'd she get off to, anyway? Is this her twelve-step meeting tonight?"

The door shut behind them and Darcy made a face as she tried shifting her weight on the old mattress. The wound on her thigh stung like a son of a bitch. She should've asked the Doc for some sleeping pills. Screw it, the way her mind had been racing since the altercation in the barn, she doubted she'd sleep anyway, pills or no pills. Try to remember, Darce, try to remember! You walked into the barn, the door swung shut behind you, you heard a whisper or maybe a breath, very remote, and the next thing your leg had been cut and you were on the ground kicking and screaming, flailing away at the knife. And then you heard Thaine or Cody hollering and come running toward the barn. And then they, whoever it was, disappeared, like that! Gone, vanished–out the back door like a coyote fleeing the rabbit hutch. And that odd scent left behind. Spicy and sweet, plus a little like wet wood after the rain. What was that?

Hearing a small thud at the door, Darcy glanced over to see Pettus stick his head inside the room.

"You got a minute, or you off to Dreamland?"

"I wish I could sleep. Where's Delilah's old pill stash when you need it?"

Pettus scooted a chair over and sat by the bed. He held a bottle of Wild Turkey in one hand, and two Jiffy peanut butter glasses in the other. "I know you feel like shit, here." Pettus carefully poured, then handed the amber liquid to Darcy.

"Better'n downers any day." They clinked glasses. "Just take it easy for a while and don't worry 'bout Carol Ann or the Dusty Rose or none of it."

Darcy shivered imperceptibly as the Turkey warmed her insides. "Easy for you to say."

"Look, I know you're in a tight. I been there a jillion times myself. You just gotta roll with the stink and pray for a little abundance down the line. When have we ever had a surplus of anything good in this family? Money, brains, luck...love. We got the short stick on all of it...well, but..." Pettus's thought drifted away.

"But?"

Pettus crossed his legs and reflected thoughtfully, "I've had my fair share of persuasion with the ladies."

Darcy snorted, "Where'd that get ya? Two divorces, one alimony settlement and a front-page adultery lawsuit. I'll take cash over romance any day."

Pettus looked bewildered. "You ain't never getting married?"

"Not if I can help it. The Lyndecker sisters, married? Who'd take on that freak show? Delilah's got the church and Darlene's too nut job for these dumbshit cowboys round here. I just want peace and quiet and something to call my own...something nobody can ever take away."

Pettus exhaled sharply. "Well since I can't get none of y'all married off, I guess I'll have to go another route. What if you had the money to fix up the Rose and make it so Carol Ann's place looked like the shitter fell on it?"

Darcy laughed. "What if the Queen of England came in here riding a goat sidesaddle? What if, what if?"

Pettus nodded solemnly. "Give your old brother a little time–he might just surprise you." Starting to rise, he turned back to Darcy and said, "And be nicer to Lilah, she's not smart like you. She's your twin sister, chrissake–help her!"

Darcy stared in wonder as Pettus shut the door. What the hell was that about? What money? When did Pettus the Benevolent suddenly appear? Darcy finished her bourbon and sat the glass on her nightstand. Pulling the coverlet over her shoulders, she said a silent prayer thanking God for sparing her the dubious blessing of having testosterone overload toss another boulder on the daily afflictions of her life.

*** 

Chito pulled off to the side of the road just at the entry to the Lyndecker ranch and jumped out of his rented Lexus. A rusted cattle guard with a partially open pipe swing bar that served as a gate drooped listlessly, blocking his entry. Swaying in the breeze, a buckshot-riddled Texas and Southwestern Cattle Raisers Association metal sign clung tentatively to the pipe bar with baling wire. As he nudged open the entrance, he couldn't recall the last time he'd felt heat, real heat, this intense scalding of his neck, head and arms. The pipe itself was as blistering as a clothes iron as he poked it forward.

"They must have asbestos in their veins," he thought to himself as he hurried back to the chilled environ of the Lexus. Driving slowly on the caliche road, he thought of Delilah and her bizarre request. Buy a flower shop? In this town? Madness! Surely Tom hadn't meant for something that *outré* as the final repository of his financial largesse. He'd always spoken of the town as peculiar, demented even, but how was anyone, a stranger no less, supposed to decipher this Gordian knot of Texan perplexity before him?

Chito slammed on the brakes as a large, curly blond male emerged from the brush pulling an enormous hog on a rope. Shirt off, his muscles gleamed on his nut-brown shoulders like a buttered hamburger bun. Chito lowered the window and stammered, "H...hello. I was looking for the main house. I'm supposed to meet with Pettus Lyndecker."

The large blond man stared at Chito as if not understanding English. Finally, he wiped his brow with his forearm and spat, "You wanna give me a lift up to the house? I'll show ya."

Chito started to answer when the man suddenly opened the side door and plopped down in the leather passenger seat, holding his arm out the window, still clutching the rope.

"The exercise'll do ole 'Spongebutt, Squarenuts' good. Third time this week he's gotten outta his pen and lit out for town. I think he's got a girlfriend over there–or he thinks he's gonna find a girlfriend–one or the other. Shit, it's hotter than a whore's bed in Piedras Negras, huh? What is this thing, a Toyota? Dodge? Nice. How much it cost?" Chito opened his mouth but again was interrupted. "Never mind. I'm not supposed to ask that."

Thaine suddenly stuck his head out the window and yelled at the hog, which was now trotting alongside the car. "Come on, you fat bastard. Move those squatty legs 'fore I light a fire under your big ass!"

Thaine put his head back in the car. "Thaine Lyndecker–I seen you up at the tank with Miz Pennebaker the other day."

Thaine reached out a sweaty left hand and shook Chito's right.

"You're one of the guys in the mud?" Chito stared in awe at Thaine.

"Yep, I guess you don't recognize me with my clothes on!" Thaine let out a guffaw that shook the car. "Wadn't that a hoot? Ole Spongebutt here woulda had a good time with us, huh?" Thaine stuck his head out the window again and whistled loud as a fire truck siren. "Move it, you sorry sack of bacon shit!" He stuck his head back in. "What brings ya out this way, Mr., Mr...."

"Sorry, it's Sosa. Chito Sosa."

"Cheeto. Never met a Cheeto before. We had a kid back in grade school we used to call 'Frito.' His real name was Arthur, but we all called him Frito."

Chito, at a loss, glanced at Thaine and nodded.

"You and Pettus working on a job together, what?" Thaine asked.

"No. Just seeking a little advice."

Thaine snorted. "Advice? From Old Iron Drawers? Hell, he watches my brother Cody and me like we was juvenile delinquents or something. I mean, we ain't squeaky clean or nothing, but shit fire, a guy's gotta have a little fun sometime, don't he?"

Chito nodded again and noticed Thaine's deeply brown skin pulled tight over his furry blonde chest still glinting from the afternoon blaze. "You don't worry about skin cancer?"

Thaine looked at Chito puzzled. "Nah. I'm too young for that shit. Only thing I worry about is pussy. Like, I ain't getting enough. Girls round here either church rats, dick teases or *putas*. *Putas* okay if you don't mind waiting in line with every other shithead in town. Nah, I gotta move to Cotulla or Corpus someday and meet a nice girl who likes to fuck. How 'bout you, you been getting any?"

Chito clutched the steering wheel and smiled faintly. Where is there an overhead drone to capture these moments in life when needed?

Pulling up in front of the Lyndecker home, it looked to Chito like some unhappy marriage between a livestock barn and a doublewide mangled by a tornado. Littered with "stuff"– old chairs, clothing, boxes, half a bicycle, a discarded clothes rack, tires, a wading pool, pots of flowers, cactus, several dog houses, a nude store mannequin, 55-gallon drums and an upside-down barbeque grill–Chito marveled at the Hieronymus Bosch nightmare of disorganized perfection. Nothing was missing–including the myriad of chickens, ducks, guinea hens, peacocks, dogs, cats and now one very large hog, meandering blissfully about in their very own Shangri-La.

Pettus appeared from around an abandoned refrigerator. "Looks like you found us. I've told Thaine not to hitch rides with the hog, but he don't listen."

Pettus glared at Thaine, now standing beside the car and kicking a scuffed boot in the dirt. He grinned sheepishly. "Old Cheeto don't mind. He's good people."

A twenty-five-watt bulb clicked on in Thaine's head. "Hey, we ought to fix him up with the bank president's daughter. She's got a gimp leg but it don't stop her on the dance floor, no way. Man, she can tear it up good!"

Pettus stared at Thaine wearily, "Go find a hole to sit in." Thaine frowned and stumbled off toward the barn, leading Spongebutt.

"Nice talking to ya, Mr. Cheeto. Sorry if I stunk up your car." He let out a ringing cackle. "Keep the windows down on your way home!"

As Thaine and the hog disappeared around a cluster of hackberry saplings, Pettus motioned toward the house. "Why don't we go sit in the front room? Helluva lot cooler than out here."

Stepping through the labyrinth yard, the two men stumbled into the ancient farmhouse, with Chito once again wide-eyed in wonder. The room erupted with...antiques? Walk-sideways-as-you-enter FILLED with antiques! Armoires, sewing machines, iron stoves, rocking chairs, bookshelves, books, kitchen tables, bowls, pots, urns–enough junk to sink the Lusitania again.

"Looks like someone is a collector."

"This is all my mother's. She had a thing for old stuff." Chito took in a broken cuckoo clock. "'Cept for the time she ran off with a man half her age." He sighed, "Just can't bring myself to throw it all away. I reckon everybody's got a sentimental streak in 'em somewhere, huh? Let's sit over by the window unit."

They made their way through the heirloom canyon till they finally reached a La-Z-Boy and a barber stool adjacent to a Carrier window unit. Pettus offered the La-Z-Boy to Chito, but it was obvious that this was where the Master normally reclined, so Chito stepped up into the barber chair instead. Settling in, the two men studied each other momentarily. "So, Mr. Sosa, sir–what brings ya out this way?"

Chito studied Pettus's reclining form. It was as if he were auditing a master class in masculine privilege. Pettus embraced the easy, natural air of a born eminence. Not cocky, not obnoxious, not feigned. There was nothing for him to prove. The proof was apparent. He was a man comfortable with his own essence. An essence that veered toward sexual quintessence like no one Chito had ever been around. "I...I wanted to discuss with you a few things about my relationship with Tom Pennebaker."

Pettus looked at Chito, confused. "Tom? Why me?"

Chito cleared his throat. "Marty told me you were from one of the oldest families in the area. You know the people around here as well as anybody. Tom had an idea before he died that he wanted to do something for Rita Blanca...I guess I'm here to help make it happen."

Pettus studied Chito with a discerning gaze. He fished a wooden match out of his shirt pocket and stuck it in the corner of his mouth. Chewing lightly on the wooden stem, he finally spoke in a low murmur. "You and Tom...y'all boyfriends?"

Chito half-smiled. "We were married, actually."

Pettus let the announcement sink in then smiled back. "Well, congratulations...and my condolences. Hope you guys were happy while it lasted. Old Tom was good people, sure nuff. I always knew he was gay but he wouldn't of spoke of it no more than a horse thief would tell ya where he kept his corral." Pettus grinned and appeared to ponder a faraway anecdote. "You mind if I tell ya something?" Chito shook his head. "I shouldn't talk outta school, but you'll appreciate this." Pettus stared at Chito, savoring the suspense. "Tom and I got it on, way back when. You know, Boy Scout stuff–playing around, pulling each other's willies–kid stuff. But we had a good time while it lasted...sure did!"

Chito nodded. "I know."

Pettus looked at Chito surprised. "He told you?" Chito nodded. "Well, I'll be damned. I don't think I've ever told a soul 'til right now."

Chito smiled. "Were you ashamed?"

Taken aback, Pettus stammered, "Ashamed? Of what? Two guys having a little fun–who gives a shit? Nothing to be ashamed of."

"Some people might see it differently."

"Not me. Sex is sex–I don't care who or where or how. Just gotta be some feeling behind it. Gotta care about the other person–otherwise you're just pullin' your pud under a raincoat."

Chito looked at Pettus. "Mind if I tell you something?"

Pettus stopped chewing on his match and squinted at Chito. "You not gonna make me cry, are ya?"

Chito laughed. "Promise. You had a big impact on Tom's life. Apparently, you were the only one around here that ever showed him any...interest."

Pettus flushed and shifted in his La-Z-Boy. "Hell, it wadn't no big thing. I knew what he wanted and I didn't mind going along with it. No big thing."

"But it was to him. More than you know."

Pettus flicked the match to the floor and sighed. "Like I say, Tom was good people. Sorry he couldn't find what he needed round here, but you know what? We all got shit we're carrying in a bucket. I like women...a lot. I like everything about 'em- from their hair to their ears to their toenails. Fact is-I'm plum crazy over Tom's sister, Marty. She's as fine as they come and I'd pretty near walk on broke glass if it'd brighten her day. But here's the shit stick-she doesn't care no more 'bout me than I did Tom! I'm just a long afternoon's retreat. Retreat from..." Pettus stared at the wall, "...all that's pretty much unavoidable." Pettus turned to Chito. "That too heavy for ya?"

Chito shook his head. Without a doubt, Rita Blanca, Texas, was the loneliest place he'd ever been.

***

The Pennebaker living room was filled with muffled voices, anxious movement and mounting distress. Sheriff Al Naylor, Deputy Wayne Canfield, Dr. Finley and his elderly nurse, Mrs. Castillo, attorney Bill Seiffert, even Preacher Waddell from the United Methodist-all stood around the little wide-eyed girl and the man they found lying beside her in the brush, now tousled and flattened into the chintz sofa like two forsaken mummies. Who were they? Where were they from? What in God's name were these two doing out in the middle of the remote Texas brush country in the summertime-no water, no shoes, no hat. Where were they trying to get to-or return from?

"It's no use. She doesn't understand Spanish." Mrs. Castillo looked up at Dr. Finley as she rubbed the little girl's arm. "They're not from Mexico or Central America. I don't know where they're from."

Dr. Finley held the man's wrist as he studied his watch. "Heart's still racing. Wonder we didn't lose them both to heat stroke. Don't give the child any more water, she'll get hyponatremia." He turned to Pete. "It's good you got us all out here, Pete, but this man needs to be in the hospital."

Sheriff Naylor interrupted. "We're gonna have to run 'em both into town and book 'em, first."

Pete growled, "Albert, I didn't call ya out here to go gettin' all Marshal Dillon on us. I need some advice, not a verdict. We know nothing 'bout these people. They might even be American citizens from up north, hell, looking for mushrooms or *nopalitos* or God knows what all? Just cause they don't speak English don't make them illegals."

"You running for Nancy Pelosi's position?" Sheriff Naylor smirked. The deputy standing alongside him grinned. Pete took a few steps toward Sheriff Naylor and aimed an index finger toward his shirt pocket.

"Naw, I ain't running for nothing...and neither will you if I forget to give you the same campaign donation I laid out for your last election, *comprende*?"

Marty had witnessed Pete's *mano-a-mano* intimidations numerous times in the past. She edged forward to once again fulfill her birth role of pacifist intermediary. "Sheriff Al, I think the important thing here is to get this man some medical attention. That cut on his hand looks pretty bad. He's obviously in shock–let's try and get him to the hospital first."

Dr. Finley frowned as he continued examining the man's cut wrist. "He's gonna need stitches, and something to fight infection."

The man continued to stare blankly ahead, the little girl pressed tightly by his side. He appeared to be in his mid-to-late forties, though it was hard to be sure. Could be younger–but the beard, the lined face, his weathered, exhausted aspect in general defied certainty. The little girl, however, was most likely five or six. Dressed in a corduroy (corduroy in June!) jumper and short sleeve tee, she looked as if she walked out of playschool and into the Dust Bowl. She rubbed the man's left hand, as if calming a spooked pet.

Jacinta approached them both with a plate of sandwiches and the little girl looked at it, hesitant. The man finally spoke softly. "*Wahid faqat.*" The little girl slowly reached her hand out and pulled back a half pimento cheese on whole wheat. She looked at it curiously then nibbled at a corner. Chewing, a tiny smile appeared as she nuzzled even closer to the man beside her.

"*Ai, pobrecita, que linda.* Such beautiful eyes, like a little doe." Jacinta touched the girl's knee then turned to offer the plate to the man. He slowly reached for a sandwich.

"Thank...you."

Pete exhaled sharply. "Damn, he does speak English!"

"Why hadn't he said something before?" the deputy interrupted.

"He's in shock, that's why," said Pastor Waddell.

"Still gonna have to run him in now that I know he can talk." Sheriff Naylor leaned into them as if he were about to pick them up by the scruff of their necks.

Attorney Bill Seiffert took off his Stetson and ran his fingers through his white hair. Clearing his throat, he spoke in a deep Texas twang. "Now Al, I'm not sure Pete here hadn't already gainfully employed this gentleman and his little companion to come out to *Los Abuelos* and work for him for a time. I'm not even sure they're not just friends of the family down for a little visit–idn't that right, Pete?"

Pete nodded, slowly grasping the narrative.

"So these people don't need to be going nowhere–'cept maybe to the hospital for a little mending. They're friends of the family! No complaint has been lodged, no warrant issued, no charges brought by the Pennebaker family. See Sheriff, Pete here did us all a favor by informing the community in advance that his guests are simply here on a little visit. There's no confusion in the matter as far as the law sees it."

Sheriff Al bit on the inside of his mouth momentarily then put his hat back on. "We'll see. Thanks for the information,

Bill. Mr. Pete...we'll be sure and keep an eye on your 'guests' while they're here, sure nuff will."

Sheriff Al and Deputy Wayne turned and exited out the front door as Marty followed them. Returning, she glanced at Seiffert and shook her head. "You earned your money today, Bill, you really did. You've turned probable illegal aliens into our long-lost cousins. Nice job."

Bill smiled. "At this point, idn't anybody in Texas can't prove these fine people for sure ain't your kin–or just old friends come for a visit."

Pastor Waddell pulled up an ottoman in front of the man. "What is your name, sir?"

He answered slowly, "Adnan"

"Is this your child?"

"Yes, Haya."

"How old is Haya?"

"Five."

"Where are you from?"

"Syria."

Marty glanced over at her father, who appeared utterly confounded. The pastor continued.

"Why...what are you doing here?"

"On our way to...freedom."

"You've just come to America?"

Adnan shook his head sharply. "No. We are leaving America!"

The pastor glanced briefly at the others then continued. "I don't understand. You're leaving America?"

"We are not wanted here. We have been asked to leave. I cannot return to Syria. We will find a new life in Mexico...or elsewhere."

"How...how did you get here?"

"We paid a man to take us to the border. He took everything–our money, our clothes, our food–our water. Why would he take the water? We walked for almost two days, mostly at night. There were snakes, animals–very hot!   I would have given up, but for her."

"Where is her mother?"

His face remained impassive. "Dead. With our two sons– in Syria. Everyone dead."

Slowly comprehending the horror, the pastor reached out a hand to grasp Adnan's.

Pete moved next to them both. "But where were you coming from–just now?"

Adnan looked up at him blankly. "Where? A place called Indiana. Evansville. We were there for nine months. I am...baker. I bake bread, cakes, *baklava*–is my life. One day, they came from the government and said we were not allowed to stay. They tried to take me then. I ran from the room and escaped. I ran and ran 'til I found Haya. We left with just a small suitcase that very day. I will not–CAN NOT return to Syria! It will be the final death."

Pete kneeled to take Haya's hand. "Does your little girl speak English?"

"She is learning."

Pete squeezed her hand. "Honey, you don't have to go nowhere, understand? God brung you to the just-right place. I'm gonna look after you and your papa. You got my word." Pete studied her wise and wondrous face, taken aback by her long, exotic lashes and green tea-colored eyes. "You think you could give me a hug...just to let me know you understand?"

The little girl looked up at her father, puzzled. He spoke to her, "*Yuried minky an tuanekeeh.*"

She answered back, "*Howa da elshee' momken?*"

Adnan nodded, "Yes."

Haya smiled shyly and put her arms around Pete. At that very moment, 86-year-old Pete Pennebaker felt for the first time in his life that his heart might burst and fracture into a thousand fragments of Syrian confection.

# CHAPTER EIGHT

Carol Ann Jansky sat in the last booth of the Dairy Queen stabbing at her Hawaiian Blizzard ice cream like it was something evil. She pondered as she poked. "I shouldn't be eating this. How many billions of calories are in this thing? I'll have to swim twenty more laps in the pool when I get home." She nudged her Valentino rip-off rhinestone sunglasses further up her nose and sighed gloomily. She hated being seen inside the Dairy Queen at any hour, especially mid-afternoon–too many cowboys, truck drivers and church ladies staring a hole in her head. She was strictly a drive-thru gal. Get it and go. How many times had a Diet Coke float saved her sanity during those long, endless, life-sucking summers in Rita Blanca?

She glanced at her watch, then her iPhone, then at the clock on the wall. All were in agreement–Cody Lyndecker was late. Was she surprised? Time to a Lyndecker was like ocean to a tuna–just is. She thought about leaving. It was a crazy idea meeting Cody at the Dairy Queen! Why not meet on the lawn of the courthouse with a boom box screaming their arrival? I must be insane. Well, it was his stupid idea in the first place. "Sure, I'll meet ya, Carol Ann. You buy me a Belt Buster and some fries?" The way to a Lyndecker's brain was thru their gut–followed by the fly of their jeans.

Suddenly, as if a twisting dust devil had blown open the door, Cody Lyndecker stepped inside the Dairy Queen with all the delicacy of a Cape buffalo storming a Church of Christ. Everyone turned to gape. At twenty-one years of age, Cody Lyndecker was built like an NFL Linebacker and bore a strong resemblance to one of those Australian surfer actors with forgettable names who continually wash up in Hollywood. He took off his Dallas Cowboys gimme cap and swatted the dust on his jeans as he nodded past patrons, aiming for Carol Ann in the back. "No doubt about it," Carol Ann thought, "they breed 'em high, wide and handsome out there on that godforsaken Lyndecker dog pile. Too bad they all got shorted in the brains department." She shrugged. "Well, what good's having a big dick anyway if you have to analyze its every up and down?"

"Hey, girl."

"Hey, boy."

"You order me a Belt Buster?"

"Sure did."

Cody eased his big frame into the Formica-clad booth, knocking knees with Carol Ann.

"You look like a dirt bomb just hit you. Where'd all that grime come from?" she asked.

"Tractor broke down this morning, then the pickup got a flat out in the back pasture, then I had to pull a calf got stuck in her mama's ass. Same shit, different day." Cody flashed a big, goofy grin that was all kid with a new yo-yo. "Damn, I'm hungry!"

Carol Ann looked up. "Here she comes."

Approaching the table carrying a red hamburger basket, side of fries and a large Coke was a tiny, sad-eyed, whippet-thin server.

"Hey, Sandra."

"Hey, Sandy."

"Hey, y'all."

She set the tray down and glanced at Cody. "You need more catsup or mustard?"

"Naw, that's good."

"Sorry to hear 'bout your little brother getting run over, Sand."

Sandy shrugged. "He's up in the Hospital in San Antone. They think he can come home next week."

"Was that Omar or Julio?"

"Memo, the baby."

Cody's mouth twisted into something circling thoughtful accord. "Sucks, Sandy. Y'all come out and go fishing at the tank this week."

"Thanks." Sandy stared at the floor briefly. "Well, if y'all need anything, holler." She turned and drifted back toward the front register, a ghost floating on a cloud of fried potatoes and stale cooking oil.

Cody took a monster bite of burger. "Damn, I didn't know that about Memo."

"Family spends more time in the hospital than they do in their own home. Bad luck–all they've ever known."

Cody nodded and swallowed hard. "Meat's tough...tastes okay. What'd you wanna see me about?"

Carol Ann took off her rip-off sunglasses and stashed them in their rip-off case and put them inside her rip-off Donna Karan bag. She clicked the clasp shut. "I need you to do me a big favor."

"Oh yeah, what's that?"

"I want you to burn down the Dusty Rose."

Cody's burger froze midair. "Say what?"

"You heard."

"You shittin' me?"

"No sir, I am not."

Cody sat the burger back in the basket. "What's this all

about?"

Carol Ann leaned forward and murmured softly, "What it's about, boy mine, is this: Your sisters have a killer insurance policy on that building, covers everything. I know! We go to the same agency. They're losing money hand over fist right now. You know it and I know it. I'm trying to help 'em out here! They get replacement cost on everything. They can start all over if they want to or just pocket the change and live life for once."

Cody's forehead wrinkled deeply. It was as if he were auditing a class in Mandarin. "What's in it for you, Carol Ann?"

She smiled. "I get a breather at last to let my place have a fair chance to grow. They can rebuild the Dusty Rose–hell, I don't care! But it gives me the time to get established and let fair enterprise succeed."

Cody nodded. "Fair enterprise?"

"Hell, yes! They get to cash out like they just won 'Let's Make A Deal.' I'm the one putting every nickel on the line here."

Cody slowly shook his head. "Nah, I ain't going back to juvenile detention again. It'll be even worse this time."

"Everything'll be an accident! Don't you get it? You leave a coffeemaker on overnight, with a short in the wire next to a bunch of dead flowers they forgot to throw out. You leave a scented candle burning next to a pile of bills on the desk. The gas stove top in back gets left on unintentionally and the AC blows the lace curtains over it. My God, there's a hundred ways to burn down a building!"

Cody stared in disgust. "These are my sisters, Carol Ann. I can't go burning their business down."

Carol Ann sneered. "Wasn't it you that turned Delilah in on that last drug deal of hers?"

"That's different! I was trying to get her help and into rehab."

"And we all know Darcy rides your ass 24/7. Miss Bitchy

never once came to see you when you were in that detention center for a whole year, did she?" Cody shook his head.

"Look, I'm asking you to help your sisters out, not hurt them. Give them–and me–a fresh start!"

"Yeah? And what do I get out of all this besides a trip back to the Gainesville State School–only it won't be Gainesville this time but Huntsville with the real sweethearts?"

Darcy opened her pink purse and pulled out an envelope. She slid it toward Cody. "There's a thousand dollars in there for you to think it over. There's fourteen thousand more when you've made up your mind."

Cody stared at the envelope, frozen. A thousand dollars! He thought about all the wonderful things he could do with a thousand dollars. Fix his motocross bike, shocks for the pickup, a new thirty-aught-six rifle, ostrich cowboy boots...

He slowly slid the envelope back toward Carol Ann. "Cain't."

Carol Ann sighed. "I didn't think you'd say yes right off the bat." She slid the envelope back toward him again. "Just think about it awhile." Carol Ann stood and pulled her purse strap over her shoulder. "Why don't you come out to the house tonight? Mama and Daddy are in Houston for the weekend. We finally got the margarita machine fixed. Bring your swim trunks–or not. I like it better without, don't you?" She smiled again and strolled out the front door.  Cody stared at the envelope intently. Money, margaritas and skinny-dipping with a hot blonde. Cody shook his head in distress. "I'm twenty-one, Lord–don't turn me into a wise old sumabitch just yet."

***

Marty stood behind Chito as he scrutinized every detail of Tom's old bedroom. It was as if he were digging for fossils–hoping to retrieve some long-lost souvenir of his departed partner that might resolve a host of unanswered questions. As he picked up a small silver Brahma bull on a pedestal, Marty said, "Tom was class valedictorian, and our mascot was the proud Brahma bull. This was our version of the Academy Awards. He always used to say, 'Being valedictorian in a graduating class of thirty-six knuckleheads is the equivalent of running a mile under four minutes on a bicycle.'"

"He never told me he was valedictorian."

Marty shrugged. "I was valedictorian my year too. Not a biggie–kind of a big nothing actually. You didn't feel you'd really done anything exceptional–you just didn't royally fuck up."

Chito studied the carefully constructed wall poster montage over Tom's bed. Whitney Houston was there, and Michael Jackson, George Strait, Madonna and Shania Twain along with Andy Warhol, Joe Dallesandro, Christopher Atkins in a loincloth in *The Blue Lagoon*, and a shirtless Dallas Cowboy, Troy Aikman. Chito smiled. "Pretty much the mind of any teenage boy from twenty-five years ago. I had the same pictures."

"I did too. Except I threw in Joan Jett and Tanya Tucker for a little symmetry."

Chito turned and spun a globe on the perfectly ordered pine desk. Neat, precise–not a book, pillow or pencil holder gone awry. The room of a teenage monk. "Is this where he stayed even as an adult?"

Marty nodded. "Always."

"Odd to be frozen in an adolescent world for so long."

"Odd, but not abnormal for this family. We tend to dwell in the burrow we're most comfortable in."

Chito walked over to the closet and brushed the perfectly ordered, color-coordinated assemblage–long-sleeved shirts, short-sleeved shirts, pants, suits, sports coats, overcoats, jackets, ties, shoes, etc.–a display rack from Nordstrom or Banana Republic.

"But why not give this all away? Donate to the church,

Salvation Army–why keep it?"

"That you'd have to ask my father. The only one that ever comes in here is Jacinta to dust and vacuum. Although I did see Pete in here one time just sitting on the bed, staring out the window."

"He can't let him go, can he?"

Marty shook her head. Chito as well sat on the edge of the bed and stared ahead in bewilderment. Marty suppressed the desire to sit beside him and comfort him, stroke his head and fondle his shiny black hair. She wanted to put her arm around him and draw him close. To feel his warmth and breathe his scent. The thought of his skin touching hers sent spikey impulses coursing inside her. Marty put the brakes on her idyll. What was this? Middle-aged infatuation with your dead brother's gay husband? Don't even go there, Marty. You're way too smart for such absurdity.

"May I sit beside you?" Chito looked up at Marty blankly then patted the coverlet beside him.

"Of course."

Marty sat circumspectly on the bed, a good foot and a half away. "I can only imagine how sad all of this must be for you. I just want you to know...I personally am glad you're here. That we can get to know you better. That...you'll come to see us as your family. We love you, Chito."

Wrong! All wrong. Creepy, icky, needy. Marty wanted to roll the tape back and give it a more reasoned, benign delivery. "Dear friend, we're so happy to have you here. Please–our home is yours. Anything at all we can do to make your stay more agreeable and restful, do not hesitate to ask!" Yes, it needed much more Emily Post, less *Bridges of Madison County.*" But like all unfortunate preambles in life, we're branded with the first wretched utterances that disgorge like sausage from a grinder.

"I love you all, too," he said. "In such a short time I never thought I'd say that, never. Tom told me so many times what a funny, crazy family he had–he loved you all so much. How could he not?"

How could he not? Marty let that sink in for a millisecond then silently watched a house burning in her head. We had everything BUT love around here. Anger, bickering, accusation, sulking, silence, blame, tears, guilt, threats–ALL were in inordinate supply growing up. Love was never mentioned by either of her parents, to her, to Tom or to themselves as far as she knew. It just wasn't done. Like intestinal gas, aberrant political rumination and discussions of religious fallacy–simply not done, ever.

"Well...love is such a funny word."

"It is?"

"Sure...I mean, 'I love apple pie' is so different from...I love...you know...a person."

Chito smiled. "You Americans are so funny. We Latins don't break it down into little boxes. When we love, we LOVE! I LOVE apple pie, I LOVE Michael Jackson, I LOVE my nose this morning, I LOVE being here in this house, in this room, on this bed. I LOVE being with you, Marty!" Beaming Chito suddenly took Marty's ears in his hands and pulled her forward, kissing her quickly on the forehead. Like a child teasing a puppy, he suddenly burst out laughing. "See. It's so simple to LOVE! But I warn you...with love comes hate. When we hate, we really HATE! I HATE Kylie Minogue's music, I HATE beet salad, I HATE the way my one eye is smaller than the other, I HATE my hairy feet!"

By now they were both laughing so hard Chito collapsed back on the bed, and after only the slightest hesitation, Marty fell alongside him. They gasped as their laughter became giggles, then sighs, then slow, measured breathing. Gazing into the void of the shadowy ceiling above them, Marty felt something she thought just might be, could be, that odd sensation so long absent in her life. Was it...really...love?

\*\*\*

Pete Pennebaker hated three things in life–Brussels sprouts, tight pants and pretension. The sprouts and the pants were an easy fix–avoid them. Pretension, however, showed up not infrequently in numerous uninvited circumstances–platinum credit card offers, beer commercials where some gray-bearded old fart claimed to be The Most Interesting Man in the World, and cherished but deluded individuals who sometimes assumed "traditional" meant biased, "humble" meant conformist, and "conservative" meant oblivious. "How did it get so screwed up in this country?" Pete wondered aloud as he approached the ranch horse corral behind the main barn at *Los Abuelos*. He could remember a time when it was okay to be "arty" so long as the subject matter wasn't dirty or uncouth. Being liberal was tolerated if God and country were respected with equal fervor. Hell, he'd even known gay people his whole life and never had a problem with any of it till they decided one day to get all up in your face, shaking their tallywackers. Now why do I want to see somebody else's sex organ? I see mine every day and it doesn't do a damn thing for me! Why did everything have to be torn down just for the sake of having to rebuild it again? Yes, there were injustices everywhere. Always had been, always would be. Does it solve a problem to try and deal with it, or is it better just to stand back and scream at it?

He swung open the old wooden gate and hobbled slowly toward *Dulce*, his twenty-year-old prize roping mare. In her day, she was a champion. Pete let the local cowboys, those who knew how to rein her properly, compete with her in all the area rodeos. And she'd take home the blue ribbon nearly every time. She was as swift and alert in those days as a red cardinal on a frosty winter morning. Pete loved that horse as much as he loved anything. Deliberate in movement and now routed with age, *Dulce* exhibited only a hint of her former distinction.

Still, Pete patted her nose and rubbed her neck with utmost pride. She was a winner and always would be.

"Come on, sweetheart. Let's get you some of that good 'Equine Senior' ration you like." The two slowly plodded back toward the hay barn. In the opposite pen, the other horses followed along the fence hoping to snag a treat from Pete as well. "Y'all gonna have to wait your turn. Heah! Caesar, quit biting Charlotte's butt!" Truth be told, Pete would rather mess all day with his horses than just about anything else. Some people had golf, some liked to fish, some collected stamps– Pete had his *remuda* of equestrian misfits to while away the hours. He loved the names of horse colors–bay, sorrel, *grulla, pinto, criollo, blanca,* chestnut, dun, buckskin, palomino, roan, appaloosa–all lyrical, all aristocratic, all names invented for melancholy cowboys to wax poetic on a forlorn winter's eve.

Pete lifted the heavy wooden lid of the feed bin and measured out about two coffee cans of ration for *Dulce.* She impatiently rubbed her nose against Pete's back. "Hold on, bossy. You knock me over and we all gonna go hungry. Now quit that! Heah!"

*Dulce* continued to nudge Pete till he finally bopped her once on the nose. *Dulce* jerked back, appalled by such insolence. Can't you see I'm hungry? Get with the vittles, *viejo!*

Pete shook the feed bucket and led *Dulce* out toward the back horse trap. Pouring the pellets into a long wooden trough, he stood alongside and patted her rump. "There. Eat to your heart's content–and quit poking me like I'm a bale of hay." Pete reached forward to scratch her withers and watched as her muscles shuddered and quivered.

He sat the small bucket alongside the fence and mopped his brow with a frayed handkerchief. Squinting toward the tank down in the draw, he could make out one of the Beefmaster bulls stretching under a motte of soapberry trees. He spit and sighed; all was right at the Pennebaker *hacienda*– all, he figured, but what to do with the two refugees? He couldn't just turn them over to Immigration. Hell, he watched TV news too. Lord knows where they'd end up. Probably separated; Adnan might never see his daughter again and she'd grow up an orphan–where? He didn't doubt for a minute Adnan's life would be finished if he got sent back to Syria. And finding work in Mexico? A man who speaks no Spanish, has no money and no connections whatsoever? Had it gotten so bad that they were now leaving America for the void of living in eternal Mexican limbo? What do you do with these people? Pete wasn't a transgressor, an activist or a radical of any kind. He believed in the law and in justice. But where was the justice for these two lost souls? Who wouldn't run for their lives if they saw annihilation on the horizon? It's easy to sit in one's recliner and moralize over all these "rapists and bad hombres" until the day comes they show up at your own front door. That's when all the hypothesizing meets the hard pavement of inevitability. You're either an unfeeling robot of dubious Christian virtue–or you take matters into your own hands because the option of silently witnessing a human dumpster consume guiltless lives is not someone else's problem anymore–it's yours.

Pete lumbered back into the barn to grab a couple handfuls of carrot cubes for the other horses. They followed his route along the fence in giddy anticipation. Ice cream time! Pete knew from an early age you could stand in front of a horse with both hands out, one hiding a treat, and they'd remain there unblinking for an eternity, certain that kismet was inevitable.

Pete questioned his decision to notify the town leaders as he'd done. Was it not better to be direct in one's intentions rather than covert in committing an actual good deed? Had he not grown up his whole life dealing with wetbacks? It was a fact of South Texas ranch life as common as mesquite beans and fire ants. Tired, dirty, worn-out men (and it was nearly always men in those days) came through the ranch looking for food, water and shelter. Which is what you provided, and, hopefully, got a little something in return–a few days' work clearing brush, hoeing the garden, painting outbuildings– whatever was needed. Sometimes they stayed, sometimes they lit out right after supper. There was no set pattern to any of it. Political misdeeds, natural disasters, famine, misfortune in general–all were the cause of such sporadic migrations north. And they all came looking for a break, a chance, some hope. Ranchers who couldn't or wouldn't relate to such basic human want were simply lying to themselves. How to feed, clothe, doctor, house and educate the millions who wanted to follow suit–that was a different matter altogether. Pete had no answer to such a predicament. None whatsoever. He could only try to save two at a time.

He rested his forearms on the corral fence and breathed deeply. At least if they threw the book at him, they couldn't say he was hiding anything. From the good-hearted doctors and nurses at the Kokernot County Hospital that sewed up Adnan's gash, the preacher's wife who rocked Haya in her arms, and even the sheriff's deputy who brought out some of his kids' old clothes for Haya–everyone who was aware of the situation had treated the two wayfarers with decency and respect. At least, so far. And now the next step. What to do with them now?

\*\*\*\*

Pettus passed Marty surging down Main Street, with its usual sparse traffic, in the Montego and blew his horn. She glanced around and waved. Motioning for her to pull over, he made a sharp U-turn and steered up behind her. Marty let the window down as he got out, ambling toward her.

"Been making yourself pretty scarce. Where ya been?"

Marty smiled. "We got a world of activity going on out at the ranch. I'm sure you've heard all about our visitors that turned up?"

Pettus looked down and scratched his boot toe in the gravel. "I heard. Illegals?"

Marty shrugged. "We're trying to find out a lot of things, we still don't know."

"Yeah, well...I been missing ya. Wondering when I'd see ya again."

Marty looked apprehensively at Pettus. Why was sharing a little mutual desire with someone who obviously cared for you so fraught with angst? Why couldn't she just accept him for being Pettus and not, say, Chito, for example?

"For sure," she said, which was safer than breaking into candor. "Just have to let things settle down for a bit."

"Sounds like you're getting tired of me."

Marty looked surprised. "Why you saying that?"

"Pretty obvious." He dug his boot further in the dirt. "Well, I'm not going anywhere. I'm here 'til the bitter end, I reckon."

"I'm not going anywhere either. Don't be so dramatic." Marty put her hand over his, resting on the car door.

He looked back at her anxiously. "Look, I need to talk to ya. It's kind of urgent."

Marty was hoping to avoid another long exposition of "who's avoiding who" but she saw the determination on his face and surrendered. "I need to run this prescription home to Daddy, but if it's not going to take too long, hop in. My air conditioning is in better shape than your pickup." Pettus walked around to the passenger side and slid in.

"What's up, Pettus? Sky falling out your way?"

Pettus gazed intently ahead. "I want to make you an offer. A good deal for you–for all y'all. I want to sell you those hundred acres down along the creek bottom. You and your daddy been talking 'bout needing a good hay field for years now. Best piece of land I own. Hell, you can grow anything on it. Soybeans, corn, cotton, watermelons–you name it. It backs up to the old county road, so you'd have easy access. What do you think?"

Marty was genuinely shocked. "Pettus–our people, you and I–we don't sell land, ever."

"Wouldn't sell it to anyone but you, that's a fact. I know you'll take better care of it than we ever could."

"Where's this coming from? You need money, I can loan you some money, Pettus. That's not a problem."

"It's not just the money. It's time somebody in this family did something to help push us out of the hole we've been stuck in for more'n a hundred years."

Pettus's eyes fixed on the shimmering car hood radiating before him in the afternoon heat. "Cody and Thaine...they're nothing more than peon slaves. They have no idea what they're capable of. How could they? Never been anywhere, never seen anything–not educated enough to even know what they're missing. Maybe I could get 'em into ag school somewhere or let 'em learn a trade they can make decent money at." Pettus shook his head. "Darcy and Delilah–God bless–stuck in that shithole flower morgue trying to make a go of it. I'll say this for Carol Ann, she's opened their eyes to possibility!" He finally turned to Marty. "Don't ya see? I can help them out with a little financing to turn that place of theirs around. Make it happen, make it be something–something to be proud of!"

Marty had never seen Pettus so impassioned. It was a thoroughly unfamiliar aspect of an individual she'd always felt she knew quite well.

"And what about you, what do you want, Pettus?" He continued staring at the silver glint of sun dancing on the car hood.

"I'd like to be more deserving of you." Marty was speechless. He spoke with such sincerity and tenderness, it froze any response she could instantly invoke.

"Pettus, I...I feel that..." Marty stopped and simply stared at Pettus. After a self-conscious pause, he swung open the

heavy car door and stepped out onto the pavement. He
lowered his head back inside the car.

"Just think about it, is all. I'll go with market value. I've
had offers before–don't make me wait too long." With that he
slammed the door shut and walked back toward his pickup.
Pulling out from behind Marty, he blew his horn and ginned
off down Main Street. Marty sat for a long time,
contemplating. Was there some better angel inside Pettus
fighting those internal demons to bring a little virtue back into
his world? If so, why–why now? If so...really? It fascinated
Marty to see this new wrinkle in Pettus's character, but she
had to wonder that if indeed the leopard can change his spots,
what else might he change?

\*\*\*

Darcy dragged her sore leg across the floor of the Dusty
Rose and shook her head. "Lilah, what if we moved that
refrigerator case over here next to the sink? Would that make
it feel more commodious in here?"

Delilah twisted her face. "No, I do not think putting the
commode in front will help things. I think if we knocked the
wall out here and moved EVERYTHING into the back of the
store, we could have more displays–candles, vases, incense,
dried flowers, figurines–you know, sass up the entry."

Darcy looked drained. "Sass it up? The only thing that's
gonna sass it up around here is if we hire a bunch of topless
Hooter babes to give away free cocktails."

Delilah wrinkled her nose. "Oh, that just
sounds...unsanitary."

Darcy folded her arms. "I hate to say it, but I think I'm
defeated. Nothing we do is going to make us outshine Carol
Ann. We're old and tired and dried up." She crumpled a dead
sunflower in her hand and sighed. "Am I too old to become a
stewardess?"

"They're not called stewardesses anymore. They're flight hostesses, I read it in *In Touch Weekly*."

Darcy exhaled again and stared out the front window. "I wonder what witchcraft Old Pink Pussy's up to today? Maybe she's boiling babies in a cauldron–gonna serve it up as Fountain of Youth elixir."

Delilah looked puzzled. "Oh Darcy, how awful! What would you do with it, drink it?"

Darcy nodded. "Uh-huh, shampoo with it. Put it on chapped lips, hemorrhoids–anywhere you need that baby fresh glow."

Darcy suddenly focused on someone approaching in the street. "Oh shit. Shit!" She whirled around. "Look busy–do something!" Darcy tossed Delilah a Styrofoam wreath. "Here, put silver balls on this."

"We don't have any silver balls."

"Stick pinecones in it then–just look busy!"

"What's going on?"

Darcy grabbed a nearby push broom and began weaving unsteadily across the room. She glanced over at Delilah, who stood bewildered. Darcy hissed, "Find some G.D. pinecones for chrissake and look creative!" At that very moment, the front door swung open and in hobbled Pete Pennebaker followed by his ranch hand Nestor and another swarthy-looking man holding a little girl's hand.

"Morning ladies. Y'all look busier than a fat boy at a Methodist picnic. Business must be good."

Darcy turned to look up with exaggerated surprise. "Why, Mr. Pennebaker, you startled me! Yes indeed, no rest for the weary round here. Lilah and I barely have time for a cup of tea in the afternoon."

Delilah looked appalled. "Tea?"

Darcy leaned the broom up against a display case and wiped her hands on her jeans. "What can I do for you gentlemen? I bet somebody's got a birthday or an anniversary or a get-well surprise coming up and y'all are looking to amaze 'em with one of our beautiful bouquets?"

"Not exactly." Pete motioned toward Nestor. "You know my right-hand man here..."

Darcy shook hands. "Course. How you doing, Nestor?" Nestor nodded politely.

"And this fella here come all the way from Syria, Mr. Adnan Hakim."

Darcy shook Adnan's hand. "Well, I'll be. Howdy, welcome."

"And this little one here is his precious daughter, Haya."

Darcy bent over and took Haya's hand in hers. "Well, if you're not the cutest little thing. Lilah, come over and look at the most beautiful eyes on the planet. Gorgeous!"

Haya clung to her father as Delilah approached with a tiny rosebud in her hand. She knelt before Haya. "Here, sweetheart, you put this in a bowl of water when you get home and it'll open up like a big red kiss. Isn't that magic?"

Haya spoke to her father. "*Alsayidat latifa?*"

"She says you are nice and she doesn't want to leave here."

Delilah grinned. "Well bless her heart. Course you don't have to go anywhere, for goodness sake."

Pete interrupted, "I'm glad to hear it. I knew you girls would do the right thing." Darcy stared at Pete blankly. "I want you to give old Adnan a job here."

Darcy continued staring. "I'm sorry?"

"A job! Work, employment–he needs to earn some money."

Darcy straightened up slowly and answered in a hoarse voice, "A job? You want us to give this gentleman a job...here in our store?"

"That's right. Man's gotta work. He can do all kinds of things, but his number one skill is, he's a baker! Y'all got a little kitchen back here somewhere, doncha?"

Delilah chirped in, "Yes, we do. It's not very big but there's a gas range and a refrigerator and a double sink and…"

"Hold it, hold it…" Darcy held her hand in the air. "Now Mr. Pete, I don't mean to be fresh, you know me better'n that, but we're about at the end of the road here trying to keep this show going. We're broke! We couldn't afford to pay Mr. Hakim no more than the man in the moon. I think maybe you ought to try Carol Ann's Thunderbutt Walmart across the way. She can afford it better'n us, for sure."

Pete shook his head. "Nope. It's gotta be y'all. Carol Ann's a beautiful girl but I wouldn't trust her with a pack of Life Savers."

Darcy smiled. "Well, I agree with you there, Mr. Pennebaker, but…" Darcy waved her hand around the shop listlessly, "…maybe YOU should offer him a job!"

Pete curled his lips into a tight little smile. "That's exactly what I intend to do. I'm gonna pay you to pay him and he's gonna pay me back with part interest in his little bakery here. We've already worked it out!"

Darcy stared wide-eyed. "You have?"

Pete nodded, grinning. "Ain't it sweet? Hey, that's what you ought to call your little bakery here, 'Ain't It Sweet.' Wonderful name, catchy."

"I like it!" Delilah smiled at Adnan, who smiled shyly back.

Again, Darcy held her hand in the air, futilely trying to nip manifest enthusiasm in the bud. "Whoooa–you're gonna pay us–to pay him. What's our cut of the deal?"

Pete removed his Stetson and scratched his balding head. "Well now, I'll tell ya, my daddy always used to say, 'Pete, don't ever go to a whorehouse without enough silver in your pocket to close the deal!' and I ain't referring to you fine young ladies neither cause we all go to the same church, idn't that right?"

"Amen," murmured Delilah.

"So, I figured–hell, I'm just an old country boy and I never knew much about higher math an such–would an extra $4000 a month sweeten the deal for ya? Thousand dollars a week."

Delilah squealed, "Yes!"

Darcy's face was blank. "You'll pay us $4000 a month, cream off the top, to let Mr. Hakim run his bakery in back here?"

"All right, I'll throw in another $500–but I'll give ya just six months! You gotta make this thing go and blow in six months or I'm pulling out."

Darcy made quick mental calculations as Delilah began to hop behind the counter. "That kitchen needs a lot of work back there. He's gotta get some kind of food license from the state. What about in here? We need a little help modernizing in here, too."

Pete looked around the room and rubbed his chin. "Aw, it won't take much. I'll get Jacinto to bring some of the boys from the ranch to paint in here, tidy it up a bit. You'll need some chairs and tables to sit at; coffeemaker, drink dispenser, whatnot. It won't be highfalutin–but it'll sure nuff be better'n serviceable."

Darcy crossed her arms, frowning. She looked at everyone in the room then turned to Delilah. "What do you think, Lilah?" Delilah walked around the counter and placed a hand on Darcy's shoulder.

"What do I think? I think you'd be crazier than a can of bent nails if you turned this down."

Darcy smiled and patted Delilah's hand. "Deal, Mr. Pennebaker! You got yourself some new partners, Mr. Adnan."

Adnan exhaled deeply and wiped his eyes. Shaking hands with the Lyndecker sisters, he turned to Pete and gave him a hug, nearly knocking him over.

"All right, all right–settle down now. Y'all got work to do and I got to get back to the ranch." Pete began shuffling with his cane back toward the front door when Haya suddenly put her hand on his and shouted in a loud voice, "Deal!"

# CHAPTER NINE

"The thing about running a ranch is you can't ever let the horseshit get to ya. Every day there's some new crap bomb poking you in the eye–windmill broke, fence down, sick cow, ruptured bull, well gone dry, no rain, too much rain, freeze burst the pipes, freeze killed the crop, truck throws a rod, tractor gets a flat–you follow me?"

Chito nodded as they strode atop the narrow catwalk above the ancient cypress cattle pens built by Pettus's dad and granddad. Today they were worming just-weaned heifers with a liquid pour-on, Cydectin, that killed both internal and external parasites.

"Should be done three times a year to be most effective," Pettus intoned, "but as per usual–it's catch as catch can around the Lyndecker estate."

"Thaine, run that big bald-faced muley heifer over here," Pettus hollered as Thaine smacked the orange rump of a passing cow with a four-foot leather stock switch.

"Git in there, you fractious ole bitch!" Thaine slammed the chute gate as Cody, straddling a side fence, tapped the cow's rib with a battery-powered cattle prod. She whirled around in dismay then turned and whirled back and ran into the two-

and-a-half-foot wide cutting chute. Cody instantly rammed the pipe bar behind her legs, blocking her exit. Chito, now standing at a safe distance alongside the chute, marveled at the sheer dance of it all. Quick, abrupt, exact–everyone expressly conscious of their roles and positions. It was both thrilling and startling to a city boy like Chito. His father was a paunchy elitist who had sat behind a desk his entire adult life, dispensing orders and maxims. Physical activity meant a round of golf at *Las Misiones* in Monterrey. Chito wanted to learn, to understand what this had all meant to Tom. Mostly he enjoyed the rough and ready, unpolished camaraderie of the Lyndecker men. So utterly different from the life of a London investment banker. So completely different from any reality he'd ever experienced.

"Hey, Chito man."

Thaine squinted from beneath his crumpled, sweat-stained straw hat. "I'd hate to see you mess up those pretty new boots of yours, but you're about to step in a big ole pile of cow shit. Oops, too late!"

Without realizing, Chito had suddenly backed into a steaming heap of fresh manure.

Thaine whistled loudly. "You're a Texan now boy!" Cody joined in, cackling with laughter.

"That cow shit's better'n cologne if you wanna get the gals all hot and bothered."

Pettus smiled. "Can't live on a ranch without stepping in cow shit. And son, looks like you found the biggest pile on the place!" Chito suddenly felt absurd in his new boots, new jeans, new snap-button shirt and new straw hat. What did it matter? He was a greenhorn; shouldn't he look the part? Without hesitation he immediately stuck his other boot in the cow pie and twisted it.

"Now they match."

All three of the Lyndeckers hooted, delighted with Chito's level-headed sensibility.

Pettus called to him, "Good! You ready to get dirtier? Come over here and hold this bottle for me."

Chito walked over and Pettus handed him the plastic flask of purple liquid. "Now we're just gonna ease this little sister up a bit and get her to stick her old head in the opening there."

Chito watched, totally riveted as the cow stood motionless, staring at the semi-opening before her. The head gate was a vise-like aperture that opened and closed by an outside pull lever and yanked down around the cow's neck as she tried to escape. Cody reached over the side railing and grabbed the cow's dung-crusted tail in his bare hand and yanked it up.

"Come on, Mama–we don't have all day." With that, the heifer raced forward, fleeing her confinement. Pettus slammed down the trap door lever with a loud bang. The cow kicked, twisted and bellowed momentarily, then froze in silence.

"Hell, she's lost her tag. Thaine, bring me that tag bucket and the nose pliers. Chito, you think you can stand up on that first pipe there and pour about three-quarters of that side cylinder on her back?"

Chito looked at the bottle, gripped the receptacle and squeezed it, which instantly emitted the purple chemical into the smaller side repository. Standing above the panting heifer, he surveyed her back as if about to perform surgery.

"Just start at her neck and slowly trace a line down to her tail. Make sure she gets all the medicine." Pettus spoke as Chito commenced pouring, shaking the last bead onto her tail.

"How 'bout that?" Chito grinned. "Now get over here and hold this rope while I stick these pliers in her nose." Chito looked startled.

"Why do you want to do that?"

"You'll see."

Chito stood behind Pettus as he watched the cow jerk her wedged neck sideways inside the trap door. Instantly Pettus snapped the pliers in the cow's nostrils and pulled her head up, wrapping the joined rope around a raised pipe and handing the lead to Chito. "Hold on to this."

In another continuous motion, Pettus fished a numbered ear tag from the bucket, attached it and a holding pin to an applicator, and returned to the cow's ear, perforating the flesh with a bright yellow earmark reading "329." The heifer bawled and snorted indignantly.

"You do it fast and tidy–they think a bee stung 'em. Let go the rope!" Chito dropped the line and stepped back. Pettus jerked free the pliers from the cow's nose and sprung open the catch doors. The heifer flew out with a twist of her hips like a samba dancer. Pettus laughed and removed his hat, mopping his forehead with an already soaked-with-sweat shirtsleeve. He smiled at Chito. "That's how it's done in the Old West, pardner."

Chito grinned back. What else did they do in the Old West? He was more than ready to learn.

\*\*\*

Adnan and Haya walked around their temporary new home at the Pennebaker hunting camp. They took in with awe and apprehension all the "things" surrounding them. Things like the elaborate coffeemaker, microwave, flat-screen TV, dishwasher, side-by-side refrigerator/freezer, handheld electric broom, massage chair, satellite radio...it was all decisively overwhelming. Adnan had only a vague idea of what most of it was or what its intended purpose was. Still, he analyzed all of it with high regard.

Haya, holding up a hair dryer, spoke to her father in Arabic. "What is this? A toy?"

Adnan examined the hair dryer and handed it back to Haya. "You know what it is, remember? It dries your hair and your clothes. You point it and it dries."

Haya nodded. "Oh yes, I forgot." She turned and walked

back to the Bathroom, where she'd been rummaging through drawers.

"Don't be mischievous. None of this is ours. Leave things where they are. This is not our home–just a temporary roof." Silence. "Do you hear your father, Haya?"

A small voice, no doubt lost in discovery, drifted in from the bathroom. "Yes, father."

Adnan picked up a square Lucite cube on the coffee table with a dandelion seed encased perfectly in the middle. He marveled at the accomplishment.

"Incredible. Americans make the frail immortal. Genius." He sat the cube down and turned to stare out the window at the miles and miles of chaparral extending before him. Curiously, it reminded him of Syria. The heat, the dryness, the dust and shimmering mirages he saw rising sporadically as they walked slowly toward, he had hoped, the border with Mexico. Surely they don't arrest you for swimming the other way into Mexico? He could find work there, he knew it. He had skills, training, talent. No, it was impossible to stay in a country that didn't want you, despised you, feared you, separated you from your family and most of all suspected you of being a terrorist. A terrorist! He was running from the terrorists! The last thing on earth he identified with was terrorism. They killed his wife, his two sons–they nearly killed him. America? Why would he stay here when it was only a matter of time before they sent him back to his own execution. What future then for Haya–orphan, street urchin, prostitute–what would her fate be? No, you don't wait for the lion to eat you–you stay ahead of the annihilator with eyes open, tireless nerves and the blade of a sharp knife by your side at all times.

Haya walked back into the room holding up a pink enema bag. "Is it a balloon? How do you blow it up?"

Adnan took the rubber object from her and swatted her rear. "What have I told you? Not to get into trouble! These are not your things." Haya began to cry.

"But I want to play! There's nothing for me to do." Adnan looked at her, flustered, then pulled her into his arms, kissing her head. He rocked her gently.

"My sweet girl...I'm not fussing at you, but we have to be respectful of these people and their things. They are trying to help us, don't you see? Do you want to go for a walk, okay? Let's go for a walk. They will be here shortly to take us back into town. No tears now. Let me see. I still see one!" Haya began to laugh as she pushed her father away.

"I'm thirsty, Papa." Adnan stood and walked toward the massive refrigerator as Haya followed.

"Let's see if they have something for you." Opening the large stainless door, the only thing immediately visible was...beer. Shelf after shelf after shelf lined with chilled cans of...beer.

Adnan shook his head, "How about some water?" Haya nodded and Adnan began filling a glass at the sink.

"These Texans like their beer," Adnan conjectured aloud. "Come on, let's look around a bit. Ah now, your shoelace is undone." Adnan bent down to tie Haya's shoe as she sipped her water.

"I like this place, Daddy."

"Really...why?"

"Because–I think it will be our new home." Adnan looked up at her.

"Why?"

"Because we'll be happy here." Adnan continued to stare at her, then patted her back. "Good, I hope you're right. Come."

As they started for the front door, Adnan reached down, as he routinely did when departing a room, and felt for the knife he carried invariably in his right pant pocket. It was there–steadfast, accessible.

\*\*\*

Marty sat on the tile floor of the Pennebaker house patio and carefully examined her father's bare foot.

"I still can't see it."

"It's there, I can feel it." Marty picked up the tweezers beside her and pinched Pete's big toe.

"Ow! That's my toe, not the goddam thorn."

Marty frowned. "I don't know how many times I've told you not to wear your house slippers down to the cow pens. You don't listen. One of these times you're gonna step on a nail or a piece of glass and it'll be lockjaw for sure."

"Good. Sooner the better. Old people need to make way for the new–especially when they don't understand a goddam thing about anything anymore. Ow!"

Marty squinted. "I think I got it. What is it you don't understand? No, change that–I don't want to know! We'll just get into another fight. Stand up and see if it's gone."

Pete stabbed his cane on the tile and slowly hoisted himself from the kitchen chair. "I can't tell."

"Well, walk around."

Pete hobbled slowly in a circle. "Yeah, I 'spect it's...ow! Damn, it's still there."

Marty shook her head. "Sit down." Pete shuffled back to the chair and Marty spoke softly. "Had a talk with Pettus Lyndecker, yesterday." Pete grunted and stared at his foot. "He'd like to sell us those hundred acres down on San Miguel Creek. Make a fine hay field, horse trap–fatten some steers and yearlings up real nice."

Pete looked stunned. "Sell? Why, in God's name? Lyndeckers ain't never sold an inch of land, never. They're as bad as we are...worse!"

Marty shrugged. "I guess he needs the money."

"They ALWAYS need money! Poor, hard-ass bunch of

scoundrels."

Marty kept her head down. "That why you're giving Darcy and Delilah forty-five hundred dollars a month to keep the Dusty Rose open?"

Pete, for once, was nearly speechless. "Mary rode a mile. You fart around here and it's in the paper next day. Who told you?"

"Oh, Daddy, you can't keep a secret in this town, you know better than that. It's your money–you can do whatever you want with it."

"Damn right. I just don't want people thinking I'm getting soft on illegals."

And there it was. The extra special, unambiguously American dilemma of "wall-up-the-border but, maybe, on the sly, help the poor sonsabitches already here." Tea Partier by day, nascent liberal by night.

Marty frowned. "Don't worry. Your dirty little secret is safe with me."

"What secret?"

"Oh, Lord," Marty said. "Why do so many of y'all keep waving this rah-rah, 'Murica,' love-it-or-leave-it, one-size-fits-all flag? What did you and Mother teach me as a child? Respect the poor, help the poor, ALL God's children are created in God's image, 'Do unto others as you would have them do unto you.' And now? It's 'Fear the poor, hate the different, mistreat the needy, lock up the unfortunate.' Where does all this hostility come from?"

Pete slowly began pulling on his sock. "The world is changing–too fast. Everything I knew as a boy is catawampus. You just want to slow it down before it all explodes. Yes, you have to help the less off, no question–but it don't mean you have to invite every single one of 'em over for dinner, does it? I can't do nothing about the hell in Syria and Honduras and Nigeria and Sudan and Jesus Lord knows where all else. But if God puts a man and child near death on my land and I don't try to help lessen their misfortune in some way, shape or form, then I'm a sorrier bastard than even my enemies suppose."

Marty smiled at Pete. "I never got the thorn out."

"And you won't. I'm used to thorns–keep me motivated." Pete started back toward the living room then suddenly turned to Marty. "What do you see in that Lyndecker boy?"

Marty flushed at the surprising query. "What do you mean?"

"I guess you think I don't know you been seeing Pettus for quite some time now. What do you see in that rangy outlaw?"

"I don't think it's any of your business what I see in Pettus or anyone else, for that matter."

Pete nodded wearily. "Sure, sure–you want me to spend a barn full of money on his property, but you don't want to tell me the real reason why."

"There is no 'real reason'–it's a business proposition, that's all."

"You gonna marry Pettus?"

Marty was dumbfounded. "Don't be crazy!"

Pete looked at her gravely. "Never thought I'd say this–but you could do worse. Least he knows what a cow's udders are for."

Marty shook her head and rose up from the tile floor. "Now I've heard absolutely everything. No! I'm not interested in marrying Pettus Lyndecker; not now, not ever. And he wants your 'barn full' of money to help out his POOR family. 'Help the poor'–remember?"

Pete nodded unconvincingly and slowly shuffled back into the cool shadows of *Hacienda Los Abuelos*. He exhaled sharply as he limped, "The world is changing too fast...you just want to slow it all down before it..."

Just then, Jacinta called from the kitchen, "Lunch is ready! *Ven a comer!*"

\*\*\*

Darlene kneeled in the dirt at the edge of the house, beside the kitchen door, and called out to Thaine, "Do you see her?"

Thaine bellowed back, "No! And if I get snake bit, you're taking my ass all the way up to San Antonio 'cause round here they'll just amputate."

"I promise. But you won't get snake bit. I put a pink light around your life force."

"Put one round my nuts too. Crawling through this shit, no telling how many ticks I'll get on my gonads."

Darlene laughed and called again, "You see her? She's the calico, not the black one."

"Wait a minute...hold on...damn! She's had babies again."

Darlene was incredulous. "Again? She just had a litter a few months ago."

"Well, she done it again...four, five...I count six babies. Cute little monkeys, but they're wild as hell."

Darlene leaned in closer to squint at the cool darkness under the house. "Does she need anything?"

Thaine suddenly reappeared. "Yeah, her tubes tied and a good worming." He hurriedly shook the dirt and cobwebs out of his hair and britches. "Next time, you're going under there. Man, it's all kinds of nasty."

Darlene looked grateful. "Thank you, Thaine. If I wasn't on my way to work, I'd a scooted under there to look for sure. We haven't seen her for over two weeks! I was worried sick."

Thaine frowned. "You can stop worrying. She's alive and still pumping 'em out. You need to get her and all the rest of these mangy cats over to Doc Andrus 'fore we turn into some kinda Wildlife Park for Feral Freeloaders." Thaine scratched his head. "Damn, I think I got fleas." He headed up the kitchen steps as Darlene spoke.

"Thank you."

Thaine mumbled, "Forget it" and continued on.

"Thaine?" He turned back around. "I want you to meet someone."

"Who?"

"You don't know her. Her mom's a new nurse at the clinic."

Thaine rolled his eyes and grunted, "Oh God, not another four-eyed goofus with buck teeth and hairy legs. I can't take any more of your blind dates."

"That's not nice at all. Sheila really liked you, and you were rude."

"I was not rude. I told her she wadn't my type, that's all."

"Your type? You mean a Playboy centerfold with no brains and low morals?"

"Damn right! I want something fine as wine–not some uptight priss grabbing her shirt and drawers like I was a two-headed monster blowing fire outta my nose."

Darlene nodded. "And that's exactly what it looks like to these girls when you get all slobbery and grabby on a first date. If you'd lay off watching porn and practice being with a real woman, you'd be amazed at how much you'd like it."

"Yes, Mama." Thaine lowered his head and squinted. "What's her name?"

"Lucille."

Thaine bellowed, "Aw Jesus, she already sounds like somebody's grandmother!"

"Suit yourself. I wasn't even going to tell you she came in third in the swimsuit competition for Miss Buccaneer Days in Corpus two years ago."

"You got any pictures?"

Darlene held up her hand. "I'm through with you. I don't know how you're ever going to meet anyone stuck out here hiding in the bushes but suit yourself. Thank you for finding Miss Eudora and her babies for me." Darlene headed toward her Chevy van parked in front of the house.

"Hey," Thaine called to her. Darlene turned back around. "Is she pretty?"

Darlene crossed her arms. "Well now, I guess we'll never know, will we? When you take a long shower, comb your hair and put on something clean to wear, you're a nice-looking guy, Thaine. Women want to meet you. But not that immature, one-thing-on-his-mind fiend you seem to like better. It's your life." Darlene turned back toward the van.

Thaine stared sullenly ahead then began scratching vigorously at his underarms. "Damn fleas."

\*\*\*

Carol Ann nudged open the sliding glass door with her elbow and stepped out onto the poolside patio carrying two extra-large pink drinks. Cody glanced up from the chaise lounge he was reclining on and grinned. "Sure don't look like a beer to me."

"Beer makes you fat. It's a strawberry mojito–full of protein...and rum." Carol Ann sat beside Cody and handed him the icy drink. He took a sip and smiled again. "Damn, sweet as pie–at least you managed to spill a little alcohol in it."

"More'n a little, hon–more'n a little." Carol Ann slowly relaxed back into the chaise beside Cody and flipped aside her gauzy caftan, exposing the spray-tanned leg nearest him. Duly noted, Cody tugged impatiently at his knee-length polyester workout shorts–endemic to all South Texas men below the age of thirty. "God forbid they should show a little thigh," Carol Ann thought to herself. Somehow it was deemed unmanly, not done. She blamed it on the San Antonio Spurs. Well, the entire NBA, to be accurate. In her father's day, guys wore short shorts on all the teams; cool, sexy, liberating. Then someone decreed (who was it, Michael Jordan?) they all had to wear these ridiculous skirt/kilt/leg curtains that hung on them like sad drapes in Grandmother's parlor. About as sexy as a diaper.

"You mind if I take these off?" Cody tugged at his wet, billowy pantaloons and grinned. "You did say, swimsuit optional."

Carol Ann stirred the straw in her drink. "I thought you'd never ask." Cody grinned again then stood and slowly slid his shorts to the ground, revealing snow-white muscled legs and a marble ass ready for the Louvre. Carol Ann stopped stirring and gaped in awe.

"My God boy, you want me to spray some sunblock on those alabaster cheeks? Your heinie's gonna be cherry red."

Cody dove into the pool and surfaced on the other side. He sputtered as he wiped the hair from his eyes, "I'll let you rub some lotion on, if you'd like." Cody beamed as he cuffed waves of water around the pool.

"Sorry, plum out of lotion. Maybe you better put your long johns back on?"

"Nah. This feels too good–why don't you join me?"

"Thinking about it." Carol Ann sipped her drink languidly.

"Well, don't take all day. My cheeks are getting pinker and pinker!"

Carol Ann rose and turned her back to Cody. She let the caftan drop to the tile, revealing a white bikini. Cody had to admit, Carol Ann wasn't the prettiest girl or the beneficiary of the most outstanding body he'd ever seen–but he was fairly sure, in her own unique way, she was about the sexiest thing he'd ever laid eyes on. She turned to him and nonchalantly unhooked her top and let it drop to the chaise. She dove into the water and resurfaced next to Cody.

"Didn't you forget something?"

"What?

"You're still wearing your bikini panties."

"Oh, that. No, I didn't forget. A girl's got to have some modesty."

"Or what?"

Carol Ann smiled. "Or people might get the wrong idea

about her." She pushed off from the side of the pool and backstroked to the opposite end. Cody paddled after her till finally, his outstretched arms straddled her shoulders, resting on the pool edge.

"A fellow can only take so much teasing, Carol Ann."

"Then what happens?"

Cody grinned. "Nature takes over."

"Nice to know some things still work. You give anymore thought to what I said?"

Cody looked at Carol Ann blankly for a moment then pushed away in a huff, leaving a large swell in retreat.

"Nah, can't do it." Cody stood with the water level just below his navel. His chiseled, lightly haired chest was only a shade darker than his ivory legs. His arms and neck, however, were a deep golden brown. Carol Ann dunked her head under the water again and rose to display her generous and apparently real-deal breasts in all their un-siliconed glory. Cody stared at them with the intensity of a mongoose sizing up a cobra. He couldn't have looked away even if the heavens had parted and the hand of God reached down to smack him. As he slowly extended his arms toward the breasts of his dreams, one thought suddenly surfaced above his immediate, staggering carnal desire. "Maybe, maybe...just one trifling, no-count trash fire in the alleyway behind the Dusty Rose...maybe that'll be enough."

# CHAPTER TEN

Chito shook his head, laughing. "That's exactly the way Tom would've put it."

Marty tossed the box of random bran flakes into her shopping cart.

"What?"

"'So much display, so little displayed.' He used to say things like that all the time. What does it mean exactly?"

"That was our mother's *bon mot*. She hated ostentation and at the same time never seemed to mind the occasional lapse in good taste, especially if there was some genuine enthusiasm behind it."

"Is that kind of like putting on airs with nothing to show for it?"

"Exactly." Marty waved her hand at the endless row of Walmart cereal.

"Look at all this! Nine thousand boxes of the same stuff—give or take a frosted flake or a granola cluster. Boundless deception. The only ones paying attention are the kids."

"I think we all live in hopes of finding a free toy in a box, no?"

Marty nodded. "Sure. Just no guarantee you'll get the toy

you want." Marty continued pushing the grocery cart and wondered what Chito must think of such colossal American behemoths as Walmart. There were four small groceries in Rita Blanca when she was growing up. There were maybe a dozen cereals to be had, six kinds of bath soap, three brands of toilet paper and only iceberg lettuce–*just* iceberg lettuce. Now the small groceries are all gone, the hardware stores are gone, the garden store is gone; the radio station, the burger joints, the picture show, the Ben Franklin, the old elementary, junior and high schools, all gone–extinct like wooly mammoths. Only imagined now, or in washed-out photographs.

"We have Walmart in Monterrey, you know?"

Marty looked up, surprised. It was as if he had read her thoughts. "Of course you do. I hadn't really thought about it, but since they're everywhere–of course you do."

"And Home Depot and Starbucks, Costco, Victoria's Secret, Baskin Robbins–you name it, we either have it or we rip it off and call it '*Panchos.*'"

Marty laughed. "So why did you want to come with me and see this monstrosity today?"

Chito shrugged. "Just to be with you. To see what your day's like. To see how you react, what you're going to say–you're so much like Tom. It's very entertaining!"

Marty stopped pushing the cart and studied Chito's face. "You know, it's ridiculous for you to be at that Best Western. You need to come out and stay at the ranch. We've got all kinds of room. You can have Tom's room."

He shook his head. "No, no–you'd all think I was some kind of freeloader and I really don't want to impose..."

Marty held up a hand. "It's settled. I'm ashamed I didn't think of it sooner. We'd love to have you. You're family! What kind of Texas hospitality could we claim if we don't offer hearth and home to kinfolk?"

"But what about...your father?"

"Pete? You let me handle *el Patron*. He likes you, Chito, I know. And he doesn't cotton to people right off the bat."

Chito looked puzzled. "Cotton?"

"Cotton, it's a southern expression. Means someone or something you take a liking too...right away."

Chito nodded. "I never heard this word." He grinned and pulled up a bag of oranges from the shopping cart. "I cotton oranges!"

Marty laughed. "Right."

Chito reached for more fruit but came up with something else. "I cotton Ice Blue Secret Deodorant."

"Okay."

"I cotton...Saltines! I cotton...Campbell's Chunky Vegetable! I cotton...Colgate Optic White Mouthwash!"

"Stop!" Marty covered her mouth with laughter. Chito suddenly pointed his finger directly at her.

"I cotton you." Marty froze. Startled, she didn't have a clue how to react. Was this a brotherly-sisterly friendliness thing? An "I want to be your pal" gesture? You're a nice person and I'd like to get to know you better? Or maybe...let's hop in the sack, shall we?

"I've embarrassed you," he said.

"Not at all. Don't be silly."

"Is it? You seemed very surprised at what I said? Was I wrong? I don't always say the right thing. Please, tell me."

Marty grasped the handle of the shopping cart firmly. "I 'cotton' you too, Chito. Very much. I would just say...maybe we're both kind of...you know...raw, right now. Maybe it's just best we...you know...keep it...simple."

Chito nodded slowly. "Yes, I understand. I'll...'cotton' less."

Marty stared at Chito, then burst out laughing again. "No! You cotton whatever, whomever you want! I am not the 'cotton regulator' for God's sake. Cotton away!"

They were both laughing loudly as an elderly woman passed them in her motorized cart in front of the frozen vegetable aisle. She glanced up at Marty.

"Hon, can you hand me that small bag of corn. That's right...the little one there. Oh, they're on sale! I'll take one more, please. That's right...thank you, sweetheart. Do you know which way the bird food is?"

* * *

Adnan and Delilah finished shoving the refrigerator back into its new corner in the cramped but now more professional-looking kitchen of the Dusty Rose. A new paint job, a large worktable, a larger commercial oven, cooling racks, hanging pots and pans, a used but proficient restaurant dishwasher, even new gingham curtains–it was all starting to look-competent. Constricted, but competent.

"You sure you'll have enough room to work back here? It still looks a little crowded." Delilah glanced around the kitchen.

"Perfect. You should have seen my kitchen in Evansville. Half this size!"

"No!"

"Yes! But we made it work. We made the best breads and sweets in all of Indiana."

Delilah rubbed her hands slowly on the apron she was wearing over her blouse and skirt. "Tell me, Mr. Hakim, why did you have to leave...if you don't mind my asking?"

Adnan smiled. "Why? Because maybe there are people who don't like people of the Muslim faith in this country–in this world. When I found out that our asylum papers were revoked, I ran. What would you do? We gave up everything to come here. I think sometimes it's hard for Americans to imagine what it's like to live in constant fear that you could die at any moment for no good reason. It's madness, and it's happening in places all over the world. The only sane choice one has is to run–run for your life."

Delilah shook her head slowly. "But, did you do something horrible in your country that they would want to...kill you? I don't understand."

"I'm not political. I want to live my life in peace. But there are others who fight for what they believe in–and the rest of us, we have to pay for being in the middle. Haya is all I have left. I will run for as long as I can to keep her alive. When they come for me, I will be one step ahead."

Haya entered the kitchen carrying an enormously obese cat in her arms. *"Unzor ya aboy, ladaya sadique jadied!"*

*"Papa, momken ala'b ma' alqut?"*

Adnan looked at Delilah. "She wants to play with the cat. Is it all right?"

Delilah smiled. "I don't think Popo plays much anymore. He basically eats and sleeps."

"Will she bother the cat?"

"Oh, he'll let her know if she gets too grabby. He's had all his shots; sure, let her play."

*"Naem, momken telaby mae 'Popo,' bas la tedayaeeh."*

Haya squealed with delight, *"Popo! 'Ana baheb 'Popo!'"*

Adnan started to speak but Delilah interrupted him. "I understand–'friends for life.'" Adnan smiled and Haya ran from the room clutching Popo, who appeared to be melting through her fingers.

"Would you like to try a *barazik?* It's a sesame cookie, delicious! I made this morning." Adnan beamed as he opened the Tupperware lid of a large container and presented it to Delilah.

"Sesame? I don't think I've ever had a sesame cookie." Delilah took a bite and beamed. "Oh my..."

"You like?"

"Oh...so wonderful. Sweet, nutty, buttery. Everything you want!"

Adnan's face beamed with pride. Then he asked hesitantly, "Your name, Delilah. It's from the Bible, no?"

Delilah finished the last bite and nodded. "She-or her servant-cut the hair of the great Samson, thus rendering him powerless. I never really understood why cutting one's hair takes away somebody's strength, do you? Men get haircuts all the time and they still manage to throw their weight around like puffed-up gorillas."

"I saw the movie by the great Cecil B. DeMille when I was a child. We do not have this story in my faith."

Delilah spoke sincerely. "I really don't know much about Muslims. Do you believe in God?"

"Of course we do! There is only one God."

"Yes. But do you believe in Jesus, the son of God?"

"Jesus was a great prophet. A master. He was a true holy one-that cannot be denied."

"But...not the son of God?"

Adnan smiled. "We are all sons and daughters of God, no? Isn't that what your Bible teaches? 'For as many as are led by the Spirit of God, they are the sons of God,' Romans 8:14."

"You must've read the Bible a lot."

"Oh I've read lots of holy books-The Koran, The Torah, The Bhagavad Gita-I even read 'The Autobiography of Martin Luther King Jr.,' a very wise man indeed." Adnan studied Delilah's thoughtful expression. "And what is your faith?"

"I'm a member of Church of Our Lord Jesus of the Apostolic Faith. We believe in the Lord with all our heart, mind and soul. Jesus is Lord!"

Adnan nodded slowly. "It is good to have faith, no?

"Yes...it is good."

At that moment, a loud wail emanated from the front room. Popo came racing through the kitchen, jumped on the counter and out the back window, desperate as a drowning victim gasping for oxygen. Delilah looked at Adnan and shook her head. "I guess his patience isn't boundless." They both grinned and turned to investigate the continuing wails in the next room.

\*\*\*

"He's still gotta have some kind of papers, don't he, Al?" Deputy Wayne Canfield was scrolling through the laptop on his desk looking for answers. "It's so damn screwed up in Washington right now, I doubt anybody–least of all the President–has any idea how to handle this immigration goat-fuck rodeo." Sheriff Naylor spit the wad of snuff he'd squirreled away in the corner of his mouth into a nearby coffee can. "Read me that last part again."

Deputy Wayne squinted as he read, "*The <u>United States</u> recognizes the <u>right of asylum</u> for individuals as specified by international and federal law. A specified number of <u>legally defined</u> <u>refugees</u> who either apply for asylum from inside the U.S. or apply for refugee status from outside the U.S., are admitted annually.*"

"Read that other part about papers."

"*If an asylum seeker is inside the United States and has not been placed in removal proceedings, he or she may file an application with U.S. Citizenship and Immigration Services, regardless of his or her legal status in the United States. However, if the asylum seeker is not in valid immigration status and USCIS does not grant the asylum application, USCIS may place the applicant in removal proceedings, in that case a judge will consider the application anew.*"

Deputy Canfield looked up and removed his glasses. "So don't he say he was on the run? They came for him and he took off with the kid."

"He's still gotta have his day in court. 'Regardless of his or her legal status.' That's the law."

"So there's our answer, huh?"

Sheriff Al shrugged. "Well, he hadn't broken any city or county laws...yet. Can't charge him with trespassing if Pennebaker don't ask for it. No vagrancy, no disturbing the peace, no inciting a riot, no littering–he's just a G.D. illegal, that's all."

"Guess we just leave 'em be."

Al glowered at the Deputy. "You have no idea what kind of hell this nation is in for. They're gonna be coming in boatloads, tractor trailers, buses–hell, millions of 'em just walking over each other to get across the Rio Grande. You want one of your kids to marry a Muslim?"

Wayne shook his head, confused. "I hadn't really thought about it."

"Course you hadn't. You go home at night and settle into your massage chair and watch 'Dancing With The Stars' with Tanya and the kids and you don't give it two hoots in hell."

Mouth open, Wayne said, "Uh-huh."

"You're like every other asleep-at-the-wheel American who doesn't, or won't, see the impending disaster coming our way."

Wayne smiled and cleared his throat. "You know, Al, I did vote Democrat in the last election."

"And you admit it! That's the part of you, Canfield, that I just don't have a clue where you're coming from. You seem normal in every other way–and yet you vote Democrat?"

"Bothers you, doesn't it?"

"Bothers me that you take the easy way out."

"How so?"

"You're soft on the issues that truly stand for something in this country–illegal immigration, religious freedom, less government interference in our lives..."

"Which bathroom to use if you don't look the part labeled on the door?"

"It's not funny, none of it. We're in a crisis the likes of which I've never seen and never hope to again. People need to wake up."

Wayne closed his laptop and stood up from the desk. "Well, I'm not gonna let it give me indigestion over lunch. You coming to the Dairy Queen?"

Albert stared at Wayne, frustrated.

"Bring me a chili dog and a Big Red. Diet Big Red. I got paperwork to do."

"You got it." Wayne put on his Stetson and started for the door, then he suddenly turned back toward the sheriff. "Al, you know why we can't all be fine, upstanding Republicans like you in this state? Who would we blame for all the crappy Hollywood movies if not the pinko liberals?" Wayne chuckled and walked out. Al grumbled to himself slumped before his aged, desktop computer. He slowly typed into Google Search, "Buxom babes in crotch-less panties." Staring at it for a moment or two, he deleted the previous line and typed in "Dealing with illegal immigrants for Texas County Sheriffs." Al then reached behind and directed the AC window vent to blow cool air on the back of his neck. He waited patiently for the data to rise up and edify.

***

Doc Finley finished snipping the last of the eight stitches now shadowed in pink ridges on Darcy's thigh. "Good as new. You got a free tattoo on your leg now and a Dum Dum sucker from the nurse on your way out. Life is good, ain't it?"

Darcy examined her itchy and still sore thigh. "Peachy. You gonna give me anything more for the pain?"

"No ma'am. That's why we have aspirin."

Darcy began pulling up her sweatpants. "Not near as fun as that codeine stuff you gave me. Man, did I sleep!"

Doc Finley nodded. "I bet you did–had some nice dreams, too."

"The best! Oh, I totally get how Delilah could get strung out on all her crack." She shook her head. "I'm just too control freaky. I don't have time to lose my mind. Sometimes wish I could, but I'd be living in a dumpster in about two weeks.

Lyndeckers can't do anything halfway. We never learned that talent."

The doctor smiled. "Is there any more on who did this to you?"

"Nope."

"Got any ideas?"

Darcy laughed. "We've ruled out the Easter Bunny and Santa Claus. Other than that–nada."

"Well, with our fine local 'vice squad' doing the necessary due diligence, I'm sure it won't be long before a suspect is uncovered."

"Uh-huh–and I'll be wearing a hairnet and orthopedic shoes by then. Later, Doc."

"So long, Darcy. Go easy on that leg, you hear?"

\*\*\*

Leaving the doctor's office, Darcy crossed Nueces Street and limped ever so slightly back toward the Dusty Rose. In certain areas of her life, things had definitely turned from the darkened corner that only recently defined her existence. The out-of-left-field offer from Pete Pennebaker was a stunner. Though she hadn't quite committed herself wholeheartedly to the idea of a bake shop (a Syrian bake shop!) adding to the Dusty Rose's overall prestige, she had to admit things were slowly turning around. And what to make of the bewildering announcement from Pettus: "Give your old brother a little time–he might just surprise you." What surprise? Lyndecker men were unsurpassed at exactly three things–steer roping, coyote shooting and beer drinking. Darcy couldn't possibly imagine what surprise might be fashioned from such singular talents. She sighed. "Never a dull moment, never a moment to dwell." Life in Rita Blanca was all about just staying on the Tilt-A-Whirl of life long as you could.

Crossing Nueces Street onto the courthouse square, Darcy

noticed from the corner of her eye Carol Ann Jansky getting out of her gold Jaguar coupe. She was hauling box after box of merchandise from the trunk, sitting each gently on the sidewalk like shipments of pirate gold. Her heart sank. How long had it been since Darcy had experienced the giddy joy of opening boxes of adornment: gifts, frills, trimmings–those extra special accessories that made a flower shop distinctive. She suppressed the urge to run across the lawn and pummel her royal blondeness. Not today Darcy, not today.

Just as she was about to push open the front door to the Shoppe, she glanced around again to see Carol Ann standing beside her trunk, hands on her hips, gazing intently at Darcy. It was so odd and peculiar, Darcy froze for a moment. Carol Ann suddenly waved a slow homecoming queen gesture at her then turned to retrieve her boxes. Darcy couldn't tell if it was a "fuck you" or a "have a nice day," or both? It genuinely threw her.

"This town gets crazier by the minute. We're all heading for the State Home for the Pixilated, no question."

\*\*\*

As she entered the Rose, Darcy noticed the air was permeated with something vaguely familiar. What was that? Spicy-sweet, like...

Adnan stuck his head out the kitchen door. "Oh yes, hello! I'm back here baking *gorayba* shortbread. Would you like to try?"

"Sure. What is that smell? It's very...I know that scent."

Adnan smiled. "Cardamom. It's a spice we use a lot in the Middle East. Here, try."

Darcy stared at Adnan as if he'd just unpacked a long-concealed armoire and laid the contents methodically before her. She slowly extended her hand as if robotically manipulated.

"Careful, they're still hot. What do you think?"

Darcy raised the cookie to her lips and bit gingerly. It was indeed delicious: spicy, sweet, bittersweet, almost pleasantly...woodsy.

"I've never tasted anything like it–but it's–familiar."

Adnan looked puzzled, then quickly changed the subject.

"Delilah said she had to run to the bank. She took Haya with her; they'll be back in just a few minutes." Adnan turned back to the kitchen. In an instant he brought Darcy something that looked like a steaming pita.

"It's *manoushi* bread. Try."

Darcy took the hot pita-shaped bread and bit another small piece. She bobbed her head in approval, sucking in gulps of air with each bite. She finally swallowed and studied Adnan's face. "I feel like I've learned quite a bit more about you today."

"How so?"

"You really are who you say you are. A very fine baker from the Middle East." Adnan smiled. "Who loves his daughter very much and would do just about anything to protect her." His smile turned to an expression of uncertainty.

Darcy swallowed again and grinned. "We need to get you advertised–get the word out. Rita Blanca needs to know there's a new star chef in town!"

Adnan's face suddenly fell. "Yes, but–my 'status.' Will it cause problems?" Darcy thought for a moment. "We'll tell everybody you're our cousin by marriage...from back east."

"But the sheriff, the deputy, pastor...they all know."

"They don't know anything till they see some papers, right?"

"Yes, but I don't have."

"I don't have papers either! Hell, I was born here, and I don't have anything to prove it. I'm sure there's a birth certificate in some courthouse, somewhere–but on my person? Nothing. Don't worry about it."

Adnan was not convinced. He nodded his head to show he understood, but not in agreement. He suddenly motioned to her leg.

"How is your...wound?"

Darcy looked down at where it lay bandaged under her jeans. "Itches a little–it's fine."

"I'm glad...glad you're better."

Darcy studied Adnan for a moment then began moving a collection of twigs and faux berries off the register counter. "I've probably told Delilah five thousand times to keep this counter clean. Does she listen? No. Do I always end up cleaning her mess? Yes."

The front door swung open and in walked Delilah and Haya, each holding an ice cream cone, followed by Deputy Canfield. Delilah spoke cheerfully. "Look who I ran into at the Dairy Queen!"

\*\*\*

Pete Pennebaker, Marty Pennebaker, Pettus Lyndecker and Nestor Morales stepped out of the Pennebaker ranch truck and stretched their legs. Pettus pointed as he began to speak.

"From that cluster of *Chapote* trees back yonder, along the fence, over that draw and down into the tank bottom...you see it?"

Pete nodded, shifting his cane from one hand to the next. Pettus continued, "...up along that ridge there and just this side of the pear flat–that's all of it. Best land we've got. Two years ago we planted the whole thing in fall legumes–peas, clover, soybeans. Finally got some rain, had a hell of a crop. Loaded the soil with nitrogen."

Pete spit. "How much you asking again?"

Pettus lifted his Stetson and rubbed a forearm across his brow. He wiped his hand inside the hatband and placed it back on his head. "We hadn't had it appraised, really no need to. I can let it go for what other folks been getting in the area."

Pete frowned and spit again. "Robbery."

Pettus pursed his lips and glanced at Marty. "I couldn't argue with you on that count, Mr. Pete, but it's not twenty years ago, not ten years ago–not even five years ago. Land around here today doesn't go for less than four thousand an acre."

"Robbery."

"I might could let it go for thirty-eight hundred.

"You could, could ya?

Marty, fully aware of the male knife dance she was about to broach, spoke carefully. "Daddy, I did hear that's what old man Clayton got awhile back for his place up on *Guajalote* Creek."

Pete jerked his head around, indignantly. "You did, huh? Did ya also know Bob Clayton was an old horse thief who never made an honest dollar his whole life? He sold that sorry place of his to a Dallas banker that wanted a bird lease for his grandkids to go hunting. Ain't no ranch people around here no more–all bankers and lawyers and 'sportsmen.'" Pete spoke the word 'sportsmen' as if it were an abscessed tooth bothering him.

"Well, Mr. Pete," Pettus ventured, "my people been here long as your folk. We ain't been near as fortunate as you, but we've held on to it all these years."

Pete dug his cane in the dirt again then turned to look squarely at Pettus. "I knew your dad, I knew your granddad. Tell ya the God's honest truth, I wouldn't a pissed on either one if they was running down the road on fire." Pete removed his hat and ran his fingers through his sparse dome. "But I'll say this for you, Pettus–you're a hell of a cowman. I seen ya working down at the sale barn, I seen ya picking up slack work on neighbors' ranches–you understand cattle and it may not mean much to a Dallas banker, but it means a hell of a lot to me."

Marty noted Pettus's expression. A rare-as-gold benediction from Lord Pennebaker had just been passed, and Pettus appeared genuinely moved. He coughed, hacked an squinted into the distance.

"I appreciate that, Mr. Pete...coming from you."

"Tell me why you're selling again? Something wrong with these hundred acres you're not telling me?"

Pettus shook his head. "No sir, look around. You can see for yourself–all improved pasture. I need to do some things for my family, that's all."

Pete rubbed his chin. "You know I'm already lending a hand to your two flower shop sisters."

"Yes sir. I appreciate that. But this is different."

Pete eyed Pettus a moment longer, then called out, "Nestor, we got any cold beer left in that cooler? *Traednos a todos un* Tall One."

Nestor scrambled into the truck bed and opened the massive Yeti cooler that Pete had welded in a cage to the sidewall. He retrieved four ice-cold bottles of Shiner and quickly uncapped each one with a chain-attached opener. This being Texas during the apex of summer heat, no one thought it the least bit odd having a cold beer at ten in the morning.

Raising his bottle, Pete toasted the others, "Deal, Mr. Lyndecker. I'll give ya $4,000 an acre. Not even going to haggle about it. Hurts my heart to see any of the old places start to break up. But I'd rather it be me than some G.D. real estate developer from Houston or Fort Worth."

Pettus took a long swig of beer and held the bottle to his forehead, contemplating. What must it be like to have enough money to drop four hundred thousand dollars on a poor man's butt like it was nothing more'n grocery store change?

Marty sipped her beer and smiled at Pettus. "Daddy, I think the least we ought to do is hire Cody and Thaine to come and 'rome' disc all this before planting a fall crop."

"I 'spect." Pete eyed Pettus. "Think you can talk those two

knuckleheads into making me a deal? I'm too poor now to pay 'em government wages."

Pettus laughed. "Sure, Mr. Pete, we'll make you a deal. Not a problem."

Pete took another gulp of beer and wiped his mouth on his long-sleeved cotton shirt. He studied Pettus again for a long moment, then spoke. "Mr. Lyndecker, if you'd accommodate an old man for just a moment–would you mind telling me what your intentions are toward my daughter?"

Marty nearly choked on her beer. Her face was crimson from embarrassment. "Have you lost your mind?"

"It's an honest question. He can answer or not. Is it some secret we're not supposed to know about?"

Marty shouted, "It's nobody's business, especially yours! I'm not somebody's chattel, for God's sake."

"You're my daughter, my sole heir! I don't have an interest where your life is headed? It's a question, not a threat–he can answer if he wants to."

Marty glanced at Pettus. He resembled a man thrown into a lion's den with nothing more than a nail clipper for armor.

"Well..." He cleared his throat. "I'll tell ya, Mr. Pete. I do...uh...I do love your daughter."

Marty turned away, unsure who, where or what to focus on. She finally fixated on her scuffed boot toe, unable to lift her head.

Pettus continued in a low drawl. "I've felt that way about her for some time now, but...but it's never the right time to say it, seems like."

"Hell, man, what you waiting for–bluebonnets at Christmas? I don't know the whole story between you two– don't need to know. But you shouldn't have to hide around like a buncha teenagers when everybody in the county knows about it."

Marty continued staring at her boot. "Why don't you ask me? Ask me what I think?" She glanced up at Pettus and felt enormous empathy for his obvious mortification. A rush of emotions tumbled forth–sadness, kinship, fealty–everything but the one sentiment noticeably missing. Love.

"I think the world of Pettus. Deep down, he's a fine man who's never gotten his due, not around here anyway. I like you a lot, Pettus, I do–I just don't like you in the way that you'd want me to. Like a wife. I can't make myself feel something that's not there. It wouldn't be fair to you or me or anyone. Don't you see?"

Pettus looked at Marty a moment longer, then stared off into the distance. The hurt in his eyes immediately made Marty regret saying anything. Damn you, Pete Pennebaker! Why do you always have to bat at everyone else's hornets' nest? She felt overwhelming remorse. The very last thing she intended to do this morning was kick Pettus Lyndecker in the stomach.

Pete sighed. "Well, the lady has spoken her piece. I 'spect there's no more on the subject to be divulged. I rest my case."

Pettus turned to Marty angrily. "You say you don't love me, fine. But I know women–that's one thing I do know. I know when someone's faking and I know when it's real, and you have never not been anything but completely real with me. That is a fact! You can call it whatever you want but it was never a lie between us. Never!" Pettus threw his drained beer bottle into the bed of the pickup and began walking off down the dirt road.

After a moment's silence, Pete spoke solemnly. "You reckon that boy's gonna walk the three miles back to his house?"

Marty winced. "I would think he'd like to be alone right now. Daddy, how could you? Today, of all days. He's finally got some money to help his clan out. He's trying to turn the 'Lyndecker Luck' around–why do this today?"

Pete took his handkerchief out and blew his nose. "Sorry if I hurt your feelings, but I'd like to see you with something more than a fat bank account when I go. I messed up with your brother; I don't have to relearn that lesson." Pete turned and hollered, *"Nestor, vamos a la casa!"*

Nestor immediately placed the spare bottles back into the ice chest and returned to the driver's seat. Pete got in beside him and Marty walked over to the back passenger door of the Super Cab, still bewildered by all the morning's events. Not even noon yet–slight beer high, one broken heart, numerous splintered confessions, high finance and a down-the-road dejected wayfarer to retrieve. Life in Rita Blanca was many things, but predictable? Never.

*** 

Carol Ann stared up at the ceiling trying to catch her breath. Her most recently completed round of intense lovemaking with Cody had almost blown the café curtains off their rods. She was certainly no novice in the arena of carnal knowledge–an ex-husband and a slew of hit or miss Lotharios had trained her not to expect flawlessness in the bedroom. Just keeping track of where the ball was during a heated scrimmage was achievement enough. But Cody...Cody was...astonishing! The boy knew every button, every lever, every trick conceivable to transform Carol Ann into a wobbly heap of deep sighs.

"I think I may have a little gas." Cody grunted as he rubbed his stomach.

"What is it with you Lyndeckers and your stomachs? You want some Pepto?"

Cody shook his head. "What do you mean?"

Carol Ann leaned over and played with Cody's chest hair. "Now you know I used to date your brother. No big deal. He had a sensitive stomach too, that's all."

Cody sat up in bed, scratching his head. "Damn, you had to bring that up? Not exactly what a guy wants to hear after making love."

"But you were sooo much better, Cody. I mean it–I think you're the best I've ever had."

"Yeah, sure."

"Why would I lie? You're amazing."

"Because you want me to do something I'm not sure I ought to be doing."

Carol Ann pulled him toward her. "Baby, this is different! We just made mind-blowing love. Let's not talk about other worries when there's more important things at hand."

"Like?"

"Like where did a cowboy like you learn to be such a good kisser?"

Cody grunted, pushing his bangs off his forehead. "Practiced on my horse."

"Lucky horse."

Cody leaned over and cupped Carol Ann's breast in his hand. "I'll say this, woman–you do know how to get a boy excited."

Carol Ann feigned surprise. "Again?"

He smiled. "Must be one of those Lyndecker things." Carol Ann giggled. Time to saddle up again and ride to the ridge where the West commences.

\*\*\*

Chito stood at the sink and examined his just-shaved face. It was a decent face–clean, friendly, some interesting character lines, good eyebrows, nice smile. Since he was a boy, people had called him "handsome." He felt he looked all right, sure, but handsome? Handsome was manly, broad-shouldered, deep-voiced...and lots of other not quite definable features, like those of, say...Pettus. Now there was a man. Shameful the era of popular Western films had waned. Pettus would've been a major star with his rugged good looks and self-effacing charm. He loved to watch him do anything–walk, sit, talk, smile, frown–it was all quite captivating to Chito. Instinctive magnetism, that sly smile, a totally natural, non-gym-ballooned physique, those roguish eyes...stop!

Chito finished drying his face and putting on sunblock. Like all good gays, he moisturized religiously. Sure, we're all going to get old and pruney–but does it have to happen tomorrow? A little routine everyday–you can visually knock off a number of years from your age. Not that age was so intimidating anymore. He was forty and glad to be forty. All that youthful posing and pretense! Pretty to look at–not so pretty to be desperately chasing one's former glory with denial and surgery.

He stepped into Tom's bedroom and looked around again. Was it a mistake coming here? Was he overstepping boundaries, appearing too needy, in search of some kind of paradoxical consent from the mythical Pennebaker clan? It was more than generous of Marty to make the offer and he accepted after only a brief deliberation. But still, was he himself now slowly, senselessly, drifting toward another version of "house arrest" as Tom had so tersely labeled his developmental years at *Los Abuelos*?

Putting on a clean shirt and pants, he walked into the hallway and aimed for the kitchen. The house appeared to be empty. Where was everyone? Entering the butler's pantry, he could see Jacinta out the back window watering canna lilies at the far end of the yard. Passing the Sub-Zero, he opened the massive doors and retrieved a bottle of water. Damn, you could store three months of groceries in here, he surmised, observing the copious shelves of produce. He then turned and walked back toward the living room. Passing the hallway cactus paintings, the horse paintings, the cattle in green pastures paintings and the Frederic Remington rip-offs–it was clear to Chito who held majority rule in art acquisition at present–and it wasn't Marty. Nothing wrong with Western art, he thought, but it was kind of like collecting Hummels. A little less is a little more.

Chito approached the front door, followed closely by the house dogs who were sniffing and snorting in hopes he might be concealing bacon somewhere on his person. He waved his hand futilely. "Get back...down! *Olvidate!*"

Opening the door, Chito searched around the front porch for the likelihood of a newspaper, a magazine, even an advertising flyer stuck in the mail he could pass the time with. What he saw instead was Pettus Lyndecker sitting on the front alcove bench, staring back at him dolefully.

"I rang the bell, nobody came."

Chito blinked, unsure if he was actually seeing the real deal or some apparition. "I was in the back bathroom shaving. Jacinta's out watering in the yard, come...come in." Pettus rose slowly and began walking as if in some kind of haze, ignoring the horde of canines now turning their full attention on him.

"Get back dogs, get back! How long have you been out there?"

Pettus shrugged. "Ten, fifteen minutes. Marty here?"

"No, I don't think so. I slept late this morning and when I got up everyone was gone."

"How long you been staying out here?"

"Just a few days. Marty invited me and...well, it's a little nicer than the motel."

Pettus nodded and looked around the living room, his eyes taking in every detail with methodical consideration. "They got a lot of stuff, don't they?"

Chito started to speak and Pettus interrupted, "We got a lot of stuff too, but it's all crap. Pennebakers' got taste, money buys taste...that's what they say."

Chito stuffed his hands in his pockets awkwardly, "What brings you out this way?"

Pettus turned to Chito looking as if every misery on earth were dragging him deep into hell. "You ever been in love?"

"I was married."

Pettus huffed, "I was too, twice–but I wouldn't call it love. More like getting your rocks off on a semi-regular basis. Not too romantic, huh? Well, now I am truly, deeply, undeniably in love–I suspect for the first time in my life and it's eating at me like battery acid." Pettus stared at Chito with such fierce determination it caused him to flinch. "How do I get Marty to love me back?"

"I don't know. I don't know if such a thing is possible."

Pettus continued, undeterred. "I have money now! We have the best sex I've ever known! We're both from here, this is our country–hell, we look *right* together! It's like it's meant to be and she can't, won't, accept it."

Chito looked at Pettus helplessly. What could he possibly say that would make any difference? "Would you like...something to drink? A glass of water?"

Pettus turned resolutely. "Got any whiskey?"

Chito's eyes widened. Nine in the morning? This is dead serious. "I have a bottle of scotch in my room, Tom's room...would you?" Chito motioned down the hall and Pettus began lumbering toward the rear bedroom, weaving slightly. "Have you already had a few this morning?"

Pettus shook his head. "Just a belt outside–in the pickup. Knocks the cobwebs out."

They entered Tom's room, which suddenly seemed claustrophobic with melancholy. Chito wished he'd taken down some of the '90s teenage ephemera, at least to diminish the overall sad museum impact.

"So this is Tom's room. Never seen it before." He shook his head, gazing at the wall art. "Man, they don't want to let him go, do they?"

Chito walked toward the bathroom. "There's a couple of glasses in here. You take it straight or a little water?"

"Straight, neat. You sleeping in Tom's old bed–what's that like?"

Chito stuck his head out the door, "Lonely."

"I'll bet."

Chito pulled the bottle of Johnnie Walker out of his suitcase and poured, handing one of the glasses to Pettus. "I don't think I've ever had scotch this early in the morning."

Pettus took a long swallow, then wiped his mouth. "First time for everything, isn't there? I mean, don't get me wrong-sex is wonderful, but when you finally meet someone that you connect with here..." He pointed to his heart and then his head "...and here. Well, that's what we all want, isn't it?"

Chito nodded. Pettus patted the bed beside him. "Sit."

Chito sat hesitantly on the opposite edge of the twin daybed. Pettus put a hand on his shoulder. "You're good people, Chito. There's so many bullshitters around here, feels like living in a latrine sometimes. You don't mind me talking this way, do ya?"

"No."

"You got a little more?" Pettus held up his glass and Chito poured.

"Thing is-I'm tired of playing the field. Really and truly, God's honest truth. I just want to settle down with one gal and have a nice, peaceful, sweet little life. Anything wrong with that?"

"No." Pettus moved his hand to Chito's neck and began rubbing. "Maybe you can put in a good word for me with Marty. She likes you a lot." Chito immediately rose from the bed.

"Yes, I'll put in a good word for you. Sure will. You do a favor for me as well? Respect my feelings too, okay?" Pettus looked dumbfounded.

"Course...what?"

Chito shook his head in frustration. "Pettus...I told you...I'm a gay man."

"So?"

"So. I have feelings, too."

"Course you do."

Chito shook his head. "What if...what if I had feelings for you...in the way you feel about Marty?" Pettus looked at Chito blankly, then slowly fell back on the twin bed, his head bumping the wall and his mouth half-open in stupefaction. Slowly, methodically, he began connecting the dots.

"Oh man, man...I'm sorry..."

"Don't be sorry! Anything but pity."

"There's no pity. No way–I mean it. I think you're a really cool guy. I don't want there to be any weird stuff between us."

Chito exhaled sharply. "Forget it.   Let's just forget it." Pettus suddenly rose up from the bed.

"Aw man, no hard feelings, really. How 'bout a hug." Chito wanted to run from the room. What kind of torture was this?

"No, it's okay, really..." In an instant Pettus had his long arms around Chito, pulling him close in a "brotherly" embrace. He smelled of man and Johnnie Walker. After a moment's pause, Chito lifted his hands from his sides and placed them tentatively on Pettus's waist.

And then it was over.

"Buds? We buds?" Pettus grinned at Chito. Chito felt himself slowly falling back into his body. About a zillion neurons got lit on that squeeze. Did Pettus have any idea of what had just occurred on the opposite side of that impromptu embrace? Chito couldn't decide if it was a deliberate tease or just some straight guy placating a gay boy.

"Sure...buds."

"Damn, Chito, you're a good-looking guy. I imagine you could have your pick anywhere you went."

"Think so?"

"I knew a single gay guy up in San Antonio a few years back but I've lost track of him."

"Really."

Pettus frowned, studying Chito's expression. "Tell me– what do you see in other guys? Big muscles, hairy chest–guess it goes without saying, a big dick?"

"Why not? The main parts are here...and here, as you put it." He replicated Pettus's previous head-to-heart gesture. Pettus smiled.

"Gotcha. Well, bud, I honestly wish I could be gay sometimes. True! I've had nothing but bad luck with the ladies. I love 'em to death but I usually get kicked in the teeth."

Chito shook his head. "Why would it be different if you were gay?"

Pettus shrugged. "I guess I could kick back and it wouldn't seem near as awful, would it?"

Chito laughed. "So now you know how I feel. I just hope you're not going to make me suffer because I was upfront with you."

"Hey, man." Pettus reached out once more to embrace Chito and Chito stepped back.

"Ah-ah...you keep doing that and I'm not going to be responsible."

Pettus laughed. "I told ya Tom and I messed around. Hell, I was in prison for a year–I didn't sit on my hands the whole time reading the Bible. Nobody did!"

"When did you read the Bible, last?" Marty suddenly entered the room carrying dry cleaning and a Walmart shopping bag followed by a passel of dogs. "Hello, Pettus. What are you guys up to?"

Chito quickly moved toward Marty while Pettus abruptly transformed into a full-on mute.

"Pettus came by to visit. I was showing him around some; I hope it's all right."

"Of course. Pettus, you've seen the house before, haven't you?"

Pettus stared blankly. "Not really."

"Well, let me get rid of this stuff and I'll give you the two-dollar tour."

He shook his head. "I gotta go."

Marty looked surprised. "You don't have to run off." She noticed the bottle of scotch sitting by the bed. "Are we celebrating, mourning, or both?"

Chito half-smiled. "We were just...toasting to Pettus's recent business sale."

Marty nodded. "Ah. Well–don't let me get in the way of the celebration. Pettus, won't you stay for lunch?"

They both looked at Pettus, who still appeared unable to formulate words. "I...gotta go."

"Right. Well, good of you to drop by. I'll just..." Marty motioned down the hall with her hands full. "...Later." As she walked away, Chito turned to Pettus, baffled.

"Why didn't you say something? I thought you wanted to see Marty?"

Pettus, dazed, shook his head. "I do, I did...I just...can't get it out. She's already down the road on me, for sure." He suddenly reached out, grabbing Chito with both hands. "You gotta help me!"

"Help you?"

"You and Marty are friends. Talk to her about me. Tell her I'm sincere, tell her I'm not a bad guy...man, don't you see...I love her!"

Chito stepped back, shaking his head. "I'm here to settle issues of my own. Sorry, but I'm not the one to be your go-between."

Pettus put his hand on Chito's neck and pulled him close, whispering in his face. "Help me, I'm dying here. I'll do anything...anything."

# CHAPTER ELEVEN

Deputy Canfield removed his Stetson and fanned his face. "Hot one out there today, for sure. Darcy, you doing okay?"

"Great. How you been, Wayne?"

"Fine, fine. Ran into your sister here...and the little girl down at the Dairy Queen. Reminded me I needed to pay y'all a visit."

"That's nice. You come to buy some flowers for that beautiful wife of yours?"

Wayne blushed. "Well, I probably ought to. Actually, I wanted to address a rumor going round."

Darcy snorted, "In this town? No way!"

"Way. Word has it you're opening up a bakery here."

"A bakery! Do tell. I wonder who started that story?"

"It doesn't really matter, I guess the point is...sure smells like something's been cooking in here."

Darcy waved her hand at Adnan, standing in the kitchen door. "I believe you've met Mr. Hakim. Yes, he's been doing some baking for us. Adnan, why don't you offer Deputy Canfield one of those wonderful breads you just made?" Adnan turned back into the kitchen. Delilah, finishing her ice cream cone, spoke up.

"You've never tasted such wonderful things in your life, Wayne. Oh, he's a magician in the baking department."

Wayne scratched his chin. "I'll bet, I'll bet. I'm afraid we have a little problem though." Darcy and Delilah's eyes were suddenly glued on Deputy Canfield. "Seems you don't have a permit to run a bakery out of here."

At that moment Adnan appeared, smiling, with the *manoushi* bread in a paper napkin. He handed it to the deputy, who self-consciously took a bite.

"Good. Real good."

Darcy spoke. "Isn't that incredible? And you should try his cookies. He made a pistachio cake the other day that was out of this world...How much is the license?"

Wayne finished chewing, then swallowed. "Not as simple as all that. You got to be inspected–health department, fire department, restrooms, adequate ventilation, parking, sanitation–all that's got to be addressed before you can get a permit to open a food service establishment in Rita Blanca. Hell, in all of Texas!"

Darcy shook her head. "Now, isn't that wonderful. Lived here my whole life and never knew local and state government was taking such good care of us. My goodness, that string of lowlife beer joints out near the Interstate must be run like the Mayo Clinic to have been operating as long as they have."

"They get inspected–when necessary."

"Uh-huh. So, what are we talking here?"

"First you gotta apply for a Sales Tax Permit. Then you need a Facilities Permit–zoning, construction and occupancy regulations. Then you need a Certified Food Manager–someone to insure safe handling of food by staff. Lastly, you need a Retail Food Establishment Permit. Oh yeah–and a three-compartment sink, commercial dishwasher, employee bathroom, properly operating and monitored cooking and food-storage equipment–and I think that's it. You still want to open a bakery?"

Darcy smiled. "More than ever."

"Suit yourself." Wayne nodded to Adnan. "Thank you Mr....Hakim, sure was good. We'll be checking back with you to see how it's going. In the meantime, make sure you're not selling any baked goods out of the Dusty Rose."

Deputy Wayne started to leave then turned back around. "Oh, nearly forget...one more thing. Sheriff Naylor's pretty much made up his mind he's going to have to see some paperwork from Mr. Hakim and the little girl. Just to make sure everything's on the up and up. Last thing anybody wants round here is the Feds snooping and trying to stir things up, know what I mean? Well–bye."

Darcy nodded with an exhausted expression as Wayne shut the door behind him. "Merry fucking Christmas. The high price of doing business in the Rita Blanca metroplex!"

Delilah spoke quietly. "But...Adnan has no papers. What does it mean?"

"Means just what you think. Well, it's not gonna happen! Not to them or anybody else."

Adnan shook his head. "We will go. God provides."

"You're not going anywhere. Lilah, watch things around here till I get back."

"Where you going?"

"Pete Pennebaker, who else? You got a better idea? What good's having all that money of his if he can't do something with it? Sell some flowers, huh?"

Darcy exited with a slam of the door. Delilah glanced at Adnan's disconsolate expression.

"I guess the good news is...we have a little more time to make ready for the bakery's big opening."

Haya walked over to her father's side and took his hand. *"Hal hu bikhayr 'abi."*

Adnan spoke to her softly. "'It's okay, daddy.' Remember, we learn something new in English everyday–*qulha bil injlizy,* 'it's okay, daddy.'"

Haya buried her head in her father's pants leg then looked back at Delilah shyly. "It's...okay...dah-dy."

"I taught her another one today at the Dairy Queen. What did I teach you, Haya? Remember?"

Haya clung to her father's leg, then said bashfully, "D.Q. Dude."

"Yes! Smart as a whip. She'll be speaking English in no time. I think she already understands way more than she lets on."

Adnan looked down at Haya and rubbed her hair. "Miss Delilah, you and your sister have been very nice. The town has been very nice. It makes me happy to know Americans who have big hearts. I wish there were a way...I just don't see our staying here."

Delilah quickly moved to his side. "No! You can't leave. You're saving our store for us. You're going to bring in all those new customers. You're putting us back on the map–we need you here. I...need you here."

Adnan stared at Delilah, thinking to himself how pretty she was in an unaffected, modest way. No frills, no mask, just...natural. "Well...I'd like to stay and so would Haya...but you must understand, we will not go back to Syria. Ever. If there's the slightest chance they might come for us, we will be gone before anyone will know. I give you my word."

"And I give you my word. You will not have to leave, I promise."

The shop's front door suddenly swung open and in walked Cody Lyndecker smoking a fat cigar.

"Cody, put that nasty thing out! You know we don't allow tobacco in the Dusty Rose." Cody looked around for an ashtray, a trashcan, anything. Not seeing an appropriate receptacle, he opened the door again and tossed the lit stub out into the street.

"Damn, that was a good stogie too. What y'all been up to?"

"Running a dinky town flower shop–one thrill after

another. What are you doing here—why aren't you out at the ranch?"

"Even the peons get a day off once a year." Cody reached into a nearby display and stuck a daisy in his ear.

"You've met Mr. Hakim, Adnan Hakim." Cody moved to shake Adnan's hand.

"Don't think I have, pleased to meet ya. And who's this pretty little thing?" Cody squatted down in front of Haya, who was still clutching her father's leg. He put his hand out to shake. "What's your name, darlin'?"

Adnan spoke. "She doesn't speak very much English. Her name is Haya."

"Haya? Well, I believe you're the first Haya I've ever met. Sure is a pretty name." Cody patted his shirt pocket. "I bet I got something in this old pocket for you. You think you can reach in there and grab it?"

Haya grinned and stared up at Adnan. He nodded. Timidly, Haya reached out and pulled a stick of gum from Cody's shirt.

"How 'bout that? You gonna shake my hand now or just leave me here all sad and blue?" Haya unwrapped the gum, popped it in her mouth and finally offered her hand. "Thatta girl!"

Haya spoke in a whisper, "Thank you."

"You're 'bout as welcome as you can be!" Cody stood up and looked around the store. "I heard y'all had hired a baker."

Delilah started stacking boxes on the counter. "We did just that—for about five minutes."

"What's up?"

"What's up is Sheriff Naylor's got his nose out of joint about Adnan not having the right papers to be here."

"Papers? What papers?"

Delilah sighed loudly. "They're refugees, Cody. They're running away from the bad people and they don't have the proper paperwork to be here."

Cody pulled the daisy from his ear and stuck the stem in

his mouth. "Well, why don't you marry him, Lilah. That'd make him legal."

Delilah stopped lifting boxes and stared at Cody. "I wouldn't put that in my mouth if I were you. Somebody somewhere didn't wash their hands after visiting the bathroom when they picked that." Cody, stone-faced, whipped the daisy from his mouth and placed it on the counter.

"But that's an excellent idea, Cody." Delilah walked over to where Adnan was standing in the kitchen door and stopped in front of him. "Mr. Hakim, Adnan...would you consider...the possibility of...matrimony?"

Adnan flushed and squirmed, a vision of prodigious anxiety. "Well...this is...different...something I had never...considered."

"Or me," Delilah spoke softly.

"If...the time comes...when such a measure would be...agreeable...I would not be...against...at all."

Delilah smiled. "I'm glad."

Adnan smiled back. "Yes...and me."

Cody suddenly coughed, hacked and moved to the front door, opening it to spit into the street. Turning back inside, he wiped his mouth. "Shit, I nearly forgot what I come over here for. Y'all want some gum?" Cody held up his pack of Wrigley's; they declined. "Carol Ann wants to make an offer on the place here!"

Delilah stared at Cody as if she'd suddenly gone deaf. "What!"

"Carol Ann wants to buy the Dusty Rose! What do you think about that? Idn't that what y'all been looking for—someone to turn this sinking ship around?"

Delilah walked decisively toward Cody. "Thank God Darcy isn't here. She'd snatch you baldheaded if she'd heard what you just said."

"What'd I say?"

"Sell the Rose to Carol Ann Jansky? Have you lost your

ever-lovin' mind? We'd just as soon become streetwalkers than sell out to that, that...tart!"

"Now don't be saying things just to be mean. What's the problem? I thought you were up to your eyeballs in debt."

Delilah motioned to Adnan. "We have a Master Baker working with us now! We have independent financing to see it all successfully launched. We're 'evolving,' Cody! We're going to be an 'Emporium' like Carol Ann–only better, bigger, newer, neater. You can't stop momentum."

Cody shook his head. "I don't know. I don't know about all these big plans of yours. I just know I been working hard on Carol Ann to cut y'all some slack. She's hell-bent on putting y'all out of business. She's got some strange ideas and I really thought I was coming in here to make everyone's day."

"When did you and Carol Ann get so chummy?" Suddenly Delilah's face fell. "You didn't sleep with her, did you?"

Cody sheepishly studied the floor. "What if I did? That's my business."

Delilah took a deep breath. "Cody Joe Lyndecker–sleeping with the mortal enemy. I never thought I'd see the day."

"Oh hell, you didn't raise a stink when Pettus was squiring her around."

Delilah gasped. "Pettus is a man! You're still a short-drawer kid who doesn't know tit from tat."

Cody grinned. "Well, I don't know about the tit part."

"Nasty!" Delilah sat, thoroughly depleted in a nearby chair. "Unbelievable."

"Don't you even want to know how much she's offering?

"No! How much?"

"She said for one of y'all to call her and she'd tell you personally. Well, I did my part, that's what I get for trying to help. Just hope nothing bad happens."

"What does that mean?"

"Nothing. Just...be smart, Don't take anything for granted." Cody walked over and opened the door and left, slamming it behind him.

\*\*\*

In all honesty, eighteen-year-old Thaine Jerome Lyndecker had never been on an actual date in his entire life. Nobody his age really did that kind of thing anymore. They hung out, they hooked up, they partied, they met up–but "date?" Who did that stuff? It was like an aberration from some lame Drew Barrymore movie. Skeevy shit.

Thaine squirmed in the front seat of Darlene's van. No wheels of his own, broke, with zero prospects for any weekend action of any kind, he let Darlene talk him into a freakin' "date" with Lucille. Why did he always let Darlene connive him into these atrocities? He knew the outcome already. Nothing in common, nothing to talk about–two space aliens trying to learn each other's language. Maybe some sweaty petting at the end, a quick feel and then the pre-programmed, red-faced shove off. Where did she find these virginal freaks, anyway? Was there some app on the Old Movie Channel for goofy, celibate girls?

"Talk about movies. She'll like that. You like movies.  Talk about your favorite movies."

"Yes, Mother."

"And don't be all grabby! Lucy's a nice girl. Let her steer the course–not everybody's got sex on their mind."

"Yes, Mother."

"I'll be back when I get off my shift at eleven. You don't have to tell her you don't have a car. Not everybody in high school has a car. It's not a requirement, you know."

"Yes, Mo...so why don't you leave me your van and I'll come pick you up at eleven?"

"Nice try. Remember the last time I let you borrow my car to go fill it with gas? You drove all the way down to the coast with your buddies. You think I'm stupid?"

"Yes, Mother." Thaine giggled and Darlene shook her head.

Pulling to a stop in front of Lucille's home, Thaine stared at the worn double-wide trailer landlocked behind a sagging chain-link fence. "Damn, they're as poor as we are."

"Her mother, Faye, is recently divorced. She and her brother are living here for the time being. They're nice people, don't be rude!"

Thaine opened the door slowly and studied the cracked concrete sidewalk.

"Well?"

"I'm looking to see if there's any dog shit out here."

"Get out! I'll see you at eleven."

Thaine exited the van and gazed at the off-kilter front screen door as if it were a guillotine. He felt like a man on his way to a circumcision ceremony. He'd tell the girl he'd just gotten a phone call–one of his hogs ate their Chihuahua and he needed to hurry back home. Hell, he'd walk all the way. Anything was better than this looming tragedy.

Thaine knocked at the door for what seemed an eternity until finally it slowly opened and an eight- or nine-year-old boy stood there eating a bowl of cereal.

"Yeah?"

"Uh, hi...I'm here to see...um...Lucille."

"Nobody calls her Lucille except my mother and only when she's mad."

"What do they call her?"

"Jazz."

"Her name is Jazz?"

"Her name is Lucille, but they call her Jazz."

"So, do you think I should come in, or...what?"

"Are you the one going on a..." The kid immediately started laughing. "A date?"

Thaine nodded. "Yeah, that's me."

The kid stopped laughing and shook his head. "Oh man,

whatever." He pushed open the torn screen door and Thaine entered the shag-carpeted, wood-paneled, sparkly acoustic tile-ceilinged living room.

"What's that smell?"

"You mean the cat pee or the potpourri?"

"Smells like...cinnamon toast and...Pine Sol."

The kid shouted, "Woo-hoo! We have a winnah." He then took another bite of cereal. "My mom likes potpourri. The Pine Sol's to hide the cat pee. But I still smell it, don't you?" He held out his cereal bowl. "You want some Sour Patch cereal?"

"What is that?"

"Sour Patch candy mixed with corn flakes. It's crack for kids."

Thaine shook his head. "No thanks.  Is...Jazz around?"

"She's getting ready. So tell me...what's your gut-feeling about Joe Biden?"

"Huh?"

"I'm into politics. You think Emmanuel Macron's a complete fraud?"

"Huh?"

He sighed deeply. "Never mind." Suddenly he yelled out, "Hey, Jazz, your..." again, he burst out laughing, "date's here!"

Thaine glared at the kid. "What's your name, bud?"

"It's James, bud–but my friends call me Thelonious."

"He's lying. His name is Jimmy and his friends call him Jimmy." Thaine turned to see one of the most beautiful, red-headed women he'd ever laid eyes on–on crutches. He stood abruptly, knocking over a coffee table figurine.

"Oh, sorry. Hi...I'm Thaine."

Jimmy made a face. "What kinda name is that?"

"Jimmy, shut up. Sorry, he's always like this. And you're not supposed to be eating that crud, what did Mom tell you?"

Thaine turned to Jimmy. "It's a family name, actually. It's Scottish for 'Landowner.'" Thaine smiled. "That's what they tell me, anyway."

Jimmy belched and stuck another spoonful in his mouth. "Thrilling."

"Okay, go to the kitchen or go to your room. Out!" Jimmy leapt from his chair and walked off for the kitchen, fake-limping and singing loudly, *You take the high road, and I'll take the low road, and I'll be the one there 'afore ya!*"

"He watches lots of old movies."

Thaine nodded as he studied the cast on Jazz's leg. "What happened to you?"

"Skateboard contest in Victoria. I came in third. Would've won but I was pulling a bluntslide with a hip ollie and I slammed my ankle on the pole jam. You skate?"

Thaine stared at her with his mouth open. He was irretrievably, unimaginably infatuated for the first time in his life.

"No. Like to learn some day."

"I can teach you. You got a dirt bike? Blades? You ski, motocross...what?"

Thaine shook his head slowly. "No. We live on a ranch. We've got horses."

Jazz beamed. "Awesomeness! Oh man, I love horses! I've just never been around them much."

"I can teach you how to ride. No problem."

They stared at each other shyly. To anyone with an ounce of acuity, it was patently obvious both their "Happy Meters" were dialed on twelve noon.

Thaine pointed to her leg. "So, how long you gonna have that on?"

"My mom says another month at least. She's one of the head nurses at County Hospital."

"Yeah, she works with my sister."

"Right! I knew that–spaced for a minute."

"How come I haven't seen you around?"

"We moved here a couple of months ago from Houston. My parents got divorced. Mom got a job in Rita Blanca." Jazz gazed awkwardly out the window.

"Kinda sucks, right?" Thaine said, surprised at himself.

"It's not so bad. I mean, it ain't great either but...I guess when you got some friends..."

Thaine felt something completely unexpected welling up inside him. He suddenly wanted to protect this girl, help her, be with her. It was definitely a different sensation from the usual persistent craving for sex that permeated his tormented existence. Was this...could this be...*love*?

Jimmy entered the room again, gnawing on a Slim Jim. "I'm bored. You said we could go to the library and cruise their old DVD collection."

"Quit eating! Were gonna have dinner at six."

"I don't like frozen pizza. I want Mexican food."

"We don't have Mexican food." Jazz turned to Thaine. "I'm sorry, but Mom got called in this afternoon and I'm stuck watching him. I'm really sorry."

"No problem. I know a little Mexican food joint not too far from here. You think we could walk down there?"

Jazz smiled. "That sounds good. I can still ride my bike."

Jimmy bellowed, "Woo-hoo! Mexican food!" He then began dancing provocatively around the room. "*We're having a heat wave, a tropical heat wave. The temperatures rising, it isn't surprising, she certainly can can-can.*"

Thaine and Jazz watched him, mystified. Thaine turned to Jazz and she shrugged. "I don't know where he gets this stuff. My mom says there'll be years of therapy ahead; let them deal with it."

As Jazz started to rise from the couch she momentarily lost her balance wrangling with the crutches. Reflexively Thaine thrust his hands under her arms to balance her, and the two locked eyes.

"*Be my love, for no one else can end this yearning, this need that you and you alone create.*" Jimmy stood facing the two of them with both arms dramatically extended as he belted out

Mario Lanza.

Thaine, wide-eyed, leaned into Jazz's ear and murmured. "Your brother's definitely going places. Might be pretty interesting to see exactly where."

# CHAPTER TWELVE

Sheriff Al turned off the patrol car's ignition and raised the brim of his straw Stetson. The car's air-conditioner needed more Freon but there wasn't enough money left in the monthly allocation to sanction it. So, the AC continued to blow out semi-cool stale air and Al continued to sweat through another summer of Texas heat. And that's the way the *bolillo* rolled.

The Rita Blanca Dairy Queen was the locus of all things essential to civil existence in Kokernot County. People came here after funerals, weddings, divorces, elections, break-ups, graduations, *quinceaneras* and baptisms. They also came before clandestine affairs, car jackings, robberies, court appearances and murder raps. A consecrated temple of soft-serve ice cream egalitarianism. It was also the unofficial office of Pete Pennebaker when in town on "urban bidness."

Al entered the mercifully cool eatery and thought of nothing more satisfying than a big old double-swirl, chocolate dip ice cream cone right then and there. But he could hear his wife, Zoe, chewing him out for gaining more weight after the doctor had demanded he lose some at his last checkup. So, the thought died a hasty death. Doctors and wives–joy killers of late middle age.

Seeing Pete in his usual corner spot to the right of the front entrance, far enough away to see and still be seen, Al edged his way over, nodding at townsfolk and strangers alike.

"Hello, Marshal Dillon. Sit on down here and tell me something good." Pete grabbed Al's hand and the two shook once then released grips, avoiding the gyrations required of the newly acquainted and eager politicians.

"Wish I had some good news. Say we might get a little rain next week–'bout all I can muster."

"Dry as a can of salted peanuts. Here it is only June. We'll all be eating prickly pear come August."

Al eyed the banana split Pete was rapidly finishing. "Why is it when you're really young and really old," he pondered, "it seems you can eat anything you damn well please? Probably 'cause you don't give a hoot in hell about the consequences. Either going to live forever or you're not. Who gives a damn?"

Pete smiled. "How you doing, Sheriff Naylor?"

Al glanced up at Sandy, who was holding a glass of water. "Hello, Sandy. Omar still up at the hospital?"

"Memo. He got out two days ago. Broke a few ribs and his left hand."

"Damn, I hate to hear that. Well, I 'spect it coulda been worse. You tell your mama and daddy to come by and get all the peaches they want in my backyard. Old trees are just falling over with peaches."

"Yessir."

Pete wiped his mouth and shoved the plastic banana split bowl away. "When you and your brothers coming out to go riding again? That old sorrel mare you rode last time been looking for you."

Sandy's eyes lit up and she grinned with delight. "Yessir, real soon."

"Well, don't take too long. She's been calling for Sa-a-a-a-ndy every day now."

Sandy laughed, then turned to Sheriff Al. "You want a double-swirl chocolate dip. Cone or a cup?"

Al looked at her with the defeated capitulation of a preacher in a whorehouse. "Make it one swirl on a cone...and no chocolate."

Pete squinted at Al. "How's that diet going, *compadre?*"

"'Bout like the cattle market–one day up, one day down. What'd you want to see me about?"

Pete took a long drink of iced tea then sat his glass down. "Need you to do me a favor. Lay off this fellow from Syria. He ain't doing you or nobody else a lick of harm. Let him be. He's working for me now."

"You got papers for him?"

Pete stared at Al and slowly rubbed his chin. "Papers. You mean like Nazi Germany had papers you had to show every time you went to take a crap? No, he ain't got those. He got something better. Me. And a job that pays. And taxes and social security that goes to Uncle Sam and Uncle Texas and everyone else that gets their so-called fair share of a working man's dollar."

Al exhaled and ran his fingers through his thinning hair. "He's got to have work papers if he's going to be legally employed in this city, this county, this state, this country. And far as I know and you know, Mr. Pete, he ain't even a citizen and you for sure don't want the Feds down here stirring up that pot of piss."

Pete took a toothpick from his shirt pocket and began digging at a tooth. "Nothing more aggravating than a seed stuck somewhere you can't reach." He put the toothpick back in his pocket and smiled at Al. "Now let me tell you how this is going to play out. You're going to run for re-election next year, like you always do, and you're going to win, like you always do. And I'm going to help you, like I always do, with my usual support that comes in dollars and votes. *Comprende?* Now what you're going to do for me in order to maintain that job you've held all these years, that put three kids through college and took Zoe to Europe a couple of times–you're either gonna help me get those working papers for Mr. Adnan or you and Deputy Canfield are going to turn a blind eye to the entire situation and just say 'Good Day, Mr. Adnan' every time you see him and that precious child of his out on the street. How's that work for ya?"

"Here's your ice cream, Sheriff Al. I put just a spoonful of chocolate inside the cone for you. Kind of a little surprise." Sandra beamed at the sheriff. He turned to her, growling.

"I can't eat that. I'm on a Doctor's diet."

Sandy looked confused. "Well...I can't take it back."

"You eat it."

"I'm lactose intolerant. I can't eat dairy." Al glared at Sandy then grabbed the cone, stood and tossed it into a nearby trash receptacle. He then pulled out four dollar bills and handed them to her. "I told you I didn't want any chocolate. Pay attention next time."

Pete watched Sheriff Al's spontaneous performance with tight-eyed scrutiny. "You shouldn't oughta done that, Al. Lotta hungry people in the world."

"And they're all coming here for a free meal and a handout. Panhandling on every street corner, welfare trash. Who's paying for all that 'free' doctoring, schooling, housing–the American taxpayer, that's who!"

"You're probably right, Al, sure nuff. All I'm worried about is one man and one child–and he ain't no burden to nobody, so you can just rest easy on that one."

Sheriff Al chewed the inside of his mouth anxiously, his eyes darting back and forth between Pete and Sandra. Finally, he put his Stetson back on his head and without a word, turned and exited the Dairy Queen.

Pete exhaled deeply and took another swig of tea. "I don't think he needs to lose all that much weight, do you, Sandy?"

Sandy shrugged and began wiping a nearby table. "Maybe

a pound or two. He comes in here near every afternoon and orders an ice cream cone. Never said nothing to me 'bout a diet." Sandy stopped wiping and looked over at Pete. "How's he think we gonna pay Memo's hospital bills with no insurance and no money? My folks crossed the Rio Grande for a better life. We're not welfare trash. We're American citizens and we got a right to be treated equally." She noticed Pete's empty glass. "You want some more tea?" Pete shook his head and Sandy turned and walked back to the front counter.

Pondering Sandy's declaration, Pete stared out the window at an enormous, brand new RV hauling a bright red Jeep cautiously edging into the parking lot. "Couple of hundred thousand dollars' worth of 'entertainment value' there." Pete rubbed his stubbly chin and pursed his lips. "Oh, Sandy, baby–when has anyone in America ever been treated equally?'

\*\*\*

"*An immigrant who marries a U.S. citizen must apply for a green card (U.S. permanent residence). This is a long process involving many forms and documents. The immigrant can be refused entry if he or she is found inadmissible, perhaps because of a medical problem, criminal history, past immigration violations, or the U.S. immigration authorities' belief that the marriage is a fraud to get a green card.*"

Delilah looked up from the computer and stared at Adnan. "Well, it doesn't say we can't get married. We know that's legal anyway. It's just...we have to begin the process, that's all."

Adnan appeared worried. "Yes...process."

Delilah continued reading, "*As the spouse of a U.S. citizen (whether same-sex or opposite sex), you are what's called an immediate relative in immigration law lingo. That's good news, because there are no annual numerical limits on the green cards issued under this category, and therefore no waiting lists before you can apply.*" She again turned to Adnan. "See, it's not all doom and gloom. We just have to put our feet in the water and start swimming."

Adnan moved to her side and knelt beside her. "Delilah—you are the most wonderful thing that has happened to me in this country. You have given me hope—but more importantly—love." He rubbed her hand. "But you must be completely truthful with me. Are you sure this is what you want? It won't be easy. We will be frustrated and impatient with each other. We will no doubt have quarrels. I want for you—and myself—to be realistic."

Delilah reached out and put her hand on his face. "I do love you. I know for sure. The Bible says, *'If I have the gift of prophecy and can fathom all mysteries and all knowledge, and if I have a faith that can move mountains, but do not have love, I am nothing.'* Before you...I was nothing."

Adnan kissed her hands. *"When Allah wants two hearts to meet, he will move both of them, not just one."* He kissed Delilah. "Life is...baffling, no? But beautiful!" They embraced and held each other for a long time.

"*Laesh betukhn'au ba'dh?*" Haya entered the room, placing her hands on her hips. Adnan began laughing and Delilah looked at him, puzzled.

"What?"

"She wants to know why we're choking each other?" They both began to laugh and Haya grew indignant, stomping her feet.

"No! No good!"

Adnan walked over and smoothed Haya's hair. "It seems we have our first protester. I told you there'd be frustrations."

Delilah smiled. "Wait 'til my family finds out. There'll be fits no one's seen since Moses broke the Tablets."

\*\*\*

Marty stared at her forty-two-year-old nude body in the full-length bathroom mirror. "This is what middle-age looks like, kid. You were never Miss Hotsy to begin with, but it worked. Worked damn fine for years. You could frequently get what you wanted, and let's be honest, usually not what you needed. But in the end, you never gave this *corpus* you were born with all that much consideration. And now...now! Well, what's to be done? The sagging, the stretch lines, the wrinkles, spots, ridges, bumps, callouses, protrusions, intrusions, exclusions...I mean, what is this relentless attack of defects all about anyway? A life too well lived? They say nuns die with beautiful skin. Is wearing a shower curtain and a pillowcase on your head the beauty secret the world has been waiting for? Why doesn't Pettus recoil in horror at the sight of my degeneration? Is the man blind or just blindly infatuated? And now I've agreed to go swimming–with Chito–in the pool! Chito, the slim god of taut conquistador genes. God, I want him to like me. To see through this veneer of calamities and just...like...me. Is it asking so much? So what if he's gay? Lots of people are gay and in successful straight relationships. I mean, I don't know all that many but they're there! Why couldn't it work? We'd take cooking classes and couples yoga and travel to Puerto Vallarta. Does sex have to be everything? You know, sometimes just having a regular warm body nearby is all the serenity we can ever expect in life. And so, here I am, forty-two and never married, putting on a one-piece black swimsuit I would have snickered at my mother daring to wear outdoors. And I ask myself, "Is vodka truly the antidote to the fear and loathing we all experience on the down slope of our existence?" All I'm asking for is a little...kindheartedness...and a twist of lemon.

\*\*\*

Chito stood in front of the mirror staring at his nude forty year-old body and smiled. He never wanted to appear vain–but damn, he looked good for his age! No, he couldn't compete with the twenty-something studs that were all cock and swagger, but who wanted to mess with such one-dimensional posturing anyway? He preferred the class, brains, conversation, wit and affinity that comes with maturity. And if with maturity they were better than average attractive to boot–who's to say no to that? Indeed, if there were ever a perfect physical "type" that he was inclined to favor over another, excluding his late husband of course, it was probably Pettus Lyndecker. Of any male he'd ever crossed paths with, here was a perfectly content and at ease man totally aligned with his masculinity. He didn't try! There was no forced framework about him. He...just...was. And let's face it–most men today are complete messes. Am I confident enough, am I too confident? Am I smart enough, or trying too hard? Flirty, too flirty or just crotch dead? Cool with gay guys being raunchy, or generally incensed they might assume I was one of them. A fun guy to be with, or too full of himself to ever let anyone cross the façade barrier. On and on and on. Exhausting. Some mornings it didn't pay to even wake up.

Pulling on his black Speedo, Chito studied his reflection once more and pondered "The Marty Quandary." "I think Marty is–what's the word–maybe a little transfixed with me. A guy usually knows when someone's got a crush on them. The smiles, the extra attention, the overt niceness, a stray touch, the inadvertent bicep grab–all pretty standard obsession tactics. What to do? I've dated women, had sex with women, I like women very much. That's not the issue. If you hold a gun to my head, I just prefer men–for sex–among other fundamentals. Which is not to say sex with women is ever not satisfying. (When is sex not satisfying?) I just...what the hell do I mean? Tom always said I was a closet bisexual anyway. Maybe so. Who knows, who cares? I mean, a person can't be everything to everybody." Chito shrugged, "Unless they can."

He took one last look in the mirror and smiled. "I wonder if Marty ever invites Pettus over to go swimming?" Grabbing a towel from the bathroom, he padded barefoot down the hallway.

***

Pettus stared at his naked 45-year-old body in the cracked bathroom door mirror. Still wet from the shower, he studied the reflected landscape carefully. A purple bruise on his thigh from where the yearling kicked him, a cut on his right arm where he got caught up in barbed wire, a nick above his eye where the posthole digger fell on him and a big scabby knee–he forgot how that happened. All in all–not too ragged. Just needed a haircut, that's about it. He rubbed his hand on his flat belly and wondered what Marty was up to. God, he did enjoy that woman's entire substance!  Well, truth be told, Pettus liked sex–period. What else is there that's free, fun, exciting, passionate, satisfying, healthy and dirty all at once? And it made a body–and a mind–feel good. After a good round of lovemaking, Pettus always felt it was almost like going to church. The good part. Not the hell and damnation but the soulful, uplifting, you're-not-such-a-bad-person-after-all part. Felt like that down-to-your-toes satisfaction after a good steak dinner or watching a hell of a good ball game where skill and talent become a world of flawless ability. Or even getting that lump in your throat over some stupid movie that reminds you you're still alive and feeling. He never understood why some people seemed to feel "manly men" didn't have feelings. He had feelings all the time! He was overcome and overwrought with them daily. He just never showed it! He learned a long time ago there was no incentive in displaying outward emotion. Nobody wanted to see a grown man cry or rage. Nobody.

As he combed his hair, he thought about Chito living in the Pennebaker home. Was there some...? Nah. Chito and Marty? Not hardly. He's gay and Marty...why would she be interested in a gay guy? Ridiculous. And yet, he's there and you're not. Good-looking, Mexican movie star Chito Sosa living down the hall from Marty. The thought of the two of them–together–*that way*-made for an unfamiliar sensation. Something approaching jealousy, anger, curiosity and...*arousal*. Arousal? Did it turn him on thinking of the two of them together? Maybe. He wasn't sure. Pettus finished toweling off and stared again at his reflection in the mirror. "You going gay on me, boy?" he chuckled, then tied the towel around his waist and ambled off toward his bedroom.

***

Darcy and Uncle T.T. sat at the kitchen table and polished off what was left of the half watermelon from the fridge.

"You want a little salt on that?" T.T. held up the shaker.

"On watermelon?"

"That's the way I always eat it."

"Not me. This is too good and sweet. Where'd you get this at?"

"Old man Cantu was selling 'em outta his truck on the edge of town. Shoulda bought two."

"They are good. Thanks for saving me a piece."

"How's that leg doing today?"

"Fine, don't even notice it. Got a nice pink scar and a good story to tell."

"What's the Sheriff doing about it?"

"Sheriff Al? Case closed. He figures whoever it was is long gone. Now, if it'd happened to Marty Pennebaker, they'd have the governor down here with bloodhounds and the FBI."

Uncle T.T. nodded. "How y'all doing down at the store?"

Darcy took one more bite, sat the rind down and wiped her

mouth with a paper towel. "Tell ya the truth, I'm a little worried."

"Why?"

"We're still not getting the business we need. Mr. Pennebaker's forty-five hundred a month–divided between mortgage, utilities, phone, supplies, insurance, licenses, repairs, me, Delilah and Adnan–see where I'm going?"

"Maybe you ought to speak to Mr. Pete again? Ask him for a little more. He can afford it."

Darcy shook her head. "Not in a million years. That was a one-time shot. Up to us now."

Uncle T.T. tugged at his beard. "Your brother Cody really seeing that Jansky gal? That true?"

Darcy sighed. "That's what they tell me." She stood and rinsed her plate in the sink and placed it in the strainer. "I can understand him wanting to screw her–but do her dirty business as well? Really? My own brother?" Darcy yanked a towel from the oven door handle and began briskly wiping the counter. She stopped suddenly and turned back around. "I'll tell ya something, this family's not only crazy, we're mean and spiteful to boot. I don't know how we've all lived under this roof for so long and not killed one another. I really don't."

T.T. shoved his chair back from the table, smiling. "Don't you reckon it's cause we're the only ones around who even remotely understand each other?"

"What's that mean?"

"You don't choose your family, Darce. That's God's little gift to you. But I suspect somewhere along the way you're supposed to take the ingredients you're handed and make a meal out of it...otherwise you starve."

Darcy, frowning, turned to stare out the window, then back again at T.T. "I hate it when you go all philosophy on me. I really, really don't want to throw the towel in. We've worked too hard for too long. I know life is unfair. But once, just once, I'd like to prove to the world–to this stupid town–Lydeckers are not losers, not criminals, not trash! Just once I'd like to hear people say, 'Boy, those Lyndeckers are really chopping wood! Look at 'em go! Can't wait to see what they pull off next!'"

T.T. slid the plate of watermelon rinds before him and stared blankly at Darcy. As the oldest surviving Lyndecker male, he'd definitely experienced his measure of derision and loathing. It's true, they were never once offered the support or acceptance of the community at large. They were Lyndeckers–forever pigeonholed as county no-gooders and transgressors. And T.T. had lived up to that labelling by bungling nearly every opportunity that crossed his path. A once decent marriage, a daughter who drifted away, years of alcoholism, minor jail terms for theft and bad checks. Old and disabled now, he'd even forfeited what little land was once his, now surviving on family indulgences in a tiny back room. Darcy's words echoed in his head. "Just once–I'd like to prove to this town–Lydeckers are not losers." He pushed his chair back and stood, carrying his plate. Placing it in the sink, he placed a hand on Darcy's shoulder. She turned, surprised.

"Girl mine, you are not a loser. Never have been. Your time is coming. You just hold on and let it lie where Jesus flung it." He turned and slowly trudged back toward his bedroom. Darcy stared after him, shaking her head. "Jesus better get to flinging, Uncle T.T. This camel's back is ready to snap."

\*\*\*

Pete placed the rope halter around Dulce's neck and led her alongside the saddle room door. Sandy, Omar, Julio and Memo all stood wide-eyed and beaming as he led the big mare in front of them.

"Now, you always want to be easy 'round an old horse. No loud talk or jumping around. You gotta be calm and talk low and quiet-like."

"How old is she? She's really old, isn't she?" Julio whispered anxiously.

Pete smiled. "She's about twenty. But in her day she was a real champion, nothing else like her."

Memo, wide-eyed, with his arm still in a sling and a cast on his foot, stood behind the others timidly. "That's old."

"She's got a lotta life yet. Just like me–old as hell and still kicking." They laughed as Pete threw a thick wool blanket on her back. Dulce shook and shuddered at the sensation.

"She doesn't like the blanket," Omar spoke.

"She's just testing it out." Pete removed the halter and slipped a leather bridle over her head. He glanced at Sandy. "Sand, can you hold the reins for me? She likes it when you pet her nose." Immediately four small, brown hands reached out to stroke her. Dulce snorted once and appeared to enjoy the attention. Pete reemerged with a well-worn saddle that had definitely seen mileage. "This was my son Tom's first big boy saddle. He rode many a mile on it. Got a lot of good *juju*." Pete grunted as he slowly hoisted the saddle atop Dulce.

"What's *juju*?" Memo asked.

"Shhh! Don't talk so much." Sandra reprimanded Memo.

"It's okay. Everybody learns by asking questions. *Juju* is an African word for spirit. When you ride on Tom's saddle, you pick up a part of his spirit. That's what I believe, anyway." Pete pulled the cinch in tight and turned to his captivated audience.

"Who's first?" Everyone said "Me!" at the same time and Pete pointed to Sandra.

"I think big sister ought to go first, what do you think, Sandy?" Sandra stepped forward and stroked Dulce's mane. "Let's walk her over here to this tree stump so you can step up on it and save my old back."

"Yessir."

Together they walked toward the live oak stump, and with a small shove from Pete, Sandy flew up into the saddle. She glanced around, startled.

"Wow, it feels like I'm really tall!"

"Ride 'em, girl!" Pete led Dulce into the adjoining corral. "Just kinda walk her around in a circle. You don't have to yank on those reins. Move your hand to the right or the left and she'll follow your lead...that's it." Pete and the boys stood at the fence watching. Pete was about to call out again when a sudden pain shot up his left arm. Grimacing, he tried rubbing the ache away. Feeling dizzy, he sat down on the oak stump and lowered his head.

"Mr. Pete, you okay?"

Pete looked up at Omar, wincing. "Go get...my daughter...quick."

Omar turned and started running toward the big house. Julio and Memo stared at Pete Pennebaker, frozen. Pete glanced over at Sandra, now cantering in a circle, her face beaming with delight. He muttered aloud just before collapsing to the ground, "Ride 'em...ride 'em."

# CHAPTER THIRTEEN

Vonnie Pawlik, her daughter Tanya, and Billy Mapstone stood at the new Dusty Rose glass produce case and perused the delectables inside.

Vonnie pointed. "What's that called again?"

"*Baklava*," Adnan said, adjusting the tray of sweets.

"Yes! I had one of those in Houston once. Total mouth orgasm!"

Tanya pulled on Vonnie's pant leg. "What's...oh-gas-um, Mommy?"

Billy Mapstone patted Tanya's head. "Oh honey, it's like an adult word for fried chicken. Something you like a lot but you don't get to eat every day."

Vonnie squinted at Billy. "Brilliant." She turned back to the baked goods. "Now what's this over here?"

"*Ma'amoul*–it's made with dates, figs and walnuts."

"Oh, my. And this?"

"*Ghraybeh*–like shortbread, very tasty!"

"Decisions, decisions." Vonnie scrutinized the display case with the intensity of a bride choosing a wedding ring. "I may have to get some of everything. Tanya, don't tell your father."

Billy walked over to the far side of the store where Delilah was arranging ferns and gladiolas in a wreath. "Who died, hon?"

"Lou Emma Jenkins' Great Dane got run over out on the highway. She's having a viewing at three."

"Poor thing. I should probably run by and give her a quick blow out. Her hair's fine as lint. Takes almost a whole can of White Rain to get it right."

Delilah sighed. "I made the same wreath for her when her cat, 'Barbara Walters,' died. Oh, she cried and cried over that one, too. She'll probably need to be medicated to get through this."

Billy shook his head. "She keeps a big old bottle of Smirnoff in her dining room breakfront. That's about all the medicine she'll need. She and Smirny been friends for a looong time now." Billy turned to look at Vonnie and Adnan, then back to Delilah again.

"Little busy birdie rumor going around somebody's getting married soon."

Delilah looked up, surprised. "Who?"

"Now come on, Sugar Puss. We've known each other since kindergarten." He nodded toward Adnan. "You and Omar Sharif getting hitched?"

"Who told you that?"

"Sweetness, I know *everything*. I say bravo! 'Bout time you got a little rice in your hair."

Delilah blushed and continued with her arrangement. "Maybe. It's nobody's business."

Billy growled, "We gonna make it our business, Angel Puss! Girlfriend is NOT getting hitched without a little party-party!"

"Oh, Billy, I wish you wouldn't."

"When have you ever known me to not throw a shindig for one of my ladies 'bout to bite the bullet?" Billy glanced back at Adnan. "And from the look of things, I'd say it's a bigger than average bullet too."

"Stop."

"Let your wig down! Have some fun. I'm happy for you."
Billy suddenly grew teary. "Look at me. I'll never get married.
I'm good with it, I am. It's just...my girls are so special to me.
I want y'all to have the happiest lives possible." Billy suddenly
buried his face on Delila's shoulder and wept.

"Oh, honey. It's okay. We'll have a little party...or
something."

Billy lifted his head. "Hand me a tissue, Pumpkin. Thanks.
Sorry I lost it. But you deserve all the joy you can squeeze out
of life. You gotta take those slings and arrows and beat 'em
into rainbows! Just pound the shit out of negativity. You are
too fine to be anything less than magnificent, you hear me?"
Delilah nodded silently. "Do I look okay? Flushed? Eyes red?"
Delilah shook her head and Billy straightened his back,
exhaling. "I don't know where that came from. I've been
listening to my Marianne Williamson tapes again. So
powerful."

Haya, carrying Popo, entered from the kitchen and walked
toward Delilah with a worried expression. "Popo poo-poo."

"What, where?"

Haya pointed toward the kitchen. "*Ala al'ard fi
almatbakh.*"

Adnan approached with a concerned look and spoke to
Haya, "*Eish elly beyhasal?*"

"*Alqut beyatabawal ala ardyiet almatbakh.*"

Adnan looked at Delilah sheepishly. "She said the cat
made...an accident...on the roses in back."

"My new shipment?" Adnan nodded and Delilah raced
toward the kitchen. Billy stared at Adnan with the biggest grin
on his face. Adnan puzzled, smiled back. Suddenly, without
warning, Billy threw his arms around Adnan and buried his
face on his chest, sobbing.

\*\*\*

Cody Lyndecker strained uncomfortably at the necktie constricting his throat. He took another small bite of fish and swallowed hesitantly. Fish, other than fried catfish, really wasn't his thing. Cold-blooded mutants swimming around in all that slime? No, sir. Steak and chicken wings–good enough for any man.

Sitting at the Jansky's massive dining room table, Clayton and Barbara Jansky ate their meal in silence. Carol Ann took another sip of white wine and cleared her throat. "Did I tell you, Cody, that Daddy's John Deere dealership won the Onyx Award for being one of the top three dealers in the Southwest?"

Cody looked over at Mr. Jansky. "That's great, sir. Come with any cash or just the trophy? I had to cut back on my rodeo ropin' cause the dang prize money got so cheap. Takes a lot of cash hauling those horses around."

Mr. Jansky grunted and continued eating. Barbara spoke softly. "Would you care for some more wine, Cody?"

Cody looked worried, then laughed. "I'm not much of a wine drinker...I guess."

"Would you like something else?"

"Well...I sure wouldn't turn down a beer if you had one."

Carol Ann stood and headed for the kitchen. "I'll get it."

Clayton Jansky used his finger to remove a small bone, then wiped his mouth with a napkin. "Barbara tells me you and Carol Ann getting kinda serious."

Cody half-smiled and nervously swung a salad fork between his index and middle finger. "I guess so, yes sir."

"You got some work plans coming up?"

"Sir?"

"How are you currently employed?"

"Oh, I work on my family ranch."

"You get paid for that?"

Cody nodded, "A little."

"Make enough to support yourself, a wife and all her needs?"

Barbara pushed her chair back and rose. "I'm going to check on the dessert. May I take your plate, Cody?"

Cody handed it to her. "Thank you. No sir, I doubt that."

Clayton ran his tongue around the inside of his mouth, then used a finger to remove another small bone. "So here's the deal. Carol Ann thinks you're going to marry her."

"Now wait a minute..."

"Hold on. I'd rather see her marry a ditch digger than a Lyndecker."

"Nobody said anything about marriage!"

"Hold on. You clearly don't know my daughter. She pretty much gets what she wants and right now she wants you." Clayton muttered under his breath, "God only knows why."

"What about what I want? I'm not looking to get married."

"You want to keep seeing my daughter?"

Cody looked momentarily stumped. "Well sure, I like Carol Ann a lot, but I'm too young to get married."

"I married at twenty. Didn't know crap from cat shit. My wife and I grew up together. Marriage turns a boy into a man."

"Yes sir, but I'm not ready. No way."

"You want a job down at the dealership? I'll pay ya decent-nothing fancy. You work your way up just like everyone else. You need to cut out that rodeo shit and buckle down."

Cody's head was spinning. "Boy, that job offer sounds real good, Mr. Jansky. I just...well...maybe I should talk it over with my brother, Pettus."

Clayton slammed his hand on the table. "That sorry ass brother of yours nearly sent Carol Ann round the bend when he dropped her. I don't want to hear that bastard's name again, you hear me?"

"Yes, sir."

"Now, you use what sense God gave you and look a deal straight on. You want to continue seeing Carol Ann, you want a respectable job, you want to quit scratching a poor man's butt and grow up to make something of yourself? You better give it some deep thinking–and not too long either. Opportunity's a fickle bitch."

Carol Ann approached the table with Cody's beer. She smiled at her father. "Now what have you two been discussing?"

Clayton drained his glass of wine. "Cody seems like a reasonable fellow. I think he understands the way things work around here."

Carol Ann sat next to Cody and took his hand. "How do they work, Daddy?"

"You want something out of life bad enough, you do what it takes to make it happen. Otherwise, you're just sucking a dry titty."

Carol Ann giggled nervously. "Daddy!"

Clayton picked up his plate and stood. "There idn't a whole lot I wouldn't do for you, baby girl, but I will not abide lawbreaking, that's for damn sure."

Carol Ann looked at him, shocked. "What do you mean?"

"Everybody in town knows you're trying to run those two Lyndecker girls outta business. I don't know what it is with you and these Lyndeckers, but if y'all have some crazy-ass scheme you're dreaming up that edges on unlawful, I'll turn your devious butts in myself."

Clayton walked off toward the kitchen. Cody and Carol Ann, still holding hands, stared silently at the "Tuscan Sunrise Gold" painted wall before them.

\*\*\*

The nurse pulled the finger heartbeat monitor from Pete's hand and read aloud. "Seventy-five beats per minute. That's not too bad for an old cowboy who just had a heart attack."

Pete stared at her crossly. "What's bad is being strapped in this bed eating baby chow and farting fairy dust while some nurse tells ya everything's going to be okay."

Marty set down her magazine and rose from the chair she'd been sitting in across the room. "I told you he'd be a miserable patient."

The nurse tsk-tsked as she raised the motorized headrest on Pete's bed. "Doesn't bother me–I've had 'em all. Wait till he sees what a miserable nurse is like."

Pete looked at her askance. "You mean this is your cheery side?"

"You're about to get my laughing side when I give you your bath in a half-hour."

Pete looked at Marty, dismayed. "Jesus God–don't ever get old, Marty. Ain't no prospect in it, a'tall."

Marty straightened the comforter covering his feet. "You don't have much more to put up with. They said you could leave in two days."

The nurse snorted, "If he behaves himself."

"What do I gotta do? Make you a potholder?"

"You gotta do exactly what the doctor and I tell you. You're lucky to be alive, Mr. Pennebaker. If that ambulance had gotten stuck in San Antonio traffic another ten minutes, I doubt you'd a made it."

Pete spoke quietly. "Been all right with me if I'd a died right there in the horse corral. Hated scaring the children–but I shoulda gone right then and there."

Marty patted his leg. "Now come on. Enough of that."

The nurse picked up her tray of pills and started to exit. "They're always jolly like this after they've had that first little brush with destiny. They'll be back to their old rotten selves when we get done with 'em, idn't that right, Pappy?"

The nurse departed the room and Pete stared at Marty in horror. "One more crack outta Sunshine and I was about to take us both for a flying leap out the window."

Marty picked at some lint on her pant leg. "I talked to Pettus earlier this morning. The deeds are drawn up; he's ready for you to sign."

Pete put his hand behind his head. "Don't seem right, all these years. Poor people hanging on by their bloody knuckles and a prayer to some dried-up clump of dirt. Why now?"

"I seriously doubt the Lyndeckers are the praying kind. Why do people hold on to anything? It's usually all they have. Without something to call your own, you're what? Adrift, empty?"

Pete continued to stare at Marty, his eyes glistening. "You get it, don't you? Why don't you marry that boy? Give him something to hold onto. I know he's a little rough round the casing, but you're good with all that, Marty. Hell, you put up with me all these years!"

Marty smiled. "Just barely."

"I bet he could make a sterling individual with someone showing him a little favor. You take an old maverick bull been out in the brush since weaning; put him in a pen, fatten him up, don't wave your arms too much or yell at him–why, he'll turn into an old porch dog in due time."

Marty stood. "That's a nice image, Daddy. Too bad I can't marry someone with horns and a tail. What do you want me to say to Pettus? Shall he come by and have you sign here?"

Aggravated, Pete sunk pitifully back in bed. "Whatever you say, Marty, whatever you say. It's all gonna be yours soon enough. I've done and said all that's left in me. I'm ready to go be with your mother and brother."

"Fine. And when you're finished preaching from the pity pulpit, I'd like to get you out of this high price sickbay and back home to the ranch where you belong. I've got to run some errands. I'll be back around suppertime." Marty leaned in to kiss Pete's forehead. He turned away, slighted.

"I may or may not be here when you return. All in God's hands now, all in God's hands."

"When did you suddenly get so churchy?"

Pete glared at Marty. "Goddammit, I've always been spiritual! If you'd a spent more time around your old man instead of gallivanting around the world, you'd know what a deeply god-fearin' son-of-a-bitch I am!"

Marty shook her head, wide-eyed. "Thus endeth the lesson. I'll be back by six." She grabbed her purse and exited the room, leaving Pete to stew restlessly.

*** 

The Lyndeckers were clustered in their usual haphazard arrangement around the battered kitchen table, dining on fried Spam and SpaghettiOs, when Pettus, taking one last bite of Rainbo bread, shoved his plate back and wiped his mouth with an abandoned Kleenex.

"I have an announcement to make."

The others stopped chewing and looked at him as if they'd just spotted an Ivory-billed Woodpecker in the room.

"Where's Uncle T.T.?"

Darlene cleared her throat. "He said he had to meet someone in town." As she always did when nervous, she made the statement sound like a question.

"Delilah?"

They all glanced at each other and shrugged. "Darcy, where'd she go?"

"I don't know. She left around three and said she'd be coming back. What's the matter?"

Pettus wiped his mouth again. "I'd prefer to wait 'til everyone was here, but I need to hear from each of you now. So..." Pettus rubbed his chin and stared at his siblings. "I'm the head of this family. T.T. sold all his Lyndecker land twenty-five years ago. This here's the last of it. It ain't much, but it's ours; fence to fence, pillar to post, horsemint to horse apple. I've thought about this long and hard. Lyndeckers have always been slaves to the ranch. The cards we've been dealt. None of us was born into royalty. None of us ever got a break, a pat on the back, a 'job well done,' nada. I'm tired of scraping and scrapping. Tomorrow morning I'm meeting up with Pete Pennebaker to sell him the hundred acres in the hay field down by the creek bottom. He's paying four thousand dollars an acre–that's four hundred thousand divided by seven–fifty-seven thousand, one hundred forty-two dollars and eighty-five cents apiece!"

Silence. They continued to stare at Pettus as if now two woodpeckers were flying in the air. He spoke again. "Darlene, you got some money to put down on a new car. God knows you need one. Darce, you and Lilah can fix up that damn store for good and run Carol Ann outta town, for all I care. Cody, you and Thaine, I imagine, gonna be running this place one day along with your sisters. Get an education! I know you think you're smart enough, but you got room in those thick skulls for all kinds of knowledge. Learn a trade! Be clever. Don't be an old squanderer like me and hang out here hiding your whole life. You're good as anybody. Better. Prove 'em wrong!"

Pettus again stared intently at each of their faces. "Doesn't anybody have anything to say?"

After a long pause, Darlene spoke barely above a whisper. "You're selling part of...the ranch?"

Pettus nodded. "For you, for us...for all of us."

Darcy stared down at her plate. "What...would Mama and Daddy say?"

Pettus shook his head. "Probably not much since they're both dead." He then turned to look at Thaine and Cody. "Well?"

Cody looked up at Pettus red-faced and burst out, "Carol

Ann and I are getting married." Cody said the words so fast it sounded almost as if he were speaking a foreign language.

"WHAT?" Darcy's cry punctured the air like the dying shriek of a murdered hyena. "Have you lost your ever-loving empty-headed mind?"

"I love her! That's all there is to it."

"Love? You love her fake tits and her silicone ass, that's what you love!"

Pettus raised his hand. "All right Darcy, calm down."

Incredulous, Darcy shook her head slowly. "I don't believe it. My own flesh and blood turning against family–sleeping with the enemy!"

Cody leapt up immediately, knocking over his glass of milk. "I'm doing it as much for you, Darce! She wanted me to help her burn down your store, and I said no. And then she offered to buy y'all out, and Delilah said no. So we're leaving! She's putting the Emporium up for sale. You can take your new money and burn it down yourself." Cody threw his chair against the wall and charged out of the room.

Pettus turned to look at Thaine, who was now crying softly and dabbing his eyes with his sleeve. "What's the matter with you?"

"Nothing! I finally have somebody who loves me exactly for who I am. Even if I'm just a nobody...a nobody with a big heart. Y'all can all go to hell–I'm in love!" Thaine jumped up and ran from the room.

Pettus looked at his plate and slowly took another bite of Spam. "Well...this has been...informative. We've got Dreamsicles for dessert."

The back door to the kitchen suddenly opened and in walked Delilah, Adnan and Haya. Delilah was wearing a simple white dress with white hat and veil and carrying a small bouquet. Adnan appeared to have someone's old suit on and Haya wore a flowered dress.

"We did it!"

Darcy looked as if she'd just fled a roomful of shrieking bats. "Hol-lee shit!"

Bewildered, Darlene shook her head. "Oh...my...God."

"Hello, everybody–Reverend Korngold married us this afternoon in the Chapel of Our Lord Jesus of the Apostolic Faith."

Pettus simply looked at them, mouth open. "Why the hell didn't you tell us?"

Delilah beamed, "I wanted it to be a surprise!"

"But...you're a Christian...born again, repeatedly...isn't Adnan a...Muslim?" Darcy asked.

Delilah smiled. "Isn't it wonderful! Reverend Korngold is a 'Jews for Jesus' minister, Adnan's Muslim and I'm a fundamentalist Christian. This is how we solve the problems of the world."

"By marrying the problem?" Darlene held her hands up in exasperation.

"No! By not being afraid to love one another. I've married the sweetest, most loving man I've ever known. Aren't you happy for me?"

Darlene rose from her end of the table and walked toward Delilah and Adnan. "You couldn't have given us a little warning? This has been one hell of a supper, let me tell you."

"What'd I miss?"

Darcy shook her head. "Nothing much. Pettus is selling part of the ranch, Cody's marrying Carol Ann, Thaine's found true love with someone who likes him just the way he is–and I'm going to have myself committed right after I spend fifty-seven thousand one hundred forty-two dollars and eighty-five cents on new tits and a rubber ass."

Delilah looked bewildered. "Oh, I did miss something, didn't I?"

Adnan cleared his throat. "Please don't be upset. We didn't mean to exclude anyone, but we felt it more important that this sacred moment just be between the three of us. We want to have a big celebration, very soon."

Pettus stood and turned, facing them both. "You love my sister?" Adnan nodded. "You gonna be there for her in every rotten, unfair, stinking piece of crap life throws at you both?" Wide-eyed, again Adnan nodded. "Then I don't give a shit if you're from Mars and you worship Peppermint Patties." Pettus held out his hand and Adnan shook it vigorously.

"Yes, Mr. Pettus, yes. I love your sister and she loves me! I don't understand it but we found each other in this wonderful place called Rita Blanca. Haya and I have a home, we are a family. There is a saying in the Quran, *'And We will surely test you with something of fear and hunger and a loss of wealth and lives and fruits–but give good tidings to the patient.'* I am a patient man, Mr. Pettus, because I have love."

Pettus let go of Adnan's hand, "You just treat my sister with all the love and respect she deserves, and we'll have no quarrel between us."

Adnan smiled and Pettus gave him a hug. "Welcome." He then turned to Delilah. "Little sis, first one to fly the nut house. You be happy, shug. You deserve every good thing life's got to offer." Pettus hugged her and then turned to pick up Haya in his arms. "And you little rascal! You get any cuter and we're gonna put you in the movies!" He turned back to Delilah. "Is this my niece now? Can I call her my niece?" Delilah smiled and nodded. "Hot dog! Niece, I'm gonna show you things about a ranch you never knew existed, that's right."

As Pettus continued to fuss over Haya, Darcy made her way over to Delilah. "Congratulations. I wish you both all the best." Darcy stared at her feet. "Would've been nice if I could've worn that new dress I've been saving for so long to your wedding. My twin sister's wedding. I know we've fussed a lot through the years."

Delilah smiled. "Not a lot...but every day."

"Well, anyway–we're really the same, you know. What I do affects you, and what you do..." Darcy suddenly broke into tears and Delilah put her arms around her. "I'm sorry, I never cry. It's so...useless. But I do love you. And I do pick on you too much and I'm sorry. It's just that...you're a better person than me, Lilah, and I wish I had some of your joy in life."

Delilah hugged Darcy tighter. "Oh, Darce, now there's no point in us both crying. We'll never stop. I'm not going anywhere–we're still family."

Darlene stood behind them both. "I've always been so mean to both of you–my whole life. I was jealous of the closeness you two had. I didn't think you loved me." The three women immediately began crying together. They embraced in a tight hug.

By now Cody and Thaine had re-entered the kitchen and looked at each other, confused. "Delilah got married to Adnan." Pettus held up Haya's hand to wave at them. "Say hello to your new uncles." The brothers shared expressions of disbelief, then walked over to comfort their sobbing sisters. Unable to hold back, they both began crying as well. The entire Lyndecker clan was about to float away in a sea of tears. Pettus, still holding Haya, looked over at Adnan and said, "Thank you. I've often wondered what it would take to bring out the human side of this family."

\*\*\*

Uncle T.T. stood in the alleyway behind The Dusty Rose and once again tried to open the back door with his loop of keys. His hands were shaking so badly he couldn't get any to fit the lock. Reaching around for his back-pocket flask, he took another pinch of Wild Turkey. Maybe he'd brought the wrong damn set of keys, maybe they changed the locks. Lyndecker luck. He stared up at the open transom above the battered metal door and figured he could probably, maybe, stand on the adjacent garbage can and hoist his big butt through it. Maybe. Worth a try. He knew there was a table next to the door inside that he could slip down onto. How hard could it be? Lugging the trash can over beneath the window, he found a plastic crate nearby and stepped up on it. Steadying himself, he then mounted the garbage can and thrust the two-liter Dr Pepper bottle filled with gasoline through the open window. It fell with a dull thud inside. Flipping open the double-pane gap above the door further, he struggled, jumped and twisted his seventy-eight-year-old frame upwards as best he could, to no avail.

He turned and glanced around the alley. A second beat-up garbage can lay on its side by the building next door. Scuttling back to terra firma, T.T. retrieved the second can and dumped the contents. Slipping the first garbage can over the second one, he once again placed the plastic crate on its side and stepped gingerly atop the two metal containers. With another nip of scotch to steady his nerves, he slowly yanked himself up and peered inside the darkened room. By God, they'd moved everything around since he was in here last! Where the table sat was now a stove. What the hell, he'd just creep onto the burner, and then hop down onto the floor. It was just a question of bending his body enough in order to curl himself inside the transom and drop inside. It was tight. God knows he and flexibility parted ways years ago, but finally, after much grunting, wheezing and cursing, his boot scraped the top of the oven.

He was about to place the other foot on the stove when he fell headlong onto the floor. His boot toe shoved the range top burner knob full-on as he tumbled. Gas began filling the room with an insistent, muted hiss. T.T. didn't notice. He'd twisted his ankle and it was throbbing like hell. Dammit, just get on with it! Burn this hellhole down! All he'd heard for years was the unrelenting ordeal this godforsaken affliction had been for the girls. No money, no advertising, constant debt, unfair competition, out-of-date merchandise–just burn the sucker down! He knew the girls had Cadillac insurance on the place, had to in order to get a loan to buy it. T.T. had worked it over in his head for a very long time. Give the girls a chance at life. He was old and useless to everyone–go out with a bang! They can take the insurance money and start over–rebuild, or not. His life was at its expiration point and he knew it. What had he ever achieved, anyway? Nothing. Not a damn thing. Drank himself into uselessness, ran around on his wife, lost the only land he'd ever owned, never held a job longer than it took the boss to wise up that he'd hired another fuckup. Do something good for somebody once in your life! Give somebody else a boost, even if you've never had a helping hand once in your pitiful life! Do the right thing, Terry Tom Lyndecker–burn this sucker down!

T.T. reached for the plastic Dr Pepper container of fuel and began liberally dousing the kitchen. He then limped into the front room and flung the liquid around like it was holy water. Onto the silk roses, onto the wrapping paper, onto the raffia and ribbons and plastic reindeer–he stopped splashing only when the last droplet had been flung from the bottle. He looked around the room, stopping to catch his breath. The fumes were suddenly overpowering. He took a last sip of bourbon and tossed the bottle onto the floor. Reaching into his shirt pocket, he pulled out a small box of matches. Opening it, he squinted and laughed heartily. Empty. Flawless Lyndecker luck! Always the same shit. T.T. turned and hobbled back toward the kitchen. Pulling open several drawers, he finally located a large box of safety matches. Retrieving them, he grabbed a wooden match in his right hand and held it up. Halting momentarily, he turned back toward the alleyway door and muttered to himself, "Open door...throw match...run!"

T.T. never noticed the hissing stove top as he passed it, never smelled the gaseous odor saturating the room, never thought twice about lighting the match just before stepping outside the door and into a newer, undisclosed future.

# CHAPTER FOURTEEN

Carol Ann dabbed at her tears with her aqua silk sleeve and looked up at her mother, now holding her hand. "Why do I always fall in love with boys that are beneath me socially?"

Barbara patted her daughter's flawless, smooth skin. "I wish I knew, honey. Just once I wish you'd fall for a rich one. I guess we can't help what we want, can we?"

Carol Ann sniffed, shaking her head. "No ma'am."

"Baby, you just gotta take that old sour milk and make buttermilk pie with it. All there is to it."

"But he wants to go to agricultural college up in the Panhandle. Mother, I've never been to the Panhandle. What if I don't like it? What if they don't like me?"

"Don't like you? Why, everyone likes you, precious."

"Sometimes I wonder."

"Now stop it. You cannot afford the luxury of an unselfish thought." Barbara looked puzzled. "That's not right."

"Oh, Mother, I knew what you meant. You always put me first and I'm so grateful to you and Daddy. Where would I be without my wonderful parents?"

Barbara smiled knowingly as she stroked Carol Ann's hair. "Can you promise to keep a secret?"

Carol Ann pulled back and stared at her mother anxiously. "What? Tell me."

"Now it's not official and the whole thing may fall apart...Oh, I really shouldn't say..."

"No, Mother, what?"

"Well, we may already have a buyer for the Emporium."

"Oh, Mother, who?"

Barbara shook her head. "Nope. Your daddy made me promise, I can't."

"Oh, that's so mean! You know how I love secrets. You're just being awful."

"I know, precious, but you're just going to have to wait. Your father would kill me if I spilled the beans and it didn't come to pass." Barbara stood and smoothed her blouse. "We've got to figure this wedding of yours out. What does one wear to a Lyndecker wedding?"

Carol Ann grinned. "Whatever's on sale at Ross Dress for Less."

Barbara smirked. "That's no way to talk about your future in-laws."

"Oh God, Mother, that awful Darcy! I can handle the rest of them; they're too simple for words. But she's like something out of an evil fairy tale, broomstick and all."

"Well..." Barbara fluffed at her frosted tips with a few quick jabs, "You're just gonna have to get a bigger broomstick, Missy."

\*\*\*

Marty stepped out onto the pool patio, followed by the customary canine horde. She did suspect the spidery beach coverlet she was wearing was slightly cheesy but, hell with it, you have to approach these things with a modicum of vulgarity. Chito was at the other end of the pool doing backstrokes. Long, lissome backstrokes. Did the man have any defects? Marty was sure he was riddled with imperfections–they just weren't apparent to other human beings.

Sitting her book down (Book? A lame prop. Why not just roll out a bar trolley?) she called out cheerily, "How's the water?"

"Perfect. A little warm, but it feels great."

Marty nodded. "It's mostly a hot tub from May to October. Not much we can do about it."

"What's the latest with your father?"

"They say he can come home by the weekend. If he behaves."

"Very good. Are you coming in?"

"Sure." Marty dropped her gauzy sheath and strolled coolly to the water's edge. The dog circus followed her. "Stay back. No. You can't go in–stay!" Marty dove underwater and resurfaced on the opposite side of the pool. "I'm always afraid the lot of them are going to follow me in. The horse trough is fine for four-leggeds–not the swimming pool."

Chito, smiling, paddled toward her. "You've trained them well. They act like they're allergic to chlorine."

"They're allergic to me swatting their behinds."

Chito smiled again and floated on his back. "Can I ask you a question?"

"Probably. Shoot?"

Chito stood and wiped the hair from his eyes. "I'm just curious why you never married. Surely you had tons of offers."

Marty laughed. "Oh millions! Why are you asking?"

"I don't know. It's not unusual, is it? People do get married."

"Of course," she shrugged. "Just...didn't happen."

"I didn't think I'd ever get married. Ever."

"But you did. Happily so, no?"

"Very."

Marty shook her head. "Did I hear a slight hesitation in that 'very?'"

Chito laughed. "Are you putting pauses in my speech? No. I'm just a different person now, I guess. How could I not be?" Chito dove underwater and resurfaced.

Marty continued, "Who is that?"

"Good question."

"Figured out why you came here? What you're going to do with the money?"

Chito cuffed his hands on the surface of the water. "Maybe. I'm getting closer."

Marty shook her head. "Not ready to tell yet?"

"You'll know...soon." There was a pause as Marty continued staring at Chito. "What?"

"I'm curious about you."

"Yes."

Marty laughed. "It's none of my business. You can tell me to take a hike, whatever."

"Uh-oh, one of those questions."

Marty laughed again. "Forget it."

"Now you have my complete curiosity. Your turn...shoot."

Marty lowered her head and sighed. "Are you completely gay...or a little bi...or what?"

Chito grinned. "What a question!"

Marty shrugged. "You're right."

Chito floated on his back. "Well, it kind of depends."

"On?"

"The way I feel. Like right now I just feel–kind of open."

"Open?"

Chito nodded. "Um-hmm. Open."

Marty continued staring at Chito, then glanced off into the distance. "Oh boy–I'm not very good at this."

"At what."

"Whatever this is."

"What is this?"

"If I were to spell it out, I'd say it was...some kind of self-conscious seduction."

Chito smiled. "Nice. Am I the one being seduced?"

"I'd say yes."

Chito, still smiling, stared at Marty. She continued softly, "I like you Chito. I don't want for a second to ruin our friendship–but I do like you. Maybe, more than like."

"And I like you." Chito edged closer to Marty. "It's been a long time since I've been with a woman." He shrugged. "I don't know..."

"I don't either."

Chito laughed softly. "I'm not a virgin. But I kinda feel like one right now."

"I come from a long line of once-upon-a-time virgins. Seems like you always start with a kiss." Marty leaned in to kiss Chito softly. He closed his eyes and put his hands on her waist. They held each other, gently swaying with the water. It had been a long time indeed for Chito, and yet it felt as familiar and acquiescent as the ancient sun now warming his back.

\*\*\*

Sheriff Naylor and Deputy Canfield sat across the desk from each other, holding their cards chest high.

"Raise you ten and I'll call."

"You sandbaggin' me?"

"You're gonna find out."

Deputy Canfield placed his card on the table. "Straight."

Sheriff Naylor grinned. "Straight...flush."

"You shittin' me?"

"I shit you not."

"Why do you always deal me such a bad hand?"

"Why are you such a bad player?"

Wayne Canfield rose from his chair and walked over to the office fridge, retrieving a Diet Dr Pepper.

"Don't be sore. Your day's coming." Sheriff Naylor glanced at Wayne's soda can. "You know that shit's gonna kill you. Zoe says it's got rat poison in it."

"Sooner the better."

Naylor shrugged. "It's your life, sunshine." He pushed his chair back, "I figure you only owe me two new pickups and a riding lawnmower about now. I'm a patient man."

Wayne took a long gulp. "You'll have to be with the luck I'm having."

"What's eatin' you?"

"Nothing."

"Something's eatin' ya. You're about as agreeable as a grass sandwich."

Wayne held the cold can to his forehead and sighed, "Tanya's talking 'bout a divorce. Came straight outta nowhere. I don't know if she's serious or just trying to rattle my cage. Hell...what marriage is perfect? Not mine! Every marriage has problems." He took another sip from the can. "She says I'm not 'interesting' to her anymore. Interesting! Like I'm some magazine article she read at the doctor's office."

Sheriff Naylor stood slowly and walked over to one of the filing cabinets. "I told y'all to take that vacation to Ireland a few years back. Going to Europe saved our marriage. Zoe gets all that 'Downton Abbey' business out of her system and we're good for another couple years." He pulled out a travel brochure and tossed it on the table.

Wayne shook his head. "I don't think that's it. I think she just doesn't love me anymore."

"Damn, boy."

"Yep. Damn."

"Have you thought about counseling?"

Wayne looked at the Sheriff, chagrined. "There's nothing wrong with me!"

"Nobody said there was–don't bite my head off. Just saying...might Iron some wrinkles out, that's all."

Wayne nodded, "What, I'm an old shirt just needs a little starch, that it? How 'bout Tanya losing twenty pounds, taking a walk around the block once in a while, fixing her hair up and stop dressing like she's the entire giveaway pile down at the church?"

Albert stared at Wayne. "I see you've given this some thought."

"Sure have."

"Well...I'm just an old country yokel, don't know piss from cream soda, but I do know this–marriage is like eating a raw oyster. You gotta swallow the whole thing all at once or it just don't make any sense."

Wayne stared at Sheriff Naylor, expressionless. Suddenly they heard a muffled explosion, which gently rocked the office. Sheriff Naylor looked back at Wayne. "What was that?"

Wayne shook his head, wide-eyed. "No earthly idea."

Within seconds a loud fire siren wailed in the distance. Both men reached for their Stetsons and raced from the room.

***

Darcy stood in her nightgown stuffed into her jeans staring at the smoldering ruin of The Dusty Rose. Milling around her in various stages of grief, shock and hastily attired disarray stood Delilah, Adnan, Darlene, Pettus, Thaine and Cody.

Sheriff Naylor approached Pettus and motioned him off to the side. He removed his hat and wiped his brow. "We found T.T.'s body out in the alleyway. He was burned up pretty bad."

Pettus stared at the Sheriff in dismay. "Uncle T.T.? What the hell was he doing here?"

The Sheriff shook his head. "We were hoping you might be able to tell us something. You didn't know anything about any of this?"

"Not a damn thing. Jesus!"

"T.T. have a grudge against Darce, Lilah?"

"Oh, come on. He's their uncle. He might've been the town

drunk, but he loved his family."

"I gotta ask, Pettus, part of my job. Nothing personal."

Pettus frowned. "Everything in this pile of steaming Rita Blanca shit is personal."

"You need to watch your language, Pettus. I'm on duty right now and I'm just doing my job."

Pettus shook his head and replied sharply, "Sorry, Al, must've just lost it for a minute. How the wife and kids doing?"

\*\*\*

Delilah, tying her bathrobe tightly, approached Darcy, who was standing in what used to be the front door of The Dusty Rose. Darcy turned. "Hell of a way to spend your honeymoon, huh?"

Delilah shook her head. "Well, I'll never forget it, that's for sure."

Darcy looked at her for a moment, then put an arm around her. "What are we going to do, Lilah?"

"I guess we just start all over again."

Darcy laughed ruefully and wiped her eyes. "Yeah. Go on selling something completely needless to folks that don't need it. The American way."

Delilah stared at the smoke rising from the ashes. "Maybe we're selling a little bit of gladness in a world that really does need it. Who's to say?"

Darcy half-smiled. "Only you can find the bright side of full-on catastrophe," she shrugged. "What the hell–coulda been worse. Our new sister-in-law coulda been sitting in a folding chair across the street laughing her ass off the whole time."

Darlene walked up behind the two of them and crossed her arms. "I don't mean to be insensitive–but what happens if the insurance won't cover this?"

Darcy frowned. "What are you talking about?"

"You don't know? They found Uncle T.T.'s body in the alley. They think he set the fire."

Darcy looked incredulous. "He what...why?"

Darlene sighed deeply. "Maybe he thought...the insurance..."

Darcy shook her head. "That's crazy. If someone in the family set the fire..."

Delilah turned to Darlene. "What does it mean?"

"It means arson and insurance don't exactly complement each other. Do we know any good lawyers?"

Darcy stared at Darlene then turned and walked out into the street. Glancing back to gaze at the smoldering building, she saw the now nonchalant firemen cleaning up and repositioning their equipment. She observed the townsfolk who'd silently gathered to survey the damage like accountants squaring the ledger. She saw her family stumbling about in shock and assemblages of half-dressed ratty sleepwear. She wanted to cry and laugh and pull her hair out all at once. Lyndecker luck! Two steps forward, one giant catapult back, day in, day out, dependable as seeds on a strawberry. Nothing ever comes easy in life. Nothing. Least of all benevolence.

\*\*\*

Thaine and Jazz held each other as closely as if they were penetrating each other's cellular nuclei. Jimmy stared at them disgustedly from across the booth at Dairy Queen.

"I feel sick."

Jazz turned to look at him. "What's the matter?"

"What do you think? Watching you both gnaw on each other like two starving raccoons. I'm gonna upchuck big time."

Thaine smiled. "Haven't you ever been in love?"

"Yeah, sure, all the time. I'm nine, dude." Jimmy started singing, *"Just a gigolo everywhere I go, People know the part, I'm playing..."*

Jazz reached out her hand to stop him. "No! Do not do this."

Jimmy started singing louder, *"Paid for every dance, selling each romance, Every night some heart betraying..."*

Jazz tried grabbing his hand, but Jimmy jumped into the aisle and began gyrating wildly, *"Hummala bebhuhla zeebuhla boobuhla, Hummala bebhuhla zeebuhla bop."*

Jazz covered her face with her hands and Thaine grinned. "He's actually pretty good, ya know?"

Jazz shook her head. "Don't. He'll never shut up."

By now, people in the restaurant had turned to watch the performance. One old man was slapping his table in time to the beat. He turned to look over at Jazz and Thaine, laughing. "Ain't he a little toot?"

Another customer, nodding her head, exclaimed to no one in particular, "Whoever put the quarter in that kid sure got their money's worth!"

Jazz glared at Jimmy. "You want a Hawaiian Blizzard?"

He stopped singing. "Yeah."

"Then sit down and shut up!"

Jimmy returned to the booth and plopped into the seat. "I think I prefer the Louis Prima version over David Lee Roth, what do you think?"

Jazz snarled, "I think I'm gonna pinch your head off if you pull a stunt like that again."

A woman sitting in the booth behind them turned around, laughing. "It's so darling when they have no filters like that. Wouldn't the world be a better place if we were all as full of joy as that little dickens?"

Jimmy frowned at Jazz and stuck his tongue out.

The woman continued, "What's your name, honey?"

Jimmy rose immediately. "Robespierre. What's yours?"

The woman stared at him, suddenly confused. "Bernice."

Jimmy stuck out his hand. "Nice to meet you, Bern." He motioned to Jazz and Thaine. "This here's Fred and Wilma."

Immediately he started again, *"From the, town of Bedrock, they're a page right out of his-tor-ee..."*

"That's it." Jazz jumped from her seat and grabbed Jimmy by the collar. "Move!" Thaine downed the rest of his Coke and followed behind them. Stopping at the front door, he turned back to the crowd inside. "Thank you, ladies and gentlemen, our star has left the building but we'll be back with a new show real soon." Thaine waved his hand slowly. "Tha-tha-tha-that's all folks!"

\*\*\*

Thaine, Jazz and Jimmy sat three abreast in the front seat of the pickup. Jimmy stared out the window glumly. "You said I could have a Hawaiian Blizzard."

Jazz stared ahead. "Not with you acting like a maniac and freaking everyone out."

"They weren't freaked out."

Thaine reached over and rubbed Jimmy's head. "Well, I think you're pretty talented, Thelonious. You just gotta learn to hold it in sometimes."

"Why?"

"Cause people don't always get you. Not everybody's on your wavelength."

"That's their problem."

"Why complicate your life?"

"Why not? Isn't that what life's supposed to be about? Learning how to deal with complications? Maybe I'd rather have complications than be afraid of them." Jimmy turned back again to stare out the window.

Thaine and Jazz glanced at each other blankly as they drove on in silence.

\*\*\*

Chito lay quietly contemplating beside a softly breathing Marty. After a few collisions and some inevitable misfires, their surprising if not entirely predetermined alignment between the sheets-went off remarkably well! Chito smiled slightly at their uninhibited lovemaking. It was as if he'd suddenly given himself permission to just be; stop projecting, stop rationalizing, stop fearing-just be. It didn't have to be perfect; it wasn't. It didn't have to be the great passion of his life; it wasn't. It didn't have to be anything other than two warm bodies coming together and seeking solace in the instant. Was he truly, classically bisexual? Maybe. Great-who cares? You were faithful to Tom always-well, there was that one actor in the London gym. A physical release, nothing more. You'd even dutifully told Tom about it and he shrugged it off in that quiet, nonjudgmental Tom way. And now here you were in bed next to his sister after sweaty, passionate, uninhibited sex-what would Tom think? Chito let the thought glide around his brain. What he concluded was that Tom would've laughed and shrugged the whole thing off. Tom loved his sister, Chito knew that. They had the kind of fraternal bond that comes from repeated obstacle, constant endurance and unwavering fealty to their two-member society. In fact, Tom at this very moment from the great beyond might actually be drawing the two of them together. Who's to say? There was just one slightly nagging thought still coursing inside Chito's head and it was indeed of somewhat significance-what would it be like to have Pettus in bed with them both right now?

# CHAPTER FIFTEEN

It was a June wedding after all. June 30th, to be exact. Clayton and Barbara Jansky cordially invited a handful of friends to witness their daughter, Carol Ann, marry Cody Joe Lyndecker in the living room of the Jansky "villa." The entire Lyndecker clan showed up but for Darcy. It was simply too much for her to endure. She'd have rather attended a mating demonstration of diseased Komodo dragons than have to withstand the ordeal of seeing her kid brother marry her mortal enemy. Still, it was a lovely affair rife with joy, benevolence and not a little lurking trepidation.

"Is that a hat on that woman's head or a sewing basket?" Barbara Jansky whispered into her husband's ear as he helped himself to another generous scotch and soda. Darlene Lyndecker did indeed appear to be wearing a straw hamper of some kind perched prominently atop her head like a handwrought fascinator from Tractor Supply. Laden with figurines, tinsel and...rubber washers? Barbara, unable to resist, edged closer to Darlene, who was filling her plate with devilled eggs and mints. "I couldn't help but notice what an interesting hat you're wearing. Is that a...basket?"

Darlene grinned as she swallowed. "Easter basket. I found

it back of the closet one day and I said to myself, 'Why wouldn't you wear this somewhere special? It's just so one-off!'"

Barbara nodded slowly. "One-off...and you wear it beautifully, too."

Darlene grinned at Barbara and popped a peppermint ball in her mouth. "Not everyone can carry this kind of thing off. You gotta have tons of self-confidence. Helps if you're mildly bipolar–just sayin'."

Across the room Delilah stood with Adnan, holding his hand. "I just hope Cody knows what he's getting into. We're not in the same league as the Janskys. They're like something from 'The Housewives of Orange County'–so worldly."

Adnan frowned. "Orange County?"

"Oh, it's a fake TV show about fake people living fake lives. But it's strangely inspiring." Haya approached her father, carrying a plate laden with chicken wings, mixed nuts, cheese, pickles, cookies and a large dollop of mayonnaise.

"Food!"

Adnan looked at Haya sternly. "You'll get a tummy ache."

Delilah squeezed Adnan's hand. "Let her indulge a little. We had nothing to eat at our wedding. I'm not complaining, but sometimes a child has to have eyes bigger than their plate just to have big dreams. A person can't think small their entire life." Adnan smiled at Delilah then kissed her softly.

"Glad to see another married couple enjoying the benefits of matrimonial bliss." Delilah and Adnan turned to see a tipsy Carol Ann looking resplendent in her off-white, off-the-shoulder, off-the-charts sequined mini-skirt wedding get-up. An ensemble designed to go from church to pole dancing. "I noticed your sister didn't make it today. Not surprised. We've never seen eye-to-eye on much, well ..." She cocked her head toward Cody, smiling. "I got what I wanted."

Delilah nodded. "Yes you did, Carol Ann. And I know you love my brother and you're going to be very good to him, 'cause even though he's a little coarse sometimes, he's a good person and he deserves all the love and happiness there is in life."

Carol Ann lifted her champagne glass. "Bingo! Looks like y'all gonna make a big haul on that store insurance money too. Whatcha gonna do–rebuild, sell out–move to Cancun?"

Delilah smiled slightly. "I imagine the first thing we'll do is buy a nice headstone for Uncle T.T."

Carol Ann grinned. "Poor T.T.–wrong place at the wrong time–or maybe not. In the end, all's well that spends well, right?"

"How 'bout you Carol Ann? Is it true you have a buyer for the Emporium?"

"Signed, sealed and delivered! Hey, I'm heading off to West Texas A&M University in Canyon, Texas. I'm the wife of an agricultural science major!"

"But I thought your daddy was giving Cody a job at the dealership?"

"So did I, hon! Then all of a sudden Daddy thought we'd be much happier 600 miles away from Rita Blanca. Isn't that wild? 'Course it helped he made a donation to the school endowment–Cody's grades weren't for shit. That nice wedding gift from your brother, Pettus, will come in handy though. Near sixty thousand dollars ain't Ken-L-Ration, hon!"

Delilah stared, mouth open, at Carol Ann. The girl had gumption, no question. She could see that near sixty thousand "wedding gift" vanishing into a closet full of Prada handbags, but then, it wasn't her problem. One thing she'd fully grasped from her stint in rehab–don't offer to carry someone else's suitcases when you're jumping off a sinking ship.

Pettus Lyndecker treaded warily through the animated gathering. Friend or foe? How could one tell? More importantly, why did he even bother attending such an ordeal? He loosely justified it as some hazy mindfulness of familial duty. As the surviving patriarch of the Lyndecker tribe, he owed it to his brother to share in his transitory happiness–stressful as that might be. He'd avoided Carol Ann since their brief affair ran its course like a dog fleeing a spraying garden hose. And here they were, in this joyous moment of holy wedlock, all gussied up and edgy as sewer rats gnawing on a wheel of rancid cheese.

"I heard you sold part of your place to old man Pennebaker? Sonavabitch, why didn't you come to me?" Pettus turned to see a red-eyed and slightly weaving Clayton Jansky pointing his scotch and water at him like a pistol.

"Hello, Clayton. Didn't know you were in the market."

"I ain't! Just want to be offered the opportunity, that's all. Pete Pennebaker isn't the only multi-millionaire in town."

"No, sir."

"That brother of yours is costing me a lot of *dinero*. When Carol Ann told me she was pregnant ..."

"Pregnant?"

Clayton waved his hand. "Sh-h-h-h! Not supposed to tell anybody. Well, I guess you got a right to know if anyone does. Coulda just as easy been yours, I 'magine."

Pettus glanced over at Cody, laughing and cutting up with his high school buddies and as oblivious to the conjugal inundation about to engulf him as a moth aiming for a forest fire. Pettus shook his head, "As it should be at all weddings."

"I won't tell a soul, Clayton. Why would I? Let the happy couple make the announcement. Here's to keeping it in the family."

Pettus toasted Clayton's glass with his own scotch rocks and walked off toward the buffet table. Clayton stared after him with a confused look and pondered, "Too many damn Lyndeckers in this town–knock one off, there's two more right behind."

Pettus stood before the venison sausage and the sliced roast beef, unable to make up his mind. He picked up a pork tamale instead.

"Daddy always said a tamale's no good unless there's at

least a few javelina hairs in it."

Pettus turned to see Lurene Dornak, his third-grade teacher, nibbling from a plate of cheese and grapes. "That's exactly right, Miz Dornak. How're you doing?"

"Oh, other than my COPD and Crohn's disease, alright I guess."

Pettus nodded. "You've been dealing with it a long time, bless your heart."

"Something gets us all in the end, isn't that right? Who wants to live forever? I can barely turn on my TV anymore, it's got so many bells and whistles. You know a body can only stand so much learnin' in one lifetime."

"Yes, ma'am."

"How 'bout you, Pettus? You doing all right? It's a shame old T.T. had to burn down the Dusty Rose, but it was a shambles anyway."

Pettus stopped chewing and looked at Miss Dornak. "Who said he burned it down?"

"Well, everybody in town's been talking about it. They found his drunk bohunkus out in the alleyway charred to a fare-thee-well. If he didn't set it on fire, who did?"

Pettus swallowed slowly and wiped his mouth with a paper napkin. "Miz Dornak, we're still waiting on the insurance company to give us a decision. I'd sure appreciate it if you could nip some of those rumors going round in the bud. A judgement hasn't been made yet."

"Whatever you say, son. I'm 'bout half senseless most days anyway. All I know is I taught every kid in town to spell, do numbers and say the Pledge of Allegiance, and that's more than most. If you want to believe goat droppings are pearls and shit don't stink, fine by me." Miss Dornak turned with her plate of grapes and headed back toward the bar. Pettus watched her slight figure weaving through the room and marveled at the tenacity and resilience of all small-town survivors. He was one himself. Pick your poison: trammeled and forgotten in an uncaring metropolis, or choked slowly on a tight leash in some country burg that cares way more than it ever should.

Marty and Chito entered the room looking like a perfume ad come to life. A sudden jab pricked at Pettus as he watched the two of them greet the other partygoers. Damn, they looked good together. Like they were somehow designed to fit. What was different? Something about the two of them was changed. No question–gay guys have that cool factor–but why was Marty so-glowing?

"Hello, handsome. Nice buffet, what are you drinking? I'll have one too." Marty pecked Pettus on the cheek and headed for the bar. Chito approached from behind and offered his hand. "Did we miss everything?"

Pettus nodded. "Pretty much everything. What happened?"

"I went to the hospital with Marty. Mr. Pennebaker was having a difficult morning. Took longer than usual."

Pettus sipped from his drink and studied Chito. "Sorry to hear. How goes it out at *Casa Los Abuelos*?"

"Good." Chito glanced back. "I think you should come by more often."

"Yeah? What does Marty say 'bout that?"

Chito shrugged. "Haven't asked. Just a suggestion."

The two men eyed each other. Pettus drained his drink. "Might do that very thing. Figured out where you're going to spend Tom's money?"

Chito smiled. "Getting warmer."

Pettus nodded with a grin. "Okay."

Marty returned with her drink. "So the happy couple got shackled and no shots were fired? Oh, sand tarts, my favorite." Marty reached between Pettus and Chito and grasped one of the crumbly, powdered sugar shortbread cookies. Pettus flinched imperceptibly as he inhaled the faint scent of whatever exotic perfume she was wearing that was so much her–her chemistry, her essence–it could never have been any other woman.

Pettus mumbled, "No shots yet, but it's still early. You never know who'll get massacred at one of these social pleasantries."

Marty grinned at Pettus. "I was only joking. Aren't you happy for your little brother?"

"Sure. Always glad to see 'em  fat and sassy as they're being led to slaughter."

"Are we having one of our moods?"

Pettus stared at Marty. "Chito just invited me to come out to your place and visit more."

"He did?" Marty turned to Chito and smiled. "Why not? I guess the dam's been broken between you and Daddy. Why not?"

"Big of you."

Marty frowned. "Oh, come on now..."

"I wasn't out of line, I hope?" Chito asked.

"No!"

"I wouldn't want to put you out, make it...awkward."

"Awkward?"

"If y'all are busy, or...whatever."

"Busy?" Marty turned to Chito, who shrugged back. Suddenly a red-faced Cody, his arm around an even redder-faced Carol Ann, approached the trio and held their champagne glasses aloft.

"Brother, Marty, Chito–you're looking at the happiest man in the whole USA right now!" They each smiled back, toasting the couple.

"Brother, your glass is empty.  Let me go fill it up."

"No, it's okay. I gotta get back to the place...stuff to do."

Cody looked perplexed. "On my wedding day?"

Carol Ann brushed back the hair covering one eye and grinned. "You haven't even kissed the bride yet." Pettus grimaced. The absolute, very last thing he wanted to do at present was to kiss Carol Ann *Lyndecker* in front of an entire room of gawkers, which had now suddenly grown so still you could hear a dust bunny roll. Sensing no possibility of forestalling the inevitable, Pettus corralled his courage and leaned in to peck Carol Ann on the cheek. A sigh of relief seemed to envelop the room when Carol Ann loudly proclaimed, "You call that a kiss? That wasn't even worthy of a ninety-year-old emphysema patient. Come here!" Carol Ann grabbed Pettus's lapels and pulled him down into a lip-lock that would make Stormy Daniels squirm. For what seemed like several lifetimes, Carol Ann sucked and gurgled on Pettus's mouth like it was an underwater respirator. The look on Cody's face could only be described as...brain fucked. When finally she surfaced for oxygen and let loose Pettus's jacket, Miss Dornak could be heard muttering at the end of the bar, "Praise the Lord, I didn't think we'd ever get to the end of that porno."

Thaine and Jazz had been sitting across the room, holding hands on the sofa. Thaine shook his head slowly. "Man, that was some epic shit. Cody looked like his head was about to unscrew."

Jazz nodded. "I think your brother may need a lip transplant."

Thaine continued shaking his head. "So fucked-up. Whoa. Did I tell you how fucked-up my family is?"

"Right after I told you about mine."

"How does anybody ever have a chance?"

Jazz sighed. "You ignore it all 'cause you can't fix it. You just keep on believing in something 'cause not having anything to trust in is like dying a little every day." Both teenagers stared straight ahead at Pettus and Carol Ann. Slowly, without turning their heads, they leaned in toward one another.

***

Darcy stumbled through the ashen heap that had once been her sole purpose in life. Make people happy. Who doesn't like a flower? Colored beads? A rhinestone Jesus? Something simple, bright and cheery to ease you through another day of routine and tedium. Was it such a bad thing? Why did life have this consistent habit of smacking down any glimmers of joy?

Kicking at a pile of black muck beside her, a completely intact ceramic Easter bunny rolled out of the heap and landed at her feet. Darcy stooped to pick up the ridiculous-looking rabbit and smiled. Speaking aloud, she laughed, "Okay God, got it. For every shitty disaster there's a bunny rabbit to remind us that even this too, you will survive."

"Survive? You're gonna survive, you have to. This town needs a good flower shop." Darcy turned to see Deputy Wayne Canfield standing just inside the blackened front door.

"Hello, Wayne. Just talking to myself."

"I do it all the time. I'm pretty good company too, if I do say so."

Darcy smiled. "What brings you to the Black Hole of Rita Blanca?"

"Saw your car out front. Thought I'd say...hi."

"Hi."

"You're not over at the wedding party?"

Darcy laughed. "Nope. That's one celebration I can afford to miss."

"Right. Never thought I'd see those two married–but hey, what I know about marriage you can scribble on a pinhead. That's what my wife tells me, anyway."

Darcy turned and crossed her arms. "Sounds like a little discord in the Canfield household."

"More'n a little...actually, we're getting a divorce."

Darcy looked at Wayne, expressionless. "Well...that's that,

I guess. Sorry if I don't sound surprised."

Wayne shrugged. "Nobody's surprised. Certainly not me. It was over a long time ago. You hang on as long as you can and then you just don't. Way it is."

Darcy stared at Wayne a moment longer, then kicked at another pile of debris. "Tell me something, Wayne–we gonna get our insurance money?"

"I dunno. Doesn't look real good, finding T.T. out in the alley."

Darcy stared dazed at the pile before her. "Stupid old man. Really stupid, ya know? He never did anything worthwhile his whole life. The only thing I can say that he knew how to do...was how to love me. Uncle T.T. loved me...that he was good at."

Wayne edged slowly over and offered Darcy his handkerchief. She took it, wiping her eyes. "I'm sorry, I don't cry about anything. Well, almost never. Nothing worth crying over–'cept that crazy old man." She blew her nose and wiped her eyes again.

Wayne stared at his feet, nervously shifting his weight. "Darcy, Darcy...I..." Suddenly Wayne reached out an arm and placed it around Darcy's shoulder. "Please don't cry. I'm no good around people that cry. I get...emotional."

Darcy looked at Wayne's right hand on her shoulder and froze. Wayne Canfield, the boy she'd known her whole life? The boy she chased and held down on the baseball field and spit in his face when he called her a priss? The boy she made out with in eighth grade who was covered in pimples but still had the best smile in school? After a moment she patted his hand and stepped away.

"Thank you, Wayne. Thanks."

"You're welcome. Well, if you need anything...you know...if I can help."

"Thank you." Wayne glanced at Darcy a moment longer, then turned to walk away.

"Wayne," Darcy called out and he turned quickly, "I'd like you to have...the rabbit." Darcy held out the ceramic bunny and Wayne reached for it, smiling. "Piece of junk, but it has-survival skills! Just...keep it."

"I will. I'll keep it always." Wayne smiled the same, sweet, eighth-grade boy smile and Darcy felt something inside she thought had been extinguished so long ago it could never be restored. Gratefulness.

\*\*\*

Chito parked his Lexus across the street from the derelict wreck of the Dusty Rose and got out. Crossing the street, he entered the darkened ruin and contemplated the disaster at hand. Worse than he'd imagined. A complete tear-down. Poor souls–of all the calamities to befall a business, this was...finality. No roof, no appliances, no display cases, shattered refrigerator, broken glass everywhere, dangling wires, strewn garbage. Miserable. Still, nothing is ever totally lost if there is resolve to rebound from calamity. Could be done. Not easy, but feasible–with help. Chito nudged his shoe at a congealed amalgamation of melted glass and plastic roses. Strangely beautiful, in an unsettling way. Like viewing the splendor of a destructive volcano. Great devastation, great spectacle.

"Ah, you've come to view the funeral pyre, too?" Chito turned to see Adnan standing at the former front door.

"Yes. How are you? A terrible thing, no?" The two shook hands and Adnan gazed around slowly.

"Delilah cannot bring herself to come back and see again. She said it's like losing an arm or a leg. She's–'disfigured'–her word."

Chito nodded. "What are your plans, if any?"

Adnan smiled. "Plans? I don't make plans. Plans are for idealists."

Chito studied Adnan. The resolve to rebound from calamity-where and when exactly does such impetus arise? "I have a thought." Adnan looked at Chito. "Why don't you open a food truck?"

"A what?"

"You sell food, beverages, snacks-Syrian bread from a mobile kitchen."

Adnan laughed and shook his head. "Whoever heard of such a thing?"

"Lots! It's a proven business model in cities now all over the world. You don't pay rent, you own your profession! You move to follow the market, very little overheard, keep it simple and affordable."

Adnan grinned. "Crazy. Food from an automobile? Besides, we have no money."

"I'll finance you! Very reasonable terms. I'm not saying you won't have to work hard, but you and Delilah have already shown your commitment and determination."

Adnan stopped grinning. "But, where does one find such an automobile that bakes bread?"

"Easy! We'll go up to San Antonio, Austin, Houston-wherever. We'll find you a used one, a good one, one you can start serving in right away. Where are you living now?"

Adnan looked embarrassed. "We were staying in Mr. Pennebaker's hunting camp, but since the marriage, we are in a bedroom at the Lyndecker home."

"You can't live that way! What about your daughter? I'll speak to Marty and see about finding you a better place."

"No, please..."

"Of course, it's my duty."

Adnan was taken aback. "Duty? You're not required to save my life. God is in charge."

Chito laughed. "God's been a little busy lately. Who knows, maybe I'm an angel come to earth to rescue all the unloved food trucks." Chito smiled and held out his hand. "Take a chance?"

Adnan stared at the outstretched palm, momentarily perplexed. "*Saedny ya Rab,*" Adnan shook Chito's hand. "We have a saying in Syria, something like, 'The mouse fell from the ceiling and the cat cried, *Allah!*' I think I need to pay closer attention!"

Chito laughed. "We have a similar one in Mexico, '*Me admira que siendo gato no sepas coger ratone*'–'I'm amazed that being a cat you don't know how to hunt mice!' *Andale!*"

The two men laughed and embraced and, for an instant, standing in the scorched remnants of all former dreams, a slightly different one began to arise.

# CHAPTER SIXTEEN

Pete Pennebaker stood staring out the hospital room window. The tiny Filipino nurse bracing him upright was as resolute as the Battleship Texas. He figured it'd take a backhoe and a full work crew to disengage from her. "Hon, you're kinda digging into my belly here. Think we can readjust just a bit?"

"I let you go, you fall like Raggedy Ann!"

With all the wires, plugs, drips and monitors attached to him, Pete didn't worry so much about falling as strangling midair from all the appendages. Patient and nurse turned as one and slowly shuffled toward the hallway.

"Das right, stretch those legs. No good lying in bed all day, no good!"

"When am I getting out of here? What's it been, ten days, two weeks? You lose track, never getting sufficient nourishment."

"What you talking about? You have your very own nutritionist monitoring your dietary needs."

"Untold ways to kill a hostage. Don't y'all believe in meat? Ever hear of a chicken fried steak?"

"Too much animal fat."

"You keep starving me like this, there won't be enough hide left on me for a new pair of shoes."

Marty entered the room just as they reached the door. "Thank God! A face from my distant past come to pick out a proper coffin. Don't want anything fancy. I hear they got cardboard ones now. Quicker the worms get to me, quicker I start fertilizing the soil."

"Good, I'm all for economizing. How's he been today? Vile or just awful?"

"Oh, alright, maybe some restless."

"Well, I've got good news–you're leaving!"

Pete's mouth fell open. "Don't mess with a dying man. Truth?"

Marty nodded. "Truth. I've got Nestor out in the car with the AC on max and we're ready to blow this joint."

"Mary rode a mile–girl, get me unhooked from this torture contraption!"

"Not so fast. The doctor's coming by to see you first. You're going on a strict diet and no alcohol."

Pete began unbuttoning his pajamas. "Right."

"I mean it. They're letting you go home because I promised them you wouldn't start drinking again."

Pete turned his head sharply. "Why'd you do a fool thing like that?"

Marty sighed. "You want out of here, don't you?"

"Gotcha, tell 'em  what they want to hear. Whatever it takes."

Marty grabbed Pete's hand. "I'm serious. You can't drink anymore. Your liver's shot, your heart is busted, your kidneys are barely there–you've got prostate cancer, slow-growing but not going away." Marty squeezed his hand. "I need you to help me–really need you to tell me everything you know about running a ranch. I'm here, I'm staying. I'd like you to be as clear-headed as possible, for as long as possible. Understand?"

Pete stared at Marty as if he were seeing a long-lost

acquaintance materializing from the ether. "I'll be gaw-dam. After all this long, long time–my daughter's come home. What happened?" Pete held up his hand. "No! I don't want to know. You're here and you're staying–and you said it!" He turned to the nurse. "You heard her?" The nurse nodded in agreement. "Damn...Gaw-dam." Pete continued staring at Marty, a small smile lighting his face. Home! She's come home!

\*\*\*

"What's all this marriage nonsense about? Everyone's getting married around here. You're too young, Thaine. Eighteen is too young to take on that kind of responsibility. You ain't even graduated high school yet." Pettus spit the peach pit he'd been chewing on into a paper towel, then held up the paper sack full of peaches for the rest of the family gathered round. "Damn, those are good. Thank you, Darlene."

Darlene wiped a sleeve at the peach juice on her chin. "Should've bought another bag. Old man at the hospital was selling them out of his car trunk for near nothing."

Thaine pointed the peach he'd been munching on at Pettus. "I can pass my GED with Jazz's help this December!" He put his arm around Jazz, who sat scrunched beside him on the black, torn Naugahyde sofa in the Lyndecker "den." "'Sides, you were married at nineteen..."

"Big mistake. Look how I turned out. You wouldn't have wanted the parents I had."

Thaine shook his head, frowning. "Uh, I think we had the same parents, and besides they didn't say no to you neither."

"They should've. A guy at eighteen is ruled by his pecker–excuse me, Jazz, honey, but we're a forthright bunch around here–you're just not thinking clearly. You know what happens next? A baby. You know what a baby brings? Bills! Bills the likes of which your youthful little brain can't even fathom. Who's going to pay all these bills?"

Thaine tossed his peach pit into the plastic wastebasket before him. "I've got fifty-seven thousand, one hundred forty-two dollars and eighty-five cents coming my way. That'll take care of some bills. Plus, Jazz and I want to get a place of our own."

Pettus lowered the peach he was eating and stared at them both as if he'd been stabbed. "Sonofabitch."

Darlene rose. "He's right. You promised him–all of us–the fifty-seven thousand, free and clear."

"Not true. I made Cody and Thaine agree they'd go somewhere to college for at least two years and learn some skill other than castrating yearlings."

"And that's just what Cody's doing with the great whore of Babylon." Darcy dropped her pit also into the wastebasket and wiped her hands on her jeans. "Why would Thaine be any different?" She turned to Jazz. "And I'm not referring to you, Jazz, honey, I'm just referring to that *puta* my other brother married." Puzzled, Jazz smiled faintly.

Delilah and Adnan sat silently in the corner. Haya, in Delilah's lap, happily rubbed a smooth peach on her face. "I'd just like to say marriage is God's way of saving us from total self-absorption," Delilah spoke. "It's nice to care about someone else. I'd nearly forgotten what it's like to be happier more for another than yourself."

Darcy stood and smoothed her rumpled T-shirt. "But if you're not happy to begin with, your partner's never going to be happy enough for the two of you. I'd think long and hard, my man Thaine. Divorce runs in our family like freckles and toe fungus. Not saying you can't pull it off, just saying the hand you're dealing with ain't all that picture-perfect, know what I mean?" Darcy started to leave, then turned back to Pettus. "When exactly are we getting this fifty-thousand-dollar windfall, brother? The bills don't stop 'cause a person's world incinerates."

Pettus looked up at Darcy wearily. "It's coming. I'd

personally appreciate it if you didn't spend every dime of it on creditors. You need to plan for the future."

Darcy turned. "My future is to keep treading water long as I can. 'Bout all anyone can do when you're stranded in the middle of the ocean."

Delilah spoke softly. "You can hang on to me, Darc. I won't let you go."

Darcy glanced at Delilah, started to speak, then turned suddenly and exited the room. Pettus exhaled, "Well, our little family keeps getting smaller. Pretty soon I guess it'll just be the two eldest, Darlene and me, holding down the fort. Thaine, you're near a grown man–almost. I'm glad you and Jazz found each other. I'm happy you're happy, really and truly. But I'm telling ya, you're only going to get so many favors like this in a lifetime. Put it to good use. Don't run off and get married first thing. Sit with it a bit. If you really love each other it ain't gonna go nowhere."

Jazz slowly raised her hand. "Can I...say something?"

Pettus nodded. "Please."

"I do...I really love Thaine. We have a lot in common. And my mom likes him and my brother likes him and even more amazing is, Thaine really likes and gets along with my brother, and that means a lot to me. So, I guess what I'm saying is, I want Thaine to be his best, always. And I know he wants the same for me. So, if he'd like to go to college somewhere, I'll support that, married or not. If he wants to work at a sale barn or fix cars or drive a dump truck, I'll be there too. The money would be nice but it's not going to change our happiness either way. We're in love and there's just not much anybody can do about that."

Pettus exhaled again and glanced sideways. He then stood and walked toward the couple. He rubbed Thaine's head. "You do what you need to do. Wouldn't be your big brother if I didn't offer my two cents worth. I'll miss seeing your big butt around here."

Thaine put a hand on Pettus's pant leg. "You too."

After a moment, Adnan cleared his throat. "May I say something."

Pettus looked terrified. "Oh, God."

Adnan nervously rattled the loose change and small knife in his pocket. He quickly pulled his hand from his pants pocket then just as quickly stuck it back in, continuing to absentmindedly rattle the jangling contents. "It seems, it appears, that Delilah and Haya and I are going to be staying at the Pennebaker hunting camp once more. They're being very generous to us. Marty has offered us the rooms while we prepare the food truck."

Pettus scowled. "The what?"

"Food truck!" Delilah answered excitedly. "Mr. Chito is financing our new business. We're going to be serving Syrian baked goods out of a 1984 converted Chevy mail truck. We already have a name for it: *Seriously Scrumptious Syrian!*"

Pettus shook his head and stared absently at Darlene. "Are you moving, too?"

"Where would I go?"

"Exactly. Well, good luck to one and all, and I mean that." Pettus grabbed another peach from the paper bag and walked from the room. The remaining assemblage munched their fruit in silence. Darlene finally broke the hush.

"I saw on TV last week where a man in India ate an entire chair made out of bamboo. He died, of course. I wonder what kind of funeral service they held for him?" Not certain of what a suitable response might be, they each continued munching in silence.

***

Carol Ann, wearing a billowy caftan, stepped onto the balcony of their suite at the Cancun Ritz-Carlton and pointed to something far off in the Gulf. "Cody, is that a whale? Come here, baby, what is that?"

Cody stood naked behind her at the window and rubbed his tired, groggy face. "Where?"

"Over there. See that gray thing? Honey, put your drawers on, people will see you."

"We're on our honeymoon. People don't wear clothes on their honeymoon." Cody rubbed up against Carol Ann and kissed her neck.

"With all the conventions going on in town, if we get thrown out of here, the only thing left is the Days Inn."

"Perfect." Cody reached out both hands and grabbed Carol Ann's stomach, pulling her close.

"Cody!"

"You married me 'cause I'm such a great lover, didn't you? You can't blame a dog 'cause it wags its tail. Nature calls!" Cody lifted up Carol Ann's caftan and crawled underneath it, popping his head out behind hers. Carol Ann burst out laughing.

"You're impossible!"

He grabbed her naked breasts, moaning, "I'm never leaving here, ever! Can we go to lunch like this?"

Carol Ann loosened her arms from inside the caftan sleeves and turned to face Cody. "You're just plain bad, you know that?" They kissed.

"You knew what a rotten boy I was when you married me."

"I married you 'cause the third time's the charm. This time it's for good." They kissed again. "I've been thinking."

"Mmmm."

"Mother and Daddy have been so generous–paying for the wedding, our honeymoon–I'm just wondering..."

"Yeah?"

"Maybe you should put off going to that college for a while?"

Cody stopped nibbling her ear and stared at her. "You

serious?"

"You can still work at the dealership and I can still run the Emporium. Think of the money we'll save, especially now that there's only one florist in town!"

Cody frowned as he pulled a strand of Carol Ann's hair from his mouth, "But baby...I'm really looking forward to being a college man. I can learn some valuable things to turn our old ranch into a showplace."

"You don't have to make up your mind right this second! We've still got four more days here–let's enjoy ourselves!" Carol Ann lifted the caftan over Cody's head and walked back into the room, leaving Cody naked on the balcony. "Honey, put some clothes on. There're children down at the pool." Cody stood gazing off into the horizon. Stay in Rita Blanca? With his in-laws and his sisters pissed as hell at him? My God, he was planning, counting, on getting out of there for a while, and as quickly as possible. Man up, bro. Time to put on your Big Dad *chones* and make your case before the Supreme Court of Carol Ann.

"Baby, I was thinking..." Turning back to the room, Cody was suddenly smacked across the chest with a still wet pair of swim trunks.

"Put on your swimsuit and let's go down to the buffet; I'm starved." Cody clutched the dripping board shorts and stared at Carol Ann as she fastened her bikini top. This was going to take...deliberation.

\*\*\*

"Five thousand square feet, not too big, not too small–just right for what it is, no? Comes with everything in it or you can pick and choose what you need or don't need–which I think is super reasonable of the owner, no? There's parking all around the square and a side lot for up to eight cars–sweet, no? Utilities run about a hundred fifty to two hundred dollars a month, but if you're like me, you keep those overhead fans going during shop hours and it cuts the AC bill way down, no? Questions?"

"No. Uh, just one. They're asking too much-how much haggling room do we have?"

The realtor smiled and removed her shoulder bag, setting it on a display case. "They're asking three hundred thirty thousand dollars for everything-soup to Rolaids-but I feel confident they'll let it go for three hundred ten."

"Still too much."

"Really? You really think so? What did you have in mind?"

"Two hundred fifty thousand, not a penny more." Chito removed a handkerchief from his back pocket and wiped his forehead in the still stifling room. The realtor looked at him, shocked.

"You're not serious, no?"

Chito nodded. "No, I am."

The realtor quickly grinned and ruffled her blouse. "It IS warm in here, isn't it?"

"No-yes!"

"So, you want me to go back to the owners and ask them to take eighty thousand off their asking price?"

"Yes. It's not unreasonable, no?"

"Yes...I mean no. I mean, they're probably going to say no. But hey, in this business you never shut the door on potential. You like running a flower shop?"

"It's not for me."

"My understanding is the proprietor just got married and they're on their honeymoon and the actual owners would like to unload it as quickly as possible."

"Yes."

"I'll see what I can do, Mr. Sosa. No guarantees, but then I'm constantly surprised in this business-what people will pay and in particular what people will give up in order to make a deal happen."

"True."

The petite realtor wobbled in her four-inch heels toward the front door. "You know, you should think about getting into the real estate business. You've got great presence." She turned at the front door and smiled broadly. "You're that gentleman-type the ladies eat up. You ought to give it some thought; my company's always on the lookout for new blood." She offered her hand. "Can I show you anything else while I'm in the neighborhood?"

Chito smiled and shook her hand. "You've been wonderful."

"Three hundred ten thousand?"

"Two hundred fifty."

The realtor gazed intently at Chito. "I don't know which is killing me more, those big brown eyes of yours or my new shoes?"

"Probably the thought of losing a deal, no?"

She laughed. "Oh, you're bad–but it's good."

***

Pete Pennebaker wrestled with his walker as if it were something hostile. Shambling through the edifice that was once The Dusty Rose, he looked around in bewilderment. "Sweet Mother McCready. When they said the store was gone they wadn't shittin'. Not even a coat of paint left on the walls."

Nestor, walking behind, kicked at a burnt can of spray glitter that had somehow escaped the inferno. "They say most of the cleaning up is finished already. Just some scraps left." Nestor picked up the spray can. "My wife would like this."

"Take it. Take whatever you want. The 'Going Out of Business Sale' is over." Pete exhaled slowly. "Hard luck. Some people get all the luck in the world–long as it's bad." Pete glanced at Nestor. "What do we do about the Syrian fellow and his baby girl?"

Nestor looked surprised. "He got married, Mr. Pete! When you were in the hospital."

Pete looked genuinely bewildered. "Married?"

"Yes, to Delilah Lyndecker. Marty didn't say nothing?"

"Not a damn thing. Well I'll be...married?"

"Yes, sir."

"Damn, I guess they can fight their own battles now. Where they staying? What they gonna do?"

Nestor stared sheepishly into the distance. "They staying at *Los Abuelos,* Mr. Pete. Back at the hunting camp again. Marty didn't say nothing?"

Pete shook his head. "Not a word. I guess she's running the ranch now." He shrugged. "So it is. I'm working for the new boss now...so it is." Pete walked a few more paces, then turned. "I've seen enough. Sad to see it go, but it wadn't much. Just a cheap little old gee-gaw shop full of junk and cobwebs. Funny–you never miss nothing 'til it's totally outtasight. Wonder why that is? Why do people get attached to senseless things that never amount to nothing?"

Nestor shrugged, "Maybe it's just something we feel..." Nestor pointed to his chest, "...here. *Quien sabe?* Everybody got a soft place for something worthless. Worthless...but necessary."

Pete smiled. "You do me a lot of good, Nestor. Sometimes I get so blue I can't see my way back home again. Then–you save the day for me." Pete nodded at Nestor, then cocked his head toward the car. "*Vamanos.*"

As the two headed for the front of the building, Pete suddenly stopped. "Shit." Across the street he saw Sheriff Albert Naylor getting out of his police car. "Nearly made a clean break, now I gotta put up with this four-flusher." Pete muttered and spit.

Albert, all large teeth and pretext, approached the two men, hand extended. "Well, here's the old reprobate himself. I heard you got sprung from the doctor slammer. How you feeling, *Comandante*?" Naylor was in full-on campaign mode. Seizing Pete's hand, he oozed benevolence. "Zoe and I tried to get up to San Antonio to see you several times, but the grandkids came to town and Zoe had dental work to take care of, and...how ya doing, chief?"

Pete nodded stoically. "Fine, fine–nothing works anymore, but I don't plan on hitting the rodeo circuit no how."

Albert shook Pete's hand vigorously. "Isn't that the truth. Leave that to the younger cowboys...right, right." Albert let loose Pete's grip and stared earnestly into his eyes. "So, Pete, I got a little bit of news..."

"That so?"

"Yessir, we did some background research on your...friend...Mr. Hakim."

"That so? He's a married man now, you know. To an American taxpayer."

Albert nodded. "Yes, I heard the good news." He glanced around the blistered shop. "Somebody's gonna have a hell of a tax headache this year. Makes you wonder what old T.T. was doing out in that alleyway anyway? Well, I 'spect we'll know something soon enough. Anyhow..." Pete pursed his lips, bracing himself for the usual shit note Albert was known for dispensing. "It seems, up in Indiana, Evansville I think it was, there's a warrant out for a Mr. Hakim person wanted for...stabbing an individual."

Pete stared at Albert for a long moment. "I'll be. What become of the person got stabbed?"

"Alive. Just wants a little justice, you know. It's assault and battery charge."

"Or maybe...self-defense?"

Albert smiled. "Well you know, neither of us are lawyers. That's why we have a judicial system to sort all this out, fickle as the law usually is."

"I 'magine you'll have to speak to Mr. Hakim's lawyer."

Albert looked surprised. "He's got one?"

"He does now. My lawyer. Why don't you give old Bob Goldstein a call."

Albert's face was expressionless. "Goldstein and Boone? Outta Dallas?"

Pete nodded. "That's right. You remember, they handled the litigation I had awhile back with Exxon Mobil...that unpaid royalty screw-up. Did a fine job."

"They're handling criminal cases now?"

"Whatever I need. Good people."

Albert smiled and started to turn, then turned suddenly back around. Pete interrupted before he could speak.

"Call the lawyer."

Albert turned once again, then exited the store. He called out from the door, "Welcome home, Pete."

"Good to be back!" Pete waited until Albert was halfway across the street, then muttered, "Sorry pissant." Pete spit again and turned to Nestor. "Did we leave the cellphone in the car? Need to call my lawyer."

\*\*\*

Chito sat alone in the booth of *El Maguey* Mexican restaurant and stirred a spoon around his bowl of steaming *caldo*. It seemed to him that his life had speeded up to the point of race car barely holding the track. Here he was buying a food truck for the newlywed Hakims, putting an offer out on the Jansky building, moving in with Marty and knowing full well his London work sabbatical would be up by the end of the month. Was he losing his mind, fulfilling Tom's behest, or spectacularly achieving all in some half-assed way? And the quandary that kept him awake nearly every night was the growing compulsion inside him for a perplexity named– Pettus. Where to begin? The man, for this gay man anyway, was everything he thought he'd ever want, need or conceive of for the rest of his life. Yes, it was lust. Of course, it was lust.

From the minute he saw him naked, covered in mud and standing before God and jackrabbit like some libidinous lifeforce rising from the earth in carnal splendor–it was over for Chito. Towel tossed; game forfeited–nothing left but total submission to the sway of providence. And other than Pettus's flip confession of "boy stuff" experimentation with Tom in their youth, what remote hope was there for Chito to even aim for? He'd gone and slept with Marty. He did. And agreeable, exuberant and spontaneous as it was, it didn't, couldn't erase his compulsion for Pettus. Marty wants Chito, Chito wants Pettus, Pettus wants Marty. A recipe for madness.

Marty entered the café in a burst of energy, wearing tight jeans, a tight T-shirt and her sun-streaked hair bouncing on her shoulders–the truckers at the counter gave her a full assessment. "Sorry I'm late. Daddy went down to see the Dusty Rose and he's all in a lather about getting his lawyer involved to do something with Mr. Hakim and Sheriff Naylor and who knows what all...that looks good, how is it?" Marty pointed to his soup.

Chito glanced up, a thousand miles distant. "Haven't tried it yet. I've been...stirring."

Marty smiled. "Lot on your mind?" Chito shrugged and the waitress appeared with silverware, napkin and a glass of ice water. Marty loved that in Texas one never asked for ice water. It was mandatory, from humble roadhouse to five-star bastion. A small recompense for spending summers in hell. "Thank you, Carmen. Yes please, I'd like the *migas* with corn tortillas."

The waitress scribbled silently on her pad. "Everything okay with the soup?"

Chito looked up. "*Ta bueno,* just letting it cool."

The waitress ambled off and Marty spoke softly, "So...what's new?"

"I put a bid on the Flower Emporium."

Marty looked startled. "Why?"

"I don't know. I think...the town needs a flower shop. I've been thinking a lot about Tom and what he said about 'helping the town.' You know, it's a big responsibility; I made a vow to my husband. And it feels like–the longer I stay here–the more I'm pulled to stay here. Crazy!"

"Is it?"

"Yes! I have a job, a life. I have friends all over the world–what am I doing here?"

Marty stared at her dripping glass of ice water. "Other than fulfilling my brother's bidding, I was hoping you might say something like, 'Getting to know Marty Pennebaker has been one of the delightful, unexpected revelations of my life.'"

Chito looked at her. "Yes! But there have been other 'revelations,' as you put it. I'm in...I have...I don't know if you can call it love but it's certainly an obsession–with someone else."

The waitress appeared with chips and salsa and set them down. "Your *migas* are on the way."

After a moment Marty cleared her throat. "And you're going to say..."

"Pettus."

Marty blinked quickly, then turned to stare out the restaurant window. "Well. That kind of...surprises...and doesn't."

"Meaning?"

Marty laughed. "Well, the first thing I can think of–he's straight."

"Not entirely." Marty's eyes widened. "He played around with your brother back in the day."

Marty laughed again. "That? Oh, for God's sake! Tom told me that when he was still a teenager. Pettus would just as soon stick it in a bowl of oatmeal back then. He was 100% testosterone."

"He still is."

Marty looked back at Chito. "Have you told Pettus?"

"No."

"Will you?"

"Yes."

"And if he says..." Marty shrugged, "Thanks, but no thanks?"

"Then I'll have an answer."

Marty picked up a chip, held it in her fingers, then dropped it unexpectedly. "So, I have a confession too. Cards on the table...what if I said I loved you? What if I said from the first moment I saw you I felt something entirely new to me. First time in my life I knew that I loved a person without having the slightest conception of why. How does that happen? Maybe we have that in common."

Chito stared at Marty's hand resting on the table and reached for it. Marty whispered, "So, between us...what did that mean to you?"

Chito looked into her eyes, squeezing her hand. "Love. It felt like all kinds of love, not just one kind. I don't think I'm capable of one kind. I know I'm not."

"Hot plate." The waitress set the dish down and started to refill their water glasses. "Need anything else?" They both shook their heads silently. "Pay at the cashier, please." As the waitress walked away, Marty blew her nose into a paper napkin.

"Well, this has been one of those instructive days life seems to dole out so liberally. Never stop learning, growing..."

"Or loving." Chito stared at Marty. She slowly picked up her water glass.

Marty sighed, "Loving what we love. What's to be done about it? I guess we just keep on till the music stops, huh? And when it finally stops..."

Chito shook his head. "I don't think it ends. I think the song just changes. We change with it."

Marty held the glass to her forehead. She smiled at Chito then stared at her plate of food. "Flour tortillas. I always ask for corn, they always bring flour. What the hell—we live in anticipation." Marty picked up her fork and cut into the steaming platter of cheese, chips, eggs, onions, jalapenos and pinto beans. Lunchtime perfection.

# CHAPTER SEVENTEEN

"There's somebody here to see you." Darlene stood grinning in the doorway of the Lyndecker living room and crossed her arms. Darcy turned slowly from her seat in the rocking chair in front of the TV.

"Who?"

"You're just going to have to get up now and come find out."

"Darlene, don't be a butthead. Who is it?" Darlene smiled again, then turned with a snicker and walked off. Darcy stopped rocking. Her body felt like a sack of rocks weighing her down, down into the floor and into the very grunge beneath her toes. This is what it's like to be a hundred years old and have a bad case of influenza, she reasoned. Nothing works, nothing resonates, nothing matters. Slouching into the next room, she squinted at the sole light bulb over the front entrance.

"Hello?" Peering around the corner of the bookshelf, she stopped abruptly and called again, "Hello...Wayne?"

Wayne Canfield stood at the front door, scrubbed and shiny as she'd ever seen him. Hair combed, pressed shirt and khakis, he held out a fresh bouquet of roses before him. "Don't mean to intrude on you, but I don't see you around much anymore and I just wanted to say...hi. These are for you." He held out the roses and Darcy stared at them, shocked.

"Oh, Wayne...no one has ever brought me flowers in my whole life! Why would they? Who brings ice cream to the Dairy Queen?"

"I hope they're okay. I brought 'em down from San Antonio this afternoon."

Darcy examined the bouquet, mumbling to herself, "Nature's Cherry, Red Paris, and there's a Sweet Unique. Velvet ribbon, packet of preservative, yard of green tissue-$31.95? No, I'd say $29.90-at the grocery store, right?"

Wayne, looking only slightly deflated, shook his head. "They were almost forty dollars. I picked each rose out myself."

Darcy looked startled. "Oh, Wayne-you paid too much. We'd let this go on Valentine's Day and Mother's Day for $26, $27 dollars max."

"It wasn't about the money..."

"I hate it when these large chains rip people off. I mean, we managed to undersell Walmart when we had to. It's just so moneygrubbing...."

"Wasn't about the money...."

Darcy shook her head. "But people don't know, and they just go to any old place and let the corporate bastards rob 'em blind..."

"Darcy."

"Our only saving grace was that we didn't live in a big city and we had a captive audience 'til that whore took over..."

"Darcy!" Wayne shouted and Darcy looked at him startled. "I bought these for you. I bought these...because a man gives flowers to a woman when...he likes her."

Darcy dropped the flowers to her side. "Oh, Wayne...in the nicest way possible...isn't there anybody else you like?"

Wayne shook his head. "No. No there isn't. It's been you

since fourth grade. And I can't hide how I feel anymore. You're free to tell me to take a flying leap or burn in hell, but my feelings for you have never changed. Not once. Now I know I'm not your ideal of something wonderful. But you need to give me a chance. That's all–just give me a chance."

Darcy looked genuinely perplexed. She spoke softly. "Why do I have to give you a chance, Wayne Canfield? You're a good person, I've always liked you and we have indeed known each other forever–but I don't owe you or anyone a chance. A chance is something you give yourself."

Wayne stepped forward and cupped his hands over hers. "Here goes–I love you! Always have, always will. My divorce was finalized yesterday, so I'm a free man! How many opportunities does a body get in life?"

Darcy, mouth open, shook her head. "Wayne, I haven't been on a date in...years."

"Look–you're going to have to face it. I'm your biggest fan whether you like it or not. I'm not going anywhere and I don't think you're going anywhere. Maybe we should–at least get to know each other a little?"

Darcy didn't know where to look. She felt cornered. Escape! Where, how? She stared intently at her flip-flops and cleared her throat. "So...if you feel like walking around the VFW golf course on Sunday afternoon...I guess that'd be okay."

Wayne nodded eagerly. "That's great! I like the golf course. They've cleaned it up good since they dragged off that dead horse awhile back. Makes me think of England...or Six Flags." Wayne nodded and touched his Stetson, then exited quickly. Darcy pondered the Six Flags declaration, smiled, then returned to her rocking chair in front of the TV feeling, strangely enough, slightly less gloomy than before.

*\*\*

Adnan slowly backed the renovated Chevy mail truck to the side door of the Pennebaker hunting house. Delilah stood on the steps with a tray of bagged and wrapped breads, sweets, pastries and meat pies. Haya, next to her, clutched Popo steadfastly. Suddenly, the cat squirmed and jumped, making a mad dash to hide behind the washing machine on the carport.

"Popo!" Haya darted for the cat as Adnan instinctively slammed on the brakes. Leaping from the front seat, he reached for Haya as she passed, grabbing her.

"*Haya, waish betsawi? Kan bi'iimkani dhsk!*"

"*Alquta natat men eidy. Ana kont khayfa alaa Popo!*"

"*Enty lazem tekony hariesah. Khody balek men el sayarah.*"

Immediately the tears arose. Delilah quickly sat the tray down and moved to comfort Haya.

"It's okay, honey. Your daddy was just afraid you might get hurt."

Haya wailed and pointed. "Po-po!"

Delilah turned to Adnan. "You frightened her. She was only looking out for her friend." Popo, now sitting atop the washer, idly licked the fur on his arm.

Adnan took a deep breath. "Yes, I know. It scared me...I lost my temper. The new truck, our new home, our new lives...I'm just feeling...so much worry."

Delilah sat the tray down and put a hand on Adnan's chest. "We had a saying we used to recite to each other when I was in Rehab: *'Listen to God with a broken heart. He is not only the doctor who mends it but also the father who wipes away the tears.'* It's a good one, no?"

"Yes. Very good. I'm still learning every day what it's like to be normal in such an abnormal place...for me and Haya." Delilah nodded. "I know you will help me and I will help you and we shall both help Haya together." Delilah smiled. Adnan continued. "I am...imperfect. But I am aware of my faults,

247

truly, and I am conscious of what I must aim for in this life."

Delilah took his face in her hands and Adnan embraced her. Haya approached, putting her arms around her father's leg.

"'Ana asfa baba."

"Ma fi shei. Abaki beya'la' kteer–Hatsaadeey ma yea'la' tany?"

Adnan rubbed Haya's head. All forgiven for the moment. He nodded toward the truck. "Come, I want to show you what I've done inside. Close your eyes." Adnan led them both to the side door and helped them step up. Standing closely behind them in the middle of the cramped interior, he spoke softly, "Open your eyes!" Delilah and Haya both stared around the new kitchen-on-wheels in utter astonishment. The inside had been painted in bold stripes of red, white and black. Iridescent green stars were attached everywhere as well as hanging from the ceiling by sparkling tinsel. The oven, fryer, exhaust fan, fridge, countertops and microwave glistened. Delilah took it all in with wide-eyed amazement. "It's like a Cracker Jack box turned inside out!"

Adnan looked puzzled. "A what?"

"It's a box of candy popcorn. All shiny and sparkly. Where'd you come up with the color scheme?"

Adnan answered quietly, "It's the flag of Syria. Once upon a time it made us all very proud. Perhaps someday..." The thought quietly disappeared from Adnan's lips.

Delilah noticed an object above the door and smiled. "One of our rhinestone crosses! Where did you find it?"

"I saved it for you. It was in the alley with the rest of the trash. Somehow it survived."

Delilah touched the cross, admiring it. "Something good always survives in the end."

Haya picked up a colander and put it on her head. "Hada sayahmini lama alquta tuhawil taodhani."

"She says the strainer will protect her when Popo tries to

bite her ear again." They laughed, then suddenly a voice spoke behind them.

"Wow, oh wow, oh wow! Looks like y'all got everything in here but a piano and a pool table. Can I come in?" Darcy stepped up into the truck.

"Hey, Darce–what are you doing out this way?"

"Just came to see how my favorite twin is doing." Darcy patted Haya's colander head as she studied the interior. "Very nice." She stood at the order window. "This where all the money comes in?"

Adnan slid the window back and forth. "We can run the air conditioner if it gets too hot or just leave the windows open all day."

"Who did your menu board?" Darcy held up a painted sign plank.

"I did that. Adnan wanted something Middle Eastern around the edges but all I could think of was palm trees and camels. Does it work?"

Darcy nodded. "Perfect. You win hands down in the art department, Lilah."

Delilah grinned and Darcy continued studying the interior. "Pots, pans, Styrofoam cups, ice maker, espresso machine, sink, napkins..." She brushed one of the stars overhead. "...green stars! Just missing one thing."

They stared at Darcy.

"Me!"

Delilah shook her head. "You?"

"Me! And you don't have to pay me either. You know why? Because we're going to be working together again. Full on. You know why that is? Because Mr. Chito is buying the frigging Flower Emporium and he wants me to run it!"

Adnan and Delilah looked puzzled. Delilah tilted her head.

"Wait...Chito's buying the Emporium...and wants you to run it?"

Darcy grinned.

"So what do you need us for?"

"Did Chito not just finance y'all on this food truck? Are you not in a business relationship now with Chito? Did I just not tell you Chito is buying the Emporium? Chito wants you both to work out of the Emporium AND run the food truck too. We'll all be a team!"

Adnan and Delilah blinked at each other. Adnan spoke, mystified. "Who does this sort of thing...for strangers?"

Darcy spoke. "You yourself were a stranger not so long ago, Mr. Hakim. And now look–you're family. How? Why?" Darcy shrugged. "Why ask why?"

Delilah and Adnan stared at each other uncomfortably. Finally, Delilah spoke, "But...Darce...we were kinda thinking this would be our opportunity to become our own bosses now."

"And you will, silly! I don't want to be a part of..." Darcy waved her arms in the air, "...this! It belongs to y'all. But we can complement each other! Adnan can run the truck, you can run the bakery inside the store–whatever works best. Plus, I'm gonna need your help in the store anyway."

Delilah looked dazed. "I just don't know. It seems like maybe losing the Rose was some kind of sign we should be paying attention to."

"Exactly! So it's gone now. Not a damn thing we can do about it. An angel named Chito dropped down in our midst to give us all a second chance. The Wicked Witch is moving to the Panhandle with our sex-starved brother so now we have nothing, truly, nothing to stop us!"

Adnan cleared his throat. "May I speak?"

Darcy nodded. "Yes, you may."

Adnan put his arm around Haya and pulled her into his lap. "My daughter and I have never known such generosity. I keep thinking maybe this is a dream, a trance, that some new disaster lies just ahead. And then instead...only more blessings. Why? I don't know why." Adnan suddenly stood up, setting Haya in his chair. "But this I know. I memorized in English, in school, when I was a boy, *'The moving finger writes; and, having writ, moves on: nor all thy piety nor wit shall lure it back to cancel half a line, nor all thy tears wash out a word of it.'* The Rubáiyát of the Omar Khayyam." Adnan looked at Delilah, then at Darcy. "What is done is done. Indeed, why ask why?"

Darcy smiled and crossed her arms. "I got one too. *'Can't never could!'* Without a positive frame of mind you'll be scratching a pauper's behind your whole life. What have you got to lose?"

Delilah shared a look with Adnan. "Well?"

Adnan pursed his lips, then held out his hand to Darcy. "Partners!"

Delilah put her hand on theirs. "Partners."

Haya stood on her chair and extended her hand. "Pah-nah!"

Laughing, Delilah turned to Darcy. "Owners of the Emporium? In your entire life did you ever think such a thing?"

Darcy laughed. "Never. Thought of running an eighteen-wheeler through the front door a few times–but only if Satan's Bride was standing in it."

Haya whispered in Adnan's ear. He turned to the others. "Excuse us–Haya has to use the bathroom. For some reason she needs an escort."

Delilah spoke. "I'll go. I have to bring the rest of the baked goods out anyway."

Darcy said, "Yes, I wanted to talk with Adnan for just a minute."

Delilah took Haya's hand and they headed for the house. Adnan studied Darcy's face, curious. She suddenly reached into her pocket and pulled out a small knife. She placed it on the counter next to Adnan.

"I think maybe you dropped this at the house the other

night when we were all enjoying those peaches that Darlene brought."

Adnan looked at the knife, then quickly felt his pants pocket.

"It has the initials 'A.H.' on it. I just assumed it was yours."

Adnan hastily picked up the knife and slipped it back into his pocket. "Yes, thank you." He smiled. "I didn't realize it was missing, so much distraction lately." Darcy nodded slowly. Adnan turned to leave. "I'd better see if they need more help in there."

"Adnan...I think you and I share a little secret. I think I've seen that knife before, haven't I?"

"I couldn't say."

"Not exactly seen...felt." Adnan fixated on the truck door. Darcy continued, "Cardamom. It's such an unusual scent. Not too many people around here smell like cardamom...except you. Then when I saw this knife..."

Adnan turned to look at her. "As I've said before, I'll do what I have to do to protect my daughter. You caught us asleep. I was afraid; all I could think of was escape. You stood between us and the door. I prayed that the barn was dark enough, that your memory was clouded, that you somehow would misremember. I prayed for a miracle. A miracle of forgiveness. What are you going to do?"

Darcy remained expressionless for seemingly an eternity, then finally raised her shoulders in a sign of acquiescence. "Nothing. The same as you. I might've done the same thing. I meant it when I said it, you're family now. All I'm going to ask of you is to take that knife and go somewhere on this big ranch and drop it into a deep rock crevice and never look back. Does that work for you?"

Adnan swallowed hard, then nodded. "Yes."

"And we don't ever have to bring it up again, ever. Forgotten?" Darcy reached out her hand.

Adnan took it and they shook. "Forgotten."

Darcy craned her neck toward the camp house. "Go tell your wife and daughter I had to get back into town."

Adnan started for the door, then turned once more back to Darcy. "You are a strong woman. We say in my country only the strong can forgive, never the weak. *Inshallah.*"

\*\*\*

"Are you ever leaving?" Pettus grimaced as he yanked and pulled the single wire cable saw held tightly in his hands. Meticulously, he filed away on the old cow's horn that had grown inverted and was now touching the side of her cheek. In another month or two the horn would start piercing her skull. Not an everyday occurrence, but a common enough one with Herefords and crossbred cattle that one always had to keep an eye out.

"Would you like me to leave?" Chito stood atop the pipe fence and gazed down at Pettus's handiwork in fascination. He imagined he could no more saw a cow horn with a wire thin as a fishing line than he could perform brain surgery. Inversely, the thought of Pettus wearing a three-piece Marks and Spencer suit with Testoni loafers perched atop a desk in some posh West End office didn't seem anomalous at all to him either. Why? Could it be Alpha male masculinity pinnacles Beta male identity wherever and whenever it decides to park its size eleven feet? Possibly. In other words, one of the world's worst kept secrets–big dick men don't really have to try all that hard–ever. Why bother?

"I don't particularly care one way or the other." With one swift snap, Pettus popped eight inches of horn off the old cow's dome and sent it airborne across the head gate like a flying comma. He lifted his straw Stetson and mopped his brow. "Tell you the truth, I'm getting used to you."

Chito laughed. "How so?"

Pettus wiped his forehead with his other arm. "You're like

an old pair of shoes–you don't bother me, you don't squeak, and you don't stink yet." He pointed. "You want to grab that toolbox? Got a mama goat in the pen outside the barn, may have to pull her kid. You up for a maternity demonstration?"

Chito grimaced only slightly, nodding his head. "I'm here to learn. All of it."

Pettus opened the head gate and the whiteface Braford mama cow ambled out of the chute as casually as a Bed, Bath and Beyond shopper perusing towels. Pettus shook his head. "Wish they were all like that. I'd a been spared a half dozen broken fingers, a busted lip and a pulled groin."

"What happened?"

"I'll tell ya one day when the bourbon's chilled and my butt's in a reclining position. Come on." The two men started off for the barn. Chito, in his stiff jeans, new T-shirt and barely worn Tony Lama boots still felt entirely too city slicker to remotely compete with Pettus's tattered swagger. The Bible quote his maternal grandmother had made him memorize as a youth, "*Muchos son llamados, pocos son elegidos*–Many are called, few are chosen," came to mind. What did it mean exactly? We all wish we could secretly be a butch Texas cowboy–even if we'll never come close to making the cut?

Chito leaned sideways as he switched hands carrying the heavy toolbox. "So, I wanted to come out here today to just get a feeling about, you know, what you think about these things I'm doing with Tom's money and...stuff."

Pettus glanced at Chito. "What kind of stuff?"

Chito cleared his throat. "Just, you know, kind of see where your head's at."

"It's on my shoulders last time I looked. What's your point?"

"I, uh, well, Marty...she..."

"Yeah?"

"She...we. Well, really me..."

"Yeah."

"You know, I guess–I'd just like to know where your head's at."

Pettus stopped walking and turned to Chito, "You're not making a damn bit of sense. Tell me what you want."

Chito sat the toolbox down, his face red. He finally blurted out, "I'd like...to get to know you better."

Pettus stared at him, puzzled. "What does that mean exactly?"

Chito exhaled. "It means, you know I'm a gay man. It means I know you've had gay sex. It means, I find you attractive and it means..." He let the rest of his breath rush out like a dying inner tube. "Screw it...that's what it means."

Pettus looked as if he were trying to decipher Russian. After an exasperating interval, Pettus turned and began walking away.

Chito called out to him, "I didn't mean to offend you!"

Pettus, striding fast, called back, "I'm not offended...I'm thinking!"

Chito smiled slightly, then picked up the toolbox and hurried after him. "Well?"

"Well, what?"

"Aren't you going to say anything?"

"Sure–you a top or a bottom?"

Chito stopped walking and laughed. "Whoa! You're getting a little ahead of me here. Where'd that come from?"

Pettus stopped and turned, "You think, just 'cause I look like a redneck I gotta act stupid all the time? I know what goes on in the gay world. I read stuff. You think I'm supposed to be shocked or something? Like a guy's hitting on me and I'm supposed to...what? Bust his chops? Call the police? Tell my mama? Okay, so you like me, okay. You know where I'm at. You know what I want, I've told you."

"Marty doesn't love you." Chito immediately regretted saying it even as the words left his mouth. "Sorry, I didn't mean that, exactly."

Pettus slowly rubbed his forehead again with his sleeve. "Yes, you did, and it's true. She doesn't love me...she loves you. I'm just the son of a bitch who wipes his ass with sandpaper and eats a wild javelina for breakfast every morning. What would I know about feelings?"

"She likes you, a lot. Really."

"I want what she feels for you. That's what I want."

Chito, taken aback, muttered, "And I want what you feel for her."

The two men stared at each other utterly baffled. Finally, Pettus erupted in laughter, laughing so hard he fell to his knees. "Ain't this the godawful shits?"

Chito began to laugh with him, then nodded. "It is...ridiculous."

Pettus continued, gasping for air between hoots, "None of us...not a damn one of us wants what he already has...for nothing! And they think people in asylums are crazy. We got 'em beat all to hell!" Both men, on their knees, laughed until suddenly, completely unexpected, Pettus flung himself powerfully on Chito and kissed him hard on the mouth. No passion or enticement, just a brute, physical stunt to convey, what...frustration, dominance, fear, rage?

Pettus finally jerked back, holding his hand on Chito's neck. "That good for you? That what you wanted? How was it?"

Chito snatched his hand away and fell back, shaken. He rubbed the spit from his mouth and stared into Pettus's wild, agitated eyes. "Why did you do that?"

"You said you wanted to get to know me."

Chito spoke loudly, "You did that out of anger...some kind of asshole 'fuck you'! You decided to make my coming here some kind of pathetic joke." Chito stood, brushing himself off. "Go ahead, have a good laugh." He started walking toward his car, then turned back. "At least someone in your life was honest with you. You're not so special. You're just another guy

256

who's a master at fucking up his own life."

As Chito continued on toward his car, Pettus, still on his knees, watched, then slowly fell back on the bare ground. After a moment he coughed and spit to the side, flinging his hat skyward, sailing into the distance.

# CHAPTER EIGHTEEN

"Goody...fucking...gumdrops!" was the immediate answer Carol Ann replied after Cody uttered his previous observation: "Damn, they've really gone to town on the Emporium, haven't they?" The two stood on the street in front of the building once owned, designed and operated by Carol Ann Jansky.

She shook her head in astonishment. "How in the name of sweet Jesus did things get so almighty screwed up?"

"How so, honey?" Cody assumed his fixed expression, since their honeymoon, of consistent bewilderment.

"This was MY store, MY business, MY livelihood–how in God's name did your sisters end up with MY shop?"

Cody smiled weakly. "Well, babe, you sold it, remember?"

Carol Ann rolled her eyes dramatically. "Of course I sold it! I'm speaking metaphorically." Cody blinked, perplexed.

"That's like an 'example' kind of thing, right?"

Carol Ann thrust an arm around Cody's neck and pulled him close. "So proud of you. You have been reading that *New Word a Day* book I gave you, haven't you?"

He grinned and Carol Ann spoke again. "Well, do we go inside or just stand out here looking like two grackles waiting for a bag of Fritos to roll by?"

Although they'd been back from their honeymoon for almost two months, getting settled into school life at West Texas A & M–all the way to hell and gone up in the Panhandle–had not been easy for Carol Ann. She cried, she raged, she pouted–her only motivator had been Clayton Jansky's unstinting checkbook. That and a new Liquid Platinum Lexus RC F Sport Coupe he bought to ease her distress. But she did most sincerely want to give running the Emporium another try, particularly when she learned that the Lyndecker hobgoblins were temporarily out of business. But, as it sometimes happened when it came to Carol Ann and exceptionally handsome men of just adequate intelligence, she let her feminine instincts be swayed. She was fragile in that department, she knew. She also felt it was probably some preordained omen she'd carry till the end of her days.

Stepping inside the front door, Carol Ann couldn't believe her eyes. All her pink, pastel, lacy, rhinestone girly-girl interior was utterly decimated. In its place were sawhorses, paint drops, stacked drywall, sprayers, nail guns–it looked like the Fourth of July weekend sale at Home Depot.

"Oh...my...sweet Jesus."

Cody stared at the floor and shook his head. "I knew this was a bad idea."

"Where did all my creations go? My incense bar, my Lladro fantasy wall, the Gum Drop Gallery...?"

"Hey, let's go get a tequila sunrise down at Shorty's! You always like dropping by Shorty's." Cody, grinning madly, tried redirecting the room's rapidly descending atmosphere in his most upbeat manner. To no avail.

"I could just cry. If I started now I'd never stop. What have they done with all my talent?"

At that instant, Deliah, wearing overalls and carrying a paint roller, appeared from behind scaffolding covered in drop cloths. "Well, hi! I got so carried away with my painting I thought I heard a cat in here yowling." Catching herself, she continued, "But it was a surprise visit from y'all, how nice!"

Cody walked toward her for a hug. "Sis."

"Look at you, all educated-looking college boy!" As they embraced, Delilah smiled at Carol Ann. "I bet you don't recognize a thing in here anymore?"

Carol Ann gazed around the room, dumbstruck. "What are those...colors?"

"Isn't it wild? They match our food truck."

Cody's head spun around. "Food truck? What are you doing with a food truck?"

"Mr. Chito financed Adnan and me. We're selling lunch and sandwiches and baked goodies all over town; out at the rig sites, up at the high school, on game nights, parties–it's really taken off."

Carol Ann's mouth hung open. "You're selling Middle Eastern food in Rita Blanca?"

Delilah nodded. "Yes, ma'am, and as soon as we get the little café set up in here, we'll really be all over town."

Carol Ann looked as if she'd stepped in dog vomit. "Café? Who financed all this, Mr. Pennebaker?"

"Oh no, that was the Dusty Rose! Mr. Chito again. He's just a Mexican angel."

Carol Ann shook her head in dismay. "I don't get it. Pennebaker gives them money, Chito gives them money–what happened with the insurance on the Dusty Rose? You make a million dollars on that one?"

Darcy suddenly appeared from the back of the store in ripped jeans and a man's T-shirt. "Well, look who's back– *Nightmare on Elm Street* herself."

Cody walked between the two. "Darce, don't start. Y'all gotta make peace or you're never gonna see me again."

Darcy looked at Cody surprised. "Cody, I have nothing against your wife whatsoever. I just find it–what's the word– 'destiny,' that now we're here and y'all are way off there in– what's the name of that Panhandle town again?"

"Canyon."

"Canyon–so grand! I hope to see it one day."

Carol Ann walked to Cody and put her arm around him. "Better hurry, we're not going to be there that long. Daddy's offered Cody a management job at the dealership. We may be back way sooner than anyone thinks."

"Well good. Maybe we can find you a position here in the store then. You know–start out with a mop and a broom, but sky's the limit!"

"Thanks. I wouldn't work here if y'all were handing out solid gold vibrators and a lifetime supply of batteries."

Cody interrupted, "Okay, we're going."

Carol Ann continued, "It's too bad T.T. had to burn down your store. Arson's such a hard way to make any money nowadays."

Darcy stepped forward. "I know. And that's why they decided to go ahead and pay anyway when they determined T.T was trying to break in and put the fire out himself. He did everything he could to save the shop and lost his life instead. Even notoriously tight insurance companies can recognize an out-and-out hero when they see one."

Carol Ann shook her head in disbelief. "Come on, Cody. The paint fumes in here are making some people high."

As Carol Ann turned and began walking out of the store, Cody stared at Darcy and whispered, "Did that really happen? Did T.T. try to put out the fire?" Darcy crossed her arms and shrugged.

Carol Ann called out at the door, "Are you coming?"

Cody, as ordered, turned and followed obediently. As the door shut behind them, Darcy shuddered. "Ever feel like ripping your clothes off and diving into a cold beer? That's what I want right this minute."

Darcy headed over to an Igloo cooler in the back corner and retrieved a longneck. Delilah followed close behind. "Oh, Darce, is it true? Uncle T.T. tried to put out the fire?"

Darcy took a long swig of beer and smiled. "Lilah–Jesus walked on water, fed the hungry, raised Lazarus from the dead. Now why would God deny poor old T.T. one last chance to do something good for his kin? Miracles happen! In my book he did a good deed, and yes, it was miraculous...and that's the story we're telling here. You with me?"

Delilah nodded slowly. "Poor old T.T."

\*\*\*

Nestor held Dulce's reins and rubbed her nose. Pete Pennebaker slowly stepped up onto an overturned feed bucket then stepped gingerly onto a shortened sawhorse and eyed the final lunge before him.

Nestor spoke softly. "I can saddle one of the other mares real quick and ride with you, Mr. Pete."

Pete uncomfortably lifted his leg and slung it around Dulce with a grunt and a scowl. "Nope. I'll be fine. Just want to be all by myself for a while."

Nestor looked at him, worried. "Yes, sir."

Pete winced. "Gonna make a little 'welty' up the creek bed and round the pear trap. Don't worry 'bout me. Might even ride over to see that new hundred acres we bought. Don't worry 'bout me–I know my way around."

Nestor put a hand on Pete's leg. "Mr. Pete, I feel much better you let me ride with you. Snakes bad this time of year. The horse get spooked *y no bueno.*"

Pete reached down and touched Nestor's hand. "Thank you, Nestor, but I'll be fine. Do me a favor now and run on up to the house and tell Jacinta to make a big pot of *frijoles* for supper, with plenty of salt pork in it."

Nestor stared at Pete with a look of resignation. After near twenty-five years of interpreting and accepting Pete Pennebaker's mood swings and occasional surprising bigheartedness, he knew when to back off an entreaty. The

*Patron* knows what he knows. It's not for him or anyone else to decide another's intentions. One can question a sober man's aim just once. Beyond that, provocation.

Nestor patted Dulce's nose then released his grip on the bridle. *"Ve, mi jefe. Cuida las ramas de los árboles.* I will watch until you pass beyond the hill. I like to see you riding in the saddle. We all become young again, no?"

Pete smiled and nodded. He studied Nestor's face for a moment then turned Dulce's head around and commenced a gentle lope toward the back corral gate. Nestor squinted until he could no longer see man nor horse on the horizon. He stared moments longer as if expecting some epiphany to rise up and alleviate his mounting uneasiness.

\*\*\*

Pete rode down into the gully carved out by the backwater of the Santa Cecilia Creek that uncoiled through the ranch like a twisted intestine. How the country had changed–and not changed–in his lifetime! Today there were irrigated fields of soybeans and milo, gigantic crop circles of corn and cotton, all prodigiously watered from rapidly dwindling underground aquifers. It weighed heavily on Pete that he'd lived long enough to see his grandparents' astounded expressions when their first windmill was dug and that initial tenuous dribble of briny liquid landed in their outstretched hands. They danced and rubbed their faces and arms and wept with joy.

So many of the old ranches had been sold. "Ranchettes" were the thing. Any Jake from the city could buy thirty acres nowadays, put a travel trailer on it, dot it with deer stands and by God, he'd now become a real sumagun Texas rancher! The only thing missing was an actual cow, but why quibble over particulars. He'd seen the land before oil, and he'd seen the land after. The only meaningful comparison he could make was Padre Island before a hurricane and Padre Island after.

Same geographical upheaval, same refuse dumped, same permanent disfigurement, same environmental cataclysm-plus a huge windfall for the engineers, builders, loan brokers, appraisers and other countless middlemen of questionable employ-not the least of which was the eventual bounty destined for the landowner themselves.

And yet, in spite of all the endless upheaval, some things had remained etched in perpetuity; never changing, always reviving from youthful reminisce. The mountain laurel bloom at the end of winter. Cactus blossoms erupting in scarlet, orange, yellow and occasional mauve exuberance. The intensely sweet smell of *guajillo* flowers. The early summer dew that clung to *sacahuista* grass like sparkling jewels. Electric colored purple *ceniza* bushes erupting to announce a coming rainstorm. Always, prescient desert tortoises on ranch roads moving to higher ground to avoid an impending deluge. Fat cattle lying in the shade on perfectly still, sunny days, chewing their cud in trancelike torpor. Two bucks battling for primacy during the fall rut. Green jays that arrive from Central America every spring to screech and flutter through the oak trees on the creek bottom. A frenzied winter cardinal beating endlessly at its reflection in a truck's side mirror. The dead of winter was probably his favorite time of year. Mesquite fires, quiet, fog, mist, utter stillness everywhere-it fully transported the gray earth and bare brush into a landscape of haunting beauty-if you had eyes to see it. Leading a parched horse to water and indeed watching it drink, for some reason still one of life's more gratifying endeavors. Baby javelinas close behind their mama crossing a *sendero* in a perfectly straight line like dwarf monks on their way to chapel. Baby quail, baby deer, baby calves, baby colts, baby armadillos-God's inspiring plan to honor the permanency of life with miniature perfection.

As Pete rode on, he ruminated on many concerns that fretted unabated in his mind. He'd not been particularly exceptional at anything in life, really. Had no hobbies, no real interests outside the ranch, paid only sporadic attention to politics, mostly to bitch about. Not a regular churchgoer, not a Kiwanis/Lions/Rotary kind of guy, not the country club chap or the sports nut either. He was primarily good at one thing– being ornery. That he could do as good or better than most. And where did it get him? Very few friends, for sure. Mostly employees who took his outbursts of irritability with a shovel of salt. All gruff, no sting–largely exhibition. As an only child he'd learned early on the greater the tantrum, the quicker the reward to silence him. It worked only intermittently as he grew older; wife, Lila B., wouldn't tolerate it for long.

To be perfectly honest, he was lonely, tired, sad and old. Very old. He'd seen quite enough of this life. There was no new anything around the corner waiting to excite or challenge. Just gradual, inevitable dissolution. He'd tried making Christian amends as he was raised up to emulate. Money to the hospital, money to the schools, money to various and sundry supplicants of want who pinned him down with steadfast regularity. It didn't fill him with any great joy or charitable fulfillment. But it's what you did with vast amounts of money. You made it, you spent it, and then you gave it away. What else is it for?

Gradually, Dulce and Pete sidled up alongside the largest live oak on the creek bottom, a tree Pete had spent many an afternoon courting Lila B. beneath when they were newly wooing. Halting, man and horse gazed listlessly into the distance. Pete rubbed Dulce's neck. "Old girl...our many-a-mile together has petered down to merely-a-meander. All right, as they like to say on the TV news, 'It's a marathon, not a race'...something like that."

Pete removed his right foot from the stirrup and tried lifting his leg. It felt numb, completely asleep. He reached down to pull his foot up and slowly, tenderly he was able to swing his leg back up on Dulce's rump. Attempting to stand on his left leg and dismount, he momentarily lost balance and fell with a thud on hard, caliche rock. For an instant it thumped the wind out of him completely and he forgot where he was. Dulce jittered for a second then stood calmly by, glancing round at Pete several times to determine the predicament. Pete lay there a minute longer then slowly rolled over onto his side. Something must've popped or given way. The pain in his chest was intense.

Rising up on his knees, he turned to look back at Dulce. "It's the shits darlin'. Don't get old, no likelihood in any of it." Pete spit out a mouthful of blood and marveled at its scarlet red stain on the white caliche. He grinned and thought aloud, "Modern art. Now I get modern art!" He wheezed and wished he could've shared the moment with Marty. She'd have laughed with him. He wished he could've shared a lot of things with his only daughter. Like how to tell for sure when you're being lied to. Hunches don't lie. When to sell an old dry cow. Check her bag and her titties to see if a calf's still sucking. How groveling before arrogant bankers is one surefire way to get ahead in the world. A small price to pay for leaving your self-esteem at the door in order to one day return with "fuck you" money to wave in their faces. Lots, lots more he wanted to and needed to share, but the time and mood were rarely compatible. He'd finally stopped worrying about Marty. It was her burden now. He could've been a better father. He could've been a better everything. The spot-on lament of all humanity. It was her turn to rise and fall on her own.

Gasping, Pete managed to pull himself up by holding on to the saddle pommel. It felt like every cell in his body was dialing out for attention and the operator on duty was MIA. Slowly he unbuckled the cinch and, grabbing the horn and cantle, he shook free the saddle and blanket, letting them fall heavily to the ground. Too weak to pick up the gear, he led Dulce a few feet away and rubbed her nose. He loosened the strap under her chin and gently pulled the bridle off.

Putting his head next to hers, he spoke softly. "Now listen to me, you know how much I love you. You're the only thing left in life that matters so deeply to me. You're going to be well taken care of 'til your time comes, don't you worry. I want you to head on back to the barn now–do this for me. Don't look back, just keep moving. God bless you sweet girl...GIT!"

Pete waved the bridle in the air and Dulce ran about ten or twelve feet, then stopped and turned back to look at him. Eyes burning, Pete couldn't speak. He waved the bridle high and made a hissing sound. This time Dulce turned and walked away slowly, finally disappearing into the brush. Pete rubbed his face then slowly moved back toward the saddle and pushed it with one foot till it rested against the tree trunk. Squatting, then falling down beside the saddle, he edged his back into the seat and stared up at the sky, exhausted. It was quiet and peaceful. A good afternoon for settling the ledger. He thought about maybe saying a prayer, but it'd been too long for him to remember how exactly all that was supposed to go. Do you ask for things or do you just list all the stuff you're grateful for? He wasn't sure. And if God didn't know all that already, he was certainly doing a piss-poor job. Still, he wanted to recall something fine, peaceful and inspirational. He spat again. This time, the bloody spittle depicted mortality to him, not art. He looked up to see a roadrunner darting out from under a cactus bush holding a baby rattlesnake in its mouth. The baby snake twisted and lunged, just shy of making a strike. The roadrunner, all alert intensity, moved closer to study the old man lying under the tree. Pete stared back, fixated. Edging closer to Pete's boot, the *paisano* jerked his head back and forth, trying to make sense of the situation. The snake continued to writhe furiously and then suddenly the roadrunner dropped the snake and jumped up on Pete's boot. Pete held his breath. The snake wriggled frantically away, parallel to Pete's pant leg, aiming precisely for his arm. Pete studied the *paisano's* eyes and he, in turn, stared back at Pete with the intensity of bottled lightning. In a flash the roadrunner leapt from Pete's boot, grabbed the fleeing snake and flew off into the black brush with it still thrashing in his mouth. Pete exhaled sharply and pondered what had just occurred. Was this God's idea of a lesson? Something has to live, something has to die? Why not let the snake bite and kill the roadrunner? Same lesson, different outcome. He finally surmised that it didn't matter. He'd asked for something inspirational, not coherent. It was a good show, God, no question.

Pete reached into his shirt and slowly pulled the concealed pistol from his shoulder holster. It had belonged to his father, who'd always claimed it came from a Brigadier General in the Confederacy. An 1861 Colt revolver, a beauty in its simplicity and modest design. He'd only ever fired it a few times, but it was powerful and resolute and it knew its limits–perfect for the task at hand. He snapped open the cylinder and saw the five bullets neatly aligned. He clicked it back into position then slowly, methodically, pulled the hammer. All ready, all complete–the only thing missing, the only thing needed, was that moment of peace to surround him. He mumbled aloud, "God, if you can hear me, help an old sinner out. Show me some calm now, something whole to lead me on...and thank you." From deep, somewhere in a locked room, the door slowly opened, and Pete began to sing softly an old song his mother had taught him a long, distant time ago.

"Now when I die
Take my saddle from the wall
Put it on the pony
Lead him out of the stall

Tie my bones to his back
Head our faces toward the west
We'll ride the prairie
That we love the best

Ride her out Old Paint
I'm a leaving Cheyenne
And goodbye Old Paint
I'm a leaving Cheyenne"

\*\*\*

The Katzfy Funeral Home had exceeded all expectations. The flowers, the lighting, music, program, seating–even the air conditioning was perfect for wearing a black, light wool summer suit that wouldn't leave you drenched in perspiration within ten minutes. Alone, Marty stood before the closed coffin for a long time. The tears fell but there was no sobbing, no lamentation. Oddly, she felt like crying but couldn't seem to convince herself there was any probability in it. Why weep for an old man who was more than ready to make his earthly departure? Why be sad? He died on his ranch, his horse nearby, his saddle cradling him–he died where he belonged– why be sad? And still, the tears were unrelenting. If only they'd had that "final talk." If only she'd been more pliant, more conciliatory. If only she'd listened more, been less confrontational, remained moderately flexible. But no, she was Pete's daughter after all. To have conceded to his irascible nature would have signaled defeat and for certain his not so veiled disappointment. He needed, demanded, an heir that could stand up to him. Not that either of them particularly relished the established framework, but both understood it instinctively.

Marty suddenly felt a hand on her back and she turned to see Nestor and his wife, Yolanda, and their grown married children, Arturo, Raul and Leticia, each with their spouses and a passel of assorted babies and children in tow. Dressed in their Sunday best, Marty was unexpectedly overcome with emotion. The crying all around began in haste. Nestor and his family had been a part of her family for so long it was as if there'd never been anything before. Now that she was truly alone–who else was there? Yes, they were the employees and the Pennebakers were the employers. At some point, for a myriad of reasons, time erases boundaries, eliminates barriers and draws people closer in spite of perceived disparities. The Nestor Morales family was her family, and vice versa. You can't have survived in deep South Texas for as long as their respective lineages had endured and not share the same tenacity, same perseverance and–no other word for it–love for one another.

As she was hugging the wife of Raul, Marty looked up to see Jacinta and her son Hipolito approach. Wearing a black mantilla over her white hair, Jacinta looked for all the world like a glorified penitent from a Goya painting. Even though she herself was close in age to Pete, she always carried herself with remarkable nobility. Marty moved to embrace her and Hipolito both.

Jacinta dabbed at her eyes. "Oh *señora*, now we can say Mr. Pete is free from all this earthly *confusión*. He was so unhappy toward the last. Such *angustia* to see him suffer so!"

Marty hugged Jacinta tighter. "You were the only one–the only one–who could put up with his pigheadedness day in and day out. Believe me, if anyone's got a nonstop pass to heaven, it's you."

Jacinta smiled. "I tell you a secret, we liked each other! He's a man, what can you do? He let you know how he felt every hour, every day. We had no problems–I let him be him and he let me be me."

Marty blinked back at Jacinta. It was about the sanest reason she'd ever heard for weathering a fluctuating relationship. Simple, precise. Why in hell was it so hard for her, then, to put such certainty into practice?

And on they came. Fidencio and his second or third wife, Gloria, and their six or seven children. Marty couldn't remember exactly how many were his, how many were hers, and how many were "theirs," but they were a lively, animated bunch that brought some much-needed life to the otherwise despondent occasion.

Marty stood in the aisle for a long time greeting neighbor after acquaintance after hazy stranger until her hands pulsated from back-patting and her eyes burned with repeated emotion. Sheriff Naylor and his wife, Zoe, Deputy Canfield (minus Tanya,) Clayton and Barbara Jansky, Dr. Finley, attorney Bill Seiffert, the ladies from the Dairy Queen plus Sandy, Omar, Julio and Memo, Thaine, Jazz and Jimmy, Vonnie Pawlik, Miss Delmer, Billy Mapstone, Brittany Hinojosa, Lurene Dornak, the Mayor, the City Council, the hospital staff, the high school principal, the Ford, Chevy and Polaris ATV dealers, the ladies garden club, the local NRA chapter, the dog catcher and even the town drunk and town socialist were there. The aisles were full, the hallway was full, the lobby was full and there were people standing outside in the parking lot. It helps to die in a small town where everyone knows you or wants you dead. They all show up for the same reasons.

Marty was about to be seated in the front pew when she turned to see the aisle parting for what appeared to be a Kentucky Derby winner garland of roses being ferried toward the coffin by Darcy, Delilah and Darlene Lyndecker.

"Excuse me...sorry...'cuse!...pardon..." The women came to a halt just beside Marty.

Panting, Darcy handed Marty the card. "It's from the board of the Livestock Sale Barn. We worked on it all night. Pretty damn fabulous, huh?"

Marty nodded. "Amazing."

Delilah, out of breath, spoke quickly. "Would you like it gracing the top of the coffin or more of a casual 'flung' effect?"

Marty was stumped. "Well..."

Darlene grunted, "Y'all, this is starting to get heavy on the tail end here. What say we unload and worry about esthetics afterwards?"

Marty jumped in. "Right, how 'bout we lay it across the top here...yes...perfect!"

As the women stepped back and the assembled multitude admired, it did look incredible. Marty leaned toward Darcy, whispering, "How many roses are in that thing?"

"If you have to ask, you're too poor to handle the answer."

Marty nodded, leaning in again. "What happened to your brother? Thought for sure he'd be here?"

Darcy shrugged. "You know better than me. That one's about as predictable as a diabetic holding a sugar doughnut." Darcy hugged Marty, followed by Delilah and Darlene, and they edged their way back to the rear of the room to stand.

Preacher Waddell from the First Methodist Church, a longtime friend and *confrere* of Pete's, entered and walked onto the dais. As lapsed Episcopalians and not members of any local congregation, the Pennebakers always ran the risk of being stoned at the metaphorical city gates of Rita Blanca. Of course, being the wealthiest family in town made up for a multitude of virtuous objections. Sponsor the Little League annually and you were essentially issued the resident Christian "get-out-of-jail" card. Preacher Waddell embraced Marty and she thanked him for agreeing to deliver the *brief* eulogy, at Pete's insistence. She'd heard it a thousand times before: "I don't want any pack of lies about what a fine son of a bitch I was being propagated at my funeral. He was born on and he died on–then get with the damn shovels."

Marty was about to take her seat on the front pew again when she turned to see Chito coming down the aisle, carrying a single calla lily. He looked exceptionally handsome in his tailored black suit with a yellow rose boutonnière. Marty again silently sighed at that "Sosa dash"–coolness, grace and yes, "it's-a-funeral-but-I'm-still-breathing," sex appeal.

"I'm sorry I'm late but I had to drive to San Antonio to buy a proper suit." He smiled, shrugging. "Off the rack."

Marty smiled back and patted the seat next to her. "Please sit here." Nestor and Yolanda scooted down the pew and Chito shook their hands as he sat. Marty turned to him again and suddenly pecked him on the cheek. "Thank you."

By now the entire room had been laser-focused on what was transpiring in the front pew–the dark and handsome stranger, the flower, the kiss–it was better than reruns of *The Bachelor*. Even Preacher Waddell was momentarily sidetracked as he gaped at the couple. Catching himself, he cleared his throat, stood and walked slowly toward the podium. Suddenly another interruption arose in the back of the room. Every head turned as if on remote to see Pettus Lyndecker wearing a suit (!), hair slicked back and holding an orange calla lily, now rambling toward Marty. You could almost hear a mouse fart. He stopped beside her and held out the flower.

"Sorry I'm late. Had to pull a calf out of the cattleguard." He then leaned forward and kissed Marty on the cheek. You could almost hear a collective sigh emanating through the congregation.

Marty, flushed, took the flower and, holding it with the other flower, motioned for the others to scoot down one. Pettus then sat on the aisle, next to Marty, who sat next to Chito. The three of them gazed up at Preacher Waddell reverentially. Pettus reached behind Marty and patted Chito on the back and squeezed his neck with his hand. From near the back of the room, one could faintly hear Lurene Dornak mumbling to herself, "Lord-a-moses, just when you think you've seen everything."

Preacher Waddell cleared his throat again and began to

speak in a dry monotone. "Peter Joseph Pennebaker, born on August 12, 1933, son of Hiram and Violet Pennebaker passed into eternity on August 28th···"

Marty stared straight ahead, barely hearing a word of Preacher Waddell's sermonette. Her heart was beating so fast she thought for a second she might pass out. If there were anyone left in this town who didn't know or couldn't imagine who or what she was doing with her free time, the jig was presently up. Seated between both men, she did sense an odd kind of resolution rising from the fog. What do you call this unexpected schematic–a fractional ménage-a-trois? A vague "*Design For Living*" that comes with no road map, no instructions and no guarantee? It was uncharted and precarious territory. What it really was, was just short of exhilarating–and Marty found herself unable to stop smiling.

Chito bit his lip and stared at the minister dutifully. He couldn't understand a word he was saying. His heart was racing and he was certain his face was surpassing crimson. What did Pettus mean by the pat and the squeeze? Was this some kind of rapprochement? The three of them, pressed tightly in the pew, thigh to thigh, facing Mr. Pennebaker's embalmed corpse–in the scheme of things, it was only slightly surreal. His mind raced. What would it be like to watch Pettus and Marty make love? To have Marty watch him and Pettus make love? To have the three of them entwined in some libidinous entanglement that only God could unsnarl? It was veering dangerously close to wholesale libidinous abandon for a buttoned-up London investment banker who really wasn't all that experienced in the more prurient ways of the world. And yet he couldn't stop the gyrations in his mind. He felt a sudden jab in his side and nearly shot out of his seat. Nestor, next to him, was offering him a stick of gum. Chito anxiously took the gum and unwrapped it with unsteady fingers. '*Hijo cálmate, estoy en un funeral. No en un burdel. ¡Para!*'

Pettus pulled at the tie that was choking his Adam's apple. The suit belonged to an old high school buddy who'd stayed pretty much in the same shape as he had. Sleeves were a mile short, but it worked. Even the tie didn't belong to him. Pettus hadn't been to church since T.T.'s funeral and all he wore then was a clean white shirt. But he needed to make a statement today. It was important. He needed to up his game. He saw a light up ahead and if he followed the light, there would come a vision. A vision of attainment. And that light, strangely enough, was Chito. Why hadn't he seen it before? Marty didn't love him, she loved Chito! In her head anyway. And Chito wanted him–for what, sex, love? Why not, the entire idea of the three of them, somehow, pleasing each other, in a circuitous way–well hell, what else was there presenting itself as any kind of feasible alternative? People gonna talk whether you're happy, sad or dead–people gonna talk! Live your goddam life!

Preacher Waddell droned on in mellifluous monotone, "...and now I'd like to introduce to you some of our newest neighbors here in Rita Blanca who've asked if they may speak briefly today–Mr. Adnan Hakim and his daughter, Haya."

All turned toward the rear of the room to see Adnan and Haya make their way toward the front. Marty turned to Jacinta behind her and they shared looks of surprise. Standing before the lectern, Adnan nervously unfolded a piece of paper from his wedding suit coat pocket. He glanced out at the gathering and smiled nervously. "Please forgive my English, not the best. I asked to speak today because the first person I met in the town of Rita Blanca was Mr. Pete Pennebaker. A man who, as you say, took me under his wing, both myself and my daughter, Haya. I come from a small country in the Middle East, Syria. I won't use up your time by telling you my story because it is a long and unhappy one. What I will say is that the God we all profess to believe in led me here for a reason. Sometimes we don't know why things happen in life, or why we are in the situation that we are. And then, like prophecy, God shows us a new vision, a new way, new hope. This is what happened to us. Mr. Pennebaker never hesitated, never faltered in showing us his care and love. I have heard from others that he was very strong-willed. That he had strong opinions. What I would say is that we can never know completely what is inside another person's heart. We learn from deeds and acts. What I know about Mr. Pete is that he cared. He cared very deeply in his own way..." Adnan folded the paper and put it back in his pocket. "...and he had the God-given power to change people's lives–as he did ours." He lifted the microphone from its holder and spoke again. "My daughter wishes to say a few words."

Adnan handed the mic to Haya, and she shyly stepped forward to face the audience. She began to speak in halting English. "My name is Haya...I'm five...I love Grandpa Pete...My best time ever in Rita Blanca. Thank you, Grandpa Pete. I love you."

Haya handed the microphone back to Adnan, he placed it in the holder, and together they proceeded back to the rear. As they passed Marty, she held out a hand and touched them both. She considered Adnan's words about never knowing a person's heart. What a loss, what a terrible shame they couldn't at least have made a stab at being friends.

Preacher Waddell thanked Adnan and Haya for witnessing for brother Pennebaker and after only the briefest, mandatory proselytizing effort on behalf of the church, he asked for all to stand and sing one stanza of Violet Pennebaker's favorite hymn, "He Leadeth Me."

"He leadeth me, O blessed thought
O words with heavenly comfort fraught
Whate'er I do, where'er I be
Still 'tis God's hand that leadeth me..."

# CHAPTER NINETEEN

Three weeks after the funeral, Marty drove slowly up the bumpy, caliche road toward the derelict Lyndecker home. In all her illusory musings of how an ideal life might feasibly be sustained via some Rita Blanca crystal ball, NEVER did the prospect of Pettus Lyndecker claiming any portion of that distant chimera exist. And yet, here she was now approaching "Lyndecker Incorporated," at Pettus's behest, to discuss a prospectus that had...prospect.

Assured that no one would be around when she arrived, Marty stepped outside her faithful Montego and scrutinized the customary disarray. A mama cat unexpectedly appeared, followed by four kittens strolling nonchalantly from under an abandoned stove. Marty looked up from scratching the cat's head to see Pettus standing in cut-off shorts, a muscle T-shirt and flip-flops. He held out a drink toward her. "Gin and tonic? I know you like them."

Marty, surprised, smiled. "Why not? Won't solve anybody's problems but it sure beats a stick in the eye." She took the glass and sipped. "Um...good." She noticed Pettus's get-up. "Is this a new look for you?"

Pettus stared down at his bare, pale legs and laughed.

"What, the shorts? I don't have to do cowboy all the time, do I?"

Marty nodded. "Not at all."

"Why don't we go sit up on the porch–get out of this sun."

They weaved their way through the junk jungle and up onto the front porch which was surprisingly neat and attractively appointed. Marty glanced around, admiring. "It's sweet up here. Who made this happen?"

"This is Darlene's 'girl cave.' No one's allowed out here. You won't tell on me, will ya?"

Marty laughed. "You got my word. And be nice to Darlene–there's a budding interior decorator there waiting to blossom." Marty took another sip and glanced around the yard. "Tell me something–how'd it all end up looking like this?"

Pettus sighed and rubbed his head. "Well, it didn't happen overnight. When Mama was here, things were orderly, tidy. It just kind of got away from us, ya know? You kinda stop caring when you're hurting. Sit."

Pettus pointed to the porch swing and he took a seat in the wicker rocker nearby. "You hungry? I've got crackers and cheese, a jar of peanuts. I'll make us a sandwich."

"No, no–this is fine." Marty took another sip and pushed the swing with her feet. "So..."

Pettus smiled back. "So."

Marty stared at him for a moment. "You have very nice legs, you know that? I don't think I've ever noticed before. Strong, athletic–you're a regular Philippides."

Pettus stared blankly back then finally grinned. "Okay...I don't always get your jokes, but I do appreciate them."

"I'm not joking! Philippides was an ancient Greek runner. He ran twenty-six miles from Marathon to Athens to announce the Greek victory over the Persians...and then died from exhaustion right after delivering the news."

"Damn, talk about killing the messenger. How do you

know all this stuff?"

"I've got a million files in my head–all stored behind a door marked 'Useless.' You want to make a killing at Trivial Pursuit, I'm your girl."

Pettus stopped rocking. "I tell you what I do want–I'd like to make all of us happy. I'd like to make things right between you, me and Chito."

Marty looked at him impassively. "And how's that?"

Pettus slid to the edge of the rocker, "You know how I feel about you. I know how you feel about Chito, and I'm pretty sure I know how Chito feels about me. What's the solution? I say we make peace and give it a try. Look–you and I are stuck in this place–why not make a go of it and see if we can at least try to make each other happy. Is it too much to ask?"

Marty slowly finished her drink and sat the glass down. "What about you and Chito? What about that?"

"What about it? Honestly, it's not the first or last thing I think about every day, but if it means I'm closer to you, that's enough." Pettus rose from the rocker and moved to kneel before Marty. "There's no manual for this. I don't know if I'm right or wrong. I just know I love you and I can do whatever it takes to keep that alive. I'm being completely honest–I'm willing to try anything."

Marty idly reached out and brushed Pettus's hair. "Have you had this discussion with Chito?"

He shook his head. "I wanted to talk with you first."

Marty exhaled and stared into the distance. "So give me a 'maybe, kinda, sorta' here–how does all this play out in your head?"

Pettus grinned. "I don't know! Not a clue. I mean–we could all try living together..."

"In this town?"

"Exactly! They already hate us–you've got too much money and I'm too redneck even for the rednecks. Why give a shit what 'they' think?"

Marty laughed. "Where would we live?"

"We could buy a house! I've got some money now, remember? You decide."

Marty rubbed her knees briskly, stood, walked a few steps and turned back. "I'm not saying yes; I'm not saying no. It's obvious you've got some homework to do with Chito."

"Does that mean..."

"It means—you probably need to put some action behind those words if you're truly sincere. Ball's in your court, *amigo*. Let's see how good your negotiating skills are, first."

Marty bounded down the porch steps, calling back to Pettus. "Philippides ran twenty-six miles and it killed him. You're only half that far from town—get those running shoes on, boy!"

Marty blew the Montego horn and slowly backed away. Pettus watched, transfixed, as she disappeared down the road. Something had changed, something wonderful and unimaginable that only hours before had seemed impossible. The future looked almost promising. He turned to retrieve the drink glasses when an odd thought suddenly entered his head. What does a guy bring to another guy on a first date?

\*\*\*

The Dusty *Nopalito* opened with all the huzzah Rita Blanca could muster for the much-anticipated reincarnation of the former Dusty Rose in the former Carol Ann Jansky's once flowering Flower Emporium. It was a day of celebrating, congratulating...and not a little sweet revenge, for Darcy anyway. Delilah and Adnan were swamped serving up coffee and sweets in the tiny Seriously Scrumptious Syrian pocket-cafe in the store's rear. They barely had time to catch their breaths, much less socialize. Haya weaved between the tables passing out free samples, shadowed by Popo, sharp-eyed for any spillage. Wayne Canfield was given a smock to wear and instructed to spritz customers with essential oils as they entered. It got awkward only once when he accidentally sprayed Justin McKelvy, who he'd arrested only the week before for drunk driving. Sheriff Albert and wife, Zoe, arrived and departed hastily after a cursory once-over. Zoe declared the store "interesting" and Sheriff Albert gave Adnan the stink-eye after loudly declaring he was on a diet when Haya held up the sampler tray. On the way out the door, Albert reminded Wayne that even though it was his day off, a law officer needed to maintain propriety at all times. Wayne grinned and said he thought of that very proviso every time the sheriff and Zoe went to Las Vegas for one of their frequent "lost weekends." They then both departed as glumly as they had arrived.

To Darcy's amazement, Barbara Jansky entered the store, alone. Glancing around wide-eyed, she took it all in as if she were capturing a documentary in her head. Darcy quietly slipped behind her. "How're you doing, Miz Jansky? Nice to see you."

Barbara turned quickly. "Oh, Darcy, hello. How different it all looks."

"Indeed."

Barbara continued to scan the room, pondering thoughtfully, "Indeed, indeed...time waits for no man. Opportunity knocks, advantage enters–achievement wins the day." She turned back to Darcy. "No hard feelings, I hope," then suddenly laughed. "Did you ever think we'd be family one day?"

Darcy laughed also. "Honestly–that thought NEVER entered my mind, not once."

Barbara finished chuckling, "Well, at least y'all got that insurance money. That made up for a lot, I'm sure."

Darcy stared at Barbara, puzzled, "Insurance money? We haven't gotten a dime on the Dusty Rose. Delilah and I pooled our funds from the land sale to Mr. Pennebaker, and Mr. Sosa helped with the rest."

Barbara blinked. "You DIDN'T get any insurance money?"

"No ma'am, not yet. Probably won't. Actually, Uncle T.T. did us a big favor." Darcy continued looking at Barbara. "And in a way, so did Carol Ann. We were in a rut at The Dusty Rose. Everyone knew it but Lilah and me. We needed a complete start over, a real resurrection. Funny how it all turns out."

At that moment Wayne passed by and shook his head. "Nobody's buying the Cucumber Mint but I've sold three Key Lime, four Sage/Lilac and one Nantucket Night."

Darcy grinned. "Must be that animal magnetism of yours making 'em spend money. You know Miz Jansky?"

"I certainly do, how you been?"

"Fine, fine–I could use a little animal magnetism, so what do you recommend?"

"Cucumber mint."

"I was afraid you'd say that. Well, let's have it. If my husband even bothers to notice I'll come back and buy all you got." Wayne smiled and he and Barbara walked off toward the register

Thaine and Jazz entered the store with Jimmy in tow. Jazz murmured, "You touch anything, and I'll break your neck. Do-Not-Touch-A-Thing!"

Affronted, Jimmy recoiled. "What do you think I am, some out of control newt?"

"Exactly." Jazz turned to Thaine, whispering, "What's a newt?"

Thaine shrugged. "Some kind of new cereal?"

Darcy hugged Thaine's neck, then Jazz, and finally Jimmy. Jimmy made a face. "Why does it smell in here?"

"Because that's what adults like. Something that doesn't remind them of their old bedroom slippers."

"Oh. I thought you were just covering up for cat pee."

Darcy nodded. "That too." She turned to Thaine. "Do me a favor. Go see if your sister needs any help. Looks like they're getting slammed back there. I gotta watch the front door."

"I don't know anything about Syrian food."

"You don't know anything about the 'Secret Sauce' in a Quarter Pounder either, but you manage to consume one on a regular basis. Just follow your gut–it's never let you down before."

The three of them dutifully marched to the rear. Darcy watched as Jimmy picked up a diminutive porcelain bell and stuffed it in his jeans pocket. She nodded to herself, "That's $5.95, you little bandit. I'm going to shake you upside down 'fore you ever get out of here."

Delilah looked up from her tray of cappuccinos and lattes. "Oh hey, Thaine. Do me a favor, hon, and go see what Adnan's calling for back there. Hi, Jazz! That's such a pretty blouse you've got on. And there's Mr. Jimmy. Jimmy, have you met Haya?"

At that moment Haya appeared with one piece of *Namoura* cake left. She held it toward Jimmy. Jimmy flinched. "I don't want that."

Jazz pushed his arm toward the tray. "Take it!"

Jimmy flinched, slowly lifting the cake like it was something dead. Jazz leaned in, threatening, "Take a bite or we're going home."

Jimmy made another face then nibbled a tiny morsel. His expression swiftly altered. "Not bad. I'm not saying it's great, but it's swallowable."

Delilah called back, "I gotta drop these off. Jazz, honey, there's another apron in back if you're feeling motivated."

Jazz nodded. "Sure!" She turned back to Jimmy sternly as she aimed for the serving area. "Don't touch anything, don't get into trouble and don't make me tell Mom!"

Jimmy frowned and turned back to Haya. "My name's Atticus."

Haya smiled. "Haya."

Jimmy laughed. "Hiya, Haya!"

Haya grinned. "Haya."

"You want to see the cool bell I found?" Jimmy reached in his pocket and pulled out the china ringer.

Haya's grin grew bigger and she pointed to her chest. "Haya."

"Yeah, I got it. What do you do for fun around here?"

Haya again patted her chest. "Haya!"

Jimmy rolled his eyes and put the bell back in his pocket muttering, "Why do I always get the space cadets?"

Unobserved, Chito quietly entered the store and stepped off to the side to peruse the goings-on. He wasn't a hundred percent certain even now, but he definitely felt he was on the right track in achieving Tom's request. "Help the town, make something good happen...bring about change!"

"You buying or just looking?" Darcy squeezed Chito's hand, then gave him a hug. "Come on, don't hide back here, let me introduce you to a few people."

"No, no! I like...observing, really. I'm actually a bit shy."

Darcy shook her head, gazing at his leading-man features. "Okay. I'll let you in on a little secret: Me, too. Seriously. I learned a long time ago that I had to make myself stand out if I was ever going to milk any likelihood from this so-called life. You're looking at sheer willpower over mortal chicken-shit!"

Chito laughed. Darcy squeezed his hand again. "You've changed all our lives. You and Mr. Pennebaker. I don't know where we'd be if not for you both. Sometimes I think you're some kind of disoriented spirit who got lost and spilled all your glad tidings here accidentally."

Chito shook his head. "Don't thank me, thank Tom Pennebaker."

Darcy nodded slowly. "It was hard for him here. None of us knew how to help and I'm ashamed to say none of us ever really tried." She pressed her hands to her chin. "I wish you could stay–I don't know why you ever would–but it would be wonderful."

Chito shrugged. "I have a job, too, and my time is up. I've done what I promised I would, and it's been–brilliant! All of it."

Darcy reached for his elbow. "Come on, you're not leaving yet. I have to introduce you to just a few people." As they weaved their way into the throng of shoppers, looky-loos and well-wishers, the door opened once more and Pettus Lyndecker stepped in. He didn't enjoy seeing all these people clustered in one room like a herd of grunting goats. These things made him itch with anxiety. Being artificially pleasant was never his strong suit, but he clearly understood what today's assignment was–show up, congratulate the girls, be polite, say hello, play nice–and find Chito. He was a man on a mission, and he was prepared to fight like hell for whatever precarious chance at potential happiness presented itself.

Scanning the room, he finally saw the back of Chito's head. He was talking to Old Man Vickers, the high school science teacher. It impressed Pettus how easily Chito could ingratiate himself with perfect strangers. Where does that come from? Is it taught, built-in, just assumed? He himself didn't possess such a talent. It was agonizing having to come up with polite conversation with people you didn't know, didn't care about and clearly didn't want to know further. He sidled up behind Chito and placed a hand on his shoulder. Chito turned and stared at Pettus as if they'd never met.

Pettus smiled nervously. "Hey, I thought you might be here."

"Have you met Mr. Vickers?"

Pettus extended his hand. "How you doing sir, been a long time."

Mr. Vickers squinted. "It has, it really has. You're Herman Lyndecker's boy, isn't that right?"

"Yes, sir."

"I taught your daddy and your mama both."

"Yes, sir, you sure did, Mr. Vickers. You taught me too.

Afraid I was a terrible student."

"But a hell of a ball player! You really coulda gone pro. You were the best we had for a long time."

Pettus flushed. "That's good of you to say."

Mr. Vickers turned to Chito. "You shoulda seen this boy in his prime. He was like a little Texas Greek god." He turned back to Pettus. "The girls were all after your tail, sure nuff."

Self-conscious, Pettus put his hand back on Chito's shoulder. "Great seeing you again, Mr. Vickers. I need to speak with Chito for just a sec if you'll excuse us."

The two men walked over to an area behind the front display case. Pettus nervously rubbed his palms on his pant legs. "I need to see you alone; it's important."

"Why not tell me now?"

Pettus glanced around at the crowd. "No. It's not a good place."

"What is it? You want to apologize for being an asshole when you gave me that 'fuck you' kiss? Apology accepted. I've been doing a lot of thinking the last few days. I've been a real fool..."

"Don't."

"...I've got a job waiting for me, friends I haven't seen, places I need to go. I need my life back again. What I don't need is more confusion."

"Listen to me, I'm as serious as I've ever been in my life–I want you to stay. I need you to stay."

Chito stared at Pettus. "Why?"

"Meet me at the ranch tomorrow. Please."

Chito shook his head and looked away. "Man, if you only knew..."

Pettus answered, "I do...I really do."

"Hey, pal, can you hand me that super big pinecone up there? I'm thinking of buying it for my friend Haya."

The two men looked down to see Jimmy and Haya standing on the other side of the counter. Pettus reached for the pinecone, noticed the price tag, and handed it to Jimmy.

"Whew, ten dollars, that's a lot of bubble gum."

"Ten dollars? I got twenty-three big ones in my pocket, Jake, chump change. Come on, Haya, let's skidoo." The two of them strolled off as Jimmy placed a hand on Haya's shoulder, leading the way.

\*\*\*

The last customer departed, the last Syrian delectable devoured, the last trinket sold, the last bouquet ordered–the opening day celebration of The Dusty *Nopalito* had been a thundering triumph.

Darcy finished adding up the till. "Three thousand eight hundred seventy-nine dollars and sixty-two cents! A one-day world record for the Lyndecker sisters!"

Delilah, Adnan, Wayne and Darcy sat around a small café table in back sipping beer and iced tea. Haya, clutching an enormous pinecone, was fast asleep in Adnan's arms.

Delilah exhaled, "I've worn my feet to the bone, but it was worth it. After all we've been through, well, it's a blessing from God."

Adnan nodded. "*Inshallah.*"

Wayne held up his beer and toasted Adnan. "Amen, brother."

Darcy shook her head. "I can't get over it. All our old customers were back. It's like The Emporium was just a bad, rotten dream."

Delilah took a sip of iced tea and rubbed her foot. "I think we should send our sister-in-law a big bouquet thanking her for marrying our brother and leaving town. I really do."

Darcy shook her head. "She'll be back, mark my words. I can promise right now she's stirring a cauldron of dead kittens and planning her next attack."

Wayne winced. "Sweet."

Delilah suddenly stood. "We need to get home and get someone to bed. You need me to lock everything up?"

Darcy shook her head and rubbed Haya's leg. "I've got it, go. Who gave her the pinecone?"

Adnan smiled. "The young boy walking around with the motorcycle jacket and the cowboy boots with spurs."

Wayne nodded. "Oh yeah, they moved to town a while back. Cute kid. Wait 'til he's a teenager-that'll be fun."

"Well, he was very sweet with Haya–although she kept calling him 'Attic' for some reason. Let's go."

Delilah took the pinecone and Adnan picked up Haya and they all proceeded to the front door.

Darcy placed a hand on Adnan's arm. "You doing okay?"

He smiled. "Better than okay, you?"

"Absolutely."

Adnan studied her face for a moment then silently mouthed the words, "Thank you." She patted his back.

Delilah gave Darcy a hug. "We need to do something nice for Chito. Be thinking of something special, something out of the ordinary."

Darcy nodded. "For sure! Good night, all."

As they departed, Darcy turned to see Wayne turning out the lights in back. "You don't have to do that. I'll get to it."

Wayne approached. "You're tired, go home."

Darcy grinned. "Is that an order, officer?"

Wayne smiled. "Aw, now you're gonna be all cute with me and get my hopes up."

"I'm always nice to you, Wayne. But you've been a married man for so long, opportunities were...scarce, to say the least. Thank you for today. You didn't have to do this. You could've been with your kids..." Wayne put his hands on Darcy's waist. "...Gone fishing...washed the car"–he kissed Darcy softly– "mowed the yard."

Wayne smiled. "But I wanted to sell the hell out of that Cucumber Mint room freshener instead..."

Darcy kissed him back. "I hope you know what you're getting into. We're all crazy, you know? Every last one of us, mad as shithouse owls."

They kissed again and Wayne whispered in Darcy's ear, "Just the way I like 'em."

\*\*\*

Marty pulled back on Dulce's reins and scratched her neck. She hadn't been ridden since the evening of Pete's death when she showed up back at the barn spooked and disoriented. Marty knew exactly where to look for Pete. "Their tree" was as consequential and revered to her parents as the land itself. That Pete should end his life there seemed altogether apt. Brutal, but comprehendible.

Marty dismounted and lead Dulce up to the high caliche ridge with the surrounding view that seemed to encompass the entire world when she was a child. She used to ask Pete which was their land, and he'd always answer with the same low, ironic reply. "As far as the eye can see." It would give Marty chills, for she was certain he was joshing, but in reality, it definitely appeared true. In those days one could see for mile after endless mile–not a windmill, not a telephone pole, power line, drilling rig, pump jack, neighboring house–nothing. Nothing but raw, unadulterated, South Texas *pampas* as far as the eye could see. It filled her with awe and pride–and always, the same burden of inescapable apprehension. Who was she to lay claim to any of this? It chose her, not the other way around. When you're born into a legacy, your choices become finite. The obligation to persist, promote and thrive on a familial bequest is mandated prophecy. And the remaining child knows it best of all.

Marty tied Dulce's reins loosely around her neck and let her graze on the nearby bluestem grass. She then squatted on her haunches, cowboy style, and plucked a nearby stalk to chew on. "I could live anywhere if I had someone, something to fall back on. I don't even know what love is anymore! I do know what 'like' is. Maybe if I 'like' someone and they 'like' me back, it's all a body needs. I'm for sure not ready to be alone the rest of my life! Caught in all this vastness, this stillness, day after day, year after year–it'll turn you mad as a snared coyote. We're all looking for a little peace and fulfillment. However, it presents itself, whoever offers it–it's what we all crave."

# CHAPTER TWENTY

Pettus was waiting for Chito in his pickup at the front gate of the Lyndecker ranch. As Chito approached slowly, he drove across the cattleguard and rolled down his window.

"Didn't think you wanted to meet right here on the highway."

Pettus grinned and patted the door of the pickup. "I don't. Pull off on the side here and come get in."

Chito squinted at Pettus, puzzled. "Where we going?"

"You'll see."

Chito nodded slowly then rolled up the window, parking the Lexus just inside the gate. Pettus stepped outside the pickup and Chito observed he was dressed more for the pool than ranch life. Sunglasses, swim trunks, undershirt, flip-flops–all that was missing was a pair of floaties.

"You heading to the beach?"

"I wish. Just trying to be cool on a blistering day."

Chito grinned. "You're cool, all right." Chito looked down at his jeans, boots and long-sleeve shirt, overdressed as usual.

"Take off anything you like if you're too hot. It's just me and you." Chito stared at Pettus, surprised. Pettus waved an arm. "Come on and get in."

Hopping in on the passenger side, Chito pulled the creaking truck door shut. "Where we going?"

"You'll see, want a beer?" Pettus reached around to the cooler in back and produced an ice-cold, dripping can of Shiner beer. By now, Chito was well familiar with the Texas custom of consuming cold beer all summer day long.

He acquiesced immediately. "Sure." Taking the beer from Pettus, he popped it open and sipped contentedly. For the next ten minutes they bounced along in agreeable silence.

Pettus finally broke the interval. "What's London like?"

Chito looked at him. "Cold, damp, busy–stimulating."

"You like it, don't you?"

Chito shrugged. "Sure."

"Seeing anybody there?"

Chito smiled warily. "You're fishing–what do you want to know for?"

"Curious is all. Can't imagine you're going through life all alone."

Chito laughed. "Nobody special. I'm picky."

Pettus nodded. "I hear that."

Both men glanced out their side windows. Chito spoke again. "So if you're asking if I have a partner, no. Would I like to have a partner? Yes. The RIGHT partner."

"Can I ask what that RIGHT partner might be like."

Chito laughed again. "Good, kind, sincere, motivated, loving, lovable–built like a Greek God!" They both laughed. "What about you? You really going to spend the rest of your days pining for the girl on the ranch next door?"

Pettus grinned. "I've decided I'm gonna start pining for you."

Chito's good-humored expression sank and he turned to the window. "Easy to be cocky when it's somebody else's problem."

Pettus looked at Chito then slowed the truck to a stop. "I'm not being cocky, I'm putting my cards right on the table. I know you like me. Well...I like you too."

Chito raised his hand. "Please, not this again..."

"Let me finish! I do like you. You're smart, you're respectable, all refined and cultured–and you're a pretty good-looking rascal too. I have no problem in getting to know you better–in the way you want. I mean it! But you gotta help me." Chito looked at Pettus, dumbfounded. "I think me and you and Marty–the three of us–could make a go of it."

Chito's mouth hung open. "What does that mean?"

"Live together! The three of us! Why not? I'd be good to you, you'd be good to Marty and Marty would be good to me. And we'd all be good to each other! Does it sound completely fucked up?"

Chito stared numbly ahead. "I need another beer."

Pettus reached a hand back and grabbed two cold ones from the Igloo, handing one to Chito.

After a notable pause, Chito turned back toward Pettus. "What would I do here?"

Pettus grinned, practically shouting. "You'd be the change in Rita Blanca you keep saying Tom wanted you to uncover! Don't you get it? YOU'RE that change!"

Chito, thunderstruck, opened the truck door and unsteadily stepped outside. He glanced up and down the road, looking utterly confused. He felt lightheaded, flushed; his legs wobbly. He turned back to look at Pettus, who stared at him worriedly.

"You okay?"

Chito didn't answer but walked a few steps then turned back toward the truck. He removed his hat and rubbed his head. He squatted on his heels and rubbed a rock into the dirt. Putting his hat back on, he walked again toward the truck and stood at the open window. His eyes welled with tears as he spoke in a cracked voice.

"That's *exactly* what he meant! He wanted ME to be the change. But it had to be my decision, not his. Oh Tom, I get it...I finally get it."

Pettus opened his door and moved around the truck to Chito's side. He put his hand on his shoulder.

"I'm sorry about Tom. Sorry you lost him. I don't like it when anybody gets hurt–but it doesn't need to stay that way." Pettus slowly pushed his hand under Chito's hat band and let the Stetson fall to the ground. He rubbed Chito's head and gently pulled his face to his chest. The two men stood there on the side of the dirt road, not saying a word, and appearing for all the world like long-lost lovers.

\*\*\*

Chito leaned his head back against the *retama* tree behind him and studied the spread before him. He was stretched out comfortably, boots off, on an old handmade quilt someone had toiled to create generations before. Alongside him were Tupperware bowls filled with fruit, cheese, fried chicken, crackers, sandwiches and cookies. Off to the side was the venerable ice chest laden with beer. The shade was deep, the mood leisurely and the setting–peerless. Next to him lay a shirtless Pettus, eyes closed, breathing softly.

"I was just thinking," Pettus spoke low, "you could probably run for mayor of Rita Blanca and get elected."

Chito laughed. "I could. I have dual citizenship from my marriage to Tom. But I'll probably pass on that one."

Pettus rolled over on his side. "Dog catcher? Always need a new dog catcher."

Chito laughed again. "I'd be a good one, too. I'm bilingual so I can yell 'sit' in both languages." They both chuckled. Chito glanced again at the profusion of edibles scattered about. "Where'd all this come from?"

"What?"

Chito spread his arms. "This!"

"You don't like picnics?"

"Of course–but you really did this all by yourself?"

"Why not? Aren't you worth homemade pimento cheese sandwiches and cold chicken wings? I've been cooking since I was a kid. Somebody had to. Wasn't much choice in the matter."

Chito rubbed his chin absently. "You kind of raised your brothers and sisters, didn't you?"

"Not kind of–did. When there's no mother and no father around, you learn to improvise in a hurry." Pettus rose up and wrapped his arms around his knees, looking into the distance. "Always wanted to be a real father, but the first wife got custody of the kids. I was off in the pen for selling pot." He inhaled deeply. "Hey–just trying to keep food on the table, you know? Never cared too much about getting high personally. Well, I learned my lesson. No damn shortcuts in life." Pettus picked up a stick and flung it. "They'll come see their old man one day, sure nuff. And we'll start a new chapter called Strangers-In-Rita-Blanca-Paradise."

Chito stood, stretching his legs. He stared around at the muddy stock tank and studied the fat cows resting on the other side. "Why'd we come here?"

Pettus looked up. "Why? This is where I first met you, remember?"

Chito nodded. "I'll have that memory burned in my brain till the day I die. Why today?"

Pettus stood and pointed at the stock tank. "Well, I thought we might go swimming?"

Chito shook his head, horrified. "In that slime? Not me...no way."

Pettus stood and stretched as well. "But you saw me in there. We've all gone swimming in there before. You want to be a real Texas native, don't you?"

"Not that much." Chito started backing up as Pettus approached him.

"Don't be afraid. I'll hold your hand."

Chito laughed nervously, "No, no, really..."

"We don't want to get your shirt dirty." Pettus began unbuttoning at the collar and Chito pushed him away, chuckling.

"Stop, really, I'm ticklish."

"Really? Here?"

"Stop!" Pettus yanked up Chito's polo shirt and tossed it on the blanket. He then proceeded to unbutton Chito's jeans.

"You sure can't go in wearing these..."

"*Basta!* Ow! Quit it. I stepped on something. Stop!"

"Off with 'em." Pettus tugged the jeans down to Chito's knees. "Feel better?"

Chito stopped struggling and looked solemnly at Pettus. "Are you...are you trying to seduce me?"

Pettus smiled. "How'm I doin'?"

Chito blinked and yanked off his jeans. "Okay, but you have to take off those ridiculous board shorts." In a heartbeat Pettus obeyed and dropped his swim trunks.

"Better?"

Chito stared brazenly at Pettus's naked torso. "Better."

"How 'bout you? You don't want to get those tighty-whities soaking wet."

Chito contemplated the notion for a half-second, then slowly slipped his thumbs inside the elastic band of his underwear and slid them down briskly, tossing them onto the quilt. Pettus appraised the situation judiciously, nodding.

"Okay. All in its original condition! Nice. They circumcised my hooded friend when I was born. Never did forgive 'em for that. I mean, what's the point, really? We don't cut your ear off 'cause you don't wash it every day, do we?" Pettus shook his head, wistfully. "So...what do you say, ready for a swim?"

Chito began stepping carefully toward the water's edge. "There's a lot of...ow...sticks, rocks...ow...something."

"Sticker burrs, you gotta watch for 'em. Here, let me help you, I'm used to it."

"No, no, it's okay…"

In three quick steps Pettus scooped up Chito and began carrying him in his arms.

Chito laughed, squirming nervously. "No really, I can walk…"

"I don't mind, you're not heavy at all."

"*Jesus Cristo, que estoy haciendo aqui*…this is crazy…I feel…"

"How do you feel?"

"I feel like some other person. I feel like a little kid. I feel like I'm daydreaming…"

"Hold on, you're about to feel wet!"

Standing thigh-deep in the water, Pettus suddenly leapt forward and both of them fell headlong into the cool, primitive baptismal of funky South Texas immersion. Upon resurfacing, laughing, gasping and chucking water, neither man gave a moment's thought to the fact that their lives had just unalterably, involuntarily changed forever.

\*\*\*

The high school football team was done practicing by late afternoon and soon enough, one, two, then three players at a time began crossing the road and approaching the colorful Syrian food truck parked adjacent to the practice field. They hovered around the painted menu staring at it with the probing intensity of a Supreme Court tribunal.

A blond, pimple-faced, Mack truck of a teenager asked warily, "What's a…*kibbeh*?"

Adnan stood at the window and smiled. "You'll like it, it's like a spicy hamburger patty without the bread. It comes with a super dipping sauce. Very good."

The kid stared at his pals and they stared back, poker-faced. "Oh, okay…I'll try one."

"Good man. Three dollars and thirty-six cents with tax.

How 'bout a Coke to go with that?" The kid nodded yes. "Okay, one dollar more, please." He handed over his money and they all watched, mesmerized as Adnan got to work preparing the nosh.

\*\*\*

At the front of the food truck, Jazz was leaning over the open hood and staring down at Thaine lying under the vehicle, fastening the oil pan back to the chassis.

"Think I got it. Man, this sucker was leaking like a son of a bitch."

Jazz called, "Just tell me when to start the engine."

"Yeah, gimme a sec. Let me crawl outta here."

\*\*\*

On the other side of the truck, Jimmy was teaching Haya English. "Now listen, when I say alphabet, repeat after me...Owl-fa-bit!"

Haya smiled brightly and repeated, "How-fa-beet."

Jimmy stared expressionlessly. "No, you're saying it wrong. How you going to make it through kindergarten if you can't speak English?"

"How-fa-beet."

Jimmy stretched his mouth as wide as he could. "OWL-FA-BIT."

"HOW-FA-BEET!"

Jimmy put his hands atop his head and made a face. "Let's go back to the flashcards."

Jimmy held up a picture. "What is this?"

"Dog!"

"And this?"

"Hell-ee-fant."

"We'll work on it. This?"

"Arm-a-dill-o."

"We'll work on it. This?"

"Everyone knows that an Arm-a-dill-o."

Jimmy stared wide-eyed. He thought for a second he'd heard incorrectly. "Excuse me?"

"That's an arm-a-dill-o. Mammals with scales. We studied it yesterday, remember?"

Jimmy continued staring, mouth open. He spoke quietly. "I'm gonna need better books. We just blew past *Green Eggs and Ham*. Girl, you rock!"

Jimmy high-fived Haya as Delilah drove up and parked next to the food truck. Getting out, she retrieved a box of baked goods from the rear seat and started for the truck door.

"Hi Jimmy, Haya–how's the English lesson going?"

Jimmy shook his head. "She's quick, real quick. Like...surprising quick."

Haya smiled broadly. "Surprising!"

Delilah smiled. "Haya starts kindergarten in a few weeks–you think she'll be ready?"

Jimmy waved his hand, palm up. "Oh...cinch. She's gonna ace it, you'll see."

Delilah nodded and disappeared around to the front. Jimmy turned back to Haya, emitting a long sigh.

"I got a new plan. You tell me a word in Arabic, and I'll tell you what it is in English, okay?"

"Okay...dude." Jimmy turned with a start and Haya laughed loudly.

***

Delilah entered the truck and dropped off her box of treats. Adnan turned from his preparations and they kissed.

"How was it at the *Nopalito?*"

"We had a good lunch, maybe fifteen, twenty people. Darce was pleased. She sold a succulent terrarium to a lady from

Houston for eighty dollars. You?"

"I'm getting through to the football team. A couple of the teachers came over for lunch. It was a good idea putting the folding chairs and table out front, no?"

"Indeed. Hey..." Adnan looked up from slicing a tomato. "You think we're going to make it?"

Adnan put down the knife and put his arms around Delilah. "Do I think? I know. Why, what do you think?"

Delilah gave him an enigmatic glance. "What if I said you were going to be a father again?"

Adnan stared at her blankly then shook his head. "No...you joking? True?"

Delilah nodded. "True."

Adnan held Delilah at arm's length and continued staring at her. "We going to have a baby?" Delilah nodded again. Adnan laughed and pulled her close. "We going to have a baby, oh my goodness!" Adnan lifted Delilah and swung her around. Together they laughed excitedly. "Oh my goodness! God is great!" Adnan shouted and kissed Delilah again and again. He stopped suddenly. "Our baby will be American citizen, yes?" Delilah nodded. "Our baby will be free to go to school, have education, practice faith, become doctor, teacher, astronaut..."

Delilah nodded. "...Flower shop owner!"

Adnan beamed. "Of course. A dozen flower shops...and one Syrian bakery!" They laughed and kissed again.

Thaine stuck his head inside the food truck. "Y'all having a wrestling match in here? What's the commotion?"

Adnan grinned. "Come brother-in-law, congratulate us! You're going to become an uncle!"

Thaine shook his head and smiled shyly. "Dang...wow...that's something, all right. Congratulations! Whew. Jazz and I kinda got a little announcement, too..." They stared at each other expectantly. "We're moving."

Delilah's expression froze. "Moving? Where?"

"Houston. Jazz is from Houston. I'm gonna get a job

working in an auto shop– she's got a cousin who's a supervisor for a big dealership."

"But you have to graduate from high school!"

"I can get my GED in Houston. I can–Jazz is smart. She's gonna help me."

Delilah looked at the two of them; so certain, so unified. One brick falls from such a carefully planned creation and the entire structure crashes. But then who was she to rain on someone else's invented desire.

"I guess I just always thought you'd stay at the ranch and help your brother."

"I'll be back! It's not that far. I'm not leaving for good, it's just for now. Besides, I finally have a little money to do a few things on my own."

Sharp as a Roman arrow piercing a recalcitrant Christian, the primal Biblical Proverb burst into her head: *"How much better to get wisdom than gold, to get insight rather than silver!"* But she didn't share, didn't proselytize; she just smiled. Had Pettus set them all on a path of improvident ruin with the unexpected 'blessing' of their now modest affluence? Delilah shivered as she reached out to hug Thaine. "Well, I know you two will make each other very happy and hopefully you'll come back to visit your new niece or nephew as often as possible."

A wavering teenage male voice was heard coming from the order window. "Excuse me, sir, we'd like to order some more, uh, *kibbeh."* The Mack truck teen anxiously thumped a ten-dollar bill on the counter.

Adnan turned, grinning. "On the house, my friend! How many are you?"

The teen looked shocked. "Five."

"Five orders coming up! Delilah, see if our gentleman customers here would like to try some of the pastries you've brought from *Nopalito*. Thaine, come–tell me what's wrong with my motor. She won't start until I kick her!"

Delilah looked at Jazz. "When we're broke from giving it all away for free, can we come live with you?"

Jazz grinned. "We may be asking you the same thing." She leaned into Delilah's ear. "I think we'll be okay, I do. We really love each other."

Delilah put a hand on Jazz's shoulder. "You hang on to that. You might end up with all the gold in the world one day, but if you don't have something you can put an arm around and squeeze–and it squeezes back–what good's any of it?"

Jazz nodded then picked up the box of baked goods. "They look like a hungry bunch out there." She turned quickly and caught Delilah's eye. "I was wondering...could you keep an eye on my little brother for me? I know he can be a real pain and not many people understand him, but I do love him. Even when I'm mad, I love him. He's totally taken with Haya. I think they're helping each other. My mom's going to freak when she hears I'm going, but I have to...I have to."

Delilah took a deep breath. "Of course I will. He's teaching Haya to read, you know. She's a very fast learner. I've learned some interesting things from your brother."

Jazz smiled. "I'll bet."

"Did you know that Ethel Merman was married to Ernest Borgnine?"

Jazz looked confused. "I don't know who those people are."

"Neither do I, but your brother read both their biographies at the library. I think they were politicians, I can't recall..."

\*\*\*

Behind the food truck, Haya was stretched out on the grass reading aloud, slowly and softly to Jimmy from *Peter Rabbit*.

*"But naughty Peter ran to Mr...."* Haya looked at Jimmy.

Jimmy read, *"McGregor's."*

*"McGregor's garden and squeezed under the gate. First, he ate some...*Haya looked up again, and Jimmy read, *"Lettuce."*

302

Haya nodded. "Okay." She continued reading, "*and French beans; then he ate some ra...ra...radishes,*" Jimmy beamed at his star pupil.

# CHAPTER TWENTY-ONE

The three sat across from each other in the living room of the Pennebaker *hacienda* and stared dolefully into the void. Silence descended once again upon the gathering; Chito cleared his throat and spoke hesitantly. "I don't snore."

"Neither do I." Pettus nodded.

"Actually, you do," Marty interrupted.

Pettus looked alarmed. "Maybe when I've got a cold or something."

"Actually..."

Chito interrupted, "Okay, let's not get bogged down in the small stuff again. Where we sleep isn't really all that important as *when* we sleep...together." They glanced at each other uneasily.

"Well, it's obvious this will be our new home. It's big enough, private enough, comfortable enough for three adults." Marty swept an arm around the room and took a sip from her iced tea.

Pettus frowned. "Not me. I mean, I can't just leave my house."

"Why?"

"It's my home. I've lived there all my life. It's where all my stuff is."

"Well, you can't move all that 'stuff' over here, that's for sure."

"I thought we agreed we were all 'living together'?" Chito queried.

"We are–it's just that I can't be here every hour of every day."

Marty raised an eyebrow. "Just at bedtime."

Chito stood, scratching his head. "Look–this is either a real marriage of diverse personalities or it's not. Either it's going to work because we will it so, or it fails miserably because we're not committed enough to the outcome."

Marty and Pettus nodded silently.

Chito continued, "So yes, it would be impractical for Pettus to move here full time because he oversees his own place as well. But you can be here every night, no?"

Pettus, pondering, widened his eyes and bobbed his head in a slow circle, "I don't see why not...sure!"

"Are you okay with that, Marty?"

Marty nodded reflectively. "Of course, I think it's only fair we all share in the household expenses."

Chito laughed. "You do realize I'm without a job now? I've given up a career, income and any immediate prospects for having one. I have savings of course, but how long will that last?"

"It seems to me the rest of the money Tom gave you should be yours by right of achieving his wish. We're here because you're here, *hombre*." Pettus took a sip from his beer.

Marty sighed. "I'm really just talking about the light bill. It's a gesture, you know? There has to be a commitment, some kind of joint obligation other than just...the physical thing." The men stared back at her blankly. "There's no guide! We're doing something that's probably going to make us town pariahs...and I don't care what the town thinks! But I do care what WE think. It's either a functioning, truthful...*blending* of three souls–or we're all just kidding ourselves."

Pettus rumbled self-consciously, "I'll help pay for the light bill...sure will."

Marty moved to sit beside Pettus. "Thank you, but I want you to understand where I'm coming from. I can afford to pay the utilities–I can afford it all! What I'm asking for is commitment. From each of us. For something more than desire and physical need. I want a pledge, a vow that's as grounded and basic as...as money."

Pettus smiled. "In other words, 'pay to play.'"

Marty smiled back. "In other words–we gotta be all in on this or it ain't gonna fly."

Pettus nodded. "I'm in."

Chito concurred. "I'm in."

Marty clapped her hands. "I'm in! Settled. We'll open a joint checking account on Monday. Now–what the hell are we all going to do with our lives between breakfast and bedtime?"

Pettus looked surprised. "I've got a ranch to run."

"So do I," said Marty. "Let me rephrase that, what is our joint purpose as a committed union–between lovemaking and paying the light bill?"

Silence fell once again. Chito finally spoke in a faint murmur. "I've been thinking...quite a lot. What will I do in this new town, this new house, this new...everything? I came up with an idea. You can tell me it's crazy, ridiculous...it's just a concept, okay?" They looked at him expectantly.

"So what if...what if I took the remainder of Tom's money, the little bit left, and we all chipped in whatever else we could as a team...and built back the ruin of The Dusty Rose? Nothing fancy; but clean, serviceable...and we put in a gallery? Western art, Texas art, Latino art...ART. Marty could oversee it because she has gallery experience from New York. And on the other side of the store would be a Texas dry goods department selling saddles, bridles, leather, boots, western wear, etc., etc. Pettus would manage that part since he knows that area best.

And in the middle, I'd have a ready-to-wear men's store! Now, don't think I've completely lost my mind because I know there's no market in Rita Blanca for fine men's wear, but it would be the *storefront* for a mail order/online catalog like Robert Redford's Sundance or Tommy Bahama or something similar. I know this world! I know marketing, distribution, development, advertising–it's my arena with bank clients." By now, Chito was beaming enthusiastically. "But you have to tell me if I've completely lost my mind. I believe it's a very American concept–'Build it, and they will come!'"

Marty and Pettus sat in silence, their faces revealing nothing. Finally, Marty spoke. "Would the...art...be tied in with catalog sales as well?"

"Exactly!"

Pettus rubbed his chin. "And the...'dry goods'...that part, too?"

Chito nodded yes. Pettus and Marty looked at each other vacantly. Finally, Marty spoke. "I think it's...feasible. Going to take a world of planning and counting every dollar but I think we can all help each other along the way." She rose to her feet and stretched both hands toward the two men. "I don't know about y'all, but I feel something remarkable here. Who can stop an idea or a three-way marriage whose time has come?"

Pettus put an arm around Chito and Marty both. "I got two people got my back, and I got theirs. First time in my life I'm not worried about a damn thing. Lord, if this is some kinda joke you're pulling here, I'll play the fool–gladly!"

The three hugged, laughed and kidded as untroubled and heedless as children out for a freshly mowed romp, their futures as indistinct and unforeseen as a hazy dream forestalled.

\*\*\*

The fourteen-member kindergarten class of Miss Jane Henry stood anxiously on the "cafetorium" stage of the Rita Blanca's Dale Evans Elementary School. Tugging at tight bow ties and starchy pinafores, the juvenile recitalists glanced repeatedly at Miss Jane, who sat serenely at the upright piano anticipating an interior musical cue, hands posed theatrically astride the keys.

Seated in the audience was an amalgamation of both greater and lesser Rita Blanca gentry. In the first row sat Delilah and Adnan Hasim, beside them Darcy and Deputy Wayne with his four kids: Darryl, Doug and the twins, Dub and Dot. In the next row was Darlene and Jazz's mother, Faye Dimmit, Jimmy, Jazz and Thaine. Behind them sat Pettus, Marty and Chito, sharing sphinxlike smiles. Interspersed on folding chairs scattered randomly throughout the hall sat Billy Mapstone, Brittany Hinojosa, Miz Delmer, Lurene Dornak, Sandy, Omar, Julio and Memo Bautista, Preacher Waddell and his wife, Charline; Dr. Finley and even Sheriff Naylor and Zoe. On the last row sat Cody and a very pregnant, very flushed Carol Ann, in for a long weekend hiatus from West Texas A & M, along with Clayton and Barbara Jansky.

Why had they all inexplicably materialized at the school on this particular night? What was the circumstance, the impetus for such a gathering? A gaggle of cowlicked, gap-toothed preschoolers, adorable as they were, was surely not the sole incentive in motivating such a crowd.

Jimmy Dimmit stood impulsively in the front row and scanned the room with laser exactitude. His mother, Faye, yanked at his shirttail. "Sit. It's about to begin."

Jimmy dropped back into his seat, grinning. "I'm going with 200 people here, maybe more. You think she'll be nervous?" Faye Dimmit smiled impassively and marveled instead at Miss Henry's pronounced stage languor; a supine cat coiled to pounce.

The occasion? Word had raced through Rita Blanca for

weeks. Jimmy Dimmit had unintentionally opened a Pandora's box of unparalleled faculty. He'd discovered Haya was astonishingly enough...a genius! An IQ alternating in the vicinity of 160 genius. When her reading went from *Peter Rabbit* to Stephen King to Shakespeare–in English–in a matter of months, Jimmy knew his pupil was some kind of child prodigy. Adnan and Delilah grudgingly took her up to the University of Texas in San Antonio for testing and evaluation. The doctors and scientist verified what they'd all come to ultimately accept–Haya was a certifiable Syrian *wunderkind*! As any pair of unsuspecting parents would be, Adnan and Delilah were simultaneously confused, proud and fearful for their five-year-old virtuoso. How does one raise a genius? In no time, Haya's name became a Rita Blanca catchphrase. "Our own whiz kid! A Middle Eastern Brainiac from Rita Blanca! The little girl that gives Einstein the willies!"

And there she stood, center stage, a three and a half foot, sweet-faced child with olive-brown eyes and a red ribbon pulling back her curly, shoulder-length hair. In appearance, she didn't seem any different from any of the other scrubbed and pressed Mexican-American children on stage, nor did she look especially exceptional to any of the other kids either. Adnan winked at Haya and bit his lip nervously. She winked back. He pondered, who in Syria would believe this moment? A better question, who was there even left to believe?

With a sudden loud report, Miss Henry launched into the prelude of the Texas State Song, "Texas Our Texas." Instantly, all in the audience rose to face the flag of Texas displayed on stage. Several of the children seemed to have trouble remembering the words, but not Haya. She sang loudly and enthusiastically as if relating a catchy pop song. At the tune's completion, Miss Henry placed her sheet music atop the piano and strode briskly toward the podium. She addressed the audience in a low, breathy voice.

"I want to extend a welcome to you all this evening to Dale

Evans Elementary and especially to our newest class of Rita Blanca young scholars." The audience applauded; Miss Henry continued. "We're so proud of these kindergarteners. We have an exceptional group of students this year who we want to show off to all our moms and dads, aunts and uncles, grandmoms and granddads, and well, everyone we can think of! We're glad you're here. We'd like to introduce ourselves first, and we'll start over here on my left in the back row with this young man."

A little boy with blond bangs touching his eyes looked panicked. "Tell us your name?"

"Curtis."

"What's your last name, Curtis?"

"Curtis."

"No, your last name."

"Johnson."

"Thank you, Curtis. Next?

"I'm Selena Cantu..."

And so it went until finally, the introductions arrived at Haya. She stepped forward, beaming.

"Haya Hakim, although in my home country we say it like '*Haya Hakim.*' Haya means 'come on!' in Arabic, which is what my father is always telling me. We are from the country of Syria, but now we are Americans. We like America very much; we like Syria too, but this is our home now. I think everything happens very fast here. I like it, but I think my father wants to slow down sometimes. Soon I'm going to have a new half-sister. I hope that she has an American name and a Syrian name because she will be both. My friend Jimmy who's sitting right there" -she pointed-"he thinks I talk too much and I think he talks too much, so-I think that's why we're friends. And..." Haya looked toward Miss Henry. "Is that enough?"

Miss Henry smiled. "Why don't we let the other children finish introducing themselves?"

"Okay." Haya stepped back and the remaining bunch

continued with their presentations. At the end Miss Henry asked each child to perform or recite a brief poem or song. Some forgot their lines, some were too embarrassed, one grew flustered and walked off stage. When it came to Haya's turn again, she stooped to pick up a large book at her feet and opened it to the middle. Waiting for Miss Henry's direction, she took a step forward and spoke confidently.

"Because my friend Jimmy has been teaching me so many things it took me a long time to decide about tonight. I like to read. I love to read. I finally chose the following...but first I would like to translate to my father in Arabic, if that's okay. I think it will mean more to him." Haya fixed her gaze on Adnan, who appeared astonished. "I'm sorry, *Abi*, some of the words..." Haya shrugged and began to read from a piece of paper, "This is by Mr. Charles Dickens, *Oliver Twist*

..."*'in al' ashkhas hadol elly manahtohum
Kol hobbi, ennahum yarkoroun fi
a'maaq quburihim. Walaken; ala
alraghm men ana
Al-Sa'ad wa Ifarha fi hayati takmun
hnak aydana, ana Im a'mol taboot min
Qalbi wa khatamtuh 'iilaa al'abad.
Ealaa 'afdal maeani. 'inna albala' alamieq
yajaalhom aqwaa faqt. Wa 'aetaqid
'anahu yjb 'annahu yasqul tabieatana.*"

At the end of her recitation, tears were streaming down Adnan's face as Delilah handed him a tissue and held his hand. Haya took a deep breath and started again in English.

"*The persons on whom I have bestowed my dearest love lie deep in their graves; but, although the happiness and delight of my life lie buried there too, I have not made a coffin of my heart, and sealed it up forever on my best affections. Deep affliction has only made them stronger; it ought, I think, for it should refine our nature."*

Haya closed the book and stepped back into line with the other pupils. The cafetorium was silent. After a beat, Miss Henry stepped once again to the podium, clearing her throat.

"Thank you, Haya...thank you. And now, the children took a vote and decided they'd like to perform their favorite song for you now. So, with your permission...are we ready, class?"

The children moved to stand around the piano as Miss Henry started playing once again. Suddenly, each child took the hand of the other and began skipping around the stage to a dance choreographed with Miss Henry's assistance.

*"Here we go loop de loop
Here we go loop de li
Here we go loop de loop
All on a Saturday night.*

*Here we go way down low
Here we go way up high
Here we go way down low
We really know how to fly.*

*Here we go round and round
Here we go fast and slow
Here we go round and round
Oh what a great way to go.*

*Here we go up and down
Here we sit side by side
Here we go up and down
Oh what a wonderful ride!"*

An odd feeling descended upon the hall as the regular citizens of Rita Blanca sat silently watching the children sing, dance and weave about the stage. It was as if a carnival mask had lifted slightly and, for a brief moment, each could see the other more clearly than ever before. Illusions mitigated, grievances disregarded; likes, dislikes, fears, accusations, all strangely diminished. There was a haunting sense that something, a spell perhaps, had gripped them and was even now fading into oblivion just as they had begun to acknowledge its presence. What was it? Slowly, unconsciously, they began to recognize one another. Men touched their wives and their wives responded gently, children put their heads in parents' laps, lovers felt each other's warmth; friends allied, enemies relinquished, strangers saluted. And suddenly, like a switched-off channel, it vanished. The abruptness of transformation left an odd disquiet in the air. As if a great purging rainstorm had passed over, leaving behind broken limbs and flooded roads. The performance concluded, the audience stood slowly, confused and drained, unsure if what they'd felt was something authentic or the familiar return to constant longing.

Standing at the door, Miss Henry shook hands and chatted briefly with the departing attendees. Delilah, Adnan and Haya, Darcy and Wayne, Darlene, Faye and Jimmy, Jazz and Thaine–all stood in an approximate circle outside on the school breezeway quietly praising the evening's star performer and silently musing whether some arcane, divine intervention had occurred just minutes before.

Cody and Carol Ann approached warily, and it was Darcy herself who spoke first.

"Hello brother, hello Carol Ann. What a surprise to see you two tonight."

Cody grinned self-consciously and put his hand on Haya's neck. "I wadn't gonna miss my only niece's big night in Rita Blanca. Carol Ann and I took the weekend off to come visit family." Cody stared sheepishly at Carol Ann. "I guess family means more to me now than it ever has. We're having a little boy. Ain't that something?"

Darcy reached out to put her arms around Cody. She then turned to face Carol Ann. "Congratulations. I mean it. I don't think you and I will ever be exactly best friends. But I do think you might make a good drinking buddy one day. I'm game if you are?"

Carol Ann, caught off guard, countered quickly, "Why not. Soon as little Cody gets born we'll plug the Margarita machine back in and have a real family get together."

Cody whistled loudly and they all chatted and hugged as the Lyndecker clan noisily made their way into the parking lot.

Jimmy caught up with Haya and held out his hand. "You did good. We gotta work on pronunciation, but the delivery was solid."

Haya smiled shyly. "Thank you. You're a very nice boy, Jimmy."

Jimmy looked surprised. "Nice? I'm not nice. I'm forceful, dynamic...animated..."

"And nice."

Jimmy rolled his eyes and took Haya's hand. "Forget it. So here's the thing I was telling you about Danny Thomas. I'm not one hundred percent sure he was born in Lebanon, but his family's definitely from there..."

***

Pettus, Marty and Chito sat in the now almost empty cafetorium and stared at the stage mutely. A lone janitor pushed a broom across the stage.

Finally, Pettus cleared his throat. "We might ought to go. We're the last ones."

Marty, remaining seated, nodded. "Yes."

Chito murmured, lost in thought. "That little girl...she really is some kind of genius, isn't she?"

They nodded in unison.

After a beat, Marty spoke again. "I want to make a

suggestion. No matter what happens between us, no matter how stupid it gets or how impossible it all becomes–we stay friends–through all of it. I'm getting too old to find new old friends. I want to work on what I've got–here, now, today. I mean it–can we promise each other we won't ever hate one another?"

Pettus looked deeply into Marty's eyes. "I promise I'll try to screw up less."

Chito placed a hand on Marty's arm. "And I promise I'll try to screw up more."

Marty grinned, her eyes filled with emotion. She rose from her seat and held out a hand to each man. "And I promise I'll try not to give a damn!"

As the three of them made their way toward the door, they suddenly clasped arms and began singing, "*Here we go loop de loop, Here we go loop de li, Here we go loop de loop, All on a Saturday night...*" Three grown adults skipping toward the exit laughing and giggling as if it were the first day of class and they had an entire lifetime ahead to learn, grow, seek and ripen. Which, of course, they did.

The janitor on the stage looked up from his broom and shook his head. He grumbled under his breath, "Californians."

# ABOUT THE AUTHOR

William Jack Sibley is a fifth generation Texan and a versatile writer whose work has spanned from writing dialogue for television's *Guiding Light* to serving as a contributing editor at Andy Warhol's *Interview Magazine,* to seeing his plays produced off-Broadway and regionally. Author of a dozen screenplays, nine stage plays, three novels (*Any Kind of Luck, Sighs Too Deep For Words,* and *Here We Go Loop De Loop*), one newspaper column and a freelance journalist, Sibley — a graduate of the University of Texas - Austin, Radio/ Television/Film Dept, alumni of the New Dramatist in New York, and member of The Dramatist Guild and the Writers Guild of America — currently serves as Secretary of the Texas Institute of Letters. Visit www.williamjacksibley.com.

# ABOUT ATMOSPHERE PRESS

Atmosphere Press is an independent, full-service publisher for excellent books in all genres and for all audiences. Learn more about what we do at atmospherepress.com.

We encourage you to check out some of Atmosphere's latest releases, which are available at Amazon.com and via order from your local bookstore:

*Saints and Martyrs: A Novel*, by Aaron Roe

*When I Am Ashes*, a novel by Amber Rose

*Melancholy Vision: A Revolution Series Novel*, by L.C. Hamilton

*The Recoleta Stories*, by Bryon Esmond Butler

*Voodoo Hideaway*, a novel by Vance Cariaga

*Hart Street and Main*, a novel by Tabitha Sprunger

*The Weed Lady*, a novel by Shea R. Embry

*A Book of Life*, a novel by David Ellis

*It Was Called a Home*, a novel by Brian Nisun

*Grace*, a novel by Nancy Allen

*Shifted*, a novel by KristaLyn A. Vetovich

*Because the Sky is a Thousand Soft Hurts*, stories by Elizabeth Kirschner